Geoffrey Chaucer

Poetical works

With memoir by Sir Harris Nicolas. Vol. V

Geoffrey Chaucer

Poetical works
With memoir by Sir Harris Nicolas. Vol. V

ISBN/EAN: 9783337124342

Printed in Europe, USA, Canada, Australia, Japan

Cover: Foto ©Andreas Hilbeck / pixelio.de

More available books at **www.hansebooks.com**

THE POETICAL WORKS OF GEOFFREY CHAUCER

WITH MEMOIR BY SIR HARRIS NICOLAS

VOL V

LONDON

BELL AND DALDY FLEET STREET

1866

CONTENTS.

VOL. V.

TROYLUS AND CRYSEYDE.

INCIPIT LIBER QUINTUS.

I.

APROCHEN gan the fatel destyné,
That Joves hath in dispossisioun,
And to yow, angry Parcas, sustren thre,
Comitteth to don execucioune ;
For whiche Criseyde most out of the towne,
And Troilus shal dwellen forth in pyne,
Til Lachesis his thred no longer twyne.

II.

The golde tressed Phebus, heigh on lofte,
Thries hadde alle with his bemes clere,
The snowes molte ; and Zephirus as ofte   10
Ybrought ayeyn the tender leves grene,
Syn that the sone of Ecuba the queene
Bygan to love hire firste, for whom his sorwe
Was alle, that she departe sholde a morwe.

III.

Ful redy was at primo Dyomede,
Criseyde unto the Grekes oste to lede ;
For sorwe of which she felt hire herte blede,

As she that nyste what was best to rede ;
And trewely, as men in bokes rede,
Men wiste never womman han the care,   20
Ne was so loth out of a town to fare.

IV.

This Troilus, withouten reed or lore,
As man that hath his joyes ek *forlore,*
Was waytynge on his lady everemore,
As she that was sothfaste, crop and moore
Of al his lust or joyes here tofore :
But Troylus, now farewel al thy joye !
For shaltow nevere se hire eft in Troye.

V.

Soth is, that while he bode in this manere,
He gan his wo ful manly for to hyde.   30
That wel unnethes it sene was in his chere ;
But at the yate ther she sholde oute ryde,
With certeyn folk he hoved hire tabide,
So *wo* bygon, al wolde he nought hym pleyne,
That on his hors unneth he sat for peyne.

VI.

For ire he quook, so gan his herte gnawe,
Whan Dyomede on horse gan him dresse,
And seyde unto hymself this ilke sawe,
‘ Allas !’ quod he, ‘ thus foule a wrechedenesse !
Whi suffre Ich it ? whi nyl Ich it redresse ?   40
Were it not bet at oones for to dye,
Than overemore in langoure thus to crye ?

VII.

‘ Why nyl I make atones rich and pore
To have inough to done or that she go ?
Whi nyl I brynge alle Troie upon a rore ?
Whi nyl I slen this Dyomede also ?
Whi nyl I rather with a man or two,
Stele hire awey ?   Whi wol I this endure ?
Whi nyl *I* holpen to myn owene cure ?’

VIII.

But whi he nolde don so fel a dede,   50
That shal I seyn, and whi hym liste it spare ;—
He hadde in herte alweyes a manere drede,
Leste that Criseyde, in rumour of this fare,
Shold han ben slayn ; lo ! this was al hise care ;
And elles certeyn, as I seyde yore,
He hadde it done withouten wordes more.

IX.

Criseyde when she redy was to ride,
Ful sorwfully she sighte, and seyde, ‘ Allas ! ’
But forth she mot, for ought that may betide,
And forth she rite ful sorwfully a pas ;   60
Ther is non other remede in this cas.
What wonder is, though that hyre soore smerte,
When she forgothe hire owen swete herte ?

X.

This Troilus, in gise of curteysie,
With hauke on hond, and with an huge route
Of knyghtes, rood and dide hyre compaynye,

Passynge alle the valeye fer withoute;
And ferther wold han riden out of doute
Ful fayn, and wo was hym to gon so soone,
But torne he moste, and it was eke to done.

XI.

And right with that was Antenor ycome
Oute of the Grekes oste, and every wight
Was of it glad, and seyde he was welcome;
And Troilus, al nere his herte lighte,
He peyned hym with *al* his *fulle* myght
Hym to with-holde of wepynge at the leeste,
And Antenor he kyste, and made feeste.

XII.

And therwithal he most his leve take,
And caste his eye upon hire pitously,
And neer he rood, his cause for to make,
To take hire by the honde al sobrely:
And Lorde! so she gan wepen tendrely!
And he ful soft and sleighely gan hire seye,
' Now hold youre day, and do me not to dye.'

XIII.

With that his curser turned he aboute,
With face *pale*, and unto Dyomede
No worde he spak, ne non of al his route;
Of whiche the sone of Tideus tooke hede,
As he that couthe moore than the crede
In swiche a craft, and by the reyne hire hente,
And Troilus to Troye homwarde he wente.

XIV.

This Dyomede, that ledde hyre by the bridel,
When that he saugh the folk of Troye awaye,
Thoughte, ' Al my laboure shal not been on ydel,
If that Y may, for somwhat shal I seye;
For at the werste, it may yit shorte oure weye;
I have herde seyde ek, tymes twyes twelve,
He is a fool that wol foryete hyme-selve.'

XV.

But natheles, this thoughte he wel ynoughe
That ' certeinliche I am aboute noughte,   100
If that I speke of love, or mak it tough;
For douteles, if she have in hire thoughte
Hym that I gesse, he may not ben ybrought
So soone aweye, but I shal fynde a meene,
That she nat wit as yet shal what I meene.'

XVI.

This Dyomede, as he that koude his goode,
When this was don, gan fallen forth in speche
Of this and that; and axed whi she stood
In swiche disese, and gan hire ek byseche
That if that he eneresse myght or eche,   110
With any thyng hyre ese, that she sholde
Comaunde it hym, and seyde he don it wolde.

XVII.

For treweliche he swor hire as a knyghte,
That ther nas thyng with whiche he myght hire
          plese,
That he nolde don his peyne and al his myght,

To don it, for to don hire hert an ese:
And preyde hire she wold hire sorwe apese,
And seyde, 'Iwis we Grekes kan have joye
To honouren yow, *as* wel as folk of Troye.'

XVIII.

He seyde ek thus:—'I woot yow thynketh
      straunge,—   120
No wonder is, for it is to yowe newe,—
Thacqueyntaunce of this Troyans to chaunge
For folk of Grece, that ye nevere knewe:
But wolde nevere God, but if as trewe
A Greke ye shold amang us al*le* fynde,
As any Troyan is, and ek as kynde.

XIX.

'And by tho *cause* I swor yow righte lo now
To ben youre frendo and help*er* to my myghte,
And for that more acqueyntaunce ek of yow
Have Ich had than another straunger wight,   130
So fro this forth I preye yow, day and nyght,
Comaundeth me, how sore that me smerte,
To don al that may like unto youre herte;

XX.

'And that ye me wolde as youre brother trete,
And taketh nought my frendeschipe in dispit.
And though youre sorwes ben for thynges grete,
Not I nat whi, but out of more respit,
Myn herte hath for tamende it grete delit;
And if I may youre harmes nat redresse,
I am right sory for youre hevynesse.   140

XXI.

'For though ye Trojans with us Grekes wroth
Han many a day ben, alwey yet, pardé!
O god of love, in soth, we serven both:
And for the love of God! my lady fre,
Whom so ye hate, as beth not wroth with me;
For trewely ther kan no wight yow serve,
That half so loth youre wreth wolde disserve.

XXII.

'And ner it that we been so neigh tho tente
Of Calkas, which that sen us bothe may,
I wold of thys yow telle alle myn entente,   150
But this enseled til another day:
Yeve me youre honde, I am and shal ben ay,
God helpe me so! whil that my lif may dure,
Youre owen, aboven every creature.

XXIII.

'Thus seyde I nevere or now to womman borne;
For God myn herte as wisly glade so!
I lovede never womman here beforne,
As paramoures, ne nevere shal no mo:
And for the love of God! beth not my fo,
Al kan I nought to yow, my lady deere,   160
Compleyne aright, for I am yit to leere.

XXIV.

'And wondreth nought myne owen lady bryghte,
Though that I speke of love to yow thus blyve;
For I have herde or this of many a wighte,

Hath loved thynge he nevere saugh his lyve :
Ek I am not of power for to stryve
Ayenis tho god of love, but hym obeye
I wol alwey, and mercy I yow preye.

· XXV.

' Ther ben so worthy knyghtes in this place,
And ye so faire, that everich of hem alle   170
Wol peynen hym to stonden in youre grace ;
But myght to me so faire a grace falle,
That ye me for youre servaunt wolde calle,
So lawely, ne so trewely yow serve
Nyl non of hem, as I shal til I sterve.'

XXVI.

Criseyde unto that purpos lite answerde,
As she that was with sorwe oppressed so,
That, in *effect*, she nought his tales herde
But here and ther, now here a worde or two :
Hire thought hire sorwful herte braste a-two ;   180
For when she gan hire fader fer espie,
Wel neigh down of hire hors she gan to sye.

XXVII.

But natheles, she thonkede Dyomede,
Of alle his travaile and his goode chere,
And that hym liste his frendschip hyre to bede ;
And she accepteth it in goode manere,
And wol do fayn that is hym lief and deere ;
And trusten hym she wolde, and wel she myghte,
As seyde she, and from hire hors shalighte.

XXVIII.

Her fader hath hire in his armes ynome,   190
And twenty tyme he kyste his doughter swete,
And seyde :—' O dere doughter myn, welcome !'
She seyde ek, she was fayn with hym to mete,
And stood forth muwet, mylde, and mansuete ;
But here I leve hire with hire fader dwelle,
And forth I wol of Troilus yow telle.

XXIX.

To Troye is come this woful Troylus,
In sorwe aboven alle sorwes smerte ;
With felon look, and face dispitouse,
Tho sodcinly doun from his hors he sterte,   200
And thorwgh his paleys, with a swollen herte,
To chaumbre he wente, of nothyng took he hede,
Ne non to hym dar speke a worde for drede.

XXX.

And ther his sorwes, that he spared hadde,
He yaf an issue large, and ' Deth !' he criede ;
And in hise throwes, frenetike and madde,
He curseth Jove, Apollo, and ek Cupide ;
He curseth Ceres, Bachus, and Cipride,
His birthe, hymself, his fate, and ek nature,
And save his lady, every creature.   210

XXXI.

To bedde he goth, and weyleth ther and torneth
In furie, as doth he Ixion in helle ;
And in this wyse he neigh til day sojourneth,

But tho bigan his herte alite unswelle,
Thorugh teres, whiche that gonnen up to welle;
And pitously he cryed upon Criseyde,
And to hym-self right thus he spake and seyde.

XXXII.

' Where is myn owene lady, lief and deere?
Where is hire white breste, where is it, where?
Where ben hir armes, and hire eyen clere,   220
That yesternight this tyme with me were?
Now may I wepe allone many a tere,
And graspe aboute I may, but in this place
Save a pilow, I fynde naught tembrace.

XXXIII.

' How shal I don? when shal sho com ayein?
I not allas! whi lete Ich hire to go?
As wolde God Ich hadde as tho ben sleyne!
O herte myn Criseyde!   O sweto fo!
O lady myn! that I love and namo,
To whom for evere mo myn herte I dowe,   230
So how I dye! ye nyl me not rescowe.

XXXIV.

' Who seth yow now, my righte lode-sterre?
Who sit right now or stante in youre presence?
Who kan conforten nowe youre hertes werre?
Now I am gon, whom yove yo audiens?
Who spoketh for me right now in my absens?
Allas! no wight; and that is al my care,
For wel woot I as yvel as I ye fare.

XXXV.

' How shold I thus ten dayes fulle endure
When I the firste nyght have al this tene?   240
How *shal* she don ek, sorwful creature?
For tendrenesse, how shal she thus sustene
Swiche wo for me?   O, pitous, pale, and grene,
Shal ben youre fresche wommanliche face,
For langour, er ye torne unto this place.'

XXXVI.

And when he fille in any sloumberynges,
Anon bygynne he sholde for to grone,
And dremen of the dredefulleste thynges
That myghte ben: as mete he were allone
In place horrible, makynge ay his mone;   250
Or meten that he was omanges alle
His enemys, and in hire honde falle.

XXXVII.

And therwithalle his body sholde sterte,
And with the sterte alle sodeynliche awake;
And swiche a tremour fele aboute his herte,
That of the fere his body sholden quake:
And therwithal he sholde a noyse make,
And seme as though he sholde *falle* depe,
From heigh of loft, and than he wolde wepe,

XXXVIII.

And rewen on hymself so pitously,   260
That wonder was to here hise fantasye.
Another tyme he sholde myghtely

Conforte hymself, and seine it was folie,
So causeles, swiche dredo for to drye;
And eft bygynne his aspre sorwes newe,
That every man myghte on his sorwes rewe.

XXXIX.

Who koude telle arighte, or ful discryve
His wo, his pleynt, his langoure, and his pyne?
Nought al the men that han or ben on lyve;
Thow redere maist thi-self fulle wele devyne,   270
That swich a wo my wit kan not defyne;
On ydel for to write it shold Y swynke,
When that my wit is wery it to thynke.

XL.

On hevene yet the sterres weren scene,
Although ful pale ywoxen was the moone;
And whiten gan the orisounte sheene
Al esterwarde, as it wonte is to done;
And Phebus, with his rosi carte, soone
Gan efter that to dresse hym up to fare,
When Troilus hath sente efter Pandare.   280

XLI.

This Pandare, that of al the day byforne
No myght han comen Troilus to see,
Although he on his hed it hadde sworne;
For with the kynge Priam alday was he,
So that it lay nought in his liberté
Nowher to gon; but on the morwe he wente
To Troilus, when that he for hym sente.

XLII.

For in his herte he koude wel devyne,
That Troilus al nyght for sorw wooke,
And that he wolde telle hym of his pyne;   290
This knew he wele ynowgh withouten booke;
For which to chaumbre streight the wey he tooke,
And Troilus tho sobrelich he grette,
And on the bed ful soone he gan hym sette.

XLIII.

'My Pandarus,' quod Troilus, 'the sorwe
Which that I drye, I may not longe endure;
I trow I shal not lyven til to morwe;
For whiche I wolde alweys, on aventure,
To the devysen of my sepulture
The fourme, and of my moble thow dispone   300
Right as the semeth best is *for* to done.

XLIV.

'But of tho fir and flaumbe funeral,
In which my body brennen shal to glede,
And of the festo and pleyes palestral
At my vigilo, I preye the take gode hede
That that be wel: and offre Mars my stede,
My swerd, my helme: and, leeve brother deere,
My shelde to Palas yef, that shyneth clere.

XLV.

'The poudre in which myn herte ybrend shal turne,
That preye I the thow tak, and it conserve   310
In a vesselle, that men clepeth an urne

Of gold ; and to my lady that I serve,
For love of whom thus pitouslyche I sterve,
So yeve it hire ; and do me this pleasaunce,
To preyen hire kepe it for a remembraunce.

XLVI.

' For wel I fele by my maladye,
And by my dremes now and yoore ago,
Al certeinly that I mot nedes dye :
The owle ek, which that hette *Ascaphilo*,
Hath efter me shright al this nyghtes two ;   320
And god Mercurie ! of me now, woful wrecche,
The soule gide, and when the list it fecche.'

XLVII.

Pandare answerde and seyde, ' Troilus,
My deere frende, as I have told the yoore,
That it is folie for to sorwen thus,
And causeles, for whiche I kan namore ;
But who so wol nat trowen rede ne lore,
I kan not sen in hym no remedie,
But lat hym worchen with his fantasie.

XLVIII.

' But, Troilus, I preye the tello me nowe,   330
If that thow trowe er this that any wight
Hath loved paramours as wel as thow ?
Ye, God woot ! and fro many a worthy knyght
Hath his lady gon, ye, a fourtenyghte,
And he not yit made halvendel the care ;
What nede is the to maken alle this fare ?

XLIX.

' Syn day by day thow maist thy-selven see
That from his love, or elles from his wyf,
A man mot twynnen of necessité,
Ye, though he love hire as his owen life ;   340
Yet nyl ho with hymself thus make stryfe ;
For wel thow woost, my leve brother deere,
That alwey frendes may nought ben ifeere.

L.

' How don this folk that seen hire loves wedded
By frendes myght, as it bitit ful ofte,
And sen hem in hire spouses bed ybedded ?
God woot, they take it wysely, faire, and soft ;
For-whi goode hope halt up hire herte oloft ;
And for they kan a tyme of sorwe endure,
As tyme hem hurt, a tyme doth hem cure.   350

LI.

' So sholdestow endure, and laten slyde
Tho tyme, and fonde to be glad and light ;
Ten dayes nys so longe nought tabide ;
And syn sho the to comen hath behight,
Sho nyl hire heste breken for no wight ;
For drede the nought, that sho nyl finden weye
To come ayein, my lif, that dorst I leye.

LII.

' Thy swevenes ek, and alle swich fantasie
Dryve oute, and late hem faren to myschaunce ;
For they procede of thy malencolye,   360

That doth the feele in slepe al this penaunce:
A straw for alle swevenes signifiaunce !
God help me so, I counte hem nought a bene,
Ther wot no man aright what dremes mene.

LIII.

‘ For prestes of the temple tellen this,
That dremes ben the revelacions
Of Goddes ; and as wel they telle ywis,
That they ben infernals illusiouns.
And leches seyn that of complexions
Proceden they, or fast, or glotonye ;
Who woot in-soth thus what they signifie ?

LIV.

‘ Ek oother seyn, that thorwgh impressions,—
As if a wight hath fast a thynge in mynde,—
That therof cometh swiche avisions :
And oother seyne, as they in bokes fynde,
That efter tymes of the yere, by kynde,
Men dreme, and that theffect goth by the moo
But leve no dremen, for it is nought to done.

LV.

Wel worth of dremes ay this olde wyves,
And, treweliche, ek augurye of thise fowcles,
For fere of which men wenen leese hire lyves,
As ravenes qualm, or schrychynge of thise owl
To trowen on it, bothe fals and foul is ;
Allas, allas, so noble a creature
As is a man, shal dreden swich orduro !

LVI.

' For which with al myn herte I the beseche,
Unto thi-self that alle this thow foryive ;
And ryse now up, withouten more speche,
And lat us cast how forth may best be dryve
This tyme ; and ek how fresshly we may lyve, 390
When that she cometh, the whiche shal be right
  soone ;
God help me so ! thy best is thus to doone.

LVII.

' Ris, lat us speke of lusty lif in Troye
That we han led, and forth the tyme dryve,
And ek of tyme comynge us rejoye,
That bryngen shal oure blisse now so bilive ;
And langour of this twye dayes fyve
We shal therwith so foryete *or* oppresse,
That wel unneth it don shal us duresse.

LVIII.

' This town is ful of lordes al aboute,   400
And trewes lasten al this mene-qwyle ;
Go we pleye us in som lusty route,
To Sarpedon, not hennes but a myle ;
And thus thow shalt the tyme wel bygile,
And dryve it forth unto that blisful morw,
That thow hire se, that cause is of thi sorwe.

LIX.

' Now ris, my dere brother Troilus ;
For certes it non honur is to the
To wepe, and in thy bed to jouken thus ;

For treweliche of o thynge trust to me,—   410
If thow thus ligge, a day, or two, or thre,
The folk wol wene that thow for cowardyse
The feynest sik, and that thow darst not rise.'

LX.

This Troilus answarde, 'O brother deere!
This knowen folk that han isuffred peyne,
That though he wepe, and make sorwful cheere
That feeleth harm and smert in every veyne,
No wonder is; and though Ich evere pleyne,
Or alwey wepe, I nam nothynge to blame,
Syn I have lost the cause of al my game.   420

LXI.

'But syn of fyne force I moot aryse,
I shal aryse, as soone as ever Y may;
And God, to whom myn herte I sacrifise,
So send us hastely the tenthe day;
For was ther nevere fowl so fayn of May
As I shal ben, when that she cometh in Troye,
That cause is of my tormente and my joye.

LXII.

'But whider is thi reed,' quod Troilus,
'That we may pleye us best in al this town?
'By God, my conseile is,' quod Pandarus,   430
'To ryde and pleyen us with kynge Sarpedoun.'
So longe of this they speken up and down,
Til Troilus gan at tho last to assente
To ryse, and forth to Sarpedon they wente.

LXIII.

This Sarpedoun, as he that honourable
Was evere hys lyve, and ful of heigh prowesse,
With al that myght yserved ben on table,
That deynté was, al cost it grete rychesse,
He fed hem day by day; that swich noblesse
As seyden bothe the meest and ek the leste,   440
Was nevere er that day wiste at any feeste.

LXIV.

Nor in this world ther is noon instrumente
Delicious, thorugh wynde, or touch on corde,
As fer as any wight hath ever wente,
That tonge teile, or herte may recorde,
But at that feste, it nas wel herd acorde
Nof ladyes ek so faire a compaignye
On daunce, er tho, was nevere yseyn with eye.

LXV.

But what availleth this to Troylus,
That for his sorwe nothynge of it roughte,   450
But evere in oon, as herte pictus,
Ful bisily Criseyde his lady soughte?
On hire was evere al that his herte thoughte,
Now this, now that, so faste ymagynynge,
That glad, ywis, kan hym no feestynge.

LXVI.

Thise laydyes ek that at this feeste ben,
Syn that he saugh his lady was aweye,
It was his sorwe up-on hem for to sen,

Or for to here on instrumentz so pleye ;
For she that of his herte bereth the keye,
Was absente, lo ! this was his fantasie,
That no wight scholde maken melodye.

LXVII.

Nor ther nas houre in al the day or nyghte,
When he was ther as no *man* myght hym here,
That he ne seyde, ' O lufsom lady bryghte,
How have ye faren syn that ye were here ?
Welcom, ywys, myn owen lady deere !'
But, walaway ! al this nas *but* a maze,
Fortune his howen entended bet to glaze.

LXVIII.

The lettres ek that she of olde tyme
Hadde hym *isente*, he wold allone rede
An hondreth sythe attwexen none and prime,
Refigurynge hire shap, hire wommanhede,
Withinne his herte, and every worde or dede
That passed was ; and thus he droofe tan ende
The ferthe day, and seyde he wolde wende.

LXIX.

And seyde, ' Leve brother Pandarus,
Intendestow that we shal here bileve,
Til Sarpedon wol forth congeyen us ?
Yet were it fayrer that we toke oure leve :
For Goddes love, lat us now soone at eve
Oure leve take, and homwarde lat us torne ;
For trewely I nyl not thus sojorne.'

LXX.

Pandare answerde, 'Be we comen hyder
To fecchen fir and rennen hom ayein ?
God help me so! I kan *nat* tellen whider
We myghte goon, if I shal sothely seyn,
Ther any wight is of us moore feyn
Than Sarpedon; and *if* we hennes hye
Thus sodeynly, I holde it vilenye.   490

LXXI.

' Syn that we seyden that we wolde bleve
With hym a wowke, and now thus sodeynly
The ferthe day to take of hym oure leve,
IIe wolde wondren on it trewely :
Lat us holden forth oure purpos fermely;
And sen that ye byhighten hym to bide,
Holde forward now, and efter lat us ride.'

LXXII.

This Pandarus, with al*le* peyne and wo
Made hym to dwelle; and at the wekes end,
Of Sarpedon they tok hire leve tho,   500
And *on* hire weye they spedden hem to wende :
Quod Troilus, ' Now Lorde me grace sende,
That I may fynden at myn home comynge,
Criseyde comen !' and therwith gan he synge.

LXXIII.

' Ye, has*il-wode !*' thoughte this Pandare,
And to hymself ful softely he seyde,
' God woot, refreyden may this hoote fare,

Er Calkas sende Troilus Criseyde !'
But natheles he jape*de* thus and seyde,
And swor, iwis, his herte hym wel bihighte,   510
She wolde com as soone as evere she myghte.

LXXIV.

When they unto the pal*e*ys were yeomen
Of Troilus, they doun of hors alighte,
And to the chaumbre hire wey than han they
          nomen ;
And into tyme that it gan to nyghte,
They spaken of Criseyde, tho lady brighte ;
And efter this, when that hem bothe *le*ste,
.They spedde hem fro tho soper unto reste.

LXXV.

O morw, as soone as day bigan to clere,
This Troilus gan of his slepe to breyde,   520
And to Pandare, his owen brother deere,
' For love of God,' ful pitously he preyed*e*,
' As go we sene tho pal*e*ys of Criseyde ;
For syn we yit may have namooro feeste,
So lat us seen hire pal*e*ys at tho leste.'

LXXVI.

And therwithalle, his moynye for to blende,
A cause he fonde in towne for to go,
And to Criseydes hous they gonnen wende ;
But Lorde ! this eely Troilus was wo !
Hym thought his sorwful herte brasto atwo ;   530
For when he saugh hire dorres spered alle,
Wel neigh for sorwe adoun he gan to falle.

LXXVII.

Therwith, when he was ware, and gan biholde
How shet was every wyndow of the place,
As frost hym thoughte his *herte* gan to colde;
For which, with chaunged deedlich pale face,
Withouten word, he forth bygan to pace;
And as God wolde he gan so faste ryde,
That no wight of his contenaunce espiede.

LXXVIII.

Than seyde he thus :—' O paleys desolat ! 540
O hous of housses, whilom beste yhight !
O paleys empti and disconsolat !
O thow lanterne, of which queynte is the light !
O payleys, whilom day, that now ert nyght !
Wel oughtestow to falle, and I to dye,
Syn she is wente that wonte was us to gye.

LXXIX.

' O paleys, whilom crowne of houses alle,
Enlumyned with sonne of alle blisse !
O rynge, fro which the ruby is out falle !
O cause of wo, that cause has ben of *blisse* ! 550
Yit syn I may no bet fayn wold I kysse
Thi *colde dores*, dorst I for this route;
And farewel shryne, of which the scint is oute !

LXXX.

Therwith he caste on Pandarus his ye,
With chaunged face, and pitous to beholde;
And when he myght his tyme aright espie,

Ay as he rode, to Pandarus he tolde
His newe sorwe, and ek his joyes olde,
So pitously, and with so dede an hewe,
That every wight myght on his sorwes rewe.   560

LXXXI.

Fro thennes-forth he rydeth up and down,
And every thynge com hym to remembraunce,
As he rode forth by the places of the town,
In which he whilom had alle his plesaunce :—
‘ Lo! yonder saugh Ich myn owen lady daunce;
And in that temple, with hire eyen clere,
Me caughte firste my righte lady deere.

LXXXII.

‘ And yonder have I herd ful lustili
My deere herte laugh; and yonder pleye
Saugh Ich hire oones ek ful blisfully;   570
And yonder oones to me gan she seye
‘ Now goode swete! love me wel, I preye;
And yonder so gladly gan she me beholde,
That to the deth myn herte is to hir holde.

LXXXIII.

‘ And at that corner in the yonder *house*,
Herde I myn alderlevest lady deere,
So wommanly, with vois melodyous,
Syngen so wel, so goodely and so clere,
That in my soule yit me thynketh Ich here
The blisful sown; and in that yonder place   580
My lady first me tooke unto hire grace.’

LXXXIV.

Than thought he thus, ' O blisful lord Cupide !
When *I* the processe have in memorye,
How thow me hast weryed on every syde,
Men myght a book mak of it lyk a story !
What nede is thee to seke on me victorye,
Syn I am thyn, and holly at thi wille ?
What joye hastow thyn owene folk to spille ?

LXXXV.

' Wel hastow, *lord*, ywroke on me thyn ire,
Thow myghty god ! and dredeful for to greve !
Now mercy, god ! thow woost wel I'desire   591
Thy grace moost, of alle lustes leeve !
And lyve and dye I wol in thi beleve ;
For which I naxe in guerdon but a boone,
That thow Criseyde ayein me sende soone.

LXXXVI.

' Destreyne hire herte as faste to retourne,
As thow doost myn to longen hire to see ;
Than woot I wel that sho nyl naught sojourne :
Now blisful lorde ! so cruwel thow ne be
Unto the blode of Troye, I preye the,   600
As Juno was unto the blode Thebane,
For which the folk of Thebes caught hire bane.'

LXXXVII.

And efter this he to the yates wente,
Ther as Criseyde oute rode a ful goode pas,
And up and doun ther made he many a wente,

And to himself ful oft he seyde, 'Allas!
Fro hennes rod my blisse and my solas!
As wolde blisful God now for his joye,
I myght hire seen ayein com into Troye!

LXXXVIII.

'And to the yonder hille I gan hire gyde;   610
Allas! and ther I took of hire my leeve;
And yonde I saugh hire to hire fader ryde,
For sorwe of which myn herte shal to-cleve;
And hider hom I com when it was eve;
And here I dwelle, out-cast from alle joye,
And shal, til I may seen her eft in Troye.'

LXXXIX.

And of hym-self ymagyned he ofte,
To be defet, and pale, and waxen lesse
Than he was wont, and that men seyde softe,
'What may it be? who kan the sothe gesse,   620
Why Troylus hath alle this hevynesse?'
And al this nas but his melencolye,
That he hadde of hym-self swich fantasye.

XC.

Another tyme ymagynen he wolde,
That every wyght that wente by the weye
Hadde of him routhe, and that they seyne sholde,
'I am right sory, Troilus wol deye.'
And thus he drof a day yit forth or tweye,
As ye han herde; swich lyf right gan he lede,
As he that stood bitwixen hope and drede.   630

XCI.

For which hym liked in his songes shewe
Thencheson of his wo, as he best myghte,
And made a song of wordes but a fewe,
Somwhat his woful herte for to lighte :
And when he was from every mannes sighte,
With softe vois, he of his lady deere,
That absent was, gan synge as ye may here.

XCII.

' O sterre, of which I lost have alle the lighte,
With herte soore, wel oughte I to bewaylle,
That evere derk in tormente, nyght by nyght, 640
Towarde my deth, with wynde in steero I saylle ;
For whiche the tenthe nyght if that I faile
The gidynge of thi bemes bright an houre,
My ship and me Caribdes wol devoure.'

XCIII.

This songe when he thus songen hadde soone
He fel ayein into his sikes olde ;
And every nyght, as was his wone to doone,
He stood, the bryghte mone to beholde ;
And al his sorwe he to the moone tolde,
And seyde, ' Iwis, when thow ert horned newe 650
I shal be glad, if alle the world be trewe.

XCIV.

' I saugh thyne hornes old ek by the morwe,
Whan hennes rode my righte lady deere,
That cause is of my torment and my sorwe ;

For which, O bryghte *Lucina* the cleere !
For love of God ! renne fast aboute thy spere ;
For when thyne hornes newe gynnen sprynge,
Than shal she come that may my blisse brynge.'

XCV.

The day is moore, and longer evere nyght
Than they ben wonte to be, hym thoughte tho ; 66
And that the sonne wente his course unright,
By longer weye than it was wonte to go ;
And seyde, ' Iwis, me dredeth everemo
The sonnes sone, Pheton, be on lyve,
And that his fader carte amys he dryve.'

XCVI.

Upon the walles fast ek wold he walke,
And on the Grekes oost he wolde se ;
And to hymself right thus he wolde talke :—
' Lo, yonder is myn owene lady free,
Or elles yonder, ther the tentes boo,   67
And thennes cometh this eyr that is so soote,
That in my soule I feele it doth me boote.

XCVII.

' And hardyly, this wynde that moore and moore
Thus stoundemele encresseth in my face,
Is of my ladys depe sykes sore ;
I preve it thus, for in noon nother place
Of al this town, save oonly in this space,
Feele I no wynde that souneth so lyke peyne ;
It seith ' Allas ! whi twynned be we tweyne ?''

XCVIII.

This longe tyme he dryveth forth right thus,   680
Tille fully passed was the nynthe nyght;
And ay bysyde hym was this Pandarus,
That bisily dide al his ful*le* myght
Hym to confort, and mak his herte light;
Yevynge hym hope alweye, the tenthe morwe
That she shal come, and stenten al his sorwe.

XCIX.

Upon that other syde eke was Criseyde
With wommen few omange the Grekes stronge,
For which ful oft a day, ' Allas !' she seyde,
' That I was borne ! wel may myn herte longe
After my deth, for now lyve I to longe ;   691
Allas ! and I ne may it not amende,
For now is wers than evere yit I wende.

C.

' My fader nyl for nothynge do me grace
To gon ayein, for nought I kan hym queme ;
And if so be that I my terme pace,
My Troilus shal in his herte deme
That I am fals, and so it may wel seme.
Thus shal Ich have unthonke on every syde ;
That I was borne, so walawey the tyde !   700

CI.

' And if that I me put in jupartye
To stele awey by nyghte, and it befalle
That I be caught, I shal be hold a spye ;

Or elles, lo ! this drede I moost of alle,
If in the hondes of som wreche I falle,
I nam but lost, al be myn herte trewe :
Now myghty God, thow on my sorwe rewe !'

CII.

Ful pale ywoxen was hire brighte face,
Her lymes lene, as she that al the day
Stood when she dorste, and loked on the place 710
Ther she was borne, and she dwelte had ay,
And al the nyght wepynge, allas ! she lay ;
And thus, despeyred oute of alle cure,
She ledde hire lyf, this woful creature.

CIII.

Ful oft a day she sighte ek for destresse,
And in hire-self she wente ay pourtreynge
Of Troilus the grete worthinesse,
And alle his goodely wordes recordynge,
Syn first the day hire love bigan to sprynge ;
And thus she sette hire woful herte afire,   720
Thorugh remembraunce of that she gan desire.

CIV.

In al this world ther nys so cruwel herte,
That hire hadde herd compleyne in hire *sorwe,*
That nold han wopen for hire peynes smerte ;
So tendrely she wepte, bothe eve and morwe,
Hire nedede non teris for to borwe ;
And this was yet the werste of al hyre peyno,
Ther was no wight, to whom she dorst hire pleyne.

CV.

Ful *rewfully* she loked upon Troye,
Byheldo the toures heigh, and ek the hallis ;   730
' Allas !' quod she, ' the plesaunce and the joye,
The which that now al tourned into galle is,
Have Ich hadde oft withinne tho yonder wallis !
O Troilus, what dostow now ?' she seyde ;
' Lord ! whether thow thynke yet upon Criseyde !

CVI.

' Allas ! I nadde ytrowed on youre lore,
And wente with yow, as ye me redde or this,
Thanne hadde I now not siked half so sore :
Who myght han seyde, that I hadde don amys,
To stele away with swich oon as he is ?   740
But al to late cometh the latuarye,
When men the cors unto the grave *carye*.

CVII.

' To late is now to speke of that matere,
Prudens, allas ! oon of thyn eyen thre
Me lakked alwey, er that I com here :
On tyme ypassed wel remembred me,
And present tyme ek koude Ich wel ysee ;
But future tyme, er I was in tho snare,
Koude I not sen ; that causeth now my care.

CVIII.

' But natheles, bitide what bitide,   750
I shal to morw at nyght, by est or weste,
Out of this oost stele, on som maner side,

And gon with Troilus, wher as hym leste;
This purpos wol I hold, and this is beste,
No fors of wikked tonges janglerye,
For evere on love han wreches hadde envye.

CIX.

' For who so wole of every worde tak hede,
Or rulen hym by every wightes wit,
Ne shal he nevere thryven, out of drede;
For that *that* som men blamen evere yit,   7
Loo! other maner folk comenden it;
And as for me, for alle swich variaunce,
Felicité clepe I my suffisaunce.

CX.

' For which, withouten any wordes moo,
To Troye I wol, as for conclusion.'
But, God it woot! er fully monthes two,
Sho was ful fer fro that entencioun!
For bothe Troilus and Troyes town
Shal knotles thorughout hire herte slyde,
For sho wol take a purpos for tabide.   7

CXI.

This Dyomede, of whom yow telle I gan,
Goth now withinne hymself ay arguynge,
With al the sleighte and alle that evere he kan,
How he may best with shortest taryinge,
Into his net Criseydes herte brynge;
To this entente he koude nevere fyne,
To fisshen hire he layde out hook and lyne.

CXII.

But natheles, wel in his herte he thoughte,
That she nas nat without a love in Troye,
For nevere sithen he hire thennes broughte,   780
Ne koude he sen her laughe, or maken joye;
He nyst how best hire *herte* for tacoie,
But for tasaie, he seyde 'nought it ne greveth,
For he that nought nasayeth, nought nacheveth.'

CXIII.

Yet sayde he to hymself upon a nyght,
'Now am I nought a fool, that woot wel how
Hire wo for love is of another wight,
And hereupon to gon asaye hire nowe,
I may wel wete it nyl not ben my prow;
For wyse folk in bokes it expresse,   790
Men shal nought wowe a wight in hevynesse.

CXIV.

'But who-so myghte wynnen swich a floure
From hym for whom she morneth nyght and day,
He myghte seyn he were a conqueroure.'
And right anon, as he that bolde was ay,
Thought in his herte, 'happe how happe may,
Al shold I dye, I wol hire herte seche;
I shal namore lesen but my speche.'

CXV.

This Dyomede, as bokes us declare,
Was in his nedes prest and corageous,   800
With stierne vois, and myghty lymes square,

Hardy, testif, strong, and chivalrus
Of dedes, like his fader Tydeus;
And som men seyn he was of tonge large,
And heire he was of Calcidoyne and Arge.

CXVI.

Criscyde mene was of hire stature
Therto of shap, of face, and ek *of* cheere,
Ther myghte be no fairer creature;
And ofte tyme this was hire manere,
To gon ytressed with hire heres clere   810
Doun by hire coler, at hire bak byhynde,
Which with a threde of gold she wolde bynde.

CXVII.

And save hire browes joyneden ifeere,
Ther nas no lakke in ought I kan espien;
But for to speken of hyre eyen clere,
Loo! trewely they writen that hire seyen,
That Paradys stood formed in hiro yen;
And with hiro riche beaute everemore
Strof love in hire, ay whiche of hem was moore.

CXVIII.

Sho sobre was, ek symple, and wyse withalle, 820
The best ynorissed ek that myghte be,
And goodely of hire speche in general,
Charytable, estatliche, lusty, and free;
Ne neveremoo no lakked hire pyté,
Tendre herted, slidynge of corage;
But trewely I kan not telle hire age.

CXIX.

And Troilus wel woxen was in heighte,
And complet formed by proporcioun,
So wel that Kynde it nought amenden myghte;
Yong, fresshe, strong, and hardy as lyon ;   830
Trew as steele in ech condicioun ;
On *of* the best enteched creature,
That is or shal, while that the world may dure.

CXX.

And, certeinly, in story it is yfounde,
That Troilus was nevere unto no wight,
As in his tyme, in no degré secunde
In during do, that longeth to a knyghte ;
Al myght a geaunt passen hym of myght,
IIis herte ay with the firste and with the beste
Stod paregal, to dure do that hym leste.   840

CXXI.

But for to tellen forth of Dyomede :—
It fel, that efter on that tenthe day
Syn that Cryseyde out of the cité yede,
This Dyomede, as fressh as braunche in May,
Com to the tente ther as Crisseyde lay,
And feyned hym with Calkas han to doon ;
But what he mente I shal yow tellen soone.

CXXII.

Criseyde, at shorte wordes for to telle,
Welcom*ed* hym, and doun by hire hym sette,
And he was ethe ynough to maken dwelle ;   850

And efter this, withouten longe letto,
The spices and the wyn men forth hem fette,
And forth they speke of this and that yfeere,
As frendes don, of whiche som shal ye here.

CXXIII.

He gan firste fallen of tho werre in speche
Bytwyxen hem and the folk of Troye toun,
And of thassege he gan ek hire beseche
To tellen him what was hire opinyoun :
Fro that demaunde he so descendeth doun
To axen hire if that hire straunge thoughte   860
The Grekis gyse, and werkes that they wroughte?

CXXIV.

And whi hire fader tarieth so longe
To wedden hire unto som worthy wighte?
Criseyde that was in hire peynes stronge,
For love of Troylus, hire owene knyghte,
Als ferfortho as sho konnynge hadde or myght,
Answerde hym tho; but, as of his entente,
It semede not sho wiste what he mento.

CXXV.

But, natheles, this ilke Dyomede
Gan in hymself assoure, and thus he seyde :—   870
' If Ich arighte have taken of yow hede,
Me thynketh thus, O lady myn Crisseyde!
That, syn I firste hond on youre bridel layde,
When ye out com of Troye by the morwe,
No koude I nevere sen yow but in sorwe.

CXXVI.

' Kan I not seyn what may tho cause be,
But if for love of som Troyan it were ;
Tho which right soore woolde athynken me,
That ye for any wighte that dwelleth there,
Sholden spille a quarter of a teere,   380
Or pitously youre-selven so bygile ;
For dredeles it is nought worth tho while.

CXXVII.

' Tho folk of Troye, as who scith allo and some,
In prison ben, as ye youre-selven see ;
Fro thennes shal not oon on lyve come,
For al tho gold atwixen sonne and see ;
Trusteth wel, and understondeth me,
Ther shal not oon to mercy gon on lyve,
Al were he lord of worldes twyes fyve.

CXXVIII.

' Swich wreche on hem for fecchynge of Eleyne
Ther shal ben take, er that we hennes wende,   891
That Manes, which that goddes ben of peyne,
Shal ben agaste that Grekes wol hem shende ;
And men shul drede, unto the worldes ende
From hennesforth, to ravysshen any queene,
So cruel shal our wreche on hem be seene.

CXXIX.

' And but-if Calkas lede us with ambages,
That is to seyn, with dowble wordes slye,
Swich as men clepe ' a worde with two visages,'

Ye shal wel knowen that I nought ne lye,   900
And al this thynge right sen it with youre ye,
And that anoon, ye nyl not trow how soone,
Now taketh hede, for it is for to doone.

CXXX.

' What ! wene ye youre wyse fader wolde
Have yeven Antenor for yow anoon,
If he ne wiste that the cité sholde
Destrued ben ? why, nay !   So mot I gon !
He knewe ful wel ther *shal* not scapen oon
That Trojan is ; and for the grete feere,
He dorst*e* not ye dwelt*e* lenger there.   910

CXXXI.

' What wol ye moore, lufsom lady deere ?
Late Troye and Trojan fro youre herte pace ;
Dryve oute that bittre hope, and make goode chere,
And clepe ayein the beauté of youre face,
That ye with salt*e* teeris so deface,
For Troye is brought in swich a jupartye,
That it to save is now no remedye.

CXXXII.

' And thenketh wel, ye shal in Grekes fynde
A moore parfite love, or it be nyght,
Thanne any Trojan is, and moore kynde,   920
And bet to serven yow wol don his myght ;
And if ye vowchesaufe my lady bryghte,
I wol ben he to serven yow me-selve,
Ye ! levere than ben a lord of Grekes twelve.'

CXXXIII.

And with that worde he gan to wexen rede,
And in his speche a litel *while* he quooke,
And easte aside a litel with his hed,
And stynte a while; and efterwarde he wooke,
And sobreliche on hire he threw his looke,
And seyde, 'I am, albeit yow no joye, 930
As gentil man as any wighte in Troie.

CXXXIV.

'For if my fader Tydeus,' he seyde,
' Ylived hadde, Ich hadde ben or this,
Of Calcidoyne and Arge a kyng, Criseyde;
And so hope I that I shal yit, ywys:
But he was slayne, allas! the moore harme is,
Unhappilye at Thebes al to rathe,
Polymyte, and many a man to scathe.

· CXXXV.

' But herto myn! syn that I am youre man,
And ben the firste of whom I seche grace, 940
To serve yow as hertely as I kan,
And evere shal, while I to lyve have space,
So er that I departe out of this place,
Ye wol me graunte that I may to morwe,
At better layser telle yow my sorwe.'

CXXXVI.

What sholde I telle hise wordes that he seyde?
He spake inowgh for a day atte meeste;
It prove*th* wel he spak so, that Criseyde

Graunted on the morwe at his requeste,
For to speken with hym atte leste,   950
So that he nolde speke of swiche matere ;
And thus she to hym seyde, as ye mow here,

CXXXVII.

As she that hadde hire herte on Troilus
So faste, that ther may it noon arace ;
And straungely she spak and seyde thus :—
' O Diomede, I love that ilke place
Ther I was borne ; and, Joves, for his grace
Delyvere it soone of alle that doth it care !
God for thi myght so lene it wel to fare !

CXXXVIII.

' That Grekes wolde hire wrath on Troye wreke,
If that they myght, I know it wel, ywis ;   961
But it schal nought byfallen as ye speke ;
And God toforne, and ferther over this,
I woot my fader wyse and redy is,
And that he me hath bought, as ye me tolde,
So deere I am the more unto hym holde.

CXXXIX.

' That Grekes ben of heigh condicioun,
I wot ek wel ; but certein men shal fynde
As worthy folk withinne Troye town,
As konnynge, as parfite, and as kynde,   970
As ben betwyxen Orcades and Inde ;
And that ye koude wele youre lady serve,
I trow ek wel hire thonke for to desserve.

CXL.

' But as to speke of love, iwis,' she seyde,
' I had a lord to whom I wedded was,
He whos myn herte al was til that he *deyde*;
And other love, as help me now Pallas!
Ther in myn herte nys, ne nevere was;
And that ye ben of noble and heigh kynrede,
I have wel herd it tellen, out of drede.   980

CXLI.

' And that doth me to han so grete a wonnder,
That ye wol scornen any womman so;
Ek, God woot, love and I ben fer asonder;
I am disposed bet, so mot I go,
Unto my deth to pleyne and maken wo;
What I shal efter done I kan not seye,
But trewelich as yet me luste not pleye.

CXLII.

' Myn herte is now in tribulacion,
And ye in armes bysi day *by* day;
Here-efter whan yo wonnen han the town,   990
Paraunter than, so it happen may,
That when I se that I nevere er sey,
Thanne wol I werke that I never er wroghte;
This word to yow ynough suffisen oughte.

CXLIII.

' To morwe eke wol I speke with yow fayne,
So that ye touchen naught of this matere;
And when yow luste, ye may com here ayeynne,

And er ye gon, thus muche I seye yow here;—
As helpe me Pallas, with hire heres clere,
If that I sholde of any Greke han routhe,   1000
It sholde be youre-selven, be my trouthe!

CXLIV.

' I say not therfore that I wol yow love,
Ny say not nay; but, in conclusioun,
I mene wele, by God that sitt above!'
And therwithal she caste hire eyen down,
And gan to syke, and seyde, ' O Troye town!
Yet bid I God, in quiete and in reste
I may yow sen, or do myn herte breste!

CXLV.

But in effect, and shortly for to seye,
This Diomede alle fresshly newe ayein   1010
Gan presen on, and fast hire mercy preye;
And efter this, the sothe for to seyne,
Hire glove he toke, of wiche he was ful fayne;
And, finaly, when it was woxen eve,
And alle was wel, he roos and tooke his leve.

CXLVI.

The brighte Venus folwed and ay taughte
The wey ther brode Phebus down alighte;
And Cynthea hire char hors over raughte,
To whirle out of the Leon, if she myghte;
And Signifer his candels sheweth brighte,   1020
When that Criseyde unto hire bedde wente,
In-with hire fadres faire bryghte tente.

CXLVII.

Retournynge in hir soule ay up and doun
The wordes of this sodeyn Diomede,
His grete estate, and peril of the town,
And that she was allon, and hadde nede
Of frendes help; and thus bygan to brede
The cause whi, the sothe for to telle,
That sche tok fully the purpos for to dwelle.

CXLVIII.

The morwen com, and gostly for to speke,   1030
This Diomede is com unto Criseyde;
And shortly, leste that ye my tale *breke*,
So wel he for hymself*e* spake and seyde,
That alle hire sykes soore adown he layde;
And finaly, the sothe for to seyne,
He ref*te* hire of the grete of al hire peyne.

CXLIX.

And efter this, the storye telle*th* us,
That she him yaf the faire bay*e* steede,
The whiche she ones wan of Troilus;
And eke a broch (and that was litel nede)   1040
That Troilus was, she yaf this Diomede;
And ek the bet from sorw hym to releve,
She made hym were a pensel of hire sleve.

CL.

I fynde ek in stories elleswhere,
When thorugh the body hirte was Dyomede
Of Troilus, tho wepte she many a teere,

When that she saugh hise wyde woundes blede,
And that she toke to kepen hym good hede,
And for to helen hym of his sorwes smerte,
Men seyn, I not, that she yaf hym hire herte. 10

CLI.

But trewelyche, the storye telleth us,
Ther made nevere womman more wo
Than she, when that she falsede Troylus;
She *seyde*, ' Allas ! for now is clene ago
My name of trouthe in love for everemo ;
For I have falsed oon the gentileste
That evere was, and oon the worthyeste,

CLII.

' Allas ! of me unto the wor*l*des ende
Shal neither ben ywriten nor ysong*e*
No good word*e*, for this bok*es* wol me shende :
*I*rolled schal I ben on many a tonge ;   10
Thorughout the world my be*lle* schal be ronge ;
And wommen most wol haten me of alle ;
Allas ! that swich a cas me sholde falle !

CLIII.

' They wol seyn, in as muche as in me is,
I have hem don dishonoure, walaway !
Al be I not the firste that dide amys,
What helpeth that to don my blame away ?
But syn I se ther is no better way,
And that to late is now for me to rewe,   1
To Dyomede algate I wol be trewe.

CLIV.

' But, Troilus, syn I no bettre may,
And syn that thus departen ye and I,
Yet preye *I* God so yeve yow right good day ;
As for the gentileste trewely,
That evere Y say, to serven faithfully,
And beste kan ay his *lady* honour kepe ;'
And with that word she braste anon to wepe.

CLV.

' And certes, yow to haten shal I nevere,
And frendes love, that shal ye han of me,   1080
And my good*e* worde, al shold I lyve evere ;
And trewely I wol *right* sory be,
For to sen yow in adversité ;
And giltelees I wot wel I yow leeve,
And alle shal passe, and thus tak I my leve.'

CLVI.

But trew*e*ly how longe it was betweyne,
That she forsoke hym for this Dyomede,
Ther is non auctour telleth it, I wene ;
Tak every man now to his bokes hede,
He shal no time fynden, out of drede ;   1090
For though that he bigan to wow hire soone,
Er he hire wan, yet was there more to doone.

CLVII.

No me ne list this sely womman chyde
Ferther thanne the storie wol devyse ;
Hire name, allas ! is pu*bl*yshed so wyde,

That for hire gilte it ought ynough suffise ;
And if I myght excuse hire any wyse,
For she so sory was for *hire* untrouthe,
Iwis I wold excuse hire yet for routhe.

CLVIII.

This Troilus, *as* I before have tolde,   110
Thus dryveth forth as wel as he hathe myght ;
But ofte was his herte hote and colde,
And namely that ilke nynthe nyght,
Whiche on the morwe she hadde hym byhight
To com ayeyn : God woot, ful litel reste
Hadde he that nyght ! nothynge to slepe hym leste

CLIX.

The laurer-crowned Phebus, with his hete
Gan in his course ay upwarde as he wente,
To warmen of the este se the wawes wete,
And Nysus doughter song, with fressh entente,
When Troilus his Pandare efter sente ;   111
And on the walles of the town thei pleyde,
To loke if they kan sen ought of Criseyde.

CLX.

Til it was none they stoode for to so
Who that ther come, and every manere wight
That com fro fer, they seyden it was she,
Til that thei koude knowen hym aright :
Now was his herte dul, now was it light,
And thus bijaped stonden for to stare,
Aboute nought, this Troilus and Pandare   112

CLXI.

To Pandarus this Troilus tho seyde,
' For ought I woot, byfor noon sykerly,
Into this town ne cometh not here Criseyde ;
She hath ynough to doen, hardily,
To wynnen from hire fader, so trow I ;
Hire olde fader wol yet make hire dyne
Er that she go, God yeve his herte pyne !'

CLXII.

Pandare answarde, ' It may wel be certein,
And forthy lat us dyne, I the beseche,
And after noon than maistow com ayein:'   1130
And hom they go, withouten moore speche,
And comen ayein ; but longe may they seche,
Er that thei fynde that they efter *gape* ;
Fortune hem bothe thenketh for to jape.

CLXIII.

Quod Troilus, ' I so wel now that she
Is taried with hire olde fader so,
That, er she come, it wol neigh even be.
Come forth, I wol unto *the* yate go ;
Thise portours ben unkonnynge everemo,
And I wol done hem holden up the yate,   1140
As nought ne were, although she come late.'

CLXIV

The day goth fast, and efter that cometh eve,
And yet com nought to Troilus Criseyde ;
He loketh forth by hegge, by tre, by greve,

And for his hed over the walle he layde,
And at the laste he torned hym, and seyde,
' By God, I wot hire menyinge now, Pandare !
Almoost iwys al newe is my care.

CLXV.

' Now, douteles, this lady kan hire good ;
I wote she meneth riden prively ;   11
I comende hire wysdom, by myn hode !
She wol not maken peple nycely   .
Gaure on hire when that she comth ; but softely
By nyght into the town she thenketh ride,
And dere brother thenke not longe tabide,

CLXVI.

' We han nought elles for to don, iwys ;
And Pandarus, now woltow trowen me ?
Have here my trouthe, I se hire ! yonde she is !
Heve up thyn eyen man, maystow not se ?'
Pandare answerde, ' Nay, so moot I the !   110
Al wronge, by God ! what seistow man ? wher arte
That I se yonde is but a fare carte.'

CLXVII.

' Allas ! thow saist right soth,' quod Troilus ;
' But hardely it is not al for nought,
That in myn herte I now rejoysse thus,
It is ayenis som good, I have a thought ;
Not I not how, but sen that I was wroughte,
Ne felt I swich a confort, dar I seye ;
She comth to nyght, my life that dorste I lye !'

CLXVIII.

Pandaro answerd, ' It may be wel ynough,'   117
And helde with hym of al that ever he seyde,
But in his herte he thought, and softly lough,
And to hymself ful sobreliche he seyde,
' From hasel woode, ther jolye Robin pleyde,
Shal com al that that thow abydest here !
And farewel al the snowgh of ferne yere !'

CLXIX.

The wardeyn of the yates gan to calle
The folk which that withoute the yates were,
And bad hem dryven in hire bestes alle,
Or al the nyght they moste bleven there ;   1180
And for withinne the nyght, with many a teere,
This Troilus gan homwarde for to ride,
For wel he seth it helpeth nought tabyde.

CLXX.

But natheles, he gladded hym in this,
He thoughte he mysacounted hadde his day,
And seyde, ' I understonde have al amys,
For thilke nyght I laste Criseyde seye,
She seyde, ' I shal ben here, if that I may,
Er that the moone, O deere herte sweto,
The Leon passe oute of this Ariete ;'   1190

CLXXI.

' For which she may yet holde al hire biheste.'
And on the morwe unto the yate he wente,
And up and down, by weste and ek bi este,

Upon the walles made he many a wente,
But al for nought ; his hope alwey hym blente ;
For which at nyght, in sorwe and sikes sore,
He wente hym home, withouten any moore.

CLXXII.

This hope al clene out of his herte fledde,
He nath wheron now lenger for to honge ;   1199
But, for the peyne, hym thought his herte bledde,
So were his throwes sharpe, and wonder stronge ;
For when he saugh that she aboode so longe,
He nyste what he juggen of it myghte,
Syn she hath broken that she hym byhighte.

CLXXIII.

The thridde, ferthe, fyfte, *and* sexte day
After tho dayes ten, of whiche I tolde,
Betwixen hope and drede his herte lay,
Yet somwhat trusten on hire hestes olde ;
But when he saugh she nold hire terme holde,
He kan now sen non other remedye,   1210
But for to shape hym sone for to dye.

CLXXIV.

Therwith the wykked spirit, God us blesse !
Which that men clepeth wode jalousie,
Gan in hym crepe, in al this hevynesse ;
For whiche, because he wolde soone dye,
He ne ete ne dranke for his melencolye,
And ek from every compaynye he fledde ;
This was the lyf that al the tyme he ledde.

CLXXV.

He so defet was, that no maner man
Unneth hym myghte knowen there he wente ; 1220
So was he leen, and therto pale and wan,
And fieble, that he walketh by potente,
And with his ire he thus hymselven shente :
But who so axed hym whereof hym smerte,
He seyde his harme was al aboute his herte.

CLXXVI.

Priam ful ofte, and ek his moder deere,
His bretheren and his sustren gonne hym freyne
Whi he so sorwful was in al his cheere,
And what thyng was the cause of al his peyne ?
But al for nought, he nold his cause pleyne ; 1230
But seyde, he felte a grevous maladye
Aboute his herte, and fayne he wolde dye.

CLXXVII.

So on a day he layde hym down to slepe ;
And so byfel, that in his slepe hym thoughte,
That *in* a forest faste he welke to wepe,
For love of hire that hym thise poynes wroughte ;
And up and doun as he that forest soughte,
He mette he saugh a boor, with tuskes grete,
That slepte ayein the brighte sonnes hete.

CLXXVIII.

And by this boor, fast in hir armes folde, 1240
Lay kyssyng ay his lady bright Criseyde ;
For sorw of which, whan he *it* gan biholde,

And for despit, out of his slepe he breyde,
And loude he criede on Pandarus, and seyde,
‘O Pandarus, now know I, crope and roote!
I nam but ded, there is non other boote!

CLXXIX.

‘ My lady bryghte, Criseyde, hath me bytrayed,
In whom I trustede moost of any wighte ;
She elleswhere hath now hire herte apeyde ;
The blisful goddes, thorwgh hire grete myghte,
Han in my drem yshewed it ful righte ;   1251
Thus, in my drem, Criseyde have I biholde ;’
And al this thynge to Pandarus he tolde.

CLXXX.

‘ O my Criseyde, allas ! what subtilté ?
What newe lust ? what beauté ? what science?
What wrathe of juste cause have ye to me ?
What guilte of me ? what fel experience
Hath fro me raft, allas ! thyn advertence ?
O trust, O feith, O depe assurraunce !
Who hath me reft Criseyde, al my plesaunce ?

CLXXXI.

‘ Allas ! whi lett Ich yow from hennes go ?   1261
For which wel neigh out of my wit I breyde ;
Who shal now trowe on any othes moo ?
God woot I wende, O lady bright Criseyde,
That every word was gospel that ye seyde !
But who may beste bigile if hym liste,
Than he on whiom men weneth best to triste ?

CXXXLII.

What shal I don, my Pandarus, allas ?
I fele newe so sharpe a newe peyne,
Syn that ther is no remedye in this cas,   1270
That bet were it I with myn hendes tweyne
My-selven slewe, *than* alway thus to pleyne ;
For thorwgh the deth my wo shold have an ende,
Ther every day with lif myself I shende.'

CLXXXIII.

Pandare answerde and seyde, ' Allas, the while
That I was born ! have I not seyde or this
That dremes many a maner man bigile ?
And whi ?   For folk expounden hem amys :
How darstow seyn that fals thy lady is,
For any dreme, right for thyn owen drede ?   1280
Lat be this thought, thow kanst no dremes rede.

CLXXXIV.

' Paraunter ther thow dremest of this boor,
It may so be that it may signifye
Hire *fadir*, whiche that old is and ek hoor,
Ayein the sonne lyth o poynte to dye ;
And she for sorwe gynneth wepe and crye,
And kysseth hym, ther he lyth on the grounde ;
Thus sholdestow thy dreme aright expounde.'

CLXXXV.

' How myght *I* than don,' quod Troilus,
' To know of this, ye, were it nevere so lite ?'   1290
' Now seyestow wisely,' quod this Pandarus ;

'My rede is this, syn thow kanst wel endite,
That hastily a letre thou hire write,
Thorugh whiche thow shalt wel bryngen it aboute
To knowe a soth of that thow ert in doute.

CLXXXVI.

'And se now why: for this I dar wel seyn,
That if so is, that she untrewe be,
I kan not trowen that *she* wol write ayein;
And if she write, thow shalt ful soone see,
As whether she hath any liberté   1300
To come ayein, or elles in som clause
If she be let, she wol asigne a cause.

CLXXXVII.

'Thow hast not writen hire syn that she wente,
Nor sche to the; and this I dorste laye,
Ther may swich cause ben in hire entente,
That hardily thow wolt thy-selven saye,
That hire abood the best is for yow tweye:
Now write hire than, and thow shalt fele soone
A sothe of al; ther is namoore to doone.'

CLXXXVIII.

Acorded ben to this conclusion,   1310
And that anon, thise ilke lordes two;
And hastily sit Troilus adoun,
And rolleth in his herte to and fro,
How he may best descryven hire his wo;
And to Criseyde, his owen lady deere,
He wroote righte thus, and seyde as *ye* may here.

THE COPY OF THE LETTER.

CLXXXIX.

‘ Right fresshe floure ! whos I ben have and shal,
Withouten part of ellesewhere servyse,
With herte, body, lyf, lust, thought, and alle !
I, woful wight, in everych humble wyse   1320
That tonge telle, or herte may devyse,
As oft as matere occupieth place,
Me recomaunde unto youre noble grace.

CXC.

‘ Liketh *it* yow to wyten, sweete herte,
As ye wel knowe, how longe tyme agon
That yo me left in aspre peynes smerte,
When that ye wente, of which *yit* boote non
Have I non had, but evere wors bigoon
Fro day to day am I, and so mot dwelle,
While it yow liste, of wele and wo my welle ! 1330

CXCI.

‘ For which to yow, with dredeful herte trew*e*,
I write (as he that sorwe drifth to write)
My wo, that every houre encresseth new*e*,
Compleynynge as I dar, or kan endite ;
And that defaced is, that may ye wite,
With teres, which that fro myn eyen reyne ;
They wolden speke, if that they koude, and pleyne.

CXCII.

‘ Yow first beseche I, that youre eyen clere,
To look on this defouled ye nat hold*e* :
And over al this, that ye, my lady dere,   1340

Wol vouche-saufe this letre to beholde ;
And by the cause ek of my cares colde,
That sleth my wit, if ought amys masterte,
Foryeve it me, myn owen swete herte.

CXCIII.

[' Yf any servaunt durst, or aught aryght
Upon hys lady pitously compleyne,
Than wene I that I oughte be that whyght ;
Considered thys, that ye thys monethes tweyne
Han taryed, there ye seyde, sothe to seyne,
But dayes ten ye nolde in hoste sojourne ;   1350
But in two monethes yit ye not retourne.

CXCIV.

' And, for as moche as me mote nedys lyke
Alle that you lust, I dar not pleyne more,
But humbly, wyth sorowful sykes syke,
You write I myn unresty sorowes sore ;
Fro day to day, desiring evermore
To knowen fully, yif youre wille it were,
How ye han ferde and don while ye ben there.

CXCV.

' Tho whos welfare and hele eke God encrece
In honour suche, that upward in *degré*   1360
Hit grow alwey, soo that it never cese,
Ryght as your herte ay can, my lady fre,
Devise, I prey *to* Gode so mote it be,
And graunt it, soone that ye upon me rewe,
As wisly as in al I am unto you trewe.

CXCVI.

' And yf it lyke yow to know*en* of the fare
Of me, whos woo ther may no wyght discryve,
I can no more, but cheste of every care,
At wrytyng of thys letre I was on lyve,
Al redy oute my wooful gost to dryve,   1370
Wych I delay, and holde hym yit in honde,
Upon the syght of matere of youre sonde.

CXCVII.

' Myn eyen twoo, in veyne wyth wych I see,
Of sorowfule terys salte ar woxen welles ;
My songe *in* pleynt of myn adversité,
My good in harme, myn ese eke woxen helle is,
My joye in wo ; I can sey you no*ught* ellys,
But tournede is, for wych my lyf I warye,
Every joye or ese in hys contrarie.

CXCVIII.

' Wych with your commyng *hom* ayen to Troye
Ye may redresse, and, more *a* thousand sithe,   1381
Than ever I hade, encrecen in me joye ;
For was ther never her*te* yit so blithe
To have hys lyf, as I shal ben as swyth
As I you see; and though no manere routhe
Com in *to* you, yit thenkyth on youre trouthe.

CXCIX.

' And yef so be my gilt dethe have deserved,
Or yf you lust no more upon me see,
In guerdon yit of that I have you served,

Beseche I you, myn owne lady free,
That herupon ye wolde write me,
For love of Gode, my ryghte lodestere,
That dethe may make an ende of al my were.

cc.

' If other cause aught dothe you for to dwelle,
Than with youre letre ye *may* me reconforte ;
For though to me youre absence is an helle,
Wyth pacience Y wyl my woo conforte,
And with youre letre of hope I wyl disporte :
Now writeth, swete, and lat me thus not ple[y]
Wyth hope, or dethe, delivereth me from pey[ne].

cci.

' Iwys, myn oune dere herte trewe,
I wote that whan ye next *upon* me se,
So lost have I myn hele and eke myn *hewe*,
Criseyde shal not *conne* knowe me ;
Iwys, myn hertes day, my lady fro,
Soo thrusteth ay myn herte to beholde
Your beauté, that unnethe my lyf I holde.

ccii.

' I sey no more, al have I for to seye
To you wel more than I tellen may ;
But whether that ye do me lyve or deye,
Yit prey I Gode so yeve you ryght gode day ;
And fareth wel, godely feyre fresshe may,
As she that lyf or deth me may comaunde,
And to your trouthe ay I me recomaunde.

CCIII.

' Wyth hele swych, but that ye yeven me
The same hele, I shal noon hele have;
In you lieth, whan you list that it so be,
The day on wyche me clothen shal my grave;
In you my lif, in youre myght for to save
Me fro disese of alle peynes smerte;   1420
And fare now wele, myn owne swete herte!
                              ' Le vostre T.'

CCIV.

Thys letre forth was sent unto Criseyde,
Of wych hir answere in effect was thys:—
Ful pitously she wrote ayen and seyde,
That al so sone as *that* she myght ywys,
She wolde come, and mende that was amys;
And finally, she wrote hym and seyde thanne,
She wolde come, ye, but she nyste whanne.]

CCV.

But in hire letre made she swich feeste,   1470
That wonder was, and swerth she loveth hym beste,
Of which he fonde but botmeles bihoste.
But Troilus thou mayst now, est or weste,
Pipe in an ivy leofe, if that the leste.
Thus goth the world; God shilde us fro meschaunce,
And every wight that meneth trouthe avaunce!

CCVI.

Encressen gan the wo fro day to nyght
Of Troilus, for tarynge of Criseyde;
And lessen gan his hope and ek his myght,

For which al doun he in his bed hym leyde ;   144(
He ne ete, ne dronk, ne slepe, no worde seyde,
Ymagynynge ay that she was unkynde,
For which wel neigh he wex out of his mynde.

CCVII.

This dreme, of which I tolde have ek biforne,
May nevere come out of his remembraunce ;
He thought ay wel he had his lady lorne,
And that Joves, of his purveiaunce,
Hym shewed hadde in slepe the signifiaunce
Of hire untrouth, and his disaventure,
And that the boor was shewed hym in figure.   145(

CCVIII.

For which he for Sibille his suster sente,
That called was Cassandre al aboute,
And al his dreme he told hire or he stente,
And hire bysought assoylen hym the doute
Of the stronge boor, with tuskes stoute ;
And finaly, withinne a litel stounde,
Cassandre bygan right thus his dreme expounde.

CCIX.

She gan first smyle, and seyde, ‘ Brother dere,
If thow a soth of this desirest knowe,
Thow most a fewe of olde stories here,   146(
To purpos how that fortune overthrowe
Hath lordes olde, thorwgh which withinne a throw(
Thow wel this boor shalt know, and of what kynd(
He comen is, as men in bokes fynde.

CCX.

'Diane, which that wroth was and in ire,
For Grekes nolde don hire sacrifise,
Ne incens upon hire auter sette afire,
So for that Greekes gonne hire so despise,
Wrak hir in a wonder cruwel wyse;
For, with a boor, as grete as ox in stalle, 1470
She made up frete hire corne and vynes alle.

CCXI.

'To slo this boor was al the contré raysed,
Omanges which ther come this boor to se
A maide, on of this worlde the beste preysed;
And Meleager, lordo of that contré,
He lovede so this fresshe mayden free,
That with his manhode, or he wolde stente,
This boor he slough, and hire the hed he sente.

CCXII.

'Of which, as olde bokes tellen us,
Ther roos a contek and a grete envye; 1480
And of this lorde descended Tideus
By ligne, or elles olde bokes lye:
And how this Meleager gan to dye
Thorwgh his moder, wol I yow nought telle,
For al to long it were for to dwelle.'

CCXIII.

She told ek how Tideus, or she stente,
Unto the stronge cité of Thebes,
To cleymen kyngdom of the cité, wente

For his felawe daun Polimytes,
Of whiche the brother daun Ethiocles   1490
Ful wrongfully of Thebes held the strengthe.
This tolde she by proces al by lengthe.

CCXIV.

She told ek how Hemonydes asterte,
When Tideus slough fifty knyghtes stoute;
She told ek al the prophecies by herte,
And how that seven kynges with hire route
Besegeden the cité alle aboute;
And of the holy serpent, and the welle,
And of the furies al*le* she gan hym telle.

CCXV

Associat profugum Tideus primus Polymycem,   1500
Tidea legatum docet insidiasque secundus,
Tercius Hemoniden canit, et vates latitantes,
Quartus habet reges incuntes prelia septem;
Mox furie lenne quinto narrantur et anguis,
Archimori bustum sexto ludusque leguntur.
Dat Grayos Thebes et vatem septimus umbris,
Octavo cecidit Tideus, spes, vita Pelasgis;
Ypomedon nono moritur cum Parthonopeo,
Fulmine percussus decimo Cappaneus superatur,
Undecimo sese perimunt per vulnera fratres,   1510
Argiva flentem, narrat duodenus et ignem.

CCXVI.

Of Archinoris buryngo, and the pleyes,
And how Amphiorax fil thorwgh the grounde,
How Tideus was slayn, lord of Argoyes,

And how Ypomedon in litel stounde
Was dreynt, and dyed Parthonope of wounde;
And also how Cappaneus the proude,
With thunder dynt was slayn, that criede loude.

CCXVII.

She kan ek telle hym how that either brother,　·
Ethiocles and Polymyte also,　　　　　　　　1520
At a scarmyche ech of hem slough other,
And ·of Argyves wepynge and hire wo,
And how the town was brente she told ek tho;
And so descendeth doun from gestes olde
To Diomede, and thus she spak and tolde.

CCXVIII.

'This ilke boor bitokneth Diomede,
Tideus sone, that doun descended is
Fro Meleagre, that made the boor to blede;
And thy lady, wher-so sehe be, ywis,
This Dyomede hire herte hath, and she *his*:　　1530
Wepe if thow wolt, or lefe, for out of doute
This Diomede is inne, and thow ert oute.'

CCXIX.

'Thow saist nat soth,' quod he, 'thow sorceresse!
With al thi false goost of prophecie!
Thow wenest ben a grete devineresse!
Now sestow nat this fool of fantasie,
Peyneth hire on ladys for to lye?
Awey!' quod he, 'ther Joves yeve the sorwe!
Thow shalt be fals paraunter yet to morwe!

CCXX.

'Als wel thow myghtest lyen on Alceste,
That was of creatures (but men lie)
That ever weren, kyndest, and the beste;
For when hire housbonde was in jupartye
To dye hymself, but if she wolde dye,
She ches for hym to dye, and gon to helle,
And starf anon, as us the bokes telle.'

CCXXI.

Cassandre goth, and he, with cruel herte,
Foryat his wo for angre of hire speche;
And from his bed al sodeynly he sterte,
As though al hool hym hadd ymade *a* leche;
And day by day he gan enquere and seche
A soth of this, with al his ful*le* cure,
And thus he driveth forth his aventure.

CCXXII.

Fortune, which that permutacioun
Of thynges hath, as it is hyre committed,
Thorwgh purveiaunce and disposicioun
Of heigh Jove, as regnes shal ben flitted
Fro folk in folk, or when they shal ben smitted,
Gan pulle awey the fetheres bright of Troie,
Fro day to day, til they ben bare of joie.

CCXXIII.

Amange al this, the fyne of the parodye
Of Ector gan *approchen* wonder blyve;
The fate wold his soule shold unbodye,

And shapen hadde a mene it out to dryve,
Ayeins which fate hym helpeth not to stryve;
But, on a day, to fighten gan he wende,
At which allas! he caughte his lyves'ende.

CCXXIV.

For which me thenketh every manere wi*g*ht
That haunteth armes oughte to bewayle
The deth of hym that was so noble a knyght:
For, as he drough a kynge by thavantaille,   1571
Un*ware* of this, Achilles, thorwgh the maylle,
And thorwgh the body, gan hym for to ryve;
And thus the worthy knyght was brought of lyve.

CCXXV.

For wh*om*, as old*e* bokes tellen us,
Was made swiche wo, that tonge it may not telle;
And namely, the sorwe of Troilus,
That next hym was of worthinesse welle;
And in this wo gan Troilus to dwelle,
That what for sorwe, and love, and for unreste,
Ful oft a day he bad his herte breste.   1581

CCXXVI.

But, natheles, though he gan hym despaire,
And drede ay that his lady was untrewe,
Yet ay on hire his herte gan repaire,
And as thise lovers don, he sought ay newe
To gete ayein Criseyde, brighte of hewe;
And in his herte he wente hire excusynge,
That Calkas caused alle hire taryinge.

CCXXVII.

And oft*e* tyme he was in purpos grete,
Hymselven like a pilgrym to degyse,   1590
To sen hire ; but he may not conterfete,
To ben unknowen of folk that weren wyse,
Ne fynde excuse aright that may suffise,
If he omange the Grekes knowen weere ;
For whiche he wepte ful oft and many a teere.

CCXXVIII.

To hire he wroot yet oft*e* tymo al newe,
Ful pitously, he left it nought for slouthe,
Besechynge hire, that syn that he was trewe,
That she wol come ayein, and hold hire trouthe ;
For which Criseyde upon a day for routhe,   1600
I take it so, touchynge al this matere,
Wroot hym ayein, and seyde as ye may here.

CCXXIX.

‘ Cupides sone, ensaumple of goodlyhede,
O swerde of knygh*th*od, sours of gentilesse,
How myght a wight in tormento and in drede,
And heleles, yow sende as yet gladnesse ?
I herteles, I sik, *I* in destresse,
Syn ye with me, nor I with yow may dele,
Yow neither sende Iche herte may, nor hele.

CCXXX.

‘ Your letres ful, tho papir al yploynted,   1610
Conceyved hath myn hertes pité ;
I have ek seyn, with teeris alle depoynted,

Youre letre, and how that ye requeren me
To come ayein ; which yet ne may not be ;
But whi, leste that this letre founden were,
No mencion ne make I nowe for fere.

CCXXXI.

' Grevous to me, God woot, is youre unreste,
Youre haste, and that the Goddes ordinaunce
It semeth nat ye take it for the beste ;
Nor other thyng nys in youre remembraunce,
As thenketh me, but oonly youre pleasaunce ; 1621
But beth not wroth, and that I yow beseche,
For that I tarye is al for wikked speche.

CCXXXII.

' For I have herde wel more than I wende
Touchynge us two, how thynges han ystonde,
Whiche I shal with dissimulynge amende ;
And, beth not wroth, I have ek understonde,
How ye ne don but holden me in honde ;
But now no fors, I kan not in yow gesse,
But alle trouthe and alle gentilesse.   1630

CCXXXIII.

' Com I wole, but yet in swich disjoynte
I stonde as now, that what yere or what day
That this shal be, that kan I nought apoynte ;
But in effect I preye yowe, as I may,
Of your good word, and of youre frendschip ay ;
For trewely while that my lif may dure,
As for a frend, ye may in me assure.

CCXXXIV.

' Yet preyo I yow, an evyl ye *ne* take
That it is short which that I to yow write;
I dar not ther I am wele letres make,   1640
Ne nevere yet ne koude I wel endite;
Ek grete effect, men write in place lite,
The entente is alle, and not the letres space;
And farth now wel, God have you in his grace!
' La vostre C.'

CCXXXV.

This Troilus this letre thought al straunge,
Whan he it saugh, and sorwfullyche he sighte;
Hym thought it like a kalendes of chaunge;
But, finaly, he ful ne trowen myghte,
That she ne wold hym holden that she hyghte;
For with ful yvel wil list hym to leve,   1651
That love*th* wel, in swiche cas, though hym greve.

CCXXXVI.

But natheles, men seyn that, at tho laste,
For any thyng, men shal tho sothe see;
And swich a cas bet*i*d, and that as faste,
That Troilus wel understood that she
Nas not so kynde as that hire oughte be;
And finaly, he woot now out of doute,
That al is lost that ho hath ben aboute.

CCXXXVII.

Stood on a day in his maloncolyo   1660
This Troilus, and in suspicioun
Of hire, for whom ho wende for to dyo;

And so bifel, that thorwghout Troie town,
As was the gyse, iborn was up and down
A manere cote armur, as seith the storie,
Biforn Deiphebe, in signe of his victorie.

CCXXXVIII.

The whiche cote, as telleth Lollius,
Deiphebe it hadde rent fro Diomede
The same day; and when this Troilus
It saugh, he gan to taken of it hede,   1670
Avysinge of the lengthe and of the brede,   .
And al the werke; but, as he gan biholde,
Ful sodeynli his herte gan to colde,

CCXXXIX.

As he that on the coler fonde withinne
A broche, that he Criseyde yaf that morwe
That she from Troie moste nedes twynne,
In remembraunce of hym, and of his sorwe;
And she hym layde ayein hir feith to borwe,
To kepe it ay; but now ful wel he wiste,
His lady nas no langer on to truste.   1680

CCXL.

He goth hym hom, and gan ful soone sende
For Pandarus; and al this newe chaunce,
And of this broche, he told hym word and ende,
Compleynynge of hire herte variaunce,
His longe love, his trouth, and his pennaunce;
And after Deth, withouten wordes moore,
Ful fast he cried, his rest hym to restoore.

CCXLI.

Than spak he thus :—' O, lady myn Criseyde,
Wher is youre feith, and wher is youre biheste?
Wher is your love, where is youre trouth?' he seyde,
' Of Diomede have *ye* now al this feeste !   1691
Allas ! I wold han trowed at the leeste,
That syn ye nold in trouthe to me stonde,
That ye thus nold han holden me in honde.

CCXLII.

' Who shal now trow on any othes mo ?
Allas ! I nevere wold han wende, or this,
That ye, Criseyde, koude han chaunged so,
Ne but I hadde agilt, and don amys ;
So cruel wende I nought youre herte, iwys,
To slo me thus ! allas ! youre name of trouthe 1700
Is now fordon, and that is al my routhe.

CCXLIII.

' Was ther non other broch yow liste lete,
To feffe with youre new*e* love,' quod he,
' But thilk*e* broch that I, with teris wete,
Yow yaf, as for a remembraunce of me ?
Non other cause, allas ! ne hadde ye,
But for despit ; and ek for that ye mente
Al outerly to showen youre entente.

CCXLIV.

'Thorwgh which I so, that clene out of youre mynde
Ye han me caste, and I ne kan nor may   1710
For al this world withinne myn herte fynde

To unloven yow a quarter of a day ;
In cursed tyme I borne was, walawey !
That yow, that dothe me al this wo endure,
Yet love I best of any creature.

CCXLV.

' Now God,' quod he, ' me sende yet the grace,
That I may meten with this Diomede !
And trewely, if I have myghte and space,
Yet shal I make, I hope, his sides blede :
O God !' quod he, ' that oughtest taken hede   1720
To ferthren trouthe, and wronges to punice,
Whi nyltow don a vengeaunce of this vice ?

CCXLVI.

' O Pandarus, that in dremes for to truste
Me blamed hast, and wonte oft ert upbreyde,
Now maistow sen thi self, if that the liste,
How trew is now thi nece, bright Criseyde !
In sondry formes, God it woot !' he seyde,
' The goddes shewen bothe joye and teene
In slepe ; and by my dreme it is now seene.

CCXLVII.

' And certeinly, withouten more speche,   1730
From hennesforth, as ferforth as I may,
Myn owen deth in armes wol I seche ;—
I recche nat how sone be the day ;
But trewely, Criseyde, swete may,
Whom I have ay with al my myght yserved,
That ye thus don, I have it not deserved.'

CCXLVIII.

This Pandarus, that al thise thynges herde,
And wiste wel he seyde a soth of this,
He nought a word ayein to hym answarde,
For sory of his frendes sorwe he is,   1740
And shamed for his nece hath don amys;
And stont astoned of thise causes tweye,
As stille as stone; a word ne koude *he* seye.

CCXLIX.

But at the laste thus he spak and seyde,
'My brother deere, I may do the namore;
What shold I seyn? I hat, iwis, Criseyde!
And, God woot, I wol hat hire everemore:
And that thow me bisoughtest don of yore,
Havynge unto myn honour ne my reste
Right no rewarde, I dide al that the leste.   1750

CCL.

'If I dide ought that myghte lyken the,
It is me liefe; and of this treson now,
God woot that it a sorwe is unto me;
And, dredeles, for hertes ese of yow,
Right faine I wolde amende it, wiste I how:
And fro this worlde, Almighty *God* I preye,
Deliver hire soone! I kan namore seye.'

CCLI.

Grete was the sorwe and pleynte of Troilus;
But forth hire cours fortune ay gan to holde;
Criseyde loveth the sone of Tydeus,   1760

And Troilus mot wepe in cares colde.
Swich is this world, who-so it kan biholde!
In ech estat is litel hertes reste!
God lene us for to take it for tho beste!

CCLII.

In many cruel bataille, out of drede,
Of Troilus, this ilke noble knyght,
(As men may in this olde bokes rede)
Was seen his knyghthod and his grete myghte;
And, dredeles, his ire day and nyghte,
Ful cruely tho Grekes ay aboughte,   1770
And alwey moost this Diomede, he soughte.

CCLIII.

And ofte tyme I fynde that they mette
With blody strokes, and with wordes grete,
Assayinge how hire speres weren whette;
And, God it woot, with many a cruel hete
Gan Troilus upon his helm to bete;
But, natheles, Fortune it nought ne wolde,
Of otheres honde that either dyen sholde.

CCLIV.

And if I hadde taken for to write
Tho armes of this ilke worthi man,   1780
Than wold Ich of his battailles endite;
But for that I to writen first bygan
Of his love, I have seyde as I can.
His worthy dedes, who-*so* lest hem here,
Rede Dares; he kan telle hem alle ifeere.

CCLV.

Besechynge every lady bright of hewe,
And every gentil womman, what she be,
That al be that Criseyde was untrewe,
That for that gilt she be not wroth with me.
Ye may hire gilt in otheres bokes se,   1790
And gladlier I wol write, if yow leste,
Penelopes trouthe, and good Alceste.

CCLVI.

Ny sey nat this al only for thise men,
But moost for wommen that betraised be
Thorwgh false folk, (God yeve hem sorwe, amen !)
That with hire grete wit and subtilité
Betraise yow: and this commeveth me
To spek ; *and* in effect yow alle I preye
Beth war of men, and herkeneth what I seye.

CCLVII.

Go, litel boke, go, litel myn tregedie !   1800
Ther God my maker, yet er that *I* dye,
So sende *me* myght to maken som comedye !
But litel book, no makynge thow nenvye,
But subgit be to alle poesie,
And kysse the steppes, wheras thow seest space,
Of Virgile, Ovyde, Omer, Lucan, and Stace.

CCLVIII.

And, for ther is so grete dyversité
In Englissh, and in writynge of our tonge,
So preye I to God, that non myswrite the,

Ne the mys-metere, for defaute of tonge !   1810
And red wher so thow be, or elles songe,
That thow be understonde, God I beseche !
But yet to purpos of my rather speche.

CCLIX.

The wrath, as I bigan yow for to seye,
Of Troilus, the Grekes boughten deere ;
For thousandes his hondes maden dye,
As he that was withouten any peere,
Save Ector in his tyme, as I kan here ;
But, walawey ! save only Goddes wille,
Dispitously hym slough the fiers Achille.   1820

CCLX.

And when that he was slayn in this manere,
His lighte gost ful blisfully is wente
Up to the holughnesse of the seventhe spere,
In convers letynge everych elemente ;
And ther he saugh, with ful avysemente,
The erratyk sterres, herkenynge armonye,
With sownes ful of hevenyssh melodie.

CCLXI.

And down from thennes faste he gan avyse
This litel spot of erth, that with the se
Embraced is ; and fully gan despice   1830
This wreched world, and helde al vanyté,
To respect of the pleyne felicité
That is in hevene above : and at the laste,
Ther he was slayn his lokynge down he caste.

CCLXII.

And in hymself he lough right at the wo
Of hem that wepten for his deth so faste,
And dampned al our werk that folweth so
The blynde luste, the which that may not laste,
And sholden al our herte on hevene caste;
And forth he wente, shortly for to telle,　　　18
Ther as Mercurie sorted hym to dwelle.

CCLXIII.

Swich fin hath, lo! this Troilus for love!
Swich fyn hath al his grete worthynesse!
Swich fyn hath his estat real above!
Swich fyn his luste, swich fyn hath his noblesse!
Swich fyn hath false worldes brotelnesse!
And thus bigan his lovynge of Cryseyde,
As I have tolde, and in this wise he deyde.

CCLXIV.

O yonge fresshe folkes, he or she,
In which that love up groweth with youre age,　18
Repeireth hom fro worldly vanyté,
And of youre herte up casteth the visage
To thilke God, that after his ymage
Yow made, and thynketh al nys but a faire,
This worlde that passeth soon, as floures faire.

CCLXV.

And loveth hym the which *that* right for love,
Upon a crois, oure soules for to beye,
First starfe and roos, and sitt in heven above,
For he nyl falsen no wight, dar I seye,
That wol his herte alle holly on hym leye;　　18

And syn he best to love is, and most meke,
What nedeth feyned loves for to seke?

CCLXVI.

Lo! here of payens corsed olde rites!
Lo! here what alle hire goddes may availle!
Lo! here this wreched worldes appetites!
Lo! here the fyn and guerdon for travaille,
Of Jove, Apollo, of Mars, *and* swich rescaille!
Lo! here the forme of olde clerkes speche
In poetrie, if ye hire bokes seche.

LENVOYE DU CHAUCER.

CCLXVII.

O MORAL Gower, this boke I directe   1870
To the, and to the philosophical Strode,
To vouchen-sauf, ther nede is, to correcte,
Of youre benignites and zeles goode.
And to that sothfast Criste that sterf on roode,
With al myn herte, of mercy evere I preye,
And to the Lord right thus I speke and seye:—

CCLXVIII.

Thow Oon, and Two, and Thre, eterne on lyve,
That regnest ay in Thre, and Two, and Oon,
Uncircumscript, and al maist circumscrive!
Us from visible and invisible foon   1880
Defende, and to thi mercy everichon,
So mak us, Jesu, for thy mercy digne,
For love of Maide and Moder thyn benigne!

EXPLICIT LIBER TROILI ET CRISEYDIS.

CHAUCERES A. B. C.

CALLED

LA PRIERE DE NOSTRE DAME.

A.

LMYGHTY and alle mercyable Quene,
To whom al this worlde fleeth for socoure
To have relees of synne, *of* sorowe, o
    tecne !
Gloriouse Virgyne, of alle floures flour,
To the I flee confounded in errour !
Help, and releve, thow mighty debonayre,
Have mercy of my perilouse langour !
Venquysshed hath me my cruel adversayre.

B.

Bountee so fix hath in thine hert his tent
That wel I wote thow wolte my socour be ;
Thow kanst not werne hym that, with good entent
Axeth thyn helpe, thyn herte is ay so free !
Thow art largesse of pleyn felicitee,
Havene and refute of quyete and of reste !
Loo how that theves seven chacen me !
Helpe, Lady bryght, er that my shippe to-breste

C.

Comfort ys noon, but in yow, Lady dere!
For loo my synne and my confusioun,
Which ought*e* not in thy presence for to appere,
Han take on me a grevouse accioun,
Of verray ryght and disperacioun!
And, as by ryght, they myghten wel sustene,
That I were worthy my damnacioun,
N*ere* mercye of yow, blysful hevenes quene!

D.

Doute is there noon, Quene of misericorde,
That thou narte cause of grace and mercye here;
God vouchedsaufe thurgh the with us tacorde:
For certes, Cristes blysful moder dere!
Were now the bowe ybent in swiche manere,
As hyt was first, of justice and of ire,
The rightful God nolde of no mercye here;
But thurgh thee han wee grace as we desire.

E.

Evere hath myn hope of refute in the be:
For here before ful often in many a wyse,
Unto mercy hastow recoyved me.
But mercy, Lady! at the grete assise,
Whan we shal come before tho hye justise!
So litel good shal then in me be founde,
That, but thou er that day correcte me,
Of verray ryght my werke wol me confounde.

F.

Fleyng, I flee for socour to thy tent,
Me for to hide fro tempest ful of drede,

Besekyng yow, that ye yow nat absente,
Though I be wikke.   O help yet at this nede !
Alle have I ben a best in wytte and dede,
Yet, Lady ! thow me clothe with thyn grace,
Thyne enemy and myn, Lady, take hede !
Unto my dethe in poynte ys me to chace.

G.

Gloriouse mayde and moder ! whiche that never
Were bitter nor in erthe nor in see,
But ful of swetnesse and of mercye ever,
Help, that my fader be nat wrothe with me !
Speke thow, for I ne dar nat him yse ;
So have I doon in erthe, allas the while !
That certes, but that thow my socour be,
To synke eterne he wol my goost exile.

H.

He vouchedesauf, telle hym, as was hys wylle,
Become a man as for oure alliaunce,
And with his bloode he wroote that blysful bille
Upon the crois, as general acquytaunce
To every penytent, in ful creaunce :
And therfore, Lady bryght ! thow for us pray,
Than shalt thou bothe stynte alle grevaunce,
And maken our foo to faylen of hys pray.

I.

I wote hyt wel thow wolt ben oure socour,
That art so ful of bountee in certeyne ;
For, whan a soule falleth in errour,
Thy pitee gooth and haleth hym ageyne,

That makestow hys pees with his sovereyne,
And bryngest him out *of the crookede strete :*
Who so the loveth he shal nat love in veyne,
That shal he fynde, as he the life shal lete.

K.

Kalendres enlumyned ben .bothe they
That in this worlde ben lyghted with thi name,
And who-so goothe with yow the ryghte wey,
Hym thar nat drede in soule to be lame ;
Now, Queene of comfort! sithe thou art that same,
To whom I seche for my medycine,
Lat not my foo no more my wounde entame ;
Myn hele into thyn hande al I resygne.

L.

Lady, thy sorwe kan I not purtreye
Under the crois, ne his grevous penaunce :
But, for youre bothe peynes, I yow preye,
Lat not our aller foo make his bobaunce,
That he hath in his lystes, with meschaunce,
Convicte that ye both han boght so dere ;
As I seyde erste, thou grounde of our substaunce !
Continew in us thy pitouse eyen clere.

M.

Moises that saugh the bussh with flambes rede
Brennynge of which there never a stik*k*e brende,
Was signe of thyn unwemmed maydenhede.
Thou art the bussh, on which ther gan discende
The Holy Goost, *the* which that Moises wende

Had ben afire : and this was in figure.
Now, Lady ! fro tho fire thou us defende,
Which that iu hello eternally shal dure.

N.

Noble princesse, that never haddest pere !
Certes yf any comfort in us be,
That cometh of the, Christes moder dere !
We han none other melodie or gle,
Us to rejoyse in oure adversite,
Ne advocate noon, that wol and dar so preye
For us, and that for *as* litel hire as ye,
That helpen for an Ave Marie or tweye.

O.

O, verray light of eyen that ben blynde !
O verray lust of labour and distresse !
O tresorere of bounté to mankynde,
The whom God chees to moder for humblesse !
From his ancile he made tho maistresse
Of heven and erthe, our bille up for to bede ;
This world awaiteth ever on thy godenesse,
For thou ne failest never wight at nede.

P.

Purpos I have sommetyme for to enquere,
Wherefore and why tho Holy Goost tho soughte,
Whan Gabrieles voys come to thyn ere ;
He nat to werre us swich a wonder wroughte,
But for to save us, that he sithen boughte :
Than nedeth us no wepene us for to save,

But oonly there as we dide nat as we ought,
Do penytence, and mercy axe and have.

Q.

Queene of comfort, yet whan I me bethynke,
That I agilte have bothe hym and thee,
And that my soule ys worthy for to synke,
Allas! I, katyf, whider may I fle?
Who shal unto thy Sone my mene be?
Who, but thy selfe, that art of pitee welle?
Thou hast more routhe on oure adversité,
Than in this world myght any tonge telle.

R.

Redresse me, Moder, and *eke* me chastise!
For certeynly my fadres chastisynge
That dar I nat abiden in no wise,
So hidouse is his ryghtful rekenynge.
Moder! of whom our mercy gan to springe,
Be ye my juge, and eke my soules leche,
For ever in yow is pitee *aboundynge*
To eche that wil of pité yow beseche.

S.

Soth is, that he no graunteth noo pitee
Withoute the; for God of his goodenesse
Foryeveth noon, but hyt lyke unto thee:
He hath the made vikaire and maistresse
Of alle this worlde, and eke governesse
Of hevene, and he represseth his justise
After thy wille: and therfore witnesse
He hath the corowned in so rialle wise.

T.

Temple devoute! ther God hathe his wonynge,
Fro whiche these misbeleved deprived been,
To yow my soule penytent I brynge,
Receyve me, I kan no ferther fleen.
With thornes venymouse, *O* hevene Quene!
For which the erthe acursed was ful yore,
I am so wounded, as ye may wel seene,
That I am lost almost, hit smert so sore,

V.

Virgyne! that art so noble of apparayle,
That ledest us into the hye toure
Of Paradyse, thou me wysse and counsayle,
How I may have thy grace and thy socoure:
Alle have I ben in filthe and in erroure,
Lady! unto that contrey thou me adjourne,
The cleped is thy benche of fressh floure,
Ther as that mercye ever shal sojourne.

X.

Christe thy Sone that in this worlde alyght
Upon a crois to suffre hys passioun,
And eke suffrede that Longius hys herte *pighte,*
And made hys herte blode to renne adoun,
And alle was this for my savacioun:
And I to him am fals and eke unkynde,
And yet he wol not my dampnacioun:
This thanke I yow, socour of alle mankynde!

Y.

Ysaac was figure of his dethe certeyne,
That so ferforth his fader wolde obeye,

That hym ne roughte nothing to be sleyne :
Ryght so thy Sone lyste, as a lambe, to deye :
Now, Lady ful of mercy ! Y you preye
Sith he his mereye mesured so large,
Be ye nat skant, for al we synge and seye,
That ye been fro vengeaunce ay oure targe.

Z.

Zacharye yow clepeth the opene welle,
That wassth synful soule out of hys gilte ;
Therefore this lesson ought I wele to telle,
That, nere thy tendre herte, we were spilt.
Now, Lady *brighte!* sith thou kanste and wilt
Been to the sede of Adam mercyable,
Brynge us to that paleyce that ys bilte
To penytentys, that been to mercye able.

EXPLICIT.

CHAUCER'S DREAM.

WHEN Flora the queene of pleasaunce,
Had*de* whole achieved thobeysaunce
Of tho fresh and new*e* season,
Thorow out every region,
And with her mantle whole covert
That winter made had*de* discovert
Of aventure, withoute light,
In May, I lay upon a night
Alone, and on my lady thoughte,
And how the lord that her wrought*e*,   1
Couth well entaile in imagery
And showed had*de* great maistry,
When he in so little space
Made such a body and a face,
So great beauty with swich features
More than in other creatures;
And in my thought*es* as I lay
In a lodge out of tho way,
Beside a well in a forest,
Where after hunting I tooke rest,   2
Nature and kind so in mo wroughte,
That halfe on sleepe they me broughte,

And gan to dreamo to my thinking,
With mind of knowliche like making,
For what I dreamed, as me thought*e*,
I saw it, and I slepte nought;
Wherefore is yet my full*e* beleeve,
That some good*e* spirit that eve,
By meano of some curious port,
Baro me, where I saw payne and sport;   30
But whether it were I woko or slept*e*,
Well wot I of, I lough and wept*e*,
Wherefore I woll in remembraunce,
Put wholo the payne, and the pleasaunce,
Which was to me axen and hele,
Would*e* God yo wist it every dele,
Or at the least, ye might o night
Of such another havo a sight,
Although it were to you a payno,
Yet on the morow yo would*e* bo fayne,   40
And wish it might*e* long*e* dure;
Then might yo say yo had*de* good cure,
For ho that dreame*th* and wene*th* ho see,
Much the better yet may heo
Wit*e* what, and of whom, and where,
And eko the lasse it woll hindero,
To thinko I seo this with mine eene,
Iwis this may not dreamo keno,
But signo or signifiaunce
Of hasty thing souning pleasaunco,   50
 For on this wise upon a night,
As yo havo heard, withoute light,
Not all wakyng, ne full on sleepe,
About such houre as lovers weepe
And crie after *here* ladies grace,

Befell me this wonder cace,
Which ye shall heare and all the wise,
So wholly as I can devise,
In playne English evill writtcn,
For sleepe writer, well ye witten,   60
Excused is, though he do mis,
More than one that waking is,
Wherefore here of your gentilnesse,
I you requyre my boistousnesse
Ye lete passe, as thing rude,
And heareth what I woll conclude;
And of the endityng taketh no heed,
Ne of the tearmes, so God you speed,
But let all passe as nothing were
For thus befell, as ye shall here.   70
    Within an yle me thought I was,
Where wall and yate was all of glasse,
And so was closed round about
That leavelesse none come in ne out,
Uncouth and straunge to beholde,
For every yate of fine golde
A thousand fanes, aie turning,
Entuned had, and briddes singing,
Divers, and on each fane a paire,
With open mouth again here;   80
And of a sute were all the toures,
Subtily corven after floures,
Of uncouth colours during aye.
That never been none seene in May,
With many a small turret hie,
But man on live could I non sie,
Ne creatures, save ladies play,
Which were such of here array

That, as me thought, of goodlihead
They passeden all and womanhead ;   90
For to behold hem daunce and sing*e*,
It seemed*e* like none earthly thing*e*,
Such was *here* uncouth countinaunce
In every play of right usaunce;
And of one age everichone
They seemed all, save onely one,
Which had of yeeres suffisaunce,
For she might*e* neyther sing no daunce,
But yet her countenaunce was so glad,
As she so fewe yeeres had had   100
As any lady that was there,
And as little it did her dere,
Of lustines to laugh and tale
As she had*de* full stuffed a male
Of disportes and new*e* playes :
Fayre had*de* she been in her daies,
And maistresse seemed*e* well to be
Of all that lusty companie ;
And so she might, I you ensure,
For one the conningest*e* creature   110
She was, and so said everichone,
That ever her knew, there fayled*e* none,
For she was sober and well avised,
And from every fault disguised,
And nothing used*e* but faith and truth ;
That she nas young it was great ruth,
For every where and in ech place,
She governed her, that in grace
She stode alway with poore and riche,
That, at a word, was none her liche,   120
Ne halfe so able maistres to be

To such a lusty companie.
 Befell me so, when I avised
Hadde the yle that me suffised,
And whole thestate every where,
That in that lusty yle was there,
Which was more wonder to devise
Than the joieux paradise,
I dare well saye, for floure ne tree,
Ne thing wherein pleasaunce mighte bee 130
There faylede none, for every wight
Hadde they desirede, day and night,
Riches, heale, beauty, and ease,
With every thing that hem mighte please,
Thinke and have, it coste no more ;
In such a country there before,
Had I not bene, no hearde telle
That lives creature mighte dwelle.
And when I hadde thus all aboute
Tho yle avised throughoute 140
The state, and how they were arayed,
In my heart I were well payed,
And in my selfe I me assured
That in my body I was well ured,
Sith I might have such a grace
To see the ladies and the place,
Which were so faire, I you ensure,
That to my dome, though that nature
Would ever strive and do her paine,
She shoulde not con no mow attaine 150
The leaste feature to amende,
Though she would all her conning spende,
That to beautie might availe,
It were but paine and lost travaile,

Such part in *here* nativitie
Was hem alarged of beautie,
And eke they had a thing notable
Unto *here* death, ay durable,
And was, that *here* beauty shoulde dure,
Which was never scene in creature,   160
Save onely there (as I trow*e*)
It hath not be *i*wist ne know*e*,
Wherefore I praise with *here* conning,
That during beautie, riche thing,
Ilad*de* they been of *here* lives certaine,
They had*de* been quite of every paine.

  And when I wende thus all have scene,
The state, the riches, that might*e* beene,
That me thought impossible were
To see one thing more than was there,   170
That to beauty or glad conning
Serve or availe might any thing;
All sodainly, as I there stood,
This lady that couth*e* so much good,
Unto me came with smiling chere,
And said*e*, " *Benedicite*, this yere
Saw I never man here but you,
Tell me how ye come hider now?
And your name, and where ye dwell*e*?
And whom ye seeke eke mote ye tell*e*,   180
And how ye come be to this place,
The soth well told may cause you grace,
And els ye mote prisoner be
Unto the ladies here, and me,
That have the governaunce of this yle:"
And with that word she gan to smile,
And so did all the lusty rout

Of ladies that stood her about.
' Madame' (quod I) ' this night *i*past,
Lodged I was and slepte fast   190
In a forest beside a well*e*,
And now am here, how should I tell*e* ?
Wot I not by whose ordinance,
But onely Fortunes purveiance,
Which put*eth* many, as I gesse,
To travaile, paine, and businesse,
And lett*eth* nothing for *here* truth,
But some sleeth eke, and that is ruth,
Wherefore, I doubt her brittilnes,
Her variance and unsteadfastnes,   200
So that I am as yet afraid,
And of my being here amaid,
For wonder thing seemeth me,
Thus many fresh*e* ladies to see,
So faire, so cunning, and so yong*e*,
And no man dwelling hem among*e* :
Not I not how I hider come,
Madame,' (quod I) ' this all and some,
What should I faine a long processe
To you that seeme such a princesse ?   210
What please you commaund or say*e*,
Here I am you to obay*e*,
To my power, and all fulfill*e*,
And prisoner bide at your will*e*,
Till y*e* duly enformed be
Of every thing ye aske me.'
    This lady there, right well apaid,
Me by the hand*e* tooke, and said*e*,
' Welcome prisoner adventurus,
Right glad am I ye have said thus,   220

And for ye doubte me to displease,
I will assay to do you ease:"
And with that word, ye anon,
She, and the ladies everichon
Assembled, and to counsailo wente,
And after that soone for me sente,
And to me said on this manere,
Word for word, as ye shall here.
   ' To see you here us thinke marvaile,
And how withoute bote or saile,   230
By any subtilty or wyle,
Ye get have entre in this yle ;
But not for that, yet shall ye see
That we gentille women bee,
Loth to displease any wight,
Notwithstanding our greate right,
And for ye shall well understonde
The olde custome of this londe,
Which hath continued many yere,
Ye shall well wete that with us here   240
Ye may not bide, for causes twaine,
Which we be purposed you to saine.
   ' Thone is this, our ordinance,
Which is of long continuance,
Woll not, sothly we you telle,
That no man here among us dwelle,
Wherefore ye mote needs retourne,
In no wise may ye here sojourne.
   ' Thother is eke, that our queene
Out of the realme, as ye may scene,   250
Is, and may be to us a charge,
If we lete you goe here at large,
For which cause the more we doubte,

To doe a fault while she is out*e*,
Or suffer that may be noysaunce,
Againe our old accustomaunce."
    And whan I had*de* these causes twaine
I-heard, O God! *lo!* what a paine
All sodainly about mine hart
There came at ones and how smart,   260
In creeping soft as who should*e* steale,
Or doe me robbe of all mine heale,
And made me in my thought so fraid,
That in courage I stode dismaid.
And standing thus, as was my grace,
A lady came more than apace,
With huge prease her about,
And told*e* how the queene without
Was arived and would*e* come in*ne*,
Well were they that thider might*e* twin*ne*, 270
They hiede so they would*e* not abide
The bridling *here* horse to ride,
By five, by sixe, by two, by three,
There was not one abode with me,
The queene to meet everichone,
They went, and bode with me not one :
And I, after a soft pase,
Imagining how to purchase
Grace of the queene, there to bide,
Till good fortune some happy guide   280
Me sende might*e*, that would*e* me bring*e*
Where I was borne to my wonning*e*,
For way no foot *ne* knew I none,
No witherward I niste to gone,
For all was sea about the yle,
No wonder though me liste not smile,

Seing the case uncouth and straunge,
And so in like a perilous chaunge;
Imagining thus walking alone,
I saw the ladies everichone,   290
So that I mighte somwhat offere,
Sone after that I drew me nere,
And tho I was ware of the queene,
And how the ladies on their kneene,
With joyous wordes, gladly advised,
Her welcomede so that it suffisede,
Though she princesse hole hadde be
Of all environed is with see :
And thus avising, with chere sad,
All sodainly I was so glad,   300
That greater joy, as mote I thrive,
I trow hadde never man on live,
Than I tho, ne hearte more light,
When of my lady I hadde sight,
Which with the queene come was there,
And in one clothing both they were,
A knight also there well bescene,
I saw that come was with the queene,
Of whome the ladies of that yle
Had huge wonder longe while,   310
Till at the last right soberly,
The queene her selfe full cunningly,
With softe wordes in good wise,
Saide to the ladies young and nise,
' My sisters, how it hath befalle,
I trow ye know it one and alle,
That of long time here have I beene,
Within this yle biding as queene,
Living at ease, that never wighte

More parfit joy have ne might*e*,
And to you been of governance,
Such as ye found in whole pleasance,
In every thing as ye know*e*,
After our custome and our low*e*,
Which how they first found*e* were,
I trow ye wote all the manere,
And who *the* queene is of this yle,
As I have been longe while,
Ech seven yeeres not of usage,
Visit the heavenly armitage,
Which on a rocke so high*e* stonds,
In strange sea out from all londs,
That to make the pilgrimage
Is called a long perillous viage,
For if the wind be not good frend,
The journey dures to the end
Of him that it undertak*eth*,
Of twenty thousand one not scap*eth*;
Upon which rock groweth a tree,
That certaine yeeres bear*eth* apples three,
Which three apples who may have,
Been from all displeasaunce save,
That in the seven yeere may fall*e*,
This wote ye well one and all*e*,
For the first apple and the hext,
Which groweth unto you next,
Hath three vertues notable,
And keepeth youth aie durable,
Beauty and looke, ever in one,
And is the best in everichone.
    ' The second apple red and grene,
Onely with lookes of your yene,

You nourish*eth* in pleasaunce
Better than partridge or fesaunce,
And feed*eth* every lives wight
Pleasantly with the sight.
  ' The third apple of the three,
Which groweth lowest on the tree,
Who it bear*eth* may not faile
That to his pleasaunce may availe.   360
So your pleasure and beauty rich,
Your during youth ever iliche,
Your truth, your cunning, and your weale,
Hath aye floured, and your good heale,
Without sicknes or displeasaunce,
Or thing that to you was noysaunce,
So that ye have as goddesses,
Lived above all*e* princesses :
Now is befall, as ye may see ;
To gather these said apples three,   370
I have not failed againe the day,
Thitherward to take the way,
Wening to speed as I had oft*e*,
But whan I come, I find alofte
My sister which that here stands,
Having those apples in her hands,
Avising hem and nothing said,
But looked as she were well paid :
And as I stood her to behold*e*,
Thinking how my joyes were cold*e*,   380
Sith I those apples have no might*e*,
Even with that so came this knight*e*,
And in his armes of me aware,
Me tooke, and to his ship me bare,
And said*e*, though him I never had*de* seen,

Yet had I long his lady been,
Wherefore I shoulde with him wende,
And he woulde to his·lives ende
My servant be, and gan to singe
As one that hadde wonne a rich thinge;   390
Tho were my spirits fro me gone,
So sodainly everichone,
That in me appearede but death,
For I felte neither life ne breath,
Ne good ne harme none I knew,
The sodaine paine me was so new,
That hadde not the hasty grace be
Of this lady, that fro the tree
Of her gentilnesse so hied
Me to comfort, I hadde died,   400
And of her three apples, one
In mine hande there put anone,
Which brought againe mind and breath,
And me recoverede from the death,
Wherefore, to her so am I holde,
That for her alle things do I wolde,
For sho was lech of all my smart,
And from great paine so quite mine hart,
And, as God wote, right as ye heare,
Me to comforte with friendly cheare   410
Sho did her prowesse and her might,
And truly eke so dide this knight,
In that he couth, and ofte said,
That of my wo he was ill paid,
And cursede tho ship that hem there broughte,
Tho mast, tho master that it wroughte;
And as ech thing mote have an end,
My sister here your brother frend,

Con with her words so womanly
This knight entreat, and conningly,   420
For mine honour and his also,
And saide that with her we shoulde go
Both in her ship, where she was brought,
Which was so wonderfully wrought,
So cleane, so rich, and so araid,
That we were both content and paid,
And me to comfort and to please,
And mine hearte to put at ease,
She toke great paine in little while,
And thus hath brought us to this yle,   430
As ye may see, wherefore echone,
I pray you thanke her, one and one,
As heartily as ye canne devise,
Or imagine in any wise.'
At once there tho men mighte seen
A world of ladies fall on kneen
Before my lady, that there about
Was left none standing in the rout,
But altogither they went at ones
To kneele, they sparede not for the stones,   440
Ne for estate, ne for *here* blood,
Well shewede there they couth much good,
For to my lady they made such feast,
With suche wordes, that the least,
So friendly and so faithfully
Said was, and so cunningly,
That wonder was, seing *here* youthe,
To here tho language they couthe,
And wholly how they governed were,
In thanking of my lady there,   450
And said by will and maundement,

They were at her commaundement,
Which was to me as great a joy,
As winning of the towne of Troy
Was to the hardy Greekes stronge,
Whan they it wan with siege longe,
To see my lady in such a place
So received as she *tho* was :
And when they talked had a while
Of this and that, and of the yle,   460
My lady, and the ladies there,
Altogether as they were,
The queene her selfe began to play*e*,
And to the aged lady say*e* :
' Now seemeth you not good it were,
Sith we be altogither here,
To ordaine and devise the best,
To set this knight and me at rest ?
For woman is a feble wight
To rere a warre against a knight,   470
And sith he here is in this place,
At my list*e*, danger or grace,
It were to me a great villany
To do him any tiranny,
But faine I would*e*, now will ye here,
In his owne country that he were,
And I in peace, and he at ease,
This were a way us both to please,
If it might*e* be ; I you beseech,
With him hereof ye fall in speech.'   480
This lady tho began to smile,
Avising her a little while,
And with glad chere she said anone,
' Madam, I will unto him gone,

And with him speake, and of him fele
What he desire*th* every dele :'
And soberly this lady tho,
Her selfe and other ladies two
She tooke with her, and with sad chere,
Saide to the knight on this manere,　　490
' Sir, the princes of this yle,
Whom for your pleasance many mile
Ye sought have, as I understonde,
Till at the last ye have her fonde,
Me sent hath here, and ladies twaine,
To heare alle thing that ye saine,
And for what cause ye have her sought,
Faine woulde she wote, and whol your thought.
And why you do her all this wo,
And for what cause ye be her fo ?　　500
And why, of every wight unware,
By force ye to your ship her bare,
That sho so nigh was agone,
That mind ne speech had*de* she none,
But as a painfull creature,
Dying, abode her adventure,
That her to see indure that paine,
Here weell say unto you plaine,
Right on your selfe ye did amisse,
Seeing how she a princes is.'　　510
This knight, the which cowthe his good,
Right of his truth moved his blood,
That pale he woxe as any lead,
And lookt as he woulde be dead,
Blood was there none in nother cheke,
Wordlesse he was and semede sicke,
And so it provede well he was,

For withoute moving any paas,
All sodainely as thing dying,
He fell at once downe sowning,   520
That for his wo this lady fraide,
Unto the queene her hyed and saide,
' Cometh on anon as have ye blisse,
But ye be wise, thing is amisse,
This knight is dead or will be soone,
Lo, where he lyeth in a swoone,
Withoute word, or answering
To that I have said, any thing
Wherefore, I doubte that the blame
Mighte be hindering to your name,   530
Which floured hath so many yere,
So longe, that for nothing here,
I would in no wise he dyede,
Wherefore good were that ye hyede
His life to save at the least,
And after that his wo be ceast,
Commaund him void, or dwelle,
For in no wise dare I more melle
Of thing wherein such perill is,
As like is now to fall of this.'   540
This queene right tho full of great feare,
With all the ladies present there,
Unto the knight came where he lay,
And made a lady to him say :
' Lo, here the queene, awake for shame !
What will ye doe, is this good game ?
Why lye ye here, what is your mind ?
Now is well seene your wit is blind,
To see so many ladies here,
And ye to make none other chere,   550

But as ye set hem all at nough*te*;
Arise, for his love that you bough*te*:
But what she said, a word not one
He spake, no answer gave her none.
The queene of very pitty tho,
Her worship, and his like also,
To save there she did her paine,
And quoke for feare, and gan to saine
For woe, ' Alas, what shall I doe?
What shall I say this man unto? 560
If he die here, lost is my name,
How shal I play this perillous game?
If any thing be here amisse,
It shall be said, it rigour is,
Whereby my name impayre migh*te*,
And like to die eke is this knigh*te*:'
And with that word her hand she laid*e*
Upon his brest, and to him said*e*,
' Awake my knight! lo, it am I
That to you speake, now tell me why 570
Ye fare thus, and this paine endure,
Seing ye be in country sure,
Among such friends that would you heale,
Your hertes ease eke and your weale,
And if I wist what you might ease,
Or know the thing that might you please,
I you ensure it should*e* not faile,
That to your heale you might availe:
Wherefore, with all my heart I pray*e*
Ye rise, and let us talke and play*e*; 580
And see! how many ladies here
Be comen for to make good chere.'
All was for nought, for still as stone

He lay, and word spoke none.
Long while was or he mighte braide,
And of all that the queene hadde said,
He wiste no word, but at the laste,
' Mercy,' twise he cryede faste,
That pittie was his voice to heare,
Or to behold his painefull cheare, 590
Which was not fained well to sein,
Both by his visage and his eyn,
Which on the queene at once he caste,
And sighed as he woulde to-braste,
And after that he shrighte so
That wonder was to see his wo,
For sith that payne was first named,
Was never more wofull payne attained,
For with voice dead he gan to plaine,
And to himselfe these wordes saine, 600
' I wofull wight full of maluro,
Am worse than dead, and yet dure,
Maugre any payne or death,
Against my will I fell my breath:
Why nam I dead sith I no servo,
And sith my lady will me sterve?
Where art thou Death, art thou agast?
Well, shall we meete yet at the last,
Though thou thee hide, it is for nought.
For where thou dwelst thou shalt be sought;
Maugre thy subtill double face, 611
Here will I die right in this place,
To thy dishonour and mine ease;
Thy manner is no wight to please,
What needes thee, sith I thee seche,
So thee to hide my payne to eche?

And well wost thou I will not live,
Who would*e* me all this world here give,
For I have with my cowardise,
Lost joy, and heale, and my servise,   620
And made my soveraigne lady so,
That while she live*th* I trow my fo
She will be ever to her end,
Thus have I neither joy ne frend ;
Wote I not whether hast or sloth
Hath caused this now by my troth,
For at the hermitage full hie,
When I her saw first with mine eye,
I hied*e* till I was aloft*e*,
And made my pace small and soft*e*,   630
Till in mine armes I had her fast*e*,
And to my ship bare at the last*e*,
Whereof she was displeased so,
That endles there seemed her wo,
And I thereof had*de* so great fere,
That me repent that I come there,
Which hast I trow gan her displease,
And is the cause of my disease :'
And with that word he gan to cry, .
'Now Death, Death !' twy or thry,   640
And motred wot I not what of slouth,
And even with that the queene, of routh,
Him in her armes tooke and sayd*e*,
' Now mine owne knight, be not evill apaid
That I a lady to you sent*e*
To have knowledge of your entent*e*,
For, in good faith, I meant*e* but well,
And would ye wist it every dele,   .
Nor will not do to you ywis ;'

And with that word she gan him kisse,   650
And prayed him rise, and saide she would*e*
His welfare, by her truth, and told*e*
Him how she was for his disease
Right sory, and faine would him please,
His lyfe to save : these wordes tho
She saide to him, and many mo
In comforting, for from the paine
She would he were delivered faine.
The knight tho up caste his een,
And whan he saw it was the queen,   660
That to him had*de* these wordes said,
Right in his wo he gan to braid*e*,
And him up dress*eth* for to knele,
The queene avising wonder wele :
But as he rose he overthrew,
Wherefore the queene, yet eft anew,
Him in her armes anon tooke,
And pitiously gan on him looke,
But for all that nothyng she say*de*,
Ne spake not like she were well payd,   670
Ne no chere made, nor sad no light,
But all in one to every wight
There was scene conning, with estate,
In her without noise or debate,
For save onely a looke piteous,
Of womanhead undispiteous,
That she showed in countenance,
For seemed her heart*e* from obeisance,
And not for that she did her reine
Him to recure from the peine,   680
And his heart*e* to put at large,
For her entent was to his barge

Him to bryng against the eve,
With certaine ladies and take leve,
And pray him of his gentilnesse,
To suffer her then*nes*forth in peace,
As other princes had*de* before,
And from then*nes*forth for evermore,
She would him worship in all wise,
That gentilnesse might*e* devise,   690
And payne her wholly to fulfill*e*,
In honour, his pleasure and will*e*.
And during thus this knight*es* wo,
Present the queene and other mo,
My lady, and many another wight,
Ten thousand ship*pes* at a sight,
I saw come over the wawy flood,
With saile and ore, that as I stood
Hem to behold, I gan marvaile
From whom might*e* come so many a saile,   700
For sith the tyme that I was bore,
Such a navie there before
Had I not scene, ne so arayed,
That for the sight my heart*e* play*e*d*e*
To and fro within my brest*e*
For joy, long was or it would*e* rest*e*,
For there was sailes full of floures,
After castels with huge toures,
Seeming full of armes bright*e*,
That wonder lusty was the sight*e*,   710
With large toppes, and mastes long*e*,
Richly depeint, and rear among*e*,
At certain times gan repaire
Small*e* birdes, downe from thaire,
And on the ship*pes* bounds about

Sate and song with voice full out,
Ballades and layes right joyously,
As they cowth in *here* harmony,
That you to write that I there see,
Mine excuse is it may not be,
For-why the matter were to long
To name the birds and write *here* song :
Whereof, anon, the tydings there
Unto the queene soone brought were,
With many alas, and many a doubt,
Shewing the ship*pes* there without.
Tho gan the aged lady weepe,
And said, 'Alas, our joy on sleepe
Soone shall be brought, ye, long or night,
For we descried been by this knight,
For certes, it may none other be,
But he is of yond companie,
And they be come him here to secche,'
And with that word her fayle*de* speeche.
'Withoute remedy we be destroid,'
Full oft said all, and gan concludo,
Holy at once at the last*e*,
That best was shit *here* yates fast*e*,
And arme hem all in good langage,
As they had*de* done of old usage,
And of faire wordes make *here* shot,
This was *here* counsailo and the knot,
And other purpose tooke they none,
But armed thus forth they gone
Toward the walles of the yle,
But or they come there long while,
They met*te* the greate lord of bove,
That called is the god of love,

That hem avised with such chere,
Right as he with hem angry wero :   750
Avayled hem not here walls of glasse,
This mighty lord let not to passe,
The shutting of *here* yates fast*e*,
 All they had ordaind was but wast*e*,
For when his ship*pes* had*de* found*e* land,
This lord anon, with bow in hand,
Into this yle with huge prease
Hied*e* fast, and would*e* not cease
Till he came there the knight *gan* lay ;
Of queene ne lady by the way   760
Tooke he no heed*e* but forth past*e*,
And yet all followed at the last*e* ;
And when he came where lay the knight,
Well shewed he he had*de* great might,
And forth tho queene called anone,
And all the ladies everichone,
And to hem said, ' Is not thus routh,
To see my servaunt for his trouth,
Thus leane, thus sicke, and in this payne,
And wot not unto whom to playne,   770
Save onely one withoute mo,
Which might him him heale and is his fo ?'
And with that word his heavy brow
He shewed*e* the queene and looked*e* row ;
This mighty lord forth tho anone,
With o looke her fault*es* echone
He can her shew in little speech,
Commaunding her to be his leoh,
Withouten more, shortly to say*e*,   779
He thought*e* the queene soone should obay*e*,
And in his hond he shoke his bow*e*,

And saide right soone he woulde be knowe,
And for she hadde so long refused
His service, and his lawes not used,
He let her wite that he was wroth,
And bent his bow and forth he goth
A pace or two, and even there
A large draught, up to his eare,
He drew, and with an arrow grounde
Sharpe and new, the queene a wounde
He gave, that piersed unto the hearte,
Which afterward full sore gan smarte,
And was not whole of many yeare;
And even with that, 'Be of good cheare,
My knight,' (quod he) 'I will thee hele,
And thee restore to parfite wele,
And for each payne thou hast endured,
To have two joyes thou art cured:'
And forth he paste by the rout,
With sober cheare walking about,
And what he said I thoughte to heare,
Well wist he which his servaunts were,
And as he passed anon he fond
My lady, and her tooke by the hond,
And made her chere as a goddesse,
And of beaute called her princesse,
Of bounty eke gave her the name,
And saide there was nothyng blame
In her, but she was vertuous,
Saving she woulde no pity use,
Which was the cause that he her soughte,
To putte that far out of her thoughte,
And sith she hadde whole richesse
Of womanhead and friendlinesse,

He said it was nothing sitting
To voide pity his owne leggyng,
And gan her preach and with her play*e*,
And of her beauty told her aie,
 And said*e* she was a creature
Of whom the name should endure,   820
 And in bookes full of pleasaunce
Be put for ever in remembraunce,
And, as me thought*e*, more friendly
Unto my lady, and goodlely
He spake, than any that was there,
And for thapples I trow it were,
That she had in possession;
Wherefore, long in procession,
Many a pace, arme under other,
He welke, and so did*e* with none other,   830
But what he would*e* commaund or say*e*,
Forthwith need*es* all must obay*e*,
And what he desired at the lest,
Of my lady, was by request ;   -
And when they long together had*de* beene,
He brought*e* my lady to the queene,
And to her said*e*, ' So God you speed,
Shew grace, consent*e*, that is need.'
My lady tho, full conningly,
Right well avised and womanly   840
Downe gan to kneele upon the floures,
Which Aprill nourished had*de* with shoures,
And to this mighty lord gan say*e*,
' That pleaseth you, I woll obay*e*,
And me restraine from other thought,
As ye woll all thing shall be wrought.'
And with that word kneeling she quoke;

That mighty lord in armes her tooke,
And said, ' Ye have a servaunt one,
That truer living is there none,
Wherefore, good were, seeing his trouth,
That on his paines ye hadde routh,
And purpose you to heare his speeche,
Fully avised him to leeche,
For of one thyng ye may be sure,
He will be yours while he may dure.'
And with that word, right on his game,
Me thought he lough, and tolde my name,
Which was to me marvaile and fere,
That what to do I niste there,
Ne whether was me bet or none,
There to abide, or thus to gone,
For well wend I my lady wolde
Imagen or deme that I hadde told
My counsaile whole, or made complaint
Unto that lord, that mighty saint,
So verily each thing unsought
He said, as he hadde knowne my thought,
And tolde my trouth and mine uncase
Bet than I couth have for mine ease,
Though I hadde studied all a weke,
Well wiste that lord that I was seke,
And woulde be leched wonder faine,
No man me blame, mine was the paine:
And when this lord had alle said,
And longe with my lady plaid,
She gan to smile with spirit glade,
This was the answere that she made,
Which put me there in double peine,
That what to do, ne what to seine

Wist I not, ne what was the best*e*,
Ferre was my herte then fro his rest*e*,
For, as I thought*e*, that smiling signe
Was token that the heart encline
Would*e* to requests reasonable,
Because smiling is favorable
To every thing that shall thrive,
So thought I tho ; anon, blive,
That wordlesse answere in no toun
Was tane for obligatioun, 890
Ne called surety in no wise,
Amongst hem that called been wise.
Thus was I in a joyous dout,
Sure and unsurest of that rout,
Right as mine heart*e* thought it were,
So more or lesse wexe my fere,
That if one thought made it wele
Another shent it every dele,
Till, at the last, I couth*e* no more,
But purposed, as I did*e* before, 900
To serve truly my lives space,
Awaiting ever the yeare of grace,
Which may fall*e* yet or I sterve,
If it please her that I serve,
And served have, and woll do ever,
For thyng is none that me is lever
Than her service, whose presence
Mine Heaven is whole, and her absence
An Hell, full of divers paines,
Whych to the death full oft me straines. 910
Thus in my thought*es* as I stood,
That unneth felt I harme no good,
I saw the queene a little paas

Come where this mighty lord *tho* was,
And kneelede downe in presence there
Of all the ladies that there were,
With sober countenaunce avised,
In fowe wordes that well suffised,
And to this lord, anon, present
A bill, wherein whole her entent   920
Was written, and how she besought*e*,
As he knew every will and thought*e*,
That of his godhead and his grace
He woulde forgive all old trespace,
And undispleased be of time past,
For she would ever be stedfast,
And in his service to the death
Use every thought while she hadd*e* breath:
And sight and wept, and saide no more:
Within was written all the sore   930
At whyche bill the lord gan smile,
And said he woulde within that yle
Be lord and syre, both east and west,
And cald it there his new*e* conquest,
And in great councell tooke the queene,
Long were the tales hem betweene,
And over her bill he reade thrise,
And wonder gladly gan devise
Her features faire and her visage,
And bad good thrift on that image,   940
And saied he trowed her comploint
Should after cause her be corseint,
And in his sleeve he put*te* tho bill*e*,
Was there none that knew his will*e*,
And forth he walke apace about
Beholding all the lusty rout,

Halfe in a thought with smiling chere,
Till at the last, as ye shall here,
He turned unto the queene ageine,
And saide, ' To morne, here in this pleine,   950
I woll ye be, and all*e* yours,
That purposed ben to weare flours,
Or of my lusty colour use,
It may not be to you excuse,
Ne none of your*es* in no wise,
That able be to my servise,
For as I said have here before,
I will be lord for evermore
Of you, and of this yle, and all*e*,
   And of all your*es*, that have shall*e*   960
Joy, peace, ease, or in plesaunce
Your lives use without noysaunce ;
Here will I in state be scene,'
And turned his visage to the queene,
' And you give knowledge of my will*e*,
And a full answere of your bill*e*.'
Was there no nay, ne wordes none,
But very obeisaunt seemed echone,
Queene and other that were there,
Well seemed it they had*de* great fere,   970
And there tooke lodging every night,
Was none departed of that night,
And some to read old*e* romances,
Hem occupied for *here* pleasances,
Some to make verelaies and laies,
And some to other diverse plaies :
And I to me a romance tooke,
And as I reading was the booke,
   Me thought*e* the sphere had*de* so run*ne*,

That it was rising of the Sun*ne*,   980
And such a prees into the plaine
Assemble gone, that with great paine
One might*e* for other go ne stand*e*,
Ne none take other by the hand*e*,
Withouten they distourbed were,
So huge and great the prees was there.
  And after that within two houres,
This mighty lord all in floures
Of divers colours many a paire,
In his estate up in the aire,   990
Well two fathom, as his hight,
He set him there in all *here* sight,
And for the queene and for the knight,
And for my lady, and every wight
In hast he sent*e*, so that never one
Was there absent, but come echone:
And when they thus assembled were,
As ye have heard me say you here,
Withoute* more tarrying, on hight,
There to be seene of every wight,   1000
Up stood among the prees above
A counsayler, servaunt of Love,
Which seemed well of great estate,
And shewed*e* there how no debate
Owe ne goodly might*e* be used
In gentilnesse, and be excused,
Wherefore, he said, his lordes wille
Was every wight there should*e* be still*e*,
And in pees, and one accord,
And thus commaunded at a word,   1010
And can his tongue to swiche language
Turne, that yet in all mine age

Heard I never so conningly
Man speake, no halfe so faithfully,
For every thing he saide there
Seemed as it insealed were,
Or approved for very trewe:
Swiche was his cunning language newe,
And well according to his chere,
That where I be, me thinke I here   1020
Him yet alway, when I mine one
In any place may be alone:
First con he of the lusty yle
Alle thastate in little while
Rehearse, and wholly every thing
That causede there his lords comming,
And every wele and every wo,
And for what cause ech thing was so,
Well shewed he there in easie speech,
And how the sicke hadde need of leech: 1030
And that whole was, and in grace,
He tolde plainly why each thing was,
And at the last he con conclude,
Voided every language rude,
And saide, ' That prince, that mighty lord,
Or his departing, would accord
Alle the parties there present,
And was the fine of his entent,
Witnesse his presence in your sight,
Which sit among you in his might:'   1040
And kneelede downe withouten more,
And not o word *ne* spake he more.
   Tho gan this mighty lord him dresse,
With cheare avised, to do largesse,
And said unto this knight and me,

' Ye shall to joy restored be,
And for ye have ben true, ye twaine,
I graunt you here for every paine
A thousand joies every weeke,
And looke ye be no lenger seeke.   1050
And both your ladies, lo, hem here
Take ech his own, beeth of good chere,
Your happie day is new begun*ne*,
Sith it was rising of the Sun*ne*,
And to all other in this place
I graunt wholly to stand in grace,
That serveth truely, withoute slouth,
And to avaunced be by trouth.'
Tho can this knight and I downe kneele,
Wening to doo wonder wele,   1060
' Seeing, O Lord, your great*e* mercy,
Us hath enriched so openly,
That we deserve may never more
The least*e* part, but evermore,
With soule and body truely serve
You and youres till we sterve."
And to *here* ladies there they stood*e*,
This knight that couth*e* so mikel good*e*,
Went in hast, and I also,
Joyous, and glad were we tho,   1070
And also rich in every thought,
As he that all hath and ought nought,
And hem besought in humble wise,
Us taccept*e* to *here* service,
And show us of *here* friendly cheares,
Which in *here* treasure many yeares,
They had*de* kept, us to great paine,
And tolde how *here* servants twaine,

Were and woulde be, and so had ever,
And to the death chaunge woulde we never,
Ne doe offence, ne thinke like ille,   1080
But fill *here* ordinance and wille:
And made our othes freshe newe,
Our olde service to renewe,
And wholly *heres* for evermore,
We there become, what mighte we more?
And well awaiting, that in slouth
We made ne fault, ne in our trouth,
Ne thoughte not do, I you ensure,
With our wille, where we may dure.   1090
      This season past, againe an eve,
This lord of the queene tooke leve,
And said he would hastely returne,
And at good leisure there sojourne,
Both for his honour and for his case,
Commaunding fast the knight to please,
And gave his statutes in papers,
And ordent divers officers,
And forth to ship the same night
He went, and soone was out of sight.   1100
And on the morrow, when the aire
Attempred was and wonder faire,
Early at rising of the Sunne,
After the night away was runne,
Playing us on the rivage,
My lady spake of her voyage,
And saide she made smalle journies,
And held her in straunge countries,
And forthwith to the queene wente,
And shewed her wholly her entente,   1110
And tooke her leave with cheare weeping,

That pitty was to see that parting :
For to the queene it was a paine,
As to a martyr new yslaine,
That for her woe, and she so tender,
Yet weepe I oft when I remember ;
She offerde there to resigne,
To my lady eight times or nine,
Thastate, the yle, shortly to telle,
If mighte it please her there to dwelle,   1120
And saide for ever her linage
Shoulde to my lady doe homage,
And hers be hole withouten more,
Ye, and all *heres* for evermore :
' Nay, God forbid,' my lady ofte,
With many conning word and softe,
Saide, ' that ever such thing shoulde beene,
That I consente shoulde, that a queene
Of your estate, and so well named,
In any wise shoulde be attamed ;   1130
But woulde be faine with all my herte.
What so befell, or how me smerte,
To doe thing that you mighte please.
In any wise, or be your ease :'
And kissede there, and bad good night,
For which leve wepte many a wight;
There mighte men here my lady praised.
And such a name of her araised,
What of cunning and friendlinesse,
What of beauty with gentilnesse,   1140
What of glad and friendly cheares,
That she used in all her yeares,
That wonder was here every wight,
To say well how they did *here* might ;

And with a prees, upon the morrow,
To ship her brought, and what a sorrow
They made, when she should under saile,
That, and ye wist, ye woulde mervaile.
Forth goeth the ship, out goeth the sonde,
And I as *a* wood man unbonde,   1150
For doubt to be behinde there,
Into the sea withouten fere,
Anon I ran, till with a wawe,
All sodenly, I was overthrawe,
And with the water to and fro,
Backward and forward travailed so,
That mind and breath nigh was *agone*
For good ne harme knew I none,
Til at the last with hookes tweine,
Men of the ship with mikel peine,   1160
To save my life, dide such travaile,
That, and ye wist, ye woulde mervaile,
And in the ship me drew on hie,
And saiden alle that I woulde die,
And laide me long downe by the maste,
And of *here* clothes on me caste,
And there I made my testamente,
And wiste my selfe not what I mente,
But whan I said had what I woulde,
And to the mast my wo all tolde,   1170
And tane my leave of every wight,
And closed mine eyen, and lost my sight,
Avised to die, without more speeche,
Or any remedy to seeche
Of grace new, as was great need :
My lady of my paine tooke heed,
And her bethought how that for trouth

To see me die it were great routh,
And to me came in sober wise,
And softly said, ' I pray you rise,
Come on with me, let be this fare,
All shall be wel, have ye no care,
I will obey, ye, and fulfille,
Holy in all that lordes wille,
That you and me not long ago,
After his list commaundede so,
That there againe no resistence
May be withoute great offence,
And, therefore, now *loke* what I say,
I am and will be friendly aye,
Rise up, behold this avauntage,
I graunte you inheritage,
Peaceably withoute strive,
During the daies of your live.'
And of her apples in my sleve
One she put, and tooke her leve
In wordes few and saide, ' Good hele,
He that all made, you send and wele :'
Wherewith my paines, all at ones,
Tooke such leave, that all my bones,
For the newe durense pleasaunce,
So as they couthe, desirede to daunce,
And I as whole as any wight,
Up rose, with joyous heart and light,
Hole and unsicke, right wele at ease,
And all forget hadde my disease,
And to my lady, where she plaide,
I went anone, and to her saide :
' He that all joies persons to please
First ordainede with parfite ease,

And every pleasure can depart*e*,
Send you madame, as large a part*e*,
And of his good*es* such plenty,
As he ha*th* done you of beauty,
With hele and all that may be thought,
He send you all as he all wrought:
Madame,' (quoth I) ' your servaunt trew*e*,
Have I ben long, and yet will new*e*,
Withoute chaunge or repentaunce,
In any wise or variaunce,   1220
And so will do, as thrive I ever,
For thing is none that me is lever
Than you to please, how ever I fare,
Mine hart*es* lady and my welfare,
My life, mine hele, my leech also,
Of every thing that doth me wo,
My helpe at need, and my surcté
Of every joy that long*eth* to me,
My succours whole in all*e* wise,
That may be thought or man devise,   1230
Your grace, madame, such have I found*e*,
Now in my need that I am bound*e*
To you for ever, so Christ me save,
For heale and live of you I have,
Wherefore is reasoun I you serve,
With due obeisaunce till I sterve,
And dead and quicke be ever your*es*,
Late, early, and at all hour*es*.'
Tho came my lady small alite,
And in plaine English con consite   1240
In word*es* few, whole her entente
She shewed*e* me there, and how she ment*e*
To me-ward*es* in every wise,

Wholly she came at *here* devise,
Withoute processe or long travell,
Charging me to keepe counsell,
As I woulde to her grace attaine,
Of which commaundement I was faine,
Wherefore I passe over at this time,
For counsell cord*eth* not well in rime,   1250
And eke the oth that I have swore,
To breake me were better unbore,
Why for untrue for evermore
I shoulde be holde, that nevermore
Of me in place shoulde be reporte
Thing that availe might, or comforte
To mewardes in any wise,
And ech wight woulde me dispise
In that they couth, and me repreve,
Which were a thing sore for to greeve,   1260
Wherefore hereof more mencion
Make I not now no long sermon,
But shortly thus I me excuse,
To rime a councell I refuse.
Sailing thus two daies or three,
My lady towardes her countree,
Over the waves high and greene,
Which were large and deepe betweene,
Upon a time me called, and saide
That of my hele she was well paid,   1270
And of the queene and of the yle,
    She talkede with me longe while,
O all that she there had*de* seene,
And of the state, and of the queene,
And of the ladies name by name,
Two houres or mo, this was her game,

Till at the last the wind can rise,
And blew so fast, and in such wise,
The ship that every wight can say*e*,
'Madame, er eve be of this day*e*,   1280
And God tofore, ye shall be there
As ye would*e* fainest that ye were,
And doubt*e* not within six*e* hours,
Ye shall be there, as all is yours.'
At which word*es* she gan to smile,
And said*e* that was no long while,
That they her set, and up she rose,
And all about the ship she gose,
And made good cheare to every wight,
Till of the land she had a sight,   1290
Of which sight glad, God it wot,
She was abashed and aboot,
And forth goeth, shortly you to tell*e*,
Where she accustomed was to dwell*e*,
And received was, as good right,
With joyous cheere and heartes light,
And as a glad new aventure,
Pleasaunt to every creature,
With which landing tho I *a*woke,
And found my chamber full of smoke,   1300
My cheekes eke unto the eares,
And all my body wet with teares,
And all so feeble and in such wise
I was, that unneth might I rise,
So fare travailed and so faint,
That neither knew I kirke ne saint,
Ne what was what, ne who was who,
Ne avised what way I would*e* go,
But by a venturous grace,

I rose and walk*e*, sought*e* pace and pace, 1310
Till I a winding staire found,
And held the vice aye in my hond,
And upward softly so can creepe,
Till I came where I thought*e* to sleepe
More at mine ease, and out of preace,
At my good leisure, and in peace,
Till somewhat I recomfort were
Of the travell and great*e* feare
That I endured had*de* before,
This was my thought withoute more, 1320
And as a wight witlesse and faint,
Withoute more, in a chamber paint
Full of stories old and divers,
More than I can now rehearse,
Unto a bed full soberly,
So as I might*e* full southly,
Pace after other, and nothing said*e*,
Till at the last downe I me laid*e*,
And as my mind would*e* give me leve,
All that I dreamed had*de* that eve, 1330
Before*n* all I can rehearse,
Right as a child at schoole his verse,
Doth after that he thinketh to thrive.
Right so did I for all my live,
I thought*e* to have in remembraunce,
Both*e* the paine and the pleasaunce,
The dreame whole, as it me befell,
Which was as ye here me tell*e*.
Thus in my thoughtes as I lay,
That happy or unhappy day, 1340
Ne wot I not, so have I blame,
Of thi*lk*e two which is the name:

Befell me so, that there a thought*e*,
By processe new on sleepe me brought*e*,
And me governed*e* so in a while,
That yet againe within the yle,
Methought I was, whereof the knight,
And of the ladies I had a sight,
And were assembled on a greene,
Knight and lady, with the queene, 1350
At which assembly there was said,
How they all*e* content and paid
Were wholly as in that thing,
That the knight there shoulde be king,
And they would all for sure witnesse
Wedded be both*e* more and lesse,
In remembraunce without*e* more,
Thus they consent*e* for evermore,
And was concluded that the knight
Depart*e* shoulde the same night, 1360
And forthwith there tooke his voiage
To journey for his marriage,
And returne with such an host*e*,
That wedded might*e* be least and most*e*,
This was concluded, written and sealed,
That it might*e* not be repealed
In no wise, but aie be firme,
And should all be within a tearme,
Without*e* more excusation,
Both feast and coronation. 1370
This knight which had*de* thereof the charge,
Anon into a little barge
I-brought was late against an eve,
Where of all he tooke his leave;
Which barge was as a man*ne*s thought,

After his pleasure to him brought,
The queene herselfe accustomed aye
In th*ilk*e same barge to play*e*,
It needeth neither mast ne rother,
I have not heard of such another,
No maister for the governaunce,
Hie sayled by thought and pleasaunce,
Withoute labour, east and west,
Alle was one, calme or tempest,
And I went*e* with at his request,
And was the first praied to the fest.
Whan he came in-*to* his countree,
And passed had*de* the wavy see,
In an haven deepe and large
He left his rich and noble barge,
And to the court, shortly to tell*e*,
He went*e*, where he wont was to dwell*e*,
And was received as good right,
As heire, and for a worthy knight,
With all*e* the states of the lond,
Which came anon at his first*e* sond,
With glade spirits full of trouth,
Loth to do fault or with a slouth,
Attaint*e* be in any wise ;
Here riches was *here* olde servise,
Which ever trow had*de* be fond*e*,
Sith first inhabit was the lond*e*,
And so received there her king,
That forgotten was no thing,
That owe to be done ne might*e* please,
Ne *here* soveraine lord do ease,
And with hem, so shortly to say*e*,
As they of custome had*de* done aye,

For seven yere past was and more,
The father, the old*e* wise and hore   1410
King of the land tooke *tho* his leve
Of all his barons on an eve,
And told hem how his dayes past
Were all, and comen was the last,
And hartily prayed hem to remember
His sonne, which yong was and tender,
That borne was *here* prince to be,
If he returne to that countree
Might*e*, by adventure or grace,
Within any time or space,   1420
And to be true and friendly aye,
As they to him hadd*e* bene alway:
Thus he hem prayd*e*, withoute more,
And tooke his leave for evermoro.
Knowen was, how tender in age,
This young*e* prince a great viage
Uncouth and straunge, honours to seche,
Tooke in hond*e* with little speeche,
Which was to seeke a princess*e*
That he desired*e* more than richess*e*,   1430
For her greate name that floured*e* so,
That in that time there was no mo
Of her estate, ne so well named,
For borne was none that ever her blamed:
Of which princes somewhat before,
Here have I spoke, and some will more.
So thus befell as ye shall heare,
Unto *here* lord they made such cheare,
That joy was there to be present
To see their troth and how they ment*e*,   1440
So very glad they were ech one,

That hem among there was no one,
That desirede more richesse,
Than for *here* lord such a princesse,
That they mighte please, and that were faire,
For fast desirede they an heire,
And saide great surety were ywis.
And as they were speaking of this,
The prince himselfe him avised,
And in plaine English undisguised,   1450
Hem shewed hole his journeye,
And of *here* counsell gan hem preye,
And told how he ensured was,
And how his day he mighte not passe,
Without diffame and greate blame,
And to him for ever a shame,
And of *here* counsell and aviso,
There he prayth hem once or twise,
And that they woulde within ten daies,
Avise and ordaine him such waies,   1460
So that it were no displeasaunce,
Ne to this realme over great grievaunce,
And that he have mighte to his feast,
Sixty thousand at the least,
For his intent within short while
Was to returne unto his yle
That he came fro, and kepe his day,
For nothing would he be away.
To counsailo tho the lords anon,
Into a chamber everychone,   1470
Togither went, hem to devise,
How they mighte best and in what wise,
Purveye for *here* lords pleasaunce
And the realmes continuaunce

Of honor, which in it before
Had*de* continued evermore.
So, at the last, they founde the waies,
How within the nexte ten daies,
All mighte with paine and diligence
Be done, and cast what the dispence 1480
Mighte draw, and in conclusion,
Made for ech thing provision.
Whan this was done, wholly tofore
The prince, the lord*es* all before
Come, and shewed what they had*de* done,
And how they couthe by no reason
Finde that within the ten daies,
He mighte departe by no waies,
But woulde be fiftcene, at the least,
Or he returne mighte to his feast : 1490
And shewed him every reason why
It mighte not be so hastily,
As he desirede, ne his day
He mighte not keope by no way,
For divers causes wonder greate :
Which, whan he heard, in such an heate
He fell, for sorow and was scke,
Still in his bed*de* whole that weke,
And nigh the tother for the shame,
And for the doubt, and for the blame 1500
That on him mighte be arct,
And oft upon his brest he bet,
And said, ' Alas, mine honour for aye,
Have I here lost cleane this day,
Dead would I be ! alas, my name
Shall aye be more henceforth in shame,
And I dishonoured and repreved,

And never more shall be beleeved :'
And made swich sorow, that in trouth,
Him to behold it was great routh :
And so endured the dayes fiftene,
Till that the lordes on an even
Him come, and tolde they ready were,
And shewed in few wordes there,
How and what wise they hadde purveyd
For his estate, and to him said,
That twenty thousand knights of name,
And forty thousand without blame,
All come of noble ligne,
Togider in a compané,
Were lodged on a rivers side,
Him and his pleasure there tabide.
The prince tho for joy up rose,
And where they lodged were, he goes
Withoute more that same nighte,
And these his supper made to dighte,
And with hem bode till it was dey,
And forthwith to take his journey,
Leving tho streight, holding the large,
Till he came to his noble barge ;
And when this prince, this lustie knight,
With his people in armes brighte,
Was comen where he thought to pase,
And knew well none abiding was
Behind, but all were there present,
Forthwith anon all his intent
He told hem there, and made his cries
Through his osto that day twies,
Commaunding every lives wight,
There being present in his sight,

To be the morow on the rivage,
Where he beginne would his viage.
The morrow come, the cry was kept,
Fewe was there that night that slept,
But trussed and purveied for the morrow,
For fault of ships was all *here* sorrow,
For save the barge, and other two,
Of shippes there saw I no mo :
Thus in *here* doubtes as they stoode,
Waxing the sea, comming the floode,   1550
Was cried, ' To ship goe every wighte,'
Then was but hie, that hie mighte,
And to the barge me thought echone
They wente, without was left not one,
Horse, male, trusse, ne bagage,
Salad, speare, gard-brace, ne page,
But was lodged and roome ynough,
At which shipping me thought I lough,
And gan to marvaile in my thought,
How ever such a ship was wrought,   1560
For what people that can encrease,
Ne never so thicke mighte be the prease,
But all hadde roome at *here* wille,
There was not one was lodged ille,
For as I trow, my selfe the last
Was one, and lodged by the mast,
And where I looked I saw such rome,
As all were lodged in a towne.
Forth goth the ship, said was the creed,
And on *here* knees for *here* good speed,   1570
Downe kneeled every wight a while,
And praiede faste that to the yle
They mighte come in safety,

The prince and all the company,
With worship and withoute blame,
Or disclaunder of his name,
Of the promise he shoulde retourne,
Within the time he dide sojourne,
In his londe biding his host,
This was *here* prayer of least and most ; 1580
To keepe the day it mighte not been,
That he appointed had*de* with the queen,
To returne withoute slouth,
And so assured had his trouth,
For whiche fault this prince, this knight,
During the time slep*te* not a night,
Such was his wo and his disease,
For doubt he shoulde the queene displease.
Forth goeth the ship with suche speed,
Right as the prince for his great need 1590
Desire would after his thoughte,
Till it into the yle him broughte,
Where in hast upon the sand,
He and his people tooke the land,
With hartes glad, and chere light,
Weening to be in Heaven that night :
But or they passed*en* a while,
Entring in toward that yle,
All clad in blacke with chere piteous,
A lady which never dispiteous 1600
Had*de* be in all her life tofore,
With sory chere, and harte to-tore,
Unto this prince where he gan ride,
Come and said, ' Abide, abide,
And have no hast, but fast retourne,
No reason is ye here sojourne,

For your untruth hath us discried,
Wo worth the time we us alliede
With you, that are so soone untrewe,
Alas, the day that we you knewe!   1610
Alas, the time that ye were bore,
For all this lond by you is lore!
Accursed be he you hider broughte.
For all your joy is turnd to nought,
Your acquaintance we may complaine,
Which is the cause of all our paine.'
' Alas, madame,' quoth tho this knight,
And with that from his horse he light,
With colour pale, and cheekes lene,
' Alas, what is this for to mene?   1620
What have ye said, why be ye wroth?
You to displease I woulde be loth,
Know ye not well the promesse
I made have to your princesse,
Which to perfourme is mine intent,
So mote I speed, as I have ment,
And as I am her very trewe,
Withoute change or thoughtes newe,
And also fully her servand,
As creature or man livand   1630
May be to lady or princesse,
For she mine Heaven and whole richesse
Is, and the lady of mine heale,
My worldes joy and all my weale,
What may this be, whence cometh this speech?
Tell me, madame, I you beseech,
For sith the first of my living,
Was I so fearfull of nothing,
As I am now to heare you speake;

For doubt I feele mine hearte breake ;   1640
Say on, madame, tell me your wille,
The remenaunt is it good or ille ?'
' Alas,' (quod she) ' that ye were bore,
For, for your love this land is lore !
The queene is dead, and that is ruth,
For sorrow of your great untruth ;
Of two partes of the lusty route,
Of ladies that were there aboute,
That wont were to talke and play,
Now aren dead and cleane away,   1650
And under earth tane lodging newe ;
Alas, that ever ye were untrewe !
For when the time ye set was past,
The queene to counsaile sone in hast,
What was to doe, and said great blame
Your acquaintaunce cause would and shame,
And the ladies of *here* avise
Prayede, for need was to be wise,
In eschewing tales and songs,
That by hem make would ille tongs,   1660
And sey they were lightly conquest,
And prayed to a poore feast,
And foule had *here* worship weived,
When so unwisely they conceivede,
Here rich treasour, and *here* heale,
Here famous name, and *here* weale,
To put in such an aventure,
Of which the sclaunder ever dure
Was like, without helpe of appele,
Wherefore they need had of counsele,   1670
For every wight of hem woulde say
Here closed yle an open way

Was become to every wight,
And well appreved by a knight,
Which he alas, without paysaunce,
Had*de* soone acheved thobeisaunce:
All this was moved at counsell thrise,
And concluded daily twise,
That bet was die withoute blame
Than lose the riches of *here* name,   1680
Wherefore, the deathes acquaintaunce
They chese, and left have *here* pleasaunce,
For doubt to live as repreved,
In that they you so soone beleeved,
And made *here* othes with one accord,
That eate ne drinke, ne speake word,
They shoulde never, but ever weping
Bide in a place withoute parting,
And use *here* dayes in penaunce,
Without desire of allegeaunce,   1690
Of which the truth, anon, con preve,
For-why the queen forthwith her leve
Toke at hem all that were present,
Of her defauts fully repent,
And diede there withouten more :
Thus are we lost for evermore ;
What should I more hereof reherse ?
Comen within, come see her herse,
Where ye shall see the piteous sight,
That ever yet was shewen to knight,   1700
For ye shall see ladies stonde,
Ech with a great rod in *hire* honde,
I-clad in black, with visage white,
Ready each other for to smite,
If any be that will not wepe,

Or who that mak*eth* countenaunce to slepe ;
They be so bet, that all-so blew*e*
They be as cloth that died is newe,
Such is their parfite repentance ;
And thus they kepe *here* ordinance,   171
And will do ever to the death,
While hem endur*eth* any breath.'
    This knight tho in armes twaine,
This lady tooke and gan her saine,
' Alas, my birth ! wo worth my life !'
And even with that he drew a knife,
And through gowne, doublet, and shert*e*,
He made the blood come from his hert*e*,
And set him downe upon the greene,
And full repent closed his cene,   172
And save that ones he drew his breath,
Without more thus he tooke his death.
For which cause the lusty hoast,
Which in a battaile on the coast,
At once for sorrow such a cry
Gan rere thorow the company,
That to the Heaven heard was the sowne,
And under therth als fer adowne,
That wild*e* beast*es* for the feare
So sodainly afrayed were,   173
That for the doubt, while they might*e* dure,
They ran as of *here* lives unsure,
From the wood*es* unto the plaine,
And from the valleys the high*e* mountaine
They sought, and ran as beast*es* blind*e*,
That cleane forgotten had *here* kinde.
This wo not ceased, to counsaile went*e*
These lords, and for that lady sent*e*,

And of avise what was to done,
They her besoughte she say woulde sone. 1740
Weeping full sore, all clad in blake,
This lady softly to hem spake,
And saide, ' My lordes, by my trouth,
This mischiefe it is of your slouth,
And if ye hadde that judge woulde right,
A prince that were a very knight,
Ye that ben of astate echone,
Die for his fault should one and one ;
And if he hold hadde the promesse,
And done that longeth to gentilnesse,   1750
And fulfilled the princes behest,
This hastie farme hadde bene a feast,
And now is unrecoverable,
And us a slaunder aye durable ;
Wherefore, I say, as of counsaile,
In me is none that may availe,
But, if ye list, for remembraunce
Purvey and make such ordinaunce,
That the queene, that was so meke,
With all her women, dede or seke,   1760
Might in your land a chappell have,
With some remembraunce of her grave,
Shewing her end with the pity,
In some notable olde city,
Nigh unto an high way,
Where every wight mighte for her pray,
And for all hers that have ben trewe ;'
And even with that she changed hewe,
And twise wished after the death,
And sight, and thus passed her breath.   1770
Then saide the lordes of the hoste,

And so conclude least and mos*te*,
That they would ever in houses of thacke
Here lives lead, and weare but blacke,
And forsake all *here* pleasaunces,
And turn all joy to penaunces,
And beare the dea*de* prince to the barge,
And named hem should have the charge ;
And to the hearse where lay the queen,
The remenaunt went, and down on kneen,
Holding *here* hon*des* on high, con crie,
' Mercy, mercy,' everich thrie,
And curse*de* the time that ever slouth
Should have such masterdome of trouth.
And to the barge a long mile,
They bare her forth, and in a while
All*e* the ladies one and one,
By companies were brought echone,
And past the sea and tooke the land,
And in new hersces on a sand,
I-put and brought were all anon,
Unto a city closed with stone,
Where it had*de* been used aye
The king*es* of the land to lay,
After they raigned in honours,
And writ was which were conquerours,
In an abbey of nunnes which were blake,
Which accustomed were to wake,
And of usage rise ech a night
To pray for every lives wight ;
And so befell as in the guise,
Ordeint and said was the servise,
Of thil*ke* prince and of the queen,
So devoutly as might*e* been,

And after that about the herses,
Many orisones and verses,
Withoute note full softely,
Said were and that full heartily,
That all the night till it was day,
The people in the church con pray   1810
Unto the holy Trinitie,
Of these soules to have pitie.
      And when the night ipast and ronne
Was, and the newe day begonne,
The yonge morrow with rayes rede,
Which from the Sunne over all con sprede,
Atempered clere was and faire,
And made a time of wholsome aire,
Befell a wonder case and strange,
Among the people and gan change   1820
Soone the word and every woo
Unto a joy, and some to two :
A bird, all fedred blew and greene,
With brighte rayes like gold betweene,
As smalle thred over every joynt,
All full of colour strange and coint,
Uncouth and wonderfull to sighte,
Upon the queenes herse con lighte,
And song full low and softely,
Three songes in her harmony,   1830
 Unletted of every wight,
Till, at the last, an aged knight
Which seemed a man in great thought
Like as he set all thing at nought,
With visage and cien all forwept
And pale, as man longe unslept,
By thilke herses as he stood

With hasty hondling of his hood
Unto a prince that by him paste
Made the bridde somewhat agast,   180
Wherefore she rose and left her song,
And departe from us among,
And spread her winges for to passe
By the place he entred was,
And in his hast, shortly to telle,
Him hurt, that backeward downe he fell,
From a window richly ipeint
With lives of many divers seint,
And bet his wings and bledde faste,
And of the hurt thus died and paste,   190
And lay there well an houre and more,
Till, at the last, of briddes a score
Come and sembled at the place
Where the window ibroken was,
And made swiche waimentacioun,
That pity was to heare the soun,
And the warbles of *here* throtes,
And the complaint of *here* notes,
Which from joy cleane was reversed,
And of hem one the glas soone persed,   200
And in his beke of colours nine,
An herbe he broughte flourelesse, all greene,
Ful of smalle leaves and plaine,
Swart and longe with many a vaine,
And where his fellow lay thus dede,
This hearbe down laide by his hede,
And dressed it full softily,
And hong his head and stood thereby,
Which hearb, in lesse than halfe an houre,
Gan over all knit, and after floure   210

Full out and wexe ripe the seed*e*,
And right as one another feed*e*
Would, in his beake he tooke the graine,
And in his fellowes beake certaine
It put, and thus, within the third,
Up stood and pruned him the bird,
Which dead had*de* be in all our sight,
And both togither forth *here* flight
Tooke singing from us, and *here* leve,
Was none disturb hem would*e* ne greve ;   1880
And when they parted were and gone
Thabbesse the seedes soone echone
I-gadred had, and in her hand
The herb she tooke, well avisand
The leafe, the seed, the stalke, the floure,
And said it had a good savour,
And was no common herb to find*e*,
And well approved of uncouth kind*e*,
And than other more vertuouse,
Who so have it might*e* for to use   1890
In his neede, flowre, leafe, or graine,
Of *here* heale might*e* be certaine ;
And laid it downe upon the herse
Where lay the queene, and gan reherse,
Echone to other that they had*de* scene,
And taling thus the sede wex greene,
And on the drie herse gan spring*e*,
Which thoughte me a wondrous thing*e*,
And after that floure and new*e* seed,
Of which the people all tooke heed,   1900
And said, it was some great miracle,
Or medicine fine more than triacle,
And were well done there to assay,

If it might ease in any way
The corses, which with torche light,
They waked had*de* there all that night.
Soone did*e* the lord*es* thero consent*e*,
And all the people thereto content*e*,
With easie word*es* and little fare,
And made the queen*es* visage bare,   191
Which showed was to all about,
Wherefore in swoone fell whole the rout,
And were so sory, most and least*e*,
That long of weeping they not ceast*e*,
For of *here* lord the remembraunce
Unto hem was such displeasaunce,
That for to live they called a paine,
So were they very true and plaine;
And after this, the good abbesse
Of the grain*es* gan chese and dresse   19
Three, with her fingers cleane and small*e*,
And in the queen*es* mouth by tale,
One after other full easily,
She putte and full conningly,
Which showed*e* soone such vertue,
That preved was the medicine true,
For with a smiling countenaunce
The queene uprose, and of usaunce,
As she was wont, to every wight
She made good cheere, for which sight   19
The people kneeling on the stones.
Thought*e* they in Heaven were soule and bone*s*
And to the prince where he lay,
They wente to make the same assay;
And whan the queene it understood,
And how the medicine was good,

She prayed*e* she might have the graines
To releve him from the paines
Which she and he had*de* both endured,
And to him went, and so him cured*e*,   1940
That within a little space,
Lusty and fresh on live he was
And in good hele and hole of speech,
And lough, and said, ' Gramercy leech,'
For which the joy throughout the town,
So great was that the bel*les* sown
Afraied the people, a journay
About the city every way,
And come and asked*e* cause and why,
They rongen were so stately ?   1950
And after that the queene, thabbesse
Made diligence, or they would*e* cesse,
Such, that of ladies soone a rout
Shewing the queene was all about,
And called by name echone and told*e*,
Was none forgotten young ne old*e* ;
There might*e* men see joyes new*e*,
When the medicine fine and trew*e*,
Thus restored had every wight,
So well the queene as the knight,   1960
Unto perfit joy and hele,
That fleting they were in such wele
As folke that would in no wise,
Desire more perfit paradise.
And thus, whan passed was the sorrow,
With mikel joy soone on the morrow,
Tho king, the queene, and every lord,
With all the ladies by one accord,
A generall assembly

Great cry through*outer* the country,
The which after as *here* intent
Was turned to a parliament,
Where was ordained and avised
Every thing and devised,
That please might*e* to most and least*e*,
And there concluded was the feast*e*,
Within the yle to be *y*hold*e*
With full consent of young and old*e*,
In the same wise as before,
As thing should*e* be withouten more ;
And shipped and thither went*e*,
And into straunge realmes sent*e*
To king*es*, queenes, and duchesses,
To divers princes and princesses,
Of *here* linage, and can pray
That it might*e* like hem at that day
Of marriage, for *here* sport,
Come see the yle and hem disport,
Where should*e* be jousts and turnaies,
And armes done in other waies,
Signifying over all the day,
After Aprill*e* within May ;
And was avised that ladies tweine,
Of good estate and well beseine,
With certaine knight*es* and squiers,
And of the queenes officers,
In manner of an embassade,
With certain letters closed and made,
Should*e* take the barge and depart*e*,
And seeke my lady every part*e*,
Till they her found*e* for any thing,
Both charged have queene and king,

And as *here* lady and maistresse,
Her to beseke of gentilnesse,
At th*ilke* day there for to been,
And oft her recommaund the queen,
And prayeth for all loves to hast*e*,
For, but she come, all woll be wast*e*,
And *al* the feast a businesso
Without*e* joy or lustinesse :⁣   2010
And tooke hem tokens and good speed
Prai*de* God send, after *here* need.
Forth went*e* the ladies and the knights,
And were out fourteene daies and nights,
And brought*e* my lady in *here* barge,
And had well sped and done *here* charge ;
Whereof the queene so hartily glad*e*,
Was, that, in soth, such joy she had*de*
When th*ilke* ship approched lond,
That she my lady on the sond   2020
I-met, and in armes so constraine,
That wonder was behold hem twaine,
Which to my dome during twelve houres,
Neither for heat ne watry shoures,
 Departe*de* not no company,
Saving hemselfe but none hem by,
But gave hem leisour at *here* case,
To rehearse joy and disease,
After the pleasure and courages
Of *here* young and tender ages :⁣   2030
And after with many a knight
I-brought were, where, as for that night,
They parte*de* not, for to pleasaunce,
Content was hert and countenaunce
Both of the queene and my maistresse,

This was that night *here* businesse :
And on the morrow with huge rout,
This prince of lordes him about,
Come and to my lady saide
That of her comming well apaid
And glad he was, and full conningly
Her thanked and full heartily,
And lough and smiled, and said, ' ywis,
That was in doubt in safety is :'
And commaunde*de* do diligence,
And spare for neither gold ne spence,
But make ready, for on the morow
Wedded, with saint John to borrow,
He would*e* be, withouten more,
And let hem wite this lesse and more.
The morow come, and the service
Of mariage, in such a wise
Said was, that with more honour
Was never prince ne conquerour
I-wedde, ne with such company
Of gentilnesse in chivalry,
Ne of ladies so greate route,
Ne so beseen, as all aboute
They were there, I certifie
You on my life withouten lie.
    And the feast hold was in tentis,
As to telle you mine content is,
In a rome, a large plaine
Under a wood in a champaine,
Betwixt a river and a wolle,
Where never had abbay, ne selle
Ben, ne kirke, house, ne village,
In time of any mannes ago :

And dure*de* three monthes the feaste,
In one estate and never ceaste, 2070
From early the rising of the Sonne,
Till spent the day was and yronne,
In justing, dauncing, and lustinesse,
And all that sownede to gentilnesse.
  And, as me thought*e*, the second morrow,
When ended was all olde sorrow,
And in surety every wight
Had*de* with his lady slept a night,
The prince, the queene, and all the rest,
Unto my lady made request, 2080
And her besought oft and praied
To mewards to be well apaied,
And consider mine olde trouth,
And on my paines have routh,
And me accept to her servise,
In such forme and in such wise,
That we both might*e* be as one,
Thus prayede the queene, and everichone:
And, for there shoulde be no nay,
They stint*e* justing all a day, 2090
To pray my lady and requere
Be content and out of fere,
And with good hearte make friendly cheare,
And said it was a happy yeare:
At which she smiled and said, ywis,
" I trow well he my servaunt is,
And woulde my welfare, as I triste,
So would I his, and would he wiste
How, and I knewe that his trouth
Continue woulde withoute slouth, 3000
And be such as ye here report,

Restraining both courage and sport,
I couthe consent at your request,
To be i-named of your fest,
And do after your usaunce,
In obeying your pleasaunce ;
At your request this I consent,
To please you in your entent,
And eke the soveraine above
Commanded hath me for to love,   3010
And before other him prefer,
Against which prince may be no wer,
For his power over all raigneth,
That other woulde for nought him paineth,
And sith his will and yours is one,
Contrary in me shall be none."
Tho (as me thoughte) tho promise
Of marriage before the mese
Desired was of every wight
To be imade the same night,   3020
To put away all maner doute
Of every wight thereaboute,
And so was do ; and on the morrow,
When every thought and every sorrow
Dislodged was out of mine herte,
With every wo and every smerte,
Unto a tent prince and princesse,
Me thoughte, broughte me and my maistresse,
And saide we were at full age
There to conclude our marriage,   3030
With ladies, knightes, and squiers,
And a great host of ministers,
With instruments and sounes diverse,
That longe were here to rehearse,

Which tent was church perochiall,
Ordaint was in especiall,
For the feast and for tho sacre,
Where archbishop, and archdiacre,
Song*e* full out*e* the servise,
After the custome and the guise,   3040
And the churches ordinaunce;
And after that to dine and daunce
Brought were we, and to divers plaies,
And for our speed ech with praies,
And merry was most and least*e*,
And said amended was the feast*e*,
And were right glad lady and lord,
Of the marriage and thaccord,
And wished us heartes pleasaunce,
Joy, hele, and continuance,   3050
And to the ministrils made request,
That in encreasing of tho fest,
They would*e* touch*en here* cords,
And with some new joyeux accords,
Moove the people to gladnesse,
And praiden of all gentilnesse,
Ech to paine hem for the day,
To show his cunning and his play.
Tho began*ne* sownes mervelous
Entuned with accords joyous,   3060
Round about all*e* tho tent*es*,
With thousand*es* of instrument*es*,
That every wight to daunce hem pained*e*,
To be merry was none that fained*e*,
Which sowne me troubled in my sleepe,
That fro my bed*de* forth I lepe,
Wening to be at thi*lke* feast,

But when I woke all was *iceast*,
For ther nas lady ne creature,
Save on the wal*les* olde portraiture
Of horsmen, haukes, and hound*es*,
And hurt*e* deere full of wound*es*,
Some like bitten, some hurt with shot,
And, as my dreame, seemed that was not ;
And when I wake, and knew the trouth,
And ye had*de* seen, of very routh,
I trow ye would have wept a weke,
For never man yet halfe so seke ;
I went escaped with the life,
And was for fault that sword ne knife
I finde no might*e* my life tabridge,
Ne thing that kervede, ne had edge,
Wherewith I might*e* my woful pain*es*,
Have voided with bleeding of my vain*es*.
Lo, here my blisse, lo, here my paine,
Which to my lady I do complaine,
And grace and mercy her requere,
To ende my wo and busie fere,
And me accept*e* to her servise,
After her service in such avise,
That of my dreame the substaunce
Might*e* once turne to cognisaunce,
And cognisaunce to very preve
By full consent and goode love,
Or el*les* without more I pray,
That thi*lke* night, or it be day,
I mote unto my dreame returne,
And sleeping so, forth aie sojourne
About the yle of pleasaunce,
Under my ladies obeisaunce,

In her servise, and in such wise,
As it please her may to devise,
And grace ones to be accept*e*,
Like as I dreamed when I slept*e*,
And dure a thousand yeare and ten,
In her good will, Amen! Amen!

FAIREST of faire, and goodliest on live,
All my secre*t* to you I plaine and shrive,
Requiring grace and of complaint,
To be healed or martyred as a saint,   3110
For by my trouth I sweare, and by this booke,
Ye may both heale and slea me with a looke.

Go forth mine owne true hart innocent,
And with humblesse, do thine observaunce,
And to thy lady on thy knees present
Thy servise new, and think how great pleasance
It is to live under thobeisance
Of her that may with her looke*s* soft*e*
Give thee the blisse that thou desirest oft*e*.

Be diligent, awake, obey, and drede,   3120
And not too wild *be* of thy countenaunce,
But meeke and glad, and thy nature feed*e*,
To do each thing that may her pleasance,
When thou shalt sleep, have aie in remembrance
Thimage of her which may with lookes soft*e*
Give thee the blisse that thou desirest oft*e*.

And if so be that thou her name find*e*
Written in booke, or el*l*es upon wall*e*,
Looke that thou, as servaunt true and kind*e*,

Thine obeisaunce, as she were there withall*e* ; 31
Faining in love is breeding of a fall*e*
From the grace of her, whose lookes soft*e*
May give the bliṣse that thou desirest oft*e*.

Ye that this ballade read*e* shall*e*,
I pray you keepe you from the fall*e*.

THE BOKE OF THE DUCHESSE;

OR, THE DETHE OF BLANCHE.

HAVE grete wonder, be this lyghte,
How that I lyve; for day ne nyghte
I may nat slepe welnygh noght,
I have so many an ydel thoght,
Purely for defaulte of slepe,
That, by my trouthe I take no kepe
Of noothinge, how hyt commeth or gooth.
Ne me nys nothynge leve nor looth;
Al is ylyche goode to me,
Joye or sorowe, wher so hyt be.   10
For I have felynge in nothynge,
But, as yt were a mased thynge,
Alway in poynt to falle adoun;
For sorwful ymagynacioun
Ys alway hooly in my mynde.
    And wel ye woote, agaynes kynde
Hyt were to lyven in thys wyse;
For nature wolde nat suffyse,
To noon erthely creature,
Nat longe tyme to endure   20
Withoute slepe, and be in sorwe.
And I ne may, ne nyght ne morwe,

Slepe ; and thys melancolye
And drede I have for to dye,
Defaulte of slepe and hevynesse,
Hath *sleyn* my spirite of quyknesse,
That I have loste al lustyhede ;
Suche fantasies ben in myn hede,
So I not what is best too doo.
  But men myght axe me, why soo
I may not sleepe, and what me is.
But natheles, who axe*th* this,
Leseth his axing trew*e*ly ;
My selven cannot tel*le* why
The soothe ; but trew*e*ly as I gesse,
I hold it *to* be a sicknes
That I have suffred this eight yere,
And yet my boote is never the nere.
For there is phisicien but one,
That may me heale, but that is done. ;
Passe we over untillo efte ;
That wil not be, mote nedes be lefte ;
Our firste matere is good to kepe.
  So whan I sawe I might*e* not slepe,
Til now late this other night
Upon my bedde I sate upright,
And bade one reche me a booke,
A romaunce, and it me toke
To rede, and drive the night away;
For me it thoughte beter play*e*,
Then either atte chesse or tables.
  And in this boke were written fables,
That clerkes had in olde time,
And other poets, put in rime,
To rede, and for to be in minde,

While men lovede the lawe in Kinde.
This boke ne speake but of suche thinges,
Of quenes lives, and of kinges,
And many other thinges smale.
Amonge al this I fonde a tale 60
That thoughte me a wonder thing.
This was the tale :—There was a king
That hight Seyes ; and had a wife,
The beste that mighte beare lyfe,
And this quene hight Alcyone.
So it befil, therafter sone,
This king wol wenden over se.
To tellen schortly, whan that he
Was in the see, thus in this wise,
Soche a tempest *tho* gan to rise, 70
That brake her maste, and made it fal*le*,
And cleft *here* schippe, and dreint hem all*e*,
That never was founde, as it telles,
Bord, ne man, ne nothing elles.
Right thus this king Seys loste his life.
Now for to speake of Alcyone his wife :—
This lady that was left at home,
Hath wonder that the king ne come
Home, for it was a longe terme.
Anone her herte began to yerne ; 80
And for that, her thought evermo
It was not wele ; her thoughte so.
She longede so after the king,
That certes it were a pitous thing
To tel her hertely sorowful life,
That she had*de*, this noble wife.
For him, alas ! she loved alderbeste,
Anone sche sente both este and weste

To seke him, but they founde him nought.
    'Alas,' quoth she, 'that I was wrought!
And where my lord, my love, be dede ?
Certes I *n*il never eate brede,
I make avowe to my God here,
But I mowe of my lord here.'
    Soche sorowe this lady to her toke,
That trew*el*y I, which made this boke,
Had*de* suche pittee and suche routhe
To rede hir sorwe, that by my trowthe
I ferde the worse al the morwe
And after, to thenken on hir sorwe.
    So whanne this lady koude here noo wo:
That no man myght*e* fynde hir lord,
Ful ofte she swouned, and sayde, 'Alas !'
For sorwe ful nygh woode she was ;
Ne she koude no rede but oon,
But doune on knees she sate anoon,
And wepte, that pittee was to here.
    'A ! mercy, swete lady dere !'
Quod she, to Juno hir goddesse,
'Helpe me out of thys distresse,
And yeve me grace my lord to se
Soone, or wete wher so he be,
Or how he fareth, or in what wise ;
And I shal make yowe sacrifise,
And hooly youres become I shal,
With gode wille, body, hert, and al.
And, but thow wilte this, lady swete,
Sende me grace to slepe and mete
In my slepe somme certeyn swoven,
Wher thorgh that I may knowe even
Whethir my lorde be quyke or ded.'

With that worde she henge doun the hed,
And felle a swowne, as colde as stoon.
Hyr women kaught hir up anoon,
And broughten hir in bed al naked;
And sche, for weped and for waked,
Was wery; and thus the dede slepe
Fil on hir, or she toke kepe,
Throgh Juno, that had herde hir bone,
That made hir to slepe sone.   130
For as she prayede, ryght so was done
Indede; for Juno ryght anone
Callede thus hir messagere
To doo hir crande, and he come nere.
Whan he was come, she bad hym thus :—
'Go bet,' quod Juno, to Morpheus;
'Thou knowest hym wel, the god of slepe;
Now understonde wel, and take kepe.
Sey thus on my halfe, that he
Go faste into the grete se,   140
And byd him that, on alle thynge,
That he take up Seys body, the kynge,
That lyeth ful pale, and nothynge rody.
Bid hym crepe into the body,
And doo hit goon to Alcyone
The quene, ther she lyeth allone;
And shewe hir shortly, hit ys no nay,
How hit was dreynt thys other day;
And do the body speke ryght soo,
Ryght as hyt was woned to doo,   150
The whiles that hit was alyve;—
Goo now faste, and hye the blyve.'
  This messager toke leve and wente
Upon hys wey, and never ne stente

Til he come to the derke valeye,
That stant betwexe roches tweye.
Ther never yet grew corne ne gras,
Ne tre, ne noght that oughte was,
Beste, ne man, ne noght elles,
Save that there were a fewe welles
Come rennynge fro the clyffes adoun,
That made a dedely slepynge soun;
And ronnen doun ryght by a cave,
That was under a rokke ygrave
Amydde the valey, wonder depe.
There these goddys lay and slepe,
Morpheus and Eclympasteyre,
That was the god of slepes eyre,
That slepe, and dide noon other werke.
  This cave was also as derke
As helle pitte, overal aboute,
They hadde good leyser for to route,
To envye who myghte slepe beste.
Some hengo her chyn upon hir breste,
And slept upryght hir hed yhedde;
And somme lay naked in her bedde,
And slepe whiles the dayes laste.
  This messager come fleynge faste,
And cried, 'O how! awake anoon!'
Hit was for noght, there herde hym noon.
'Awake!' quod he, 'Who ys lythe there?'
And blew his horne ryght in here cere,
And cried, 'Awaketh!' wonder hye.
  This god of slepe, with hys oon ye
Caste up, and axede, 'Who clepeth there?'
'Hyt am I,' quod this messagere.
'Juno bad thow shuldest goon.'

And tolde hym what he shulde doon,
As I have tolde yow here tofore,
Hyt ys no nede reherse hyt more ;   190
And went hys wey whan he had*de* sayede.
Anoon this god of slepe abrayede
Out of hys slepe, and gan to goon,
And dyd as he had*de* bede hym doon ;
Tooke up the dreynte body sone,
And bare hyt forth to Al*cy*one
Hys wife, the quene, ther as she lay,
Ryght even a quarter before day,
And stood ryght at hys beddys fete,
And called hir ryght as she hete   200
By name, and sayede :—' My swete wyfe,
Awake ! let be your sorwful lyfe !
For in your sorwe there lyth no rede ;
For certes, swete, I am but dede,
Ye shul me never on lyve yse.
But, goode swete her*te* *loke* that ye
Bury my body ; for, suche a tyde,
Ye mowe hyt fynde the see besyde.
And farewel swete, my worldes blysse !
I pray*e* God youre sorwe lysse ;   210
To lytel while oure blysse lasteth !'
     With that hir eyen up she casteth,
And sawe noght :—' Alas !' quod she, for sorwe,
And dey*e*de within the thridde morwe.
     But what she sayede more in that swowe,
I may not telle yow as now,
Hyt were to longe for to dwelle;
My first*e* matere I wil yow telle,
Wherfore I have tolde you this thynge,
Of Alcione, and Seys the kynge.   220

    For thus moche dar I saye welle,
I hadde be dolven every delle,
And ded, ryght thorgh defaulte of slepe,
Yif I ne hadde redde, and take kepe
Of this tale nexte before ;
And wol I telle yow wherfore,
For I ne myghte, for bote ne bale,
Slepe, or I hadde redde thys tale
Of this dreynte Seys the kynge,
And of the goddis of slepynge.
    Whan I hadde redde thys tale wel,
And overloked hit everydel,
Me thoghte wonder yf hit were so ;
For I hadde never herde speke, or tho,
Of noo goddis, that koude make
Men to slepe, ne for to wake ;
For I ne knewe never God but oon.
And in my game I sayede anoon,
(And yet me lyst ryght evel to pleye,)
Rather than that Y shulde deye
Thorgh defaulte of slepynge thus,
I wolde yive thilke Morphous,
Or hys goddesse, dame Juno,
Or somme wight ellis, I ne roghte who,
To make me slepe, and have some reste,—
I wil yive hym tho alder-beste
Yifte, that ever he abode hys lyve.
And here onwarde, ryght now as blyve.
Yif he wol make me slepe a lyte,
Of downe of pure dowves white,
I wil yif him a federbedde,
Rayed with golde, and ryght wel cledde,
In fyne blak satyn de owter mere,

And many a pelowe, and every bere
Of clothe of Reynes to slepe softe,
Him thar not nede to turnen ofte.
And I wol yive hym al that fallys
To a chaumbre; and al hys hallys,
I wol do peynte with pure golde,
And tapite hem ful manyfolde,   260
Of oo sute; this shal he have,
Yf I wiste where were hys cave,
Yf he kan make me slepe sone,
As did the goddesse, quene Alcyione.
And thus this ylke god Morpheus
May wynne of me moo fees thus
Than ever he wanne: and to Juno,
That ys hys goddesse, I shal soo do,
I trow that she shal holde hir payede.
    I hadde unnethe that worde ysayede,   270
Ryght thus as I have tolde hyt yow,
That sodeynly, I nyste how,
Suche a luste anoon me tooke
To slepe, that ryght upon my booke
I fil aslepe; and therwith evene
Me mette so ynly swete a swevene,
So wonderful, that never yitte
Y trow no man had*de* the wytte
To konne wel my sweven rede.
    No, not Joseph, withoute drede,   280
Of Egipte, he that red*de* so,
The kynges metynge, Pharao,
No more than koude the lest of us.
    Ne nat skarsly Macrobeus,
He that wrote al thavysyon
That he mette *of kynge* Scipion,

The noble man, the Affrikan,
Suche merveyles fortunede than,
I trowe arede my dremes even.
Loo, thus hyt was; thys was my sweven.   290
    Me thoghte thus, that hyt was May,
And in the dawnynge, *ther* I laye
Me mette thus in my bed al naked,
And lokede forth, for I was waked
With smale foules, a grete hepe,
That had afrayed me out of my slepe,
Thorgh noyse and swettenesse of her songe.
And as me mette, they sate amonge
Upon my chambre roofe wythoute,
Upon the tyles overal aboute;   300
And songe everych in hys wyse
The moste solempne servise
By noote, that ever man, Y trowe,
Had herde.   For somme of hem songe lowe,
Somme high, and al of oon acorde.
To telle shortly att oo word,
Was never herde so swete a steven,
But hyt hadde be a thynge of heven,
So mery a soune, so swete entownes,
That, certes, for the toune of Townes,   310
I nolde, but I had herde hem synge,
For al my chambre gan to rynge,
Thorgh syngynge of her armonye;
For instrument nor melodye
Was no-where herde yet halfe so swete,
Nor of acorde *ne* halfe so mete.
For ther was noon of hem that feynede
To synge, for echo of hem hym peynede
To fynde oute of mery crafty notys;

They ne sparede not her throtys.   320
And, soothe to seyn, my chambre was
Ful wel depeynted, and with glas
Were alle the wyndowes wel yglasyd
Ful clere, and nat an hoole ycrasyd,
That to beholde hyt was grete joye.
For holy al the story of Troye
Was in the glasynge ywrought thus ;
Of Ector, and of kynge Priamus,
Of Achilles, and of kynge Lamedon,
And eke of Medea and of Jason,   330
Of Paris, Eleyne, and of Lavyne ;
And alle the wallys, with colouris fyne
Were peynted, bothe text and glose,
And al the Romaunce of the Rose.
My windowes were shette echon,
And throgh the glas the sonne shon
Upon my bed with bryghte bemys,
With many glade, gilde stremys ;
And eke the welken was so faire,
Blewe, bryghte, clere was the ayre,   340
And ful atempre, for sothe, hyt was ;
For nother to colde nor hoote yt nas,
Ne in al the walkene was a clowde.
  And as I lay thus, wonder lowde
Me thoght I herde an hunte blowe,
Tassay hys horne, and for to knowe
Whether hyt were clere, or horse of soune.
  And I herde goynge, bothe uppe and doune,
Men, hors, houndes, and other thynge,
And alle men speke of huntynge,   350
How they wolde slee the hert with strengthe,
And how the hert had upon lengthe

So much embosed, Y not now what.
    Anoon ryght whan I herde that,
How that they wolde on huntynge goon,
I was ryght glad; and up anoon
Tooke *I* my hors, and forthe I wente
Out of my chambre; I never stente,
Til I come to the felde withoute;
Ther overtoke Y a grete route   360
Of huntes and eke of foresterys,
And many relayes and lymerys;
And hyed hem to the forest faste,
And *I* with hem. So at the laste
I axed oon ladde a lymere,
'Say, felowe! whoo shal hunte here?'
Quod I; and he answered ageyn,
'Sir, themperour Octovyen,'
Quod he, 'and ys here faste by.'
'A goddys halfe, in goode tyme!' quod I;   370
'Go we faste!' And gan to ryde.
Whan we come to the forest syde,
Every man didde ryght anoon,
As to huntyng fille to doon.
    The mayster hunte, anoon, fote hote,
With a grete horne blewe thre mote,
At the uncouplynge of hys houndys.
Withynne a while the herte founde ys,
I-hallowed, and rechased faste
Longe tyme; and so at the laste   380
This hart rused, and staale away
Fro alle the houndes a prevy way
The houndes hadde overshotte hym alle,
And were upon a defaulte yfalle.
Therwyth the hunte, wonder faste,

Blewe a forleygne at the laste.
　I was go walked fro my tree,
And as I wente, there came by mee
A whelpe, that faunede me as I stoode,
That hadde yfolowed, and koude no goode.　　00
Hyt come and crepte to me as lowe,
Ryght as hyt hadde me yknowe ;
Hylde doun hys hede, and joyned hys erys,
And leyde al smoothe doun hys herys.
I wolde have kaught hyt ; and anoon
Hyt fledde, and was fro me agoon.
And I hym folwed, and hyt forthe wente
Doun by a flowry grene wente
Ful thikke of gras, ful softe and swete,
With flourys fele, faire under fete,　　400
And litel used, hyt semede thus ;
For both Flora, and Zephirus,
They two, that make floures growe,
Hadde made her dwellynge ther I trowe.
For hit was on to beholde,
As thogh therthe envye wolde
To be gayer than the heven ;
To have moo floures swiche seven,
As in the walkene sterris be.
Hyt hadde forgete the povertee　　410
That wynter, thorgh hys colde morwes
Hadde made hyt suffre ; and his sorwes
Alle was forgeten, and that was sene ;
For al the woode was waxen grene ;
Swetnesse of dewe hadde made hyt waxe.
　Hyt ys no nede eke for to axe
Where ther were many grene greves,
Or thikke of trees, so ful of leves ;

And every tree stoode by hymselve
Fro other, wel ten fete other twelve.   420
So grete trees, so huge of strengthe,
Of fourty, fifty fedme lengthe,
Clene, withoute bowgh or stikke,
With croppes brode, and eke as thikke,
They were not an ynche asonder,
That hit was shadewe overal under.
And many an herte and many an hynde
Was both before me and behynde.
Of faunes, sowres, bukkes, does,
Was ful the woode, and many roes,   430
And many sqwireles, that sete
Ful high upon the trees and ete,
And in hir maner made festys.
Shortly, hyt was so ful of bestys,
That thogh Argus, the noble counter   .
Sete to rekene in hys counter,
And rekene with his figuris tonne,
For by tho figures mowe alle kenne,
Yf they be crafty, rekene and noumbre,
And tel of every thinge the noumbre,   440
Yet shulde he faylo to rekene evene
Tho wondres me mette in my sweveno.
But forthe they romede ryght wonder faste
Doune the woode ; so at the laste
I was war of a man in blak,
That sete, and hadde turned his bak
To an ooke, an huge tree.
‘ Lorde !’ thoght I, ‘ who may that bo ?
What ayleth hym to sitten here ?’
Anoone ryght tho I wente nero.   450
Than founde I sitte, oven upryght,

A wonder welfarynge knyght,
(By the maner me thoghte soo)
Of good mochel, and ryght yonge therto,
Of the age of foure and twenty yere,
Upon hys berde but lytel here,
And he was clothed al in blake.
I stalked even unto hys bake,
And there I stoode as stille as ought.
The soth to saye, he sawe me nought ;   460
For-why he henge hys hede adoun,
And with a dedely sorwful soun,
He made of ryme tenne vers or twelfe,
Of a compleynt *unto* hymselfe,
The moste pitee, the moste rowthe
That ever I herde ; for by my trowthe
Hit was gret wonder that Nature
Myght*e* suffre any creature
To have suche sorwe, and be not ded.
Ful petuose pale, and nothynge red,   470
He sayed a lay, a maner songe,
Withoute noote, withoute songe ;
And was thys, for ful wel I kan
Reherse hyt ; ryght thus hyt began :—
    ' I have of sorwe so grete wone,
That joy*e* get I never none,
    Now that I see my lady bryght*e*,
    Which I have loved with al my myght*e*,
Is fro me dede, and ys agoon.
Allas ! Dethe, what ayleth thee,   480
That thou noldest have taken me
    Whan that thou toke my lady swete ?
That was so faire, so fresh, so fre,
So goode, that men may wel se,

Of al goodenesse *s*che had*de* no mete.'
   Whan he had*de* made thus his compleynt*e*,
His sorwful hert*e* gan faste faynt*e*,
And his spiritis wexen dede;
The bloode was fled for pure drede
Doun to hys hert*e*, to make hym warme,   45
For wel hyt felede tho hert had harme;
To wete eke why hyt was adrad
By kynde, and for to make hyt glad;
For hit ys membre principal
Of the body; and that made al
Hys hewe chaunge, and wexe grene
And pale, for ther noo bloode ys sene
In no maner *l*ym of hys.
   Anoon therwith, whan I sawgh this,
He ferde thus evel there he sete,   50
I went and stoode ryght at his fete,
And grette hym; but he spake noght,
But argued*e* with his ounne thoght,
And in hys wytte disputed*e* faste,
Why, and how hys lyfe myghte laste;
Hym thought hys sorwes were so smerte,
And lay so colde upon hys herte.
   So throgh hys sorwes and hevy thoght,
Made hym that he herde me noght,
For he had*de* welnygh loste hys mynde,   55
Thogh Pan, that men clepe the god of kynde,
Were for hys sorwes never so wrothe.
But at the last, to sayne ryght sothe,
He was war of me, how Y stoode
Before hym, and did of myn hoode,
And had ygret hym, as I best koude.
Debonayrly, and nothyng lowde,

He sayde, ' I prey the be·not wrothe,
I herde the not, to seyn the sothe,
No I sawgh the not, syr, trewely.'   520
' A goode sir, no fors !' quod Y ;
' I am ryght sory, yif I have oughte
Distroubled yow out of your thoughte ;
Foryive me, yif I have mystake.'
    ' Yis, thamendys is lyght to make,'
Quod he, ' for ther lyeth noon therto ;
Ther ys nothynge mis-saydo, nor do.'
    Loo ! how goodely spake thys knyghte,
As hit hadde be another wyghte ;
And made hyt nouther towgh ne queynte.   530
And I sawe that, and gan me aqueynte
With hym, and fonde hym so tretable,
Ryght wonder skylful and resonable,
As me thoghte, for al hys bale ;
Anoon ryght I gan fynde a tale
To hym, to loke wher I myght oughte
Have more knowynge of hys thoughte.
    ' Sir quod I, ' this game is doon ;
I holde that this hert be goon ;
These huntys konne hym no wher see.'   540
    ' Y do no fors therof,' quod he ;
' My thoughte ys there on never a dele.'
' Be oure lorde !' quod I, ' Y trow yow wele ;
Ryght so me thenketh by youre chere.
But, sir, oo thyng wol ye here ?—
Me thynketh in grete sorowe I yow see ;
But certys, sir, yif that yee
Wolde ought discovre me youre woo,
I wolde, as wys God helpe me soo !
Amende hyt, yif I kan or may.   550

Ye mowe preve hyt be assay;
For, by my trouthe, to make yow hool
I wol do alle my power hool.
And telleth me of your sorwes smerte,
Paraventure hyt may ese your herte,
That semeth ful seke under your syde.'
With that he loked on me asyde,
As who sayth, ' Nay, that wol not be.'
' Graunt mercy! goode frende,' quod he,
' I thanke the, that thow woldest soo;   560
But hyt may never the rather be doo.
No man ne may my sorwe glade,
That maketh my hewe to fal and fade;
And hath myn understondynge lorne,
That me ys woo that I was borne.
May noght make my sorwes slyde,
Nought *alle* the remedyes of Ovyde,
Ne Orpheus, god of melodye;
No Dedalus, with his playes slye;
No hele me may noo phisicien,   570
Noght Ypocras, ne Galyen;
Me ys woo that I lyve houres twelve.
But whoo so wol assaye hymselve,
Whether his herte kan have pitee
Of any sorwe, lat him see me.
Y wrechche, that deth hath made al naked
Of al tho blysse that ever was maked,
Yworthe, worste of *alle* wyghtys,
That hate my dayes and my nyghtys;
My lyfe, my lustes, be me loothe   580
For al wel-fare, and I be wroothe.
The pure deth ys so ful my foo,
That I wolde deye, hyt wolde not soo;

For whan I folwe hyt, hit wol flee ;
I wolde have hym, hyt nyl nat me.
This ys my peyne wythoute rede,
Alway deyinge, and be not dede.
That Thesiphus that lyeth in helle,
May not of more sorwe telle.
And who so wiste alle, be my trouthe,   590
My sorwe, but he had*de* rowthe
And pitee of my sorwes smerte,
That man hath a fendely herte.
For whoso seeth me firste on morwe,
May seyn he hath mette with sorwe ;
For Y am sorwe, and sorwe ys Y ;
Allas ! and I wol tel*le* thee why ;
My *joye* is tourned to pleynynge,
And al my lawghtre to wepynge ;
My glade thoghtys to hevynesse,   600
In travayle ys myn ydelnesse,
And eke my reste ; my wele is woo,
My goode ys harme, and evermoo
In wrathe ys turned my pleyinge,
And my delyte into sorwynge ;
Myn hele ys turned into sekenesse,
In drede ys al my sykernesse ;
To derke ys turned al my lyghte,
My wytte ys foly, my daye ys nyghte.
My love ys hate, my slepe wakynge,   610
My merthe and meles ys fastynge ;
My countenaunce ys nyceté,
And al abawed, where so I be ;
My pees is pledynge, and in werre.
Allas, how myght I fare werre ?
My boldenesse ys turned to schame,

For fals Fortune hath pleyde a game
Atte the chesse with me, allas the while !
The trayteresse fals and ful of gyle,
That al behoteth, and nothyng halte,
She gothe upryght, and yet she halte,
That baggeth foule, and loketh faire,
The dispitouse debonaire,
That skorneth many a creature.
An ydole of fals portrayture
Ys she, for she wol soone varien.
She is the mownstres hede ywrien,
As fylthe, over ystrawed with flourys.
Hir moste worschippe and hir flourys
To lyen, for that ys hyr nature.
Withoute feythe, lawe, or mesure,
She ys fals ; and ever lawghynge
With one yghe, and that other wepynge.
That ys broght up, she sette al doun ;
I lykne hyr to the scorpioun,
That ys a fals flatterynge beste ;
For with his hede he maketh feste,
But al amydde hys flaterynge,
With hys tayle hyt wol stynge,
And envenyme, and so wol she.
She ys thenvyouse Charité,
That ys ay fals, and semeth wele
So turneth she hyr false whele
Aboute, for hyt ys nothynge stable,
Now by the fire, now at table.
For many oon hath she thus yblent,
She is pley of enchauntement,
That semeth oon, and ys not soo.
The false thefe ! what hath she doo,

Trowest thou? by oure Lorde, I wol the sey*e* :—
At the chesse with me she gan to pley*e* ;   651
With hir fals*e* draughtes dyvers
She staale on me, and toke my fers ;
And whan I sawgh my fers away*e*,
Allas ! I kouthe no lenger play*e* ;
But seyde, farewel, swete ! ywys,
And farewel, al that ever ther ys !
Therwith Fortune seyde, ' chek here !'
And ' mate' in the myd poynt of the chekkere,
With a poune errante, allas !   660
Ful craftier to pley*e* she was
Than Athalus, that made the game
First of the chesse, so was hys name.
But God wolde I had oones or twyes,
Ykoude, and knowe the jeupardyes,
That kowde the Greke Pythagoras,
I shulde han pleyde tho bet at ches,
And kept my fers the bet therby.
And thogh wherto ? for trowel*y*
I holde that wysshe not worthe a stree :   670
Hyt had*de* be never the bet for me.
For Fortune kan so many a wyle,
Ther be but fewe kan hir begile,
And eke she ys tho lasse to blame.
My selfe, I wolde have do the sam ,
Before God, *had* I be as she ;
She oght*e* the more excused be.
For this I say yet more therto,—
Had I be God, and myghte have do
My wille, whan she my fers kaught*e*,   680
I wolde have drawe the same draught*e* :
For, also wys God yive me reste !

I dar wel swere, she tooke the beste.
But throgh that draught I have lorne
My blysse; allas, that I was borne!
For evermore Y trowe, trewely,
For al my wille, my luste holly
Ys turned; but yet what to doone?
Be oure Lorde, hyt ys to deye soone;
For nothynge I leve hyt noght,
But lyve and deye ryght in this thoght.
For there nys planete in firmament,
Ne in ayre ne in erthe noon element,
That they ne yive me a yifte, echoon,
Of wepynge, whanne I am alloon.
For whan that I avise me wel,
And bethenke me everydel,
How that ther lyeth in rekenynge
Inne my sorwe for nothynge;
And how ther levyth noo gladnesse
May glade me of my distresse;
And how I have loste suffisaunce
And therto I have no plesaunce:
Than may I saye, I have ryght noght.
And whan al this falleth in my thoght,
Allas! than am I overcome,
For that ys doon is not to come.
I have more sorowe than Tantale.'

    And whan I herde hym telle thys tale
Thus pitously, as I yow telle,
Unnethe myght I lenger dwelle:
Hyt dyde myn herte so moche woo.

    ' A, goode sir!' quod I, ' say not soo!
Have some pitee on your nature,
That formede yow to creature.

Remembre*th* yow of Socrates;
For he ne countede nat thre strees
Of noght that Fortune koude doo.
' No,' quod he, ' I kan not soo.'
' Why so, good syr ? yis parde !' quod Y ;   720
' Ne *seye* noght soo ; for trewely,
Thogh ye had*de* loste the ferses twelve,
And ye for sorwe mordred your selve,
Ye sholde be dampned in this cas,
By as goode ryght as Medea was,
That slogh hir children for Jason ;
And Phillis also for Demophon
Henge hir selfe, so weylawa*ye* !
For he had*de* broke his terme deye
To come to hir.   Another rage   730
Had*de* Dydo, the quene eke of Cartage,
That slough hir selfe, for Eneas
Was fals ; which a foole she was !
And Ecquo died, for Narcissus
Noldo nat love hir ; and ryght thus
Hath many another foly doon.
And for Dalida diede Sampson,
That slough hymselfe with a piler.
But ther is no man alyve here
Woldo for o fers make this woo.'   740
    ' Why so ? quod he ; ' hyt ys not soo ;
Thou woste ful lytel what thou menyst,
I have loste more than thow wenyst.'
Loo ! sir, *how* may that be ?' quod I.
' Goode sir, telle me al hooly,
In what wyse, how, why and wherfore,
That ye have thus youre blysse lore ?'
' Blythely !' quod he ; ' come, sytte adoun !

I telle hyt the up a condicioun,
That thou shalt hooly with al thy wytte
Do thyn entente to herkene hitte.'
' Yis, syr'—' Swere thy trouthe therto—
' Glady—Do thanne holde hereto.'
' I shal ryght blythely, so God me save,
Hooly with al the witte I have,
Here yow as wel as I kan.
' A goddys halfe ! quod he, and began :—
 ' Syr,' quod he, ' sith ferste I kouthe
Have any maner wytte fro youthe,
Or kyndely understondynge,
To comprehende in any thynge
What love was, in myn oune wytte,
Dredeles, I have ever yitte
Be tributarye, and yive rente
To Love hooly, with goode entente,
And throgh plesaunce become his thralle,
With goode wille, body, hert, and alle.
Al this I putte in his servage,
As to my lorde, and did homage ;
And ful devoutely I prayed hym tho,
He shulde besette myn herte so,
That hyt plesaunce to hym were,
And worshippe to my lady dere.
 ' And this was longe, and many a yere
(Or that myn herte was set owhere)
That I dide thus, and nyste why ;
I trowe hit come me kyndely.
Peraventur I was therto moste able,
As a white walle, or a table ;
For hit ys rody to cachche, and take
Al that men wille theryn make.

Whethir so men wil*le* portrey or peynt*e*,
Be the werkes never so queynt*e*.
  ' And thilke tyme I ferde ryght so,
I was able to have lerned tho,
And to have kende as wel, or better
Paraunter, other arte or letre;
But for love came firste in my thoght.
Therfore I forgate hyt noght.
I ches love to my first*e* crafte,   790
Therfore hit ys with me *y*lafte;
For-why I toke hyt of so yonge age,
That malyce had*de* my corage
Nat that tyme turned to nothynge,
Thorgh to mochel knowlachynge.
For that tyme Yowthe, my maistresse,
Governede me in ydelnesse;
For hyt was in my first*e* youthe,
And thoo ful lytel goode Y couthe,
For alle my werkes were flyttynge,   800
That tyme, and al my thoght varyinge.
Al were to me ylyche goode
That I knewe thoo, but thus hit stode.
  ' Hit happede that I came on a day
Into a place, ther that I say
Trew*e*ly the fayrest companye
Off ladyes, that evere man with ye
Had*de* sene togedres in oo place.
Shal I clepe hyt happe, other grace,
That broght*e* me there ? nay, but Fortune,   810
That ys to lyen ful comune;
The false trayteresse pervers !
God wolde I koude clepe hir wers;
For now she worcheth me ful woo,

And I wol tel*le* sone why soo.
    ' Amonge these ladyes thus echoon,
Sothe to seyn, I sawgh oon
That was lyke noon of the route ;
For I dar swere, withoute doute,
That as the somerys sonne bryghte
Ys fairer, clerer, and hath more lyghte
Than any other planete in hevene,
The moone, or the sterres sevene ;
For al the worlde, so had*de* she
Surmountede hem al of beauté,
Of maner, and of comelynesse,
Of stature, and of so wel sette gladnesse ;
Of godelyhede, and so wel besey*e* ;
Shortly what shal Y sey*e* ?
By God, and by *his* halwes twelve,
Hyt was my swete, ryght al hir selve.
She had*de* so stedfaste countenaunce,
So noble porte, and meyntenaunce.
And Love, that had*de* wel herd my boone,
Had espyed me thus soone, .
That she ful sone, in my thoght,
As helpe me God, so was Y kaught
So sodenly, that I no toke
No maner counseyl, but at hir loke,
And at myn her*te* ; for-why hir eyen
So gladly, I trow, myn herte seyen,
That purely tho myn oune thoght
Seyde, hit were beter serve hir for noght,
Than with another to be wel.
And hyt was sothe, for every del,
I wil anoon ryght telle the why.
    ' I sawgh hir daunce so comolely,

Carole and synge so swetely,
Lawghe, and pleye so womanly,
And loke so debonairly ;   850
So goodely speke and so frendly ;
That certes Y trowe that evermore,
Nas seyne so blysful a tresore.
For every heer upon hir hede,
Soth to seyne, hyt was not rede,
Ne nouther yelowe, ne broune hyt nas ;
Me thoghte most lyke *gold* hyt was.
And which eyen my lady hadde !
Debonaire, goode, glade, and sadde,
Symple, of goode mochel, noght to wyde.   860
Therto hir looke nas not asyde,
Ne overtwert, but besette so wele,
Hyt drew and tooke up everydele
Al*le* that on hir gan*ne* beholde.
Hir eyen semed anoon she wolde
Have mercy, (foolys wenden soo)
But hyt was never the rather doo ;
Hyt nas no counterfeted thynge,
Hyt was hir oune pure lokynge,
That the goddesse, dame Nature,   870
Had*de* made hem opene by mesure,
And cloos ; for were she never so glad,
Hyr lokynge was not foly sprad,
Ne wildely, thogh that she pleyde ;
But ever, me thoght, hir eyen seyde,
‘ Be God, my wrathe ys al foryive !’
Therwith hir lyste so wel to lyve,
That dulnesse was of hir adrad.
She nas to sobre, ne to glad ;
In alle thynges more mesure,   880

Hadde never, I trowe, creature.
But many oon with hir loke she herte,
And that sate hyr ful lytel at herte ;
For she knewe nothynge of her thoght.
But whether she knew, or knew it noght,
Algate she ne rought of hem a stree.
To gete hyr love noo nerre was he
That woned at home, than he in Ynde ;
The formest was alway behynde.
But goode folke over al other,
She loved as man may do hys brother ;
Of whiche love she was wounder large,
In skilful placis that bere charge.
But which a visage hadde she thertoo !
Allas ! myn hert ys wonder woo,
That I ne kan discryven hyt.
Me lakketh both Englyssh and wit,
For to undo hyt, at the fulle ;
And eke my spiritis be to dulle,
So grete a thynge for to devyse ;
I have no witte that kan suffise
To comprehende hir beauté ;
But thus moche dar I sayn, that she
Was white, rody, fressh and lyvely hewed,
And every day hir beauté newed,
And negh hir face was alderbest ;
For, certys, Nature hadde swich lest,
To make that faire, that trewely she
Was hir chefe patrone of beauté,
And chefe ensample of al hir werke,
And mounstre ; for be hyt never so derke,
Me thynkyth I se hir ever moo.
And yet, more over, thogh alle thoo

That ever levede were now alyve,
Ne sholde han founde to diskryve
In al hir face a wikked sygne,
For hit was sad, symple, and benygne.
  ' And which a goodely, softe speche,
Had*de* that swete, my lyves leche !
So frendely, and so wel ygrounded,   920
Up al resoun so wel yfounded,
And so tretable to a*lle* goode,
That I dar swere wel by the roode,
Of eloquence was never founde
So swete a sownynge facounde ;
Ne trewer tonged, ne skorned lasse,
Ne bet koude hele, that by the masse,
I durste swere, thogh the pope hit songe,
That ther was never yet throgh hir tonge,
Man ne woman gretely harmed ;   930
As for hit was al harme hyd.
Ne lasse flaterynge in hir word*e*,
That purely, hir symple recorde,
Was founde as trewe as any bonde,
Or trouthe of any mannys honde.
Ne chyde she koude never a dele,
That knoweth al the worlde ful wele.
  ' But swiche a fairenesse of a nekke
Had*de* that swete, that boon nor brekke
Nas ther noon seen that mys-satte ;   940
Hyt was white, smothe, streght, and pure flatte,
Withouten hole or canel boon ;
As be semynge, had*de* she noon.
  ' Hyr throte, as I have now memoyre,
Semed a rounde toure of yvoyre,
Of goode gretenesse, and noght to grete,

And goode faire White she hete,
That was my lady name ryghte.
She was bothe faire and bryghte,
She hadde not hir name wronge. 950
Ryght faire shuldres, and body longe
She had ; and armes every lyth,
Fattyssh, flesshy, nat grete therwith ;
Ryght white handes, and nayles rede,
Rounde brestes ; and of good brede
Hyr hippes were ; a streight flat bakke ;
I knewe on hir noon other lakke,
That al hir lymmes nere pure sywynge,
In as ferre as I hadde knowynge.
Therto she koude so wel pleye 960
Whan that hir lyst, that I dar seye,
That she was lyke to torche bryght,
That every man may take of lyght
Ynogh, and hyt hathe never the lesse.
Of manor and of comlynesse,
Ryght so ferde my lady dere.
For every wight of hir manere
Myghte cachche ynogh, yif that he wolde,
Yif he had eyen hir to beholde.
For I dar swere wel, yif that she 970
Had amonge ten thousande be,
She wolde have be, at the lest,
A chefe meroure of al the fest,
Thogh they hadde stonde in a rowe,
To mennys eyen, that koude have knowe.
For wher so men hadde pleyed or wakyd,
Me thoghte the felysshyppe as naked
Withouten hir, that sawgh I oones,
As a corowne withoute stones.

Trewely she was to myn eye,   980
The soleyne fenix of Arabye;
For ther lyveth nevir but oon,
Ne swich as she, ne knowe I noon.
  To speke of godenesse, trewely she
Had as moche debonairyeté,
As ever had Hester in the Bible,
And more, yif more were possyble.
And sothe to seyn, therwythalle
She had a wytte so generalle,
So hoole enclyned to alle goode,   990
That al hir wytte was set by the rode,
Withoute malyce, upon gladnesse.
And therto I sawgh never yet a lesse
Harmeful than she was in doynge,
I sey not that she ne had*de* knowynge
What harme was, or elles she
Had*de* koude no good, so thenketh me.
And trewely, for to speke of trouthe,
But she had hadde, hyt hadde be routhe.
Therof she had*de* so moche hyr dele,   1000
And I dar seyn, and swere hyt wele,
That Trouthe hymselfe, over al and alle,
Had*de* chose hys maner principalle
In hir, that was his restynge place.
Therto she hadde the moste grace,
To have stedefaste perseveraunce,
And esy attempry governaunce,
That ever I knewe, or wyste yitte,
So pure suffraunt was hir wytte.
And resoun gladly she understoode,   1010
Hyt folowed wel, she koude goode.
She use*de* gladly to do wel;

These were hir maneres every del.
  'Therwith she lovede so wel ryght,
She wronge do wolde to no wyght;
No wyght myghte doo hir noo shame,
She lovede so wel hir oune name.
  'Hyr lust to holde no wyght in honde,
Ne, be thou siker, she wolde not fonde,
To holde no wyght in balaunce,   1020
By halfe word, ne by countenaunce,
But yif men wolde upon hir lye.
Ne sende men into Walakye,
To Pruyse, and to Tartarye,
To Alysaundre, ne into Turkye,
And byd him faste anoon that he
Goo hoodeles into the drye se,
And come home by the Carrenare ;
And soye ' Sir, be now ryght ware,
That I may of yow here seyn,   1030
Worshyppe, or that ye come ageyn.
  'She no usede no suche knakkes smale,
But wherfor that Y telle my tale ;—
    Ryght on thys same, as I have seyde,
Was hooly al my love i-leyde ;
For, certes, she was that swete wife,
My suffisaunce, my luste, my lyfe,
Myn happe, myn hele, and al my blysse,
My worldys welfare, and my goddesse,
And I hooly hires, and every del.'   1040
  'By oure Lorde !' quod I, ' I trowe you wel !
Hardely, your love was wel besette ;
I not how ye myght have doo bette.'
  'Bette ? no no wyght so wele,' quod he.
' Y trowe hyt wel, sir,' quod I, ' pardé !'

' Nay, leve hyt wel :'—' Sire, so do I ;
I leve yow wel, that trewely
Yow thoughte that she was the beste,
And to beholde, the alderfayreste,
Who soo hadde loked hir with your eyen.'   1050
' With myn ? nay, alle that hir seyen,
Seyde and swore hyt was soo.
And thogh they ne hadde, I wolde thoo
Have loved best my lady free,
Thogh I had hadde al the beauté
That ever had Alcibyades ;
And al the strengtho of Ercules ;
And therto hadde the worthynesse
Of Alysaunder ; and al the rychesse
That ever was in Babyloyne,   1060
In Cartage, or in Macedoyne,
Or in Rome, or in Nynyvé ;
And *ther*to also as hardy be,
As was Ector, so have I joye,
That Achilles slough at Troye ;
(And therfore was he slayn alsoo
In a temple ; for bothe twoo
Were slayne, he and Antylegyus ;
And so seyth Dares Frygius,
For love of Polixena)   1070
Or ben as wise as Mynerva ;
I wolde ever, withoute drede
Have loved hir, for I moste nede.
' Nede ? Nay trewely I gabbe nowe !
Noght nede ; and I wol telle howe.
For of goode wille myn hert hyt wolde,
And eke to love hir I was holde,
As for the fairest and the beste.

She was as good, so have I reste,
As ever was Penolopee of Grece,   1080
 Or as the noble wife Lucrece,
That was the best, (he telleth thus
The Romayne Tytus Lyvyus,)
She was as good, and nothynge lyke,
Thogh hir stories be autentyke ;
Algate she was as trewe as she.
 ' But wherfore that I telle the,
Whan I firste my lady say ?
I was ryght yonge, sothe to say,
And ful grete nede I hadde to lerne,   1090
Whan myn herte wolde yerne.
To love hyt was a grete empryse,
But as my wytte koude beste suffise,
 After my yonge childely wytte,
Withoute drede, I besette hytte,
To love hir in my beste wyse,
To do hir worshippe, and the servise
That I koude thoo, be my trouthe
Withoute feynynge, outher slouthe.
For wonder feyne I wolde hir so.   1100
So mochel hyt amended me,
That whan I sawgh hir first amorwe,
I was warished of al my sorwe
Of al day after ; til hyt were eve
Me thoghte nothyng myghte me greve,
Were my sorwes never so smerte.
And yet she sytte so *in* myn herte,
That, by my trouthe, Y nolde noght
For al thys worlde, oute of my thoght
Love my lady ; noo, trewely !'   1110
 ' Now by my trouthe, sir,' quod I,

' Me thynketh ye have suche a chaunce
As shryfte, withoute repentaunce.'
    ' Repentaunce? nay, fy !' quod he,
' Shulde Y now repente me
To love? nay, certis, than were I wel
Wers than was Achetofel,
Or Anthenor, so have I joye !
The traytour that betraysede Troye :
Or the false Genelloun,   1120
He that purchasede the tresoun
Of Rowlande, and of Olyvere.
Nay, while I am alyve here,
I nyl foryete hir never moo.'
' Now, goode syr,' quod I thoo,
' Ye han wel tolde me here before,
Hyt ys no nede to reherse more,
How ye sawgh hir firste, and where ;
But wolde ye telle me the manere,
To hire which was your firste speche,   1130
Therof I wolde yow beseche ;
And how she knewe first your thoght,
Whether ye loved hir or noght ;
And telleth me eke what ye have lore,
    I herde yow telle here before.
Yee, he seyde, ' thow nost what thou menyst,
I have lost more than thou wenyst.'
' What losse ys that ?' quod I thoo,
' Nyl she not love yow ? ys hyt soo ?
Or have ye oght doon amys,   1140
That she hathe lefte yow ? ys hyt this ?
For Goddys love, tello me alle.'
' Before God,' quod he, ' and I shalle.
I say ryght as I have seyde,

On hir was al my love leyde,
And yet she nyste hyt nat never a del,
Noght longe tyme, leve hyt wel ;
For ryght be siker, I durste noght,
For al this worlde, tel hir my thoght ;
Ne I wolde have wraththed hir trewely.   1150
For wostow why ? she was lady
Of the body ; she had*de* the her*te*,
And who hath that may not asterte.

    ‘ But for to kepe me so fro ydelnesse,
Trewely I dide my besynesse
To make songes, as I best koude.
And ofte tyme I songe hem loude,
And made songes, this a grete dele,
Althogh I koude not make so wele
Songes, ne knowe the arte al,   1160
As koude Lamekys sone, Tuballe,
That founde out firste the art of songe.
For as hys brothres hammers ronge,
Upon hys anvelot, up and downe,
Therof he tooke the firste sowne.
But Grekes seyn of Pitagoras,
That he the firste fynder was
Of the arte ; Aurora telleth soo ;
But therof no fors of hem twoo.
Algatis songes thus I made,   1170
Of my felynge, myn herte to glade :
And, loo ! thys was alther firste,
I not wher hyt were tho werste.

    ‘ Lorde ! hyt maketh myn herte lyght,
Whan I thenke on that swete wyght,
That is so semely on to se,
And wisshe to God hit myghte so be

That she wolde holde me for hir knyght,
My lady that is so fayre and bryght.
   'Now have I tolde the, sothe to say,   1180
My first*e* songe.   Upon a day,
I bethoghte me what woo
And sorwe that I suffrede thoo
For hir, and yet she wyst hyt noght,
Ne tel hir, durst I nat, my thoght.
Allas! thoght I, Y kan no rede!
And but I telle hir, I am but dede;
And yif I telle hyr, to seye ryght sothe,
I am adred she wol be wrothe,
Allas! what shal I thanne doo?   1190
   In this debate I was so woo,
Me thoght*e* myn herte brast atweyne.
So, at the last, sothe to sayne,
I bethoghte me that Nature,
Ne form*e*de never in creature,
So moche beauté trew*e*ly
And bounté, wythoute mercy.
   'In hope of that, my tale I tolde,
With sorwe, as that I never sholde,
For nedys; and mawgree my*n* hede   1200
I most have tolde hir, or be dede:
I not wel how that I beganne,
Ful evel reherse hyt I kan;
And eke, as helpe me God withalle,
I trowe hyt was in the dismalle,
That was the woundes of Egipte;
For many a worde I overskipte
In my tale for pure fere,
Lest my wordys mys-sette were.
With sorweful herte, and woundes dede,   1210

Softe, and quakynge for pure drede
And shame, and styntynge in my tale
For ferde, and myn hewe al pale,
Ful ofte I wexe bothe pale and rede ;
Bowynge to hir I heng the hede,
I durste nat ones loke hir on,
For witte, maner and al was goon.
I seyde : ' Mercy,' and no more ;
Hyt nas no game, hyt sate me sore.
  ' So at the laste, sothe to seyne,
Whan that myn herte was come ageyne,
To telle shortely al my speche,
With hool herte I gan hir beseche
That she wolde be my lady swete ;
And swore, and gan hir hertely hete
Ever to be stedfast and trewe,
And love hir alwey fresshly newe,
And never other lady have,
And al hir worshippe for to save,
As I best koude ; I swore hir this,
For youres is alle that ever ther ys,
For evermore, myn herte swete !
And never to false yow, but I mete,
I nyl, as wysse God helpe me soo !
  ' And whan I hadde my tale ydoo,
God wote she acountede nat a stree
Of al my tale, so thoghte me.
To telle shortly ryght as hyt ys
Trewely hire answere hyt was this ;
I kan not now wel counterfete
Hyr wordys, but this was the grete
Of hir answere ; she sayde, ' Nay ! '
Al outerly : allas ! that day,

The sorwe I suffred and the woo,
That trewely Cassandra, that soo
Bewaylede the destruccioun
Of Troye, and of Ilyoun,
Hadde never swich sorwe as I thoo.
I durste no more say thertoo,
For pure fere, but stale away.   1250
And thus I lyvede ful many a deye,
That trewely I hadde no nede,
Ferther than my beddes hede,
Never a day to seche sorwe;
I fonde hyt redy every morwe,
For-why I loved hyr in no gere.
  'So hit befel another yere,
I thoughte ones I wolde fonde,
To do hir knowe, and understonde
My woo; and she wele understode,   1260
That I ne wilnede thynge but gode
And worshippe, and to kepe hir name,
Over alle thynges, and dred hir shame,
And was so besy hir to serve,
And pitee were I shulde sterve,
Syth that I wilnede noon harme, ywys.
  'So whan my lady knewe al thys,
My lady yaf me, al hooly,
The noble yifte of hir mercy,
Savynge her worshippe by alle weyes;   1270
Dredles, I mene noon other weyes.
And therwith she yaf me a rynge;
I trowe hyt was the firste thynge.
 But yif myn herte was iwaxe
Gladde, that is no nede to axe.
As helpe me God, I was as blyve

Reysed, as fro dethe to lyve,
Of al*le* happes the alderbeste,
The gladdest and the moste at reste.
For trewely that swete wyght,   1280
Whan I had*de* wrong, and she the ryght.
She wolde alway so goodely
Foryeve me so debonairely,
In al my yowthe, in al*le* chaunce,
She tooke me in hir governaunce.
Therwyth she was alway so trewe,
Our joye was ever ylyche newe;
Our hertys werne so evene a payre,
That never nas that oon contrayre
To that other, for noo woo: 1290
For sothe ylyche they suffrede thoo
Oo blisse and eke oo sorwe bothe;
Ylyche they were bothe glade and wrothe,
Al was us oon, withoute were.
And thus we lyvede ful many a yere,
So wel I kan nat telle how.'
    ' Sir !' quod I, ' where is she now ?'
' Now ?' quod he, and stynte anoon ;
Therewith he waxe as dede as stoon,
And seyde, ' Allas, that I was bore !   1300
That was the losse ! *and* herebefore
I tolde thee that I hadde lorne,
Bethenke how I seyde here beforne,
Thow wost ful lytel what thow menyst,
I have lost more than thow wenyst.
God wote, allas ! ryght that was she.'
' Allas ! sir, how ? what may that be?'
' She ys ded :'—' Nay ?'—' Yis, be my trouthe !'
' Is that youre losse ? be God, hyt ys routhe !'

And with that worde, ryght anoon,   1310
They ganne to strake forth; al was doon,
For that tyme, the herte huntynge.
With that me thoghte that this kynge,
Gan homewarde for to ryde,
Unto a place was ther besyde,
Which was from us but a lyte,
A longe castel with wallys white,
Be seynt Johan, on a ryche hille,
As me mette; but thus hyt fille.
Ryght thus me mette, as I yow telle,   1320
That in the castell ther was a belle,
As hyt hadde smyte oures twelve;
Therewyth I awooke my selve,
And fonde me lyinge in my bedde;
And the booke that I hadde redde,
Of Alcyione and Seys the kynge,
And of the goddys of slepynge,
I fond hyt in myn honde ful evene.
Thoght I, thys ys so queynt a swevene,
That I wol, be processe of tyme,   1330
Founde to put this swevene in ryme,
As I kan best, and that anoon;
This was my swevene; now hit ys doon!

EXPLICIT THE BOKE OF THE DUCHESSE.

OF QUENE ANELYDA AND FALSE

ARCYTE.

THOU ferse God of armes, Mars the rede,
That in thy frosty contré called Trace,
Within thy grisly temples ful of drede,
Honoured art as patroun of that place !
With thee, Bellona, Pallas, ful of grace !
Be presente, and my songe contynew and guye ;
At my begynnyng thus I to the crye.

‘ For hit ful depe is sonken in my mynde,
With pitous hert, in Englyssh to endyte
This olde storie, in Latyn which I fynde,
Of quene Analida and fals Arcite,
That elde, which al can frete and bite,
(As hit hath freten mony a noble storie)
Hath nygh devoured out of oure memorie.

‘ Be favorable eke thou Polymnya
On Parnaso that hathe thy sustres glade,
By Elycon, not fer from Cirrea,
Syngest with vois memorial in the shade,
Under the laurer, which that may not fade,

And do that I my shippe to haven wynne,   20
First folow I Stace, and after him Corynne.

Jamque domos patrias Cithiee post aspera gentis,
Prelia laurigero subeuntem Thesea curru,
Letifici plausus missusque ad sidera vulgi, &c.

When Theseus, with werres longe and grete,
The aspre folke of Cithe had overcome,
Tho, laurer crouned, in his chare, gold bete,
Home to his contré houses is he come;
For whiche the peple blisful al and somme,
So criden, that to the sterres hit wen*te*,   30
And him to honouren dide al her ent*e*nte.

Beforne this duke, in signe of victorie,
The trompes come, and in his baner large,
The ymage of Mars; and in token of glorie,
Men myght*e* sene of tresoure mony a charge,
Mony a bright helme, and mony a spere and targe,
Mony a fresh knyght, and mony a blysful route,
On hors, on fote, in al the felde aboute.

Ipolita his wife, the hardy quene
Of Cithea, that he conquered had*de*,   40
With Emelye her yonge suster shene,
Faire in a chare of golde he with hym lad*de*,
That al the grounde about her char she sprad*de*
With brightnesse of beauté in her face,
Fulfilled of largesse and of al*le* grace.

With his tryumphe, and laurer crouned thus,
In al the floure of fortunes yevyng,

Let I this noble prince, *this* Theseus,
Towarde Athenes in his wey ryding,
And founde I wol in*ne* shortly to bringe,   50
The sley*e* wey of that I gan to write,
Of quene Anelida and fals Arcite.

Mars, whiche that thro his furiouse course of ire,
The olde wrethe of Juno to fulfille,
Hath set the peples hertis bothe on fire
Of Thebes and Grece, and everiche other to kille
With blody speres, reste*de* never stille,
But throng now her, now ther, amonge hem both*e*,
That everyche other slough, so wer*e* they wrothe.

For when Amphiorax and Tydeus,   60
Ipomedon and Prothonolope also
Wer ded, and slayn proude Campaneus,
And when the wrecches Thebans bretheren two
Were slayn, and kyng Adrastus home ago,
So desolat stode Thebes and so bare,
That no wight coude remedie of his care.

And when the olde Creon gan espye,
How that the blood roial was broght adoun,
He helde the cité by his tyrannye,
And dyd*e* the gentils of that regioun   70
To ben his frendes, and duellen in the toune.
So what for love of him, and what for awe,
The noble folke wer to the toune idrawe.

Among al*le* these, Anelida the quene
Of Ermony was in that toune duellyng,
That fairer was then is the sunne shene,

Thoroghout the worlde so gan her name spring*e*,
That her to seen had every wyght likyng*e* ;
For, as of trouthe, is ther noon her *i*lyche,
Of al the wymen in this worlde riche.   80

Yonge was this queno, of twenty yer of elde,
Of mydil stature, and of suche fairenesse,
That Nature had a joy hir to beheldo,
And for to speken of her stidfastnesse,
She passed*e* bothe Penelope and Lucresse,
And shortly, yf she shal be comprehended,
In her myght*e* nothing been amended.

This Theban knyght eke, for sothe to seyne,
Was yonge, therto withal a lusty knyght,
But he was double in love, and nothing pleyne,   90
And subtil in that crafte, overe eny wyght,
And with his kunnyng whan this lady bryght :
For so ferforthe he can her trouthe assure,
That she him trusted over eny creature.

What shuld I seyn ? she lov*eth* Arcite so
That when that he was absent eny throw,
Anoon her thoght her hert*e* brast atwo ?
For in her sight to her be bare hym low,
So that she wende have al his hert yknowe ;
But he was fals, hit nas but feyned chere,   100
As nedeth not to men suche craft to lere.

But nevertheles ful mykel besynesse
Had he, er that he myght his lady wynne,
And swor he wolde dyen for distresse,

Or from his wit he seyde he wolde twynne.
Alas the while! for hit was routhe and synne,
That she upon his sorowes wolde rewe,
But nothing thinketh the fals as doth the trewe.

Her fredom fonde Arcite in suche maner,
That al was his that she hath, both moche and lyte ;
Ne to no creatur ne made she chere,   111
Ferther then it lykede to Arcite ;
Ther was no lak with *w*hiche he myght hir wite,
She was so forforth yevin hym to plese,
That al that lyked him hit dyd her herte ese.

Ther nas to her no maner lettre isente
That touched love, from eny maner wyght,
That she ne shewed hit him er hit was brent ;
So pleyn she was, and did her ful*le* myght,
That she nyl hiden nothing from her knyght, 120
Lest he of eny untrouthe her upbreyde ;
Withou*te* bode his herte she obeyde.

And eke he made him jelouse over her,
That what that eny man had*de* to her seyde,
Anoon he wolde preyen her to swere
What was that worde, or make hym evel apaide ;
Then wend*e* she out of her wyt have breyd,
But al*le* was but sleght and flaterie ;
Withou*te* love he feynede jelousye.

And al*le* this toke she so debonerly,   130
That al his wil, her thoght hit skilful thing ;
And ever the lenger she loved him tendirly,
And did him honour as he wer a kyng.

Her hert was wedded to him with a ringe ;
For so ferforth upon trouthe is her entent,
That wher he gooth, her her*te* with him wen*te*.

When she shal ete, on him is so her thoght,
That wel unnethe of mete toke she kepo ;
And when*ne* she was to her reste broght,
On him she thoght ay til that she slepe ;   140
When he was absent, prevely she wepe.
Thus lyveth feire Anelida the quene,
For fals Arcite, that did her al this tene.

This fals Arcite, of his newfangle*nesse*,
For she to hym so louly was and trewe,
Toke lesse deynté for her stidfastnesse,
And saw another lady, proude and newe,
And ryght anon he clad him in her hewe,—
Wot I not whethir in white, rede, or grene,—
And false*de* fair Anelida the quene.   150

But neverthelesse, grete wonder was hit noon
Thogh he were fals, for hit is the kynde of man,
Sith Lamek was, that is so longe agoon,
To ben in love as fals as evere he can ;
He was the first*e* fader that began
To loven two, and was in bigamye.
And he fonde tentes first, but-yf men lye.

This fals Arcite sumwhat most he feyne,
When he wex fals, to coveren his traitorie,
Ryght as an hors, that ean both bite and pleyn ;
For he bar her on honde of trecherie,   161
And swore he coude her doublenesse espie,

And al was falsnes that she to him mente ;
Thus swore this thefe, and forthe his way he wente

Alas ! what herte myght endure hit,
For routhe or wo, her sorow for to telle ?
Or what man hath the cunnyng or the wit ?
Or what man *mighte* within the chambre duelle,
Yf I to him rehersen shal the helle
That suffreth feyr Anelida the quene,   17(
For fals Arcite, that did her al this tene ?

She wepith, waileth, and swouneth pitously,
To grounde dede she falleth as a stoon ;
Craumpyss*heth* her lymes crokedly ;
She speketh as her wit wer al agoon ;
Other colour then asshen hath she noon,
Ne non other worde speketh she moche or lyte,
But ' Mercie ! cruel herte myn, Arcite !'

And thus endureth, til that she was so mate
That she ne hath foot, on which she may sustene.
But for languisshing evere in this estate,   181
Of which Arcite hath nother routhe ne tene ;
His herte was elleswher newe and grene ;
That on her wo, ne deyneth him not to thinke ;
Him rekketh never wher she flete or synke.

His newe lady holdeth him so narowe
Up by the brydil, at the staves ende,
That every worde he dred hit as an arwe ;
Her daunger made him bothe bowe and bende,
And as her luste, made him turne or wende ;   19(
For she ne graunted him in her lyvynge,
No grace, whi that he hath lust to singe :

But drof hym forthe, unnethe list her knowe
That he was servaunt unto her ladishippe ;
But lest that he wer proude, she helde him lowe.
Thus serveth he, withoute *mete* or sippe,
She sent him now to londe, *and* now to shippe,
And for she yafe him daunger al his fille,
Therfor she had him at her oune wille.

Ensample of this, ye thriftie wymmen alle,   200
Take here Anelida and fals Arcite,
That for her list hym her dere *herte* calle,
And was so meke, therfor he loved her lyte ;
The kynde of mannes hert is to delyte
In thing that straunge is, also God me save !
For what he may not gete, that wolde they have.

Now turne we to Anelida ageyn,
That pyneth day be day in langwisshinge ;
But when she sawe that her ne gat no geyn,
Upon a day, ful sorowfully wepinge,   210
She cast her for to make a compleynyng ;
And with her oune honde she gan hit write,
And sent *it* to her Theban knyght Arcite.

THE COMPLEYNT OF FAIRE ANELYDA UPON

FALS ARCYTE.

‘ So thirled with the poynt of remembraunce,
The suerde of sorowe, ywhet with fals plesaunce,
My herte bare of blis, and blake of hewe,
That turned is to quakyng al my daunce,

My suerte into a *whaped* countenaunce,
Sith hit availeth not *for* to ben trewe:
For who-so truest is, hit shal hi*r* rewe,
That serveth love, and dothe her observaunce
Alwey to oon, and chaungeth for no newe.

' I wot my self as wel as eny wight,
For I loved oon, with al my hert and myght
More then my self an hundred thousand sithe,
And cleped him my hertis life, my knyght,
And was al his, as fer as hit was ryght,
And when that he was glad, then was I blithe,
And his disese was my deth as swithe,
And he ayein, his trouthe me had iplyght,
For everemore hys lady me to kythe.

' Alas ! now hath he left me causeles,
And of my wo he is so routheles,
That with a worde him list not ones deyne,
To bring ayen my sorowful hert in pes,
For he is caght up in another les;
Ryght as *him* list, he laugheth at my peyne,
And I ne can myn hert*e* not restreyne
That I ne love him alwey nevertheles,
And of al this I not to whom me pleyne.

'And shal*e* I pleyn, (alas ! tho harde stounde !)
Unto my fo, that yafe my hert a wounde,
And yet desireth that myn harme be more ?
Nay, certis ! ferther wol I never founde
Non other helpe my sores for to sounde ;
My destany hath shapen hit *so* yore,
I wil non other medecyne ne lore,

I wil ben ay ther I was ones bounde,
That I have seide, be seide for evermore.

' Alas ! wher is become your gentilesse ?   250
Youre wordes ful of plesaunce and humblesse ?
Your observaunces in soo low manere ?
And your awayting, and your besynesse,
Upon me that ye calden your maistresse,
Your sovereigne lady in this worlde here ?
Alas ! is ther nother worde ne chere,
Ye vouchesafe upon myn hevynesse ?
Alas ! youre love, I bye hit al to dere.

' Now certis, suete, thogh that ye
Thus causeles tho causer be,   260
Of my dedely adversyté,
Your manly resoun oght it to respite,
To slene your frende, and namely me,
That never yet in no degre
Offended yow, as wisly he
That al wote of wo my soule quyte.

' But for I shewed yow, Arcite,
Al that men wolde to me write,
And was so besy yow to delyte,
My honor safe meke, kynde, and fre,   270
Therfor ye put on me this wite :
And of me rek*ke* not a myte,
Thogh the suerde of sorow byte
My woful her*te*, thro your cruelté.

' My swete foo, why do ye so for shame ?
And thenke ye that furthered be your name,

To love a newe, and ben untrewe? Nay!
And put yow in sclaunder now and blame,
And do to me adversité and grame,
That love yow most, God wel thou wost! alway?
And come ayein, and be al pleyn somme day,   281
And turne al this, that hath be mys, to game;
And 'al foryeve,' while that I lyve may.

'Lo, herte myn, al this is for to seyn,
As wheder shal I prey or elles pleyn?
Whiche is the wey to doon yow to be trewe?
For either mot I have yow in my cheyn,
Or with the dethe ye mot departe us tweyn;
Ther ben non other mene weyes newe,
For God so wisly upon my soule rewe,   290
As verrely ye sleen me with the peyn;
That may ye se unfeyned of myn hewe.

'For thus forforthe have I my dethe soght,
My self I mourdre with my prevy thoght;
For sorowe and routhe of your unkyndnesse,
I wepe, I wake, I fast, al helpeth noght;
I weyve joy that is to speke of oght,
I voyde companye, I fle gladnesse;
Who may avaunt hir beter of hevynesse,
Then I? and to this plyte have ye me broght,   300
Withoute gilt, me nedith no witnesse.

'And shal I prey, and weyve womanhede?
Nay! rather dethe, then do so foule a dede,
And axe mercie, an giltles what nede?
And yf I pleyn what lyfe I lede,
Yow rekketh not; that know I out of drede,

And if I to yow myn othes bede,
For myn excuse, a skorne shal be my mede,
Your chere floureth, but wol not sede,
Ful longe agoon I oght have taken hede ;　　310

' For thogh I hadde yow to morowe ageyn,
I myght as wel holde Apprile fro reyn,
As holde yow to make yow be stedfast.
Almyghty God, of trouthe the sovereign!
Wher is the trouthe of man ? who hath hit slayn ?
Who that hem loveth, she shal hem fynde as faste,
As in a tempest is a roten maste.
Is that a tame best, that is ay feyn
To renne away, when he is lest agaste ?

' Now mercie, swete, yf I myssey !　　320
Have I seyde oght amys, I prey ?
I not, my wit is al awey.
I fare as dothe the songe of chanteplure ;
For now I pleyn, and now I pley,
I am so mased that I dey,
Arcite hath borne awey the key
Of al my worlde, and my good aventure.

' For in this worlde ther is no creature,
Walkynge in more discomfiture,
Then I, no more sorowe endure,　　330
And yf I slepe a furlonge wey or tweye,
Then thenketh me that your figure
Before me stont clad in asure,
Efte to sucre yet a newe assure,
For to be trew, and mercie me to preye.

' The longe nyght, this wonder sight I drye,
And on the day for this afray I dye,
And of al this ryght noght, ywis, ye reche,
Ne neveremo myn yen two be drie,
And to your routhe, and to your trouthe I crie ;
But, welawey ! to fer be they to feche,   341
Thus holdeth me my destany a wreche,
But me to rede out of this drede or guye,
Ne may my wit, so weyke is hit, not streche.

' Then ende I thus, sith I may do no more,
I yif hit up for now and evermore ;
For I shal never efte put in balaunce
My seknernes, ne lerne of love the lore ;
But as the swan, I have herd seyd ful yore,
Ayeins his dethe shal singen his penaunce,   35
So singe I here the destany or chaunce,
How that Arcite, Analida so sore
Hath thirled with the poynt of remembraunce.'

[Whan that Annelyda, this woful quene,
Hath of her hande written in this wyse,
With face deed, betwyxe pale and grene,
She fel a-swoune ; and sythe she gan to ryse,
And unto Mars avoweth sacrifyse
Within the temple, with a sorouful chere,
That shapen was, as ye may plainly here.]

EXPLICIT.

THE HOUSE OF FAME.

OD turne us every dreme, to goode !
   For hyt is wonder, be the roode,
   To my wytte, what causeth swevenes
   Eyther on morwes, or on evenes ;
And why theffecte folweth of somme,
And of somme hit shal never come ;
Why that is an avisioun,
And why this is a revelacioun ;
Why this a dreme, why that a swevene,
And noght to every man *i*-lyche evene ;   10
Why this a fantome, why these oracles,
I not : but who-so of these meracles
The causes knoweth bet then I,
Devyne he ; for I certeinly
Ne kan hem noght, ne never thinke
To besely my wytte to swinke,
To knowe of hir significaunce
The gendres, neyther the distaunce
Of tymes of hem, ne the causis,
For-why this is more then that cause is ;   20
As yf folkys complexiouns,
Make hem dreme of reflexiouns ;
Or ellis thus, as other sayne,
For to grete feblenesse of her brayne,

By abstinence, or by sekenesse,
Prisoun, stewe or grete distresse;
Or ellis by disordynaunce,
Or naturell acustumaunce,
That somme man is to curiouse
In studye, or melancolyouse;   30
Or thus, so inly ful of drede,
That no man may hym bote bede;
Or ellis that devocioun
 Of somme, and contemplacioun,
Causeth suche dremes ofte;
Or that the cruelle lyfe unsofte
Whiche these ilke lovers leden,
Oft hopen over moche or dreden,
That purely hero impressions
Causeth hem avisions;   40
Or yf that spiritis have the myght
To make folke to dreme anyght;
Or yf the soule, of propre kynde,
Be so parfit as men fynde,
That yt forwote that ys to come,
And that hyt worneth al and some
Of everyche of her aventures,
Bo avisions, or bo figures,
But that oure flessh no hath no myght
To understonde hyt aryght,   50
For hyt is warned to derkly;
But why the cause is, noght wote I,
Wel worth of this thynge grete clerkys,
That treto of this, and other werkes;
For I of noon opinioun
Nyl as now make mensyoun;
But oonly that the holy roode

Turne us every dreme to goode;
For never sith that I was borne,
Ne no man elles me beforne, 60
Mette, I trowe stedfastly,
So wonderful a dreme as I,
The tenthe day now of Decembre;
The which, as I kan yow remembre,
I wol yow telle everydele.
  But at my begynnynge, trusteth wele,
I wol make invocacioun,
With special devocioun
Unto the god of slepe anoon,
That dwelleth in a cave of stoon, 70
Upon a streme that cometh fro Lete,
That is a floode of helle unswete,
Besyde a folke men clepeth Cymerie;
There slepeth ay this god unmerie,
With his slepy thousande sones,
That alwey for to slepe hir wone is;
That to this god that I of rede,
Prey I, that he wolde me spede,
My swevene for to telle aryght,
Yf every dreme stonde in his myght 80
And he that mover ys of alle
That is and was, and ever shalle,
So yive hem joye that hyt here,
Of alle that they dreme to-yere;
And for to stonden al in grace
Of her loves, or in what place
That hem were levest for to stonde,
And shelde hem fro poverte and shonde,
And fro unhappe and eche disese,
And send hem alle that may hem plese, 90

That take hit wele and skorne hit noghte,
. Ne hyt mysdeme in her thoght,
Thorgh maliciouse entencioun.
And who-so, thorgh presumpcioun,
Or hate, or skorne, or thorgh envye,
Dispite, or jape, or vilanye,
Mysdeme hyt, pray I Jhesus God,
That dreme he barefote, dreme he shod,
That every harme, that any man
Hath had sythen the worlde began,   100
Befalle him thereof, or he sterve,   .
And graunt he mote hit ful deserve,
Loo, with suche a conclusioun,
As had of his avisioun
Cresus, that was kynge of Lyde,
That high upon a gebet dide.
This prayer shal he have of me;
I am no bet in charityé.
    Now herkeneth, as I have yow seyde,
What that I met or I abreyde.   110
Of Decembre the tenthe day,
Whan hit was nyght, to slepe I lay,
Ryght ther as I was wonte to done,
And fille on slepe wonder sone,
As he that wery was for-goo
On pilgrymage myles two
To the corseynt Leonarde,
To make lythe of that was harde.
    But as I slepte, me mette I was
Withyn a temple ymade of glas;   120
In whiche ther were moo ymages
Of golde, stondynge in sondry stages,
And moo ryche tabernacles,

And with perré moo pynacles,
And moo curiouse portreytures,
And queynt maner of figures
Of golde werke, then I sawgh ever.
But certeynly I nyste never
Wher that I was, but wel wyste I,
Hyt was of Venus redely,   130
This temple; for in portreyture,
I sawgh anoon ryght hir figure
Naked fletynge in a see.
And also on hir hede, pardé,
Hir rose garlonde white and rede,
And hir combe to kembe hyr hede,
Hir dowves, and daun Cupido,
Hir blynde sone, and Vulcano,
That in his face was ful broune.
But as I romed up and doune,   140
I fonde that on a walle ther was
Thus writen on a table of bras:—
' I wol now say yif I kan,
The armes, and also the man,
That first came, thorgh his destanee,
Fugityfe of Troy countree,
In Itayle, with ful moche pyne,
Unto the strondes of Lavyne.'
And tho began the story anoon,
As I shal telle yow echoon.   150
    First sawgh I the destruccioun
Of Troy, thorgh the Greke Synoun,
With his false forswerynge,
And his chere and his lesynge
Made the hors broght into Troye,
Thorgh which Troyens lost al her joye

And aftir this was grave, allas,
How Ilyoun assayled was
And wonne, and kynge Priam yslayne,
And Polite his sone, certayne,   160
Dispitously of daun Pirrus.
    And next that sawgh I how Venus
Whan that she sawgh the castel brende,
Doune fro the hevene gan descende,
And bad hir sone Eneas flee;
And how he fled, and how that he
Escaped was from al the pres,
And tooke his fader, Anchises,
And bare hym on hys bakke away,
Cryinge ' Allas and welaway !'   170
The whiche Anchises in hys honde
Bare the goddesse of the londe,
Thilke that unbrende were.
    And I saugh next in al hys fere,
How Creusa, daun Eneas wife,
Which that he lovede as hys lyfe,
And hir yonge sone Iulo,
And eke Askanius also,
Fledden eke with drery chere,
That hyt was pitee for to here;   180
And in a forest as they wente,
At a turnynge of a wente,
How Creusa was yloste, allas !
That dede, not I how she was;
How he hir soughte, and how hir goste
Bad hym to flee the Grekes oste,
And seyde he most unto Itayle,
As was hys destanye, sauns faille,
That hyt was pitee for to here,

When hir spirite gan appere   190
The wordes that she to hym seyde,
And for to kepe hir sone hym preyde.
  Ther sawgh I grave eke how he,
Hys fader eke, and his meynee,
With hys shippes gan to sayle
Towardes the contree of Itaylle,
And streight as that they myght*e* goo.
  Ther saugh I the, cr*e*wel Juno,
That art daun Jupiteres wife,
That hast yhated, al thy lyfe,   200
Alle the Troyanysshe bloode,
Renne and crye, as thou were woode,
On Eolus, the god of wyndes,
To blowe oute of al*le* kyndes
So lowde, that he shulde drenche
Lorde, lady, grome, and wenche
Of al the Troyan nacioun,
Withoute any savacioun.
  Ther saugh I suche tempeste arysc,
That every herte myght agryse,   210
To see hyt peynted on the walle.
  Ther saugh I graven eke withalle,
Venus, how ye, my lady dere,
Wepynge with ful woful chere,
Prayen Jupiter an hye   .
To save and kepe that navye
Of the Trojan Eneas,
Sythe that he hir sone was
  Ther saugh I Joves Venus kysse,
And graunted of the tempest *lysse*.   220
  Ther saugh I how the tempest stente,
And how with al*le* pyne he wente,

And prevely toke arryvage
In the contree of Cartage ;
And on the morwe how that he,
And a knyghte highte Achate,
Mette with Venus that day,
Goynge in a queynt array,
As she had*de* ben an hunteresse,
With wynde blowynge upon hir tresse ;   230
How Eneas gan hym to pleyne,
Whan that he knewe hir, of his peyne ;
And how *y*-dreynte his shippes were,
Or elles lost, he nyste where ;
How she gan hym comfort thoo,
And bad hym to Cartage goo,
And ther he shulde his folke fynde,
That in the see were lefte behynde.
And, shortly of this thyng to pace,
She made Eneas so in grace   240
Of Dido, quene of that contree,
That, shortly for to tel*le*, sho
Became hys love, and lete hym doo
That that weddynge longeth too.
What shulde I speke it more queynte,
Or peyne me my wordes peynte,
To speke of love ? hyt wol not be ;
I kannot of that faculté.
And eke to telle the manere
How they aqueynteden in fere,   250
Hyt were a longe processe to telle,
And over longe for yow to dwelle.
    Ther sawgh I grave, how Eneas
Tolde Dido every caus,
That hym was tyd upon the see.

And aftir grave was how shee
Made of hym, shortly at oo worde,
Hyr lyfe, hir love, hir luste, hir lorde;
And did hym al the reverence,
And leyde on hym alle dispence,   260
That any woman myghte do,
Wenynge hyt had al be so,
As he hir swore; and herby demede
That he was good, for he suche semede.
 Allas, what harme doth apparence,
Whan hit is fals in existence!
For he to hir a traytour was;
Wherfore she slowe hir selfe, allas!
 Loo, how a woman dothe amys,
To love hym that unknowe ys!   270
For, be Cryste, lo thus yt fareth;
Hyt is not al golde that glareth.
For, al-so browke I wel myn hede,
Ther may be under godelyhede
Kevered many a shrewde vice;
Therfore be no wyght so nyce,
To take a love oonly for chere,
Or for speche, or for frendly manere;
For this shal every woman fynde,
That some man, of his pure kynde   280
Wol shewen outward the fairest,
Til he have caught that what him lest;
And than wol he causes fynde,
And sweren how that she ys unkynde,
Or fals, or prevy double was.
Alle this sey I be Eneas
And Dido, and her nyce lest,
That loved al to sone a gest;

Therfore I wol seye a proverbe,
That he that fully knoweth therbe,
May savely ley hyt to his ye;
Withoute drede, this ys no lye.
    But let us speke of Eneas,
How he betrayed hir, allas!
And lefte hir ful unkyndely.
    So whan she saw al utterly,
That he wolde hir of trouthe faylo,
And wende fro hir to Itayle,
She gan to wringe hir hondes two.
' Allas!' quod sho, ' what me ys wo!
Allas! is every man thus trewe,
That every yere wolde have a newe,
Yf hit so longe tyme dure?
Or elles three, peraventure?
As thus:—of *oon* he wolde have fame
In magnyfying of hys name;
Another for frendshippe, seyth he;
And yett ther shal the thrid*de* be,
That shal be take for delyte,
Loo, or for synguler profite.'
In suche wordes gan to pleyne
Dydo of hir grete peyne,
As me mette redely;
None other auttour aleggo I.
' Allas!' quod sho, ' my swete her*te*,
Have piteo on my sorwes smer*te*,
And slee me not! goo noght awey!
' O woful Dido, weleaway!'
Quod she to hir selfe thoo.
' O Eneas! what wol ye doo?
O, that your love, ne your bonde,

That ye han sworne with your ryght honde,
Ne my crewel deth,' quod she,
' May holde yow stille here with me!
O, haveth of my deth pitee!
Ywys my dere her*te*, ye
Knowen ful wel that never yit,
As fer-forth as ever I had*de* wytte,
Agylte yowe in thoght ne dede.
O, have ye men suche godelyhede   330
In speche, and never a dele of trouthe?
Allas, that ever had*de* routhe
Any woman on any man!
Now see I wel, and tel*le* kan,
We wrechehed wymmen konne noon arte;
For certeyne, for tho more parte,
Thus we be served everychone.
How sore that ye men konne grone,
Anoon as we have yow receyved,
Certeinly we ben deceyved;   340
For, though your love laste a sesoun,
Wayte upon the conclusyoun,
And eke how that ye determynen,
And for the more part diffynen.
O, welcawey that I was borne!
For thorgh yow is my name lorne,
And al youre actes red and songe
Over al thys londe, on every tonge.
O wikke Fame! for ther nys
Nothinge so swifte, lo, as she is.   350
O, sothe ys, every thynge ys wyste,
Though hit be kevered with tho myste.
Eke, though I myghte dure ever,
That I have do rekever I never,

That I ne shal be seyde, allas,
Y-shamed be thourgh Eneas,
And that I shal thus juged be :—
Loo, ryght as she hath done, now she
Wol doo eftesones hardely.
Thus seyth the peple prevely.'
But that is do, *nis* not to done ;
For al hir compleynt ne al hir moone,
Certeynly avayleth hir not a stre.
    And when she wiste sothely he
Was forthe unto his shippes agoon,
She into hir chambre wente anoon,
And called on hir suster Anne,
And gan her to compleyne thanne ;
And seyde, that she cause was,
That she first loved *hym*, alas,
And thus counseylled hir thertoo.
But what ! when this was seyde and doo,
She rofe hir selfe to the herte,
And dyed*e* thorgh the wounde smerte.
But al the maner how she dyede,
And al the wordes that she seyde,
Who-so to knowe hit hath purpos,
Rede Virgile in Eneydos,
Or tho epistile of Ovyde,
What that she wrote or that she dyde ;
And nor hyt were to longe tendyte,
Be God, I wolde hyt here write.
    But, welcaway ! the harme, the routhe,
That hath betyd for suche untrouthe,
As men may ofte in bokes rede,
And al day so hyt yet in dede,
That for to thynke hyt a tene is.

Loo Demophon, duke of Athenys,
How he forswore hym ful falsly,
And trayied Phillis wikkidly,   390
That kynges doghtre was of Trace,
And falsly gan hys terme pace;
And when she wiste that he was fals,
She honge hir selfe ryght be the hals,
For he had doo hir suche untrouthe;
Loo! was not this a woo and routhe?
Eke lo how fals and reccheles
Was to Breseyda Achilles,
And Paris to Enone,
And Jason to Isiphile,   400
And eft Jason to Medea,
Ercules to Dyanira;
For he left her for Yole,
That made hym cache his dethe, pardé.
How fals eke was he, Theseus;
That, as the story telleth us,
How he betrayed Adriane;
The devel be hys soules bane!
For had he lawghed, had he loured,
He moste have be devoured,   410
Yf Adriane ne had ybe.
And, for she had of hym pité,
She made hym fro the dethe escape,
And he made hir a ful fals jape;
For aftir this, withyn a while,
He lefte hir slepynge in an ile,
Deserte allone, ryght in the se,
And stale away, and lete hir be;
And tooke hir suster Phedra thoo
With him, and gan to shippe goo.   420

And yet he had yswore to hire,
On alle that ever he myght*e* swere,
That so she saved hym hys lyfe,
He wolde have take hir to hys wife,
For she desirede nothing ellis,
In certeyne, as the booke tellis,
   But to excusen Eneas
Fullyche of al his trespas,
The booke seyth Mercuré sauns fayle,
Bade hym goo into Itayle,
And leve Auffrikes regioun,
And Dido and hir faire toun.
Thoo sawgh I grave how that to Itayle
Daun Eneas is goo for to assayle;
And how the tempest al began,
And how he lost hys sterisman,
Which that tho stere, or he toke kepe,
Smote overe borde, loo, as he slepe.
   And also sawgh I how Sybile
And Eneas, beside an yle,
To helle wente, for to see
His fader Anchyses the free.
How he ther fonde Palinurus,
And Dido, and eke Deiphebus,
And every torment eke in helle
Sawgh he, which is longe to telle.
Which who-so willeth for knowe,
He most rede many a rowe
On Virgile or in Claudian,
Or Daunte, that hit tell*e* kan.
   Tho sawgh I grave al the aryvayle
That Eneas had in Itaylo;
And with kynge Latyno hys tretee,

And alle the batayles that hee
Was at hymselfe, and eke hys knyghtis,
Or he had al ywonne hys ryghtis;
And how he Turnus reft his lyfe,
And wanne Lavinia to his wife;
And alle the mervelouse signals
Of the goddys celestials;   460
How mawgree Juno, Eneas
For al hir sleight and hir compas,
Acheved alle his aventure;
For Jupiter tooke of hym cure,
At the prayer of Venus,
The whiche I prey alwey save us,
And us ay of oure sorwes lyghte.
 When I hadde seene al this syghte
In this noble temple thus,
'A lorde!' thought I, 'that madest us,   470
Yet sawgh I never suche noblesse
Of ymages, ne suche richesse,
As I saugh grave in this chirche;
But not wote I whoo did hem wirche,
Ne where I am, ne what contree.
But now wol I goo oute and see,
Ryght at the wiket, yf Y kan
See oughtwhere stiryng any man,
That may me telle where I am.'
 When I oute at the dores came,   480
I faste aboute me behelde,
Then sawgh I but a large felde,
As fer as that I myghte see,
Withouten toune, or house, or tree,
Or bussh, or gras, or cryd londe;
For al the felde nas but sonde,

As smale as man may se yet lye
In the desert of Lybye;
Ne no maner creature,
That ys yformed be nature, 490
Ne sawgh *I* me to rede or wisse.
' O Criste,' thought I, ' that art in blysse,
Fro fantome and illusioun
Me save !' and with devocioun
Myn eyen to the hevene I caste.
Thoo was I war at the laste,
That faste be the sonne, as hye
As kenne myght I with myn ye,
Me thought I sawgh an egle sore,
But that hit semede moche more 500
Then I had any egle seyne.
But, this as soothe as deth certeyne,
Hyt was of golde, and shone so bryght,
That never sawgh men such a syght,
But-if the hevene hadde ywonne
Al newe of God another sonne ;
So shon the egles fetheres bryghte,
And somewhat dounwarde gan hyt lyghte.

EXPLICIT LIBER PRIMUS.

LIBER SECUNDUS.

OW herkeneth every maner man,
That Englissh understonde kan,
And listeneth of my dreme to lere ;
For now at erste shullen ye here
So sely an avisyoun,
That I saye no Cipioun,

Ne kynge Nabugodonosor,
Pharoo, Turnus, ne Eleanor,
Ne mette suche a dreme as this.
Now faire blisfulle, O Cipris,   10
So be my favor at this tyme!
And ye me to endite and ryme
Helpeth, that on Parnaso dwelle,
Be Elicon the clere welle.

    O Thought, that wrote al that I mette,
And in the tresorye hyt shette
Of my brayne! now shal men se
Yf any vertu in the be,
To tellen al my dreme aryght;
Now kythe thyn engyne and myght!   20
    This egle of whiche I have yow tolde,
That shone with fethres as of golde,
Which that so highe gan to sore,
I gan beholde more and more,
To se her beauté and the wonder;
But never was ther dynt of thonder,
Ne that thynge that men calle foudre,
That smote sommetyme a toure to powdre,
And in his swifte comynge brende,
That so swithe gan descende,   30
As this foule when hyt behelde,
That I a-roume was in the felde;
And with hys grymme pawes stronge,
Withyn hys sharpe nayles longe,
Me, fleynge, in a swappe he hente,
And with hys sours ayene up wente,
Me caryinge in his clawes starke,
As lyghtly as I were a larke,
How high, I cannot telle yow,

For I came up, Y nyste how.   40
For so astonyed and asweved
Was every vertu in my heved,
What with his sours and with my drede,
That al my felynge gan to dede;
For-whi hit was to grete affray.
    Thus I longe in hys clawes lay,
Til at the last he to me spake
In mannes vois, and seyde, 'Awake!
And be *thou* not agaste, for shame!'
And callede me *tho* by my name.   50
And for I sholde the bet abreyde,
Me mette, 'awake' to me he seyde,
Ryght in the same vois and stevene,
That useth oon I koude nevene;
And with that vois, soth for to seyne,
My mynde came to me ageyne,
For hit was goodely seyde to me,
So was hyt never wonte to be.
And herewithalle I gan to stere,
As he me in his fete to-bere,   60
Til that he felt that I had hete,
And felte eke tho myn herte bete.
And thoo gan he me to disporte,
And with wordes to comforte,
And sayede twyes, 'Seynt Mary!
Thou arte noyouse for to cary,
And nothynge nedith *it*, pardee;
For, al-so wis God helpe me,
As thou noon harme shalt have of this;
And this caas that betydde the is,   70
Is for thy lore and for thy prowe,
Let see! darst thou yet loke nowe?

Be ful assured, boldely,
I am thy frende.'   And therewith I
Gan for to wondren in my mynde.
'O God,' thought I, 'that madesto kynde,
Shal I noon other weyes dye?
Wher Joves wol me stellefye,
Or what thinge may this sygnifye?
I neyther am Ennok, ne Elye,   80
Ne Romulus, ne Ganymede,
That was ybore up, as men rede,
To hevene with daun Jupiter,
And made the goddys botiller.'
Loo, this was thoo my fantasye!
But he that bare me gan espye,
That I so thought and seyde this :—
'Thow demest of thy-selfe amys;
For Joves ys not therabouto,
I dar wel put*te* the out of doute,   90
To make of the as yet a sterre.
But er I bere the mocho ferre,
I wol the telle what I am,
And whider thou shalt, and why I cam
To do thys, so that thou take
Goode herte, and not for fere quake.'
'Gladly,' quod I.   'Now wel,' quod he:
'First, I, that in my fete have the,
Of which thou haste a fere and wonder,
Am dwellynge with the god of thonder,   100
Whiche that men callen Jupiter,
That dooth me flee ful ofte fer
To do al hys comaundement.
And for this cause he hath me sent
To the: now herke, be thy trouthe!

Certeyn he hath of the routhe,
That thou so longe trewely
Hast served so ententyfly
Hys blynde neviwe Cupido,
And faire Venus also,   110
Withoute guerdoun ever yitte,
And neverthelesse hast set thy witte,
(Although in thy hede ful lytel is)
To make songes, dytees, and bookys
In ryme, or elles in cadence,
As thou best canst in reverence
Of Love, and of hys servantes eke,
That have hys servyse soght, and seke;
And peynest the to preyse hys arte,
Although thou haddest never parte;   120
Wherfore, al-so God me blosse,
Joves halt hyt grete humblesse,
And vertu eke, that thou wolt make
A nyghte ful ofte thyn hede to ake,
In thy studye so thou writest,
And evermo of love enditest,
In honour of hym and preysynges,
And in his folkes furtherynges,
And in hir matere al devisest,
And noght hym nor his folke dispisest,   130
Although thou maiste goo in the daunce
Of hem that hym lyst not avaunce.
Wherfore, as I seyde, ywys,
Jupiter consideroth *wel* this;
And also, beausir, other thynges;
That is, that thou hast no tydynges
Of Loves folke, yf they be glade,
Ne of noght elles that God made;

And noght oonly fro ferre contree,
That ther no tydynge cometh to thee,   140
Not of thy verray neyghebors,
That duelle almoste at thy dors,
Thou herist neyther that nor this,
For when thy labour doon al ys,
And hast ymade rekenynges,
Instid of reste and newe thynges,
Thou goost home to thy house anoon,
And, also dombe as any stoon,
Thou sittest at another booke,
Tyl fully dasewyd ys thy looke,   150
And lyvest thus as an heremyte,
Although thyn abstynence ys lyte.
And therfore Joves, thorgh hys grace,
Wol that I bere the to a place,
Which that hight the House of Fame,
To do the somme disport and game,
In somme recompensacioun
Of labour and devocioun
That thou hast had, loo ! causeles,
To Cupido the rechcheles.   160
And thus this god, thorgh his merite,
Wol with somme maner thinge the quyte,
So that thou wolt be of goode chere.
For truste wel that thou shalt here,
When we be come there as I seye,
Mo wonder thynges, dar I leye,
Of Loves folke moo tydynges,
Both sothe-sawes and leysinges ;
And moo loves newe begonne,
And longe yserved loves wonne ;   170
And moo loves casuelly,

That betyde, no man wote why,
But as a blende man stert an hare;
And more jolytee and fare,
While that they fynde love of stele,
As thinketh hem, and over al wele;
Mo discordes, and moo jelousies,
Mo murmures, and moo novelries,
And moo dissymulacions,
And feyned reparacions;
And moo berdys in two oures
Withoute rasour or sisoures
Ymade, then greynes be of sondes;
And eke moo holdynge in hondes,
And also mo renoveilaunces
Of olde forleten aqueyntaunces;
Mo love-dayes, and acordes
Then on instrumentes bon cordes;
And eke of loves moo eschaunges,
Than ever cornes were in graunges;
Unnethe maistow trowen this?'
Quod he.   'Noo, helpe me God so wys!'
Quod I. 'Noo? why?' quod he.   'For hyt
Were impossible to my witte,
Though *hadde* Fame *alle* the pies
In alle a realme, and alle tho spies,
How that yet he shulde here al this,
Or they espie hyt.'—'O yis, yis!'
Quod he, to me, 'that kan I preve
Be resoun, worthy for to love,
So that thou yeve thyn advertence
To understonde my sentence.

     'First shalt thou here where she dwelleth,
And so thyn oune boke hyt tellith,

Hir paleys stant as I shal sey
Ryght even in-myddes of the wey
Betwexen hevene, erthe, and see ;
That whatsoever in al these three
Is spoken either prevy or aperte,
The aire therto ys so overte,   210
And stant eke in so juste a place,
That every soune mot to hyt pace,
Or what so cometh fro any tonge,
Be hyt rouned, red, or songe,
Or spoke in suerté or in drede,
Certeyn hyt moste thider nede.
  ' Now herkene wel ; for-why I wille
Tellen the a propre skille,
And worche a demonstracioun
In myn ymagynacioun.   220
  ' Geffrey, thou wost ryght wel this,
That every kyndely thynge that is,
Hath a kyndely stede ther he
May best in hyt conserved be ;
Unto whiche place every thynge,
Thorgh his kyndely enclynynge,
Moveth for to come to,
Whan that it is awey therfro.
As thus, loo, thou maist al day se
That any thinge that hevy be,   230
As stoon or lede, or thynge of wight,
And bere hyt never so hye on hight,
Lat goo thyn hande, hit falleth doune.
Ryght so sey I, be fire, or soune,
Or smoke, or other thynges lyghte,
Alwey they soke upward on highte,
While eche of hem is at his large ;

Lyghte thinges upwarde, and dounwarde charge.
And for this cause mayste thou see,
That every ryver to the see   240
Enclyned ys to goo by kynde.
And by these skilles, as I fynde,
Hath fyssh duellynge in floode and see,
And trees eke in erthe bec.
Thus every thinge by this reasoun
Hath his propre mansyoun,
To which he seketh to repaire,
As there hit shulde not apaire.
Loo, this sentence ys knowen kouthe
Of every philosophres mouthe,   250
As Aristotile and daun Platoun,
And other clerkys many oon,
And to confirme my reasoun,
Thou wost wel this, that speche is soun,
Or elles no man myght hyt here;
Now herke what Y wol the lere.
    'Soune ys noght but eyre ybroken,
And every speche that ys yspoken,
Lowde or pryvee, foule or faire,
In his substaunce ys but aire;   260
For as flaumbe ys but lyghted smoke,
Ryght soo soune ys *but* aire ybroke.
But this may be in many wyse,
Of which I wil the twoo devyse,
As soune that cometh of pipe or harpe.
For whan a pipe is blowen sharpe,
The aire ys twyst with violence,
And rent: loo, this ys my sentence;
Eke, whan men harpe strynges smyte,
Whether hyt be moche or lyte,   270

Loo, with the stroke the ayre to-breketh ;
Right so hit breketh whan men speketh.
Thus wost thou wel what thinge is speche.
  ' Now hennesforthe Y wol the teche,
How every speche, or noyse, or soune,
Thurgh hys multiplicacioune,
Thogh hyt were piped of a mouse,
Mote nede come to Fames House.
I preve hyt thus :—Take hede now
Be experience, for yf that thow   280
Throwe on water now a stoon,
Wel wost thou hyt wol make anoon
A litel roundelle as a sercle,
Paraventure brode as a coverele ;
And ryght anoon thow shalt see wele,
That sercle wol cause another whele,
And that the thridde, and so forth, brother,
Every sercle causynge other,
Wydder than hymself *erst* was.
And this fro roundel *to* compas,   290
Echo aboute other goynge,
Caused of othres sterynge,
And multiplyinge evermoo,
Til that hyt be so fer ygoo
That hyt at bothe brynkes bee.
Althou*gh* thow mowe hyt not ysee
Above, hyt gooth yet *ay* under,
Although thou thenke hyt a grete wounder.
And who-so seyth of trouthe I varye,
Bid hym proven the contrarye.   300
And ryght thus every worde, ywys,
That lowde or pryvee yspoken ys,
Moveth first an ayre aboute,

And of thys movynge, out of doute,
Another ayre anoon ys meved,
As I have of the watir preved,
That every cerclo causeth other.
Ryght so of ayre, my leve brother;
Everych ayre other stereth
More and more, and speche up bereth,
Or voys, or noyse, or worde, or soun,
Aye through multiplicacioun,
Til hyt be atte House of Famo ;—
Take yt in ernest or in game.
   ' Now have I tolde, yf ye have in mynde,
How speche or soun, of pure kyndo
Enclyned ys upwarde to meve ;
This mayst thou fele wel I preve.
And that sum place *or* stede, ywys,
That every thynge enclyned to ys,
Hath his kyndelyche stede :
That sheweth hyt, withoute drede,
That kyndely the mansioun
Of every speche, of every soun,
Bo hyt eyther foule or faire,
Hath hys kynde place in ayre.
And syn that every thynge that is
Out of hys kynde place, ywys,
Moveth thidder for to goo,
Yif hyt awey *may* bo therfro,
As I before have preved tho.
Hyt seweth, every soun, pardé,
Moveth kyndely to pace,
Al up into his kyndely place.
And this place of which I tello,
Ther as Famo lyst to duelle,

Ys sette amyddys of these three,
Hevene, erthe, and eke the see,
As most conservatyf tho soun.
Than ys this the conclusyoun,   340
That every speche of every man,
As Y the telle first began,
Moveth up on high to pace
Kyndely to Fames place.
  ' Telle me this *now* feythfully,
Have I not preved thus symply,
Withouten any subtilité
Of speche, or grete prolyxité
Of termes of philosophie,
Of figures of poetrie,   350
Or coloures of retorike?
Pardee, hit oughte the *wel* lyke;
For harde langage, and hard matere
Ys encombrouse for to here
Attones; wost thou not wel this?'
And Y answered and seyde, ' Yis.'
' A ha!' quod he, ' lo, so I can,
Lewdely to a lewed man
Speke, and shewe hym swyche skiles,
That he may shake hem be the biles.   360
So palpable they shulden be.
But telle me this now pray Y the,
How thenketh the my conclusyoun?'
' A goode persuasioun,'
Quod *I*, ' hyt is; and lyke to *be*,
Ryght so as thou hast preved me.'
' Be God,' quod he, ' and as I leve,
Thou shalt have yet, or hit be eve,
Of every word of thys sentence,

A preve by experience ;
And with thyn eres heren wel,
Toppe and taylle, and everidel,
That every word that spoken ys,
Cometh into Fames House, ywys,
As I have seyde; what wilt thou more?'
And with this word upper to sore,
He gan and seyde, ' Be seynt Jame,
Now wil we speken al of game.
 ' How fairest thou?' quod he to me.
' Wel,' quod I. ' Now see,' quod he,
' By thy trouthe, yonde adoune,
Wher that thou knowest any toune,
Or hous, or any other thinge.
And whan thou hast of ought knowynge,
Looke that thou warne me,
And Y anoon shal telle the,
How fer that thou art now therfro.'
 And Y adoun to loken thoo,
And behelde feldes and playnes,
And now hilles, and now mountaynes,
Now valeys, and now forestes,
And now unnethes grete bestes ;
Now ryveres, now citees,
Now tounes, and now grete trees,
Now shippes scyllynge in the see.
 But thus sone in a while hee
Was flowen fro the grounde so hye,
That al the worlde, as to myn ye,
No more semede than a prikke ;
Or elles was the aire so thikke
That Y ne myghte not discerne.
With that he spak to me as yerne,

And seyde: " Seestow any token,
Or ought that in this world of spoken ?'
  I seyde, ' Nay.' ' No wonder nys,'
Quod he, ' for half so high as this,
Nas Alexandre Macedo
Ne tho kynge, daun Cipio,
That saw in dreme, at poynt devys,
Helle and erth, and paradys;   410
Ne eke the wrechche Didalus,
Ne his childe, nyse Ykarus,
That fleegh so highe, that the hete
His wynges malte, and he fel wete
In myd the see, and ther he dreynt,
For whom was maked moch compleynt.
  ' Now turne upward,' quod he, 'thy face,
And beholde this large place,
This eyre; but loke thou ne be
Adrad of hem that thou shalt se;   420
For in this regioun certeyn,
Dwelleth many a citezeyn,
Of which that speketh daun Plato.
These ben eyrysshe bestes, lo !'
And so saw Y alle that meynee,
Boothe goone and also flee.
' Now,' quod he thoo, ' cast up thyn ye;
Se yonder, loo, the galoxie,
Whiche men clepeth the melky weye,
For hit ys white: and somme, parfeye,   430
Kallen hyt Watlynge strete,
That ones was ybrente wyth hete,
Whan the sonnes sonne, the rede,
That highte Phetoun, wolde lede
Algate his fader carte, and gye.

The carte hors gonne wel espye,
That he kouude no governaunce,
. And gan *he* for to lepe and taunce,
And beren hym now up, now doun,
Til that he sey the Scorpioun,
Whiche that in heven a synge is yit.
And he for ferde lost hys wyt
Of that, and lat the reynes goon
Of his hors ; and they anoon
Gonne up to mounten, and doun descende,
Til both the ayre and erthe brende ;
Til Jubiter, loo, atte laste
Hym slowe, and fro the carte caste.
Loo, ys it not a mochil myschaunce,
To lat a foole han governaunce
Of thing that he can not demeyne ?'
  And with this word, sothe for to seyne,
He gan upper alwey for to sore,
And gladded me ay more and more,
So feythfully to me spake he.
  Tho gan I loken under me,
And behelde the ayerisshe bestes,
Cloudes, mystes, and tempestes,
Snowes, hayles, reynes, wyndes,
And *hir* gendrynge iñ hir kyndes,
Alle the wey thrugh whiche I came ;
' O God,' quod Y, ' that made Adam,
Moche is thy myght and thy noblesse.'
  And thoo thought Y upon Boesse,
That writ of thought may flee so hye,
With fetheres of philosophye,
To passen everyche elemente ;
And whan he hath so fer ywente,

Than may be seen, behynde hys bak,
Cloude, and erthe, that Y of spak.   470
    Thoo gan Y wexen in a were,
And seyde, ' Y wote wel Y am here ;
But wher in body or in gost,
I not ywys, but God, thou wost !'
For more clere entendement,
Nas *me* never yit ysent.
And than thought Y on Marcian,
And eke of Anteclaudian,
That sooth was her descripcioun
Of alle hevenes regioun,   480
As fer as that Y sey the preve ;
Therfore Y kan hem now beleve.
    With that this egle began to crye,
' Lat be,' quod he, ' thy fantasye,
Wilt thou lerne of sterres aught ?'
' Nay, certenly,' quod Y, ' ryght naught.'
' And why ?   For Y am now to olde.'
' Elles I wolde the have tolde,'
Quod he, ' the sterres names, lo,
And al the hevenes sygnes ther to,   490
And which they ben.'   ' No fors,' quod I.
' Yis, pardee,' quod ho, ' wostow why ?
For whan thou redest poetrie,
How goddes gonne stellifye
Briddes, fisshe, best, or him, or here,
As the ravene or cyther bere,
Or Arionis harpe fyne,
Castor, Polex, or Delphyne,
Or Athalantes doughtres sevone,
How alle these arne set in hevene ;   500
For though thou have hem ofte on honde,

Yet nostow not wher that they stonde.'
' No fors,' quod Y, ' hyt is no nede,
I leve as wele, so God me spede,
Hem that write of this matere,
Alle though I knew her places here ;
And eke they semen here so bryghte,
Hyt shulde shenden al my syghte,
To loke on hem.' ' That may wel be,'
Quod he. And so forthe bare he me
A while, and than he gan to crye,
That never herd I thing so hye,
' Now up the hede, for alle ys wele ;
Seynt Julyane, loo, bon hostele !
Se here the House of Fame, lo !
Maistow not heren that I do ?'
' What ?' quod I. ' The grete soun,'
Quod he, ' that rumbleth up and doun
In Fames House, ful of tydynges,
Bothe of feire speche and chidynges,
And of fals and that soth compouned ;
Herke wel ; hyt is not rouned.
' Herestow not the grete swogh ?'
' Yis, perde,' quod Y, ' wel ynogh.'
' And what soune is it lyke ?' quod hee.
' Peter ! betynge of the see,'
Quod Y, ' ayen the roches holowe,
Whan tempest doth the shippes swalowe,
And lat a man stonde, out of doute,
A myle thens, and here hyt route.
Or elles lyke the last humblynge
After a clappe of oo thundringe,
When Joves hath the aire ybete
But yt doth me for fere swete.'

' Nay, drede the not therof,' quod he,
Hyt is nothinge wille biten the,
Thou shalt non harme have truely.'
  And with this word both he and Y
As nygh the place arryved were,
As men may casten with a spere.   540
I nyste how, but in a strete
He sette me fair *upon* my fete,
And seyde, ' Walke forth a pace,
And take thyn aventure or case,
That thou shalt fynde in Fames place.'
  ' Now,' quod I, ' while we han space
To speke, or that I goo fro the,
For the love of God, telle me,
In sooth, that wil I of the lere,
Yf thys noyse that I here   550
Be, as I have herd the tellen,
Of folke that doun in erthe dwellen,
And cometh here in the same wyse,
As I the herde, or this, devyse?
And that there lives body nys
In al that hous that yonder ys,
That maketh al this loude fare?'
  ' Noo,' quod he, ' by seynte Clare!
And also wis God rede me,
But o thinge wil Y warne the,   560
Of the whiche thou wolt have wonder.
Loo, to the House of Fame yonder,
Thou wost how cometh every speche,
Hyt nedeth noght efte the to teche.
But understonde now ryght wel this,
Whan any speche ycomen ys
Up to the paleys, anon ryght

Hyt wexeth lyke the same wight,
Which that the worde in erthe spak,
Be hyt clothed rede or blak;
And so were hys lykenesse,
And spake the word, that thou wilt gesse
That it the same body be,
Man or woman, he or she.
And ys not this a wonder thynge?'
' Yis,' quod I tho, ' by heven kynge!'
And with this worde, ' Farewel,' quod he,
' And here I wol abyden the,
And God of hevene sende the grace,
Some goode to lerne in this place.'
And I of him toke leve anoon,
And gan forthe to the paleys goon.

EXPLICIT LIBER SECUNDUS.

LIBER TERTIVS.

O God of science and of lyght,
Apollo, thurgh thy grete myght,
This lytel laste boke thou gye!
Nat that I wilne for maistrye
Here art poetical be shewed.
But, for the ryme ys lyght and lewed,
Yit make hyt sumwhat agreable,
Though somme vers fayle in a sillable;
And that I do no diligence,
To showe crafte, but o sentence.
And yif devyne vertu thow,
Wilt helpe me to shewe now,

That in myn hede ymarked ys,
(Loo, that is for to menen this,
The Hous of Fame for to descryve)
Thou shalt *tho* se *me* go as blyve
Unto the next laurer Y see,
And kysse yt, for hyt is thy tree.
Now entreth in my brest anoon.

    Whan I was fro thys egle goon,   20
I gan beholde upon this place.
And certein, or I ferther pace,
I wol yow al thys shape devyse
Of hous and citee ; and al the wyse
How I gan to *thys* place aproche,
That stood upon so hygh a roche,
Hier stant there noon in Spayne.
But up I clombe with alle payne,
And though to clymbe grevede me,
Yit I ententyf was to see,   30
And for to powren wondre low*e*,
Yf I koude eny weyes know*e*
What maner stoon this roche was,
For hyt was lyke a thynge of glas,
But that hyt shoon ful more clere ;
But of what congeled matere
Hyt was, nyste I redely.
But at the laste espied I,
And founde that hit was everydele,
A roche of yse, and not of stele.   40
Thought I, ' By seynt Thomas of Kent,
This were a feble fundament,
To bilden on a place hye ;
He ought him lytel glorifye
That heron bilte, God so me save !'

Tho sawgh I the *oon* halfe ygrave
With famouse folkes names fele,
That had yben in mochel wele,
And her fames wide yblowe.
But wel unnethes koude I knowe
Any lettres for to rede
Hir names be; for, oute of drede,
They were almost of thowed so,
That of the lettres oon or two
Were molte away of every name,
So unfamouse was wox hir fame;
But men seyn, ' what may ever last*e* ?'
    Thoo gan I in myn hert*e* cast*e*,
That they were molte awey with hete,
And not awey with stormes bete.
For on that other syde I say
Of this hille, that northewarde lay,
How hit was writen ful of names,
Of folkes that hadden grete fames
Of olde tymes, and yet th*ey* wero
As fressh as men had*de* writen hem here
The selfe day, ryght or that oure
That I upon hem gan to poure.
But wel I wiste what yt made;
Hyt was conserved with the shade,
Alle this wrytynge that I sigh,
Of a castel stoode on high;
And stoode eke on so colde a place,
That hete hyt myghte not deface.
    Thoo gan I up the hille to goone,
And fonde upon the cop a woone,
That alle the men that ben on lyve
Ne han the kunnynge to descrive

The beauté of that ylke place,
No coude casten no compace 80
Swich another for to make,
That myght of beauté be hys make;
No wonderlyche so ywrought,
That hyt astonyeth yit my thought,
And maketh alle my wytte to swynke
On thilke castel to bethynke.
So that the grete beauté
The caste, tho curiosité
Ne kan I not to yow devyse,
My wit ne may me not suffise. 90
But natheles alle the substance
I have yit in my remembrance;
For-why me thoughte, by scynte Gyle,
Alle was of stone of beryle,
Bothe castel and the toure,
And eke the halle, and every boure,
Wythouten peces or joynynges.
But many subtile compassinges,
As rabewyures and pynacles,
Ymageries and tabernacles, 100
I say ; and ful eke of wyndowes,
As flakes falle in grete snowes.
And eke in ech of the pynacles
Weren sondry habitacles,
In whiche *stode*, alle withoute,
Ful the castel alle aboute,
Of al maner of mynstralles,
And gestiours, that tellen tales
Bothe of wepinge and of game,
Of alle that longeth unto Fame. 110
    There herd I pleyen upon an harpe

That sowneth bothe wel and sharpe,
Orpheus ful craftely,
And on the syde faste by
Sat the harper Orioun
And Eacides Chiroun.
And other harpers many oon,
And the grete Glascurioun.
And smale harpers with her glees,
Saten under hym in sees;
 And gunne on hym upwardo to gape,
And countrefet hym as an ape,
Or as crafte countrefeteth kynde.
  Tho saugh I stonden hym behynde,
A-fer fro hem, alle be hemselve,
Many thousand tymes twelve,
That maden lowde menstralcies
In cornemuse and shalmyes,
And many other maner pipe,
That craftely begunne to pipe,
Bothe in doucet and in riede,
That ben at festes with the bride.
And many flowte and liltyng horne,
And pipes made of grene corne,
As han thise lytel herde gromes,
That kepen bestis in the bromes.
  Ther saugh I than Atileris,
And of Athenes daun Pseustis,
And Marcia that lost her skynne,
Bothe in face, body, and chynne,
For that she wolde envien, loo,
To pipen bet than Apollo.
  There saugh I famcs, olde and yonge,
Pipers of alle Duche tonge,

To lerne love-daunces, sprynges,
Reues, and these straunge thynges.
  Tho saugh I in another place,
Stonden in a large space
Of hem that maken blody soun,
In trumpe, beme, and claryoun ;   150
For in feight and blodeshedynges
Ys used gladly clarionynges.
  Ther herd I trumpen, Messenus,
Of whom that speketh Vergilius.
  There herd I trumpe Joab also,
Theodomas, and other mo,
And alle that usede clarioun,
In Cataloigne and Aragoun,
That in her tyme famous were
To lerne, saugh I trumpe there.   160
  Ther saugh I sit in other sees,
Pleyinge upon sondry glees,
Whiche that I kannot nevene,
Moo than sterres ben in hevene,
Of whiche I nyl not now ryme,
For ese of yow, and losse of tyme :
For tyme ylost, this knowen ye,
Be no way may recovered be.
  There saugh I pleyen jugelours,
Magiciens, and tregetours,   170
And phitonisses, charmeresses,
Olde wiches, sorceresses,
That use exorsisaciouns,
And eke thes fumygaciouns ;
And clerkes eke, which konne wel
Alle this magikes naturel,
That craftely doon her ententes,

To maken, in certeyn ascendentes,
Ymages, lo, thrugh which magike,
To make a man ben hool or syke. 180
Ther saugh I the quene Medea,
And Circes eke, and Calipsa.
Ther saugh *I* Hermes Ballenus,
Limeote, and eke Symon Magus.
(*Ther sawgh I tho, and knew by name,*
That by such art doon men han fame.)
Ther saugh I Colle Tregetour
Upon a table of sygamour
Pley*en* an uncouthe thynge to telle;
Y saugh him carien a wynd-melle 190
Under a walshe-note shale.
    What shuld I make lenger tale,
Of alle the pepil Y ther say,
Fro hennes into domesday?
    Whan I had al this folkys beholde,
And fonde me louse and noght y*h*olde,
And oft I musede longe while
Upon these walles of berile,
That shoone ful lyghter than a glas,
And made wel more than hit was, 200
To semen every thynge, ywis,
As kynde thynge of Fames is;
I gan to romen til I fonde
The castel yate on my ryght honde,
Which that so wel *y*-corven was,
That never suche another nas;
And yit it was be aventure
Ywrought, as often as be cure.
    Hyt nedeth noght yow more to tellen,
To make yow to longe duellen, 210

Of these yates florisshinges,
Ne of compasses, ne of kervynges,
Ne how they hat in masoncries,
As corbetz, (*ful of imageries.*)
But, Lord! so faire yt was to shewe,
For hit was alle with gold behewe.
But in I went, and that anoon;
Ther mette I cryinge many oon,
' A larges, larges! hald up wel!
God save the lady of thys pel, 220
Our oune gentil lady Fame,
And hem that wilnen to have name
Of us!' Thus herd Y crien alle,
And faste comen out of halle,
And shoon nobles and sterlynges.
And somme crouned were as kynges,
With corounes wroght ful of losynges;
And many ryban, and many frenges
Were on her clothes trewely.
Thoo atte last aspyed Y 230
That pursevauntes and herauldes,
That crien ryche folkes laudes,
Hyt weren; alle and every man
Of hem, as Y yow tellen can,
Had on him throwen a vesture,
Whiche that men clepen a cote armure,
Enbrowded wonderlyche ryche,
As though ther nero nought ylyche.
But noght wyl I, so mote Y thryve,
Ben aboute to dyscryve 240
Alle these armes that ther weren,
That they thus on her cotes beren
For hyt to me were impossible;

Men myghte make of hem a bible,
Twenty foote thykke Y trowe.
For certeyn who-so koude i-knowe
Myghte ther alle the armes seen,
Of famouse folke that han ybeen
In Auffrike, Europe, and Asye,
Syth first began the chevalrie.
   Loo! how shulde I now tel al thys?
   Ne of the halle eke what nede is,
To tellen yow that every walle
Of hit, and flore, and roof, and alle,
Was plated half a foote thikke
Of gold, and that nas no thynge wikke,
But, for to prove in alle wyse,
As fyne as ducat in Venyse,
Of whiche to litel al in my pouche is?
And they wer set as thik of nouchis
Fyne, of the fynest stones faire,
That men reden in the Lapidaire,
As greses growen in a medo.
But hit were alle to longe to redo
The names; and therfore I pace.
But in this lusty and ryche place,
That Fames halle called was,
Ful moche prees of folke ther nas,
Ne crowdyng, for to mochil prees.
But al on hye, above a dees,
Sit in a see imperiall*e*,
That made was of a rubee alle,
Which that a carbunele ys yealled,
Y saugh perpetually ystalled,
A femynyne creature;
That never formed by nature

Nas suche another thing yseye.
For altherfirst, soth for to seye,
Me thought*e* that she was so lyte,
That the lengthe of a 'cubite, 280
Was lengere than she *semede* be ;
This was gret marvaylle to me,
Hir *self* tho so wonderly streight*e*,
That with hir fete the erthe she reight*e*,
And with her hed she touched hevene,
Ther as shynen sterres sevene.
And therto eke, as *to* my witte,
I saugh a gretter wonder yitte,
Upon her eyen to beholde,
But certeyn Y hem never tolde. 290
For as feele yen had*de* she,
As fetheres upon foules be,
Or weren on the bestes foure,
That Goddes trone gunne honoure,
As Johan writ in thapocalips.
Hir heere that oundye was and crips,
As burned gold hyt shoon to see.
And sothe to tellen also shee
Had also fele up stondyng eres
And tonges, as on bestes heres ; 300
And on hir fete wexen saugh Y
Partriches winges redely.
　　But, Lorde ! the perry and the richesse
I saugh sittyng on this godesse !
And, Lord ! the hevenysshe melodye,
Of songes ful of armonye,
I herd aboute her trone ysonge,
That al the paleys walles ronge !
(So songe the myghty Muse, she

That cleped ys Caliope,
And hir eighte sustren eke
That in her face semen meke)
And evermo eternäally,
They synge of Fame as thoo herd Y,
'Heryed be thou and thy name,
Goddesse of renoun or Fame.'
　　Tho was I war, loo, atte laste,
As I myn eyen gan up caste,
That thys ilke noble quene
On her shuldres gan sustene
Bothe armes, and the name
Of thoo that hadde large fame.;
Alexander, and Hercules,
That with a shert hys lyfe les!
And thus fonde Y syttynge this goddesse,
In noble honour and rychesse;
Of which I stynte a while nowe,
Other thinge to tellen yowe.
　　Tho saugh I stonde on cyther syde,
Streighte doun to the dores wide,
Fro the dees many a pelere
Of metal, that shoon not ful clere,
But though they ner of no rychesse,
Yet they were made for gret noblesse,
And in hem gret sentence.
And folkes of digne reverence,
Of whiche I wil yow telle fonde,
Upon tho piler saugh I stonde.
　　Alderfirste loo ther I sighe,
Upon a piler stonde on highe,
That was of lede and yren fyne,
Hym of secte Saturnyne,

Tho Ebrayke Josephus tho olde,
That of Jewes gestes tolde;
And he bare on hys shuldres hye,
The fame up of the Jurye.
And by hym stonden other sevene,
Wise and worthy for to nevene,
To helpen him bere up the charge,
Hyt was so hevy and so large.   350
And for they writen of batayles,
As wel as other olde mervayles,
Therfor was, loo, thys pil*ere*,
Of whiche that I yow telle here,
Of lede and yren bothe ywys.
For yren Martes metal ys,
Which that God is of batayle.
And tho lede withouten faille,
Ys, loo, tho metal of Saturne,
That hath a ful large whele to turne.   360
Thoo stoden forthe on every rowe
Of hem, which that I koude knowe,
Though I hem noght be ordre telle,
To make yow to longe to duelle.
    These, of whiche I gynne rede,
There saugh I stonde, out of drede,
Upon an yren piler stronge,
That peynted was, al endelonge,
With tigres blode in every place,
The Tholauson that high*te* Stace,   370
That bare of Thebes up tho fame
Upon his shuldres, and the name
Also of cruelle Achilles.
And by him stood, withouten lees,
Ful wonder hye on a pilere

Of yren, he, the gret Omere;
And with him Dares and Tytus
Before, and eke he Lollius,
And Guydo eke de Columpnis,
And Englyssh Gaunfride eke, ywis.   380
And eche of these, as have I joye,
Was besye for to bere up Troye.
So hevy therof was the fame,
That for to bere hyt was no game.
But yet I gan ful wel espie,
Betwex hem was a litil envye.
Oon seyde that Omere *made* lyes,
Feynynge in hys poetries,
And was to Grekes favorable;
Therfor held he hyt but fable.   390
 Tho saugh I stonde on a pilere,
That was of tynned yren clere,
That Latyn poete Virgile,
That bore hath up longe while
The fame of pius Eneas.
 And next hym on a piler was
Of coper, Venus clerke, Ovide,
That hath ysowen wonder wide
The grete god of loves name.
And ther he bare up wel hys fame,   400
Upon this piler also hye,
As I myght hyt see *with* myn ye:
For-why this halle of whiche I rede,
Was woxen on high, tho length, and brede,
Wel more be a thousande dele,
Than hyt was erst, that saugh I wel.
 Thoo saugh I on a piler by,
Of yren wroght ful sturnily,

The grete poete, daun Lucan,
And on hys shuldres bare up than,   410
As high as that Y myghte see,
The fame of Julius, and Pompé.
And by him stoden alle these clerkes,
That writen of Romes myghty werkes,
That yif Y wolde her names telle,
Alle to longe most I dwelle.

　And next him on *a* piler stoode
Of soulfre, lyke as he were woode,
　Daun Claudian, the sothe to telle,
That bare up *than* the fame of helle,   420
Of Pluto, and of Proserpyne,
That quene ys of the derke pyne.

　What shulde I more telle of this?
The halle was al ful, ywis,
Of hem that writen al of the olde gestes,
As ben on trees rokes nestes ;
But hit a ful confuse matere
Were al*le* the gestes for to here,
That they of write, and how they hight.
But while that Y beheld thys syght,   430
I herd a noyse aprochen blyve,
That ferd as been doon in an hive,
Ayen her tyme of oute fleyinge ;
Ryght suche a maner murmurynge,
For al the world hyt semede me.

　Tho gan I loke aboute and see,
That ther come entryng into the halle,
A ryght grete companye withalle,
And that of sondry regiouns,
Of alles-kynnes condiciouns,   440
That duelle in erthe under the mone,

Pore and ryche.   And also sone
As they were come into the halle,
They gonne doun on knees falle,
Before this ilke noble quene,
And seyde, ' Graunte us, lady shene,
Eche of us of thy grace a bone !'
And somme of hem she grauntede sone,
And somme she wernede wel and faire ;
And somme she grauntede the contrairo
Of her axyng outterly.
But this I sey yow trewely,
What her cause was, Y nyste.
For *of* this folke ful wel Y wiste,
They hadde good fame eche deserved,
(Although they were diversely served.)
Ryght as her suster, dame Fortune,
Ys wonte to serven in comune.
    Now herke how she gan to paye
That gonne her *of* her grace praye,
And ryght lo, al thys companye
Seyden sooth, and noght a lye.
    ' Madame,' quod they, ' we be
Folke that here besechen the,
That thou graunte us now good fame,
And let our werkes han that name.
In ful recompensacioun
Of good werkes, yive us good renoun.'
    ' I werne yow hit,' quod she, ' anoon,
Ye gete of me good fame noon,
Be God ! and therfore goo your wey.'
    ' Allas,' quod they, ' and welaway !
Telle us what may your cause be.'
    ' For me *ne* lyst hyt noght,' quod she,

'No wyght shal speke of yow, ywis,
Good ne harme, ne that ne this.'
And with that worde she gan to calle
Her messangere that was in halle,
And *bad* that he shulde faste goon,
Upon the peyne to be blynde *anoon*,   480
For Eolus the god of wynde,
'*In Trace there ye shul him finde,*
And bid him bring his clarioun,
That is ful dyvers of his soun,
And hyt *is* cleped Clere Laude,
With which he won*te* is to hiraude
Hem that me list *y*preised be:
And also bid him how that he
Brynge his other clarioun,
That highte Selaundre in every toun,   490
With which he wonte is to diffame
Hem that me liste, and do him shame.
    This messenger gan faste goon,
And founde where in a cave of stoon,
In a contree *that* highte Trace,
This Eolus, with harde grace,
Helde the wyndes in distresse,
And gan hem under him to presse,
That they gonne as beres rore,
He bonde and pressed hem so sore.   500
    This messanger gan faste crie,
'Ryse up,' quod he, 'and faste hye,
Til *that* thou at my lady be;
And take thy clarioun eke with the,
And spede the forth.'   And he anoon,
Toke to a man that highte Tritoun,
Hys clarions to bere thoo,

And lete a certeyn wynde to goo,
And blewe so hydously and hye,
That hyt ne lefte not a skye   510
In alle the welkene longe and brode.
    This Eolus no where abode,
Til he was come to Fames fete,
And eke the man that Triton hete;
And ther he stode as stille as stoon.
And herwithal ther come anoon
Another huge companye
Of goode folke and gunne crie,
'Lady graunte us good fame
And lat oure werkes han that name,   520
Now in honour of gentilesse,
And also God your soule blesse!
For we han wel deserved hyt,
Therfore is ryght that we ben wel quyt.'
    'As thryve I,' quod she, 'ye shal faylle,
Good werkes shal yow noght availle
To have of mo good fame as now.
But wete ye what? Y graunte yow,
That ye shal have a shrewde fame,
And wikkyd loos and worse name,   530
Though ye good loos have *wel* deserved.
Now goo your wey for ye be served;
Have doon! Eolus, let see!
Take forth thy trumpe anon,' quod she;
'That is ycleped Sklaunder lyght,
And blow her loos, that every wight
Speke of hem harme and shrewedenesse,
In stede of good and worthynesse.
For thou shalt trumpe alle the contraire,
Of that they han don wel or fayre.'   540

Allas, thought I, what aventures
Han these sory creatures,
For they amonges al the pres,
Shul thus be shamed gilteles!
But what! hyt moste nedes be.
What dide this Eolus, but he
Toke out hys blake trumpe of bras,
That fouler than the Devel was,
And gan this trumpe for to blowe,
As al the worlde shuld overthrowe.   550
That thrughout every regioun,
Wente this foule trumpes soun,
As swifte as pelet out of gonne,
Whan fire is in the poudre ronne.
And suche a smoke gan out-wende,
Out of his foule trumpes ende,
Blak, bloo, grenyssh, swart, *and* rede,
As dothe where that men melte lede,
Loo, alle on high fro the tuelle.
And therto oo thing saugh I welle,   560
That the ferther that hit ran,
The gretter wexen hit began,
As dooth the ryver from a welle,
And hyt stank as the pitte of helle.
Allas, thus was her shame yronge,
And giltelesse on every tonge.
Tho come the thridde companye,
And gunne up to the dees to hye,
And doun on knes they fille anoon,
And seyde, ' We ben everychoon   570
Folke that *han* ful *truelly*
Deservede fame ryghtfully,
And praye yow hit mot be knowe,

Ryght as hit is, and forth y-blowe.'
 'I graunte,' quod she, 'for me leste
That now your goode werkes be wiste;
And yet ye shul han better loos,
In dispite of alle your foos,
Than worthy is, and that anoon:
Late now,' quod she, 'thy trumpe goon,
Thou Eolus, that is so blake;
And out thyn other trumpe take
That highte Laude, and blowe yt soo
That thrugh the worlde her fame goo,
Esely and not to faste,
That hyt be knowen atte laste.'
 'Ful gladly, lady myn,' he seyde;
And oute hys trumpe of golde he brayde
Anoon, and set hyt to his mouthe,
And blew it est, and west, and southe,
And northe, as lowde as any thunder,
That every wight hath of hit wonder,
So brode hyt ran or than hit stynte.
And, certes, al tho breth that wente
Out of his trumpes mouthe smelde,
As men a potte ful of bawme helde
Amonge a basket ful of roses;
This favour did he til her loses.

  And ryght with this Y gan aspye,
Ther come the fertho companye,
(But certeyn they were wonder fewe)
And gunne stonden in a rowe,
And seyden, 'Certes, lady bryghte,
We han doon wel with al our myghte,
But we no kepen have no fame.
Hide our werkes and our name,

For Goddys love! for certes we
Han certeyn doon hyt for bounté,
And for no maner other thinge.'
'I graunte yow alle your askynge,'   610
Quod she; 'let your werkes be dede.'
  With that aboute Y clywe myn hede,
And saugh anoon the fifte route
That to this lady gunne loute,
And doun on knes anoon to falle;
And to hir thoo besoughten alle,
To hiden her goode werkes eke,
And seyden, they yeven noght a leke
For no fame, ne suche renoun;
For they for contemplacioun,   620
And Goddes love, hadde ywrought,
Ne of fame wolde they nought.
  'What?' quod she, 'and be ye woode?
And wene ye for to doo goode,
And for to have of that no fame?
Have ye dispite to have my name?
Nay, ye shul lyen everychoon!
Blowe thy trumpes and that anoon,'
Quod she, 'thou, Eolus yhote,
And rynge this folkes werkes be note,   630
That alle the worlde may of hyt here.'
And he gan blowe hir loos so clere,
In his golden clarioun,
That thrugh the worlde wente the soun,
Also kenely, and eke so softe,
But atte last hyt was on lofte.
  Thoo come the sexte companye,
And gunne fast on Fame crie.
Ryght verraly in this manere

They seyden :—' Mercy, lady dere !
To telle certeyn as hyt is,
We han doon neither that ne this,
But ydel al oure lyfe ybe.
But, natheles, yet preye we,
That we mowe han as good fame,
And gret renoun and knowen name,
As they that han doon noble gestes,
And acheved alle her lestes,
As wel of love as other thynge ;
Alle was us never broche ne rynge,
Ne elles nought from wymmen sent ;
Ne ones in her *herte* yment,
To make us oonly frendly chere,
But myghten temen us *upon* bere,
Yet lat us to peple seme
Suche as the worlde may of us deme,
That wommen loven us for wode.
Hyt shal doon us a moche goode,
And to oure herte *as* moche avaylle
Tho countrepese, ese, and travaylle,
As we had*de* wonne hyt with labour ;
For that is dere boght honour,
At regard of oure gret ese.
And yet thou most us more plese ;
Let us be holden, eke therto,
Worthy, wise, and goode also,
And riche, and happy unto love.
For Goddes love that sit above,
Thogh we may not the body have
Of wymmen, yet, so God yow save,
Leet men glewe on us the name ;
Suffleeth that we han the fame.'

'I graunte,' quod she, 'be my trouthe!
Now Eolus, withouten slouthe,
Take out thy trumpe of golde,' quod she,
'And blow as they han axed me,
That every man wene hem at ese,
Though they goon in ful bad*de* lese.'
This Eolus gan hit so blowe,
That thrugh the worlde hyt was yknowe.   680

Thoo come the seventh route anoon,
And fel on knees everychoon,
And seyde, 'Lady, graunte us sone
The same thing, the same bone,
That this nexte folke han doon.'

'Fy on yow,' quod she, 'everychoon!
Ye maisty swyne, ye ydel wrechches,
Ful of roten slowe techches!
What? false theves! or ye wolde,
Be famous good, and nothing nolde   690
Deserve why, ne never ye rough*te*
Men rather yow hangen ough*te*!
For ye be lyke the swyn*te* catte,
That wolde have fissh; but wastow what*te*?
He wolde nothinge wete his clowes.
Yvel thrifte come to your jowes,
And eke to myn yif I hit graunte,
Or do yow favour yow to avaunte!
Thou Eolus, thou kynge of Trace,
Goo, blowe this folke a sory grace,'   700
Quod she, 'anoon; and wostow how,
As I shal telle *yow* ryght now.
Sey, These ben that wolden honour
Have, and do nos-kynnes labour,
Ne doo no good, and yet han lawde;

And that men wende that bele Isawde,
Ne coude hem noght of love werne;
And yet she that grynt at*te* querne,
Ys alle to good to ese her herte.'
	This Eolus anoon up sterte,			710
And with his blake clarioun
He gan to blasen out a soun,
As lowde as beloweth wynde in helle.
And eke therwith, sothe to telle,
This soune was so ful of japes,
As ever mowes were in apes.
And that went al the worlde about*e*,
That every wight gan on hem shout*e*,
And for to lawgh as they were wode;
Suche game fonde they in her hode.			720
	Tho come another companye,
That had ydoon the trayterye,
The harme *and* gret*er* wikkednesse,
That any herte kouthe gesse;
And prayed her to han good fame,
And that she nolde doon hem no shame,
But yeve hem loos and good renoun,
And do hyt blowe in a clarioun,
' Nay, wis !' quod she, ' hyt were a vice;
Al be ther in me no justice,			730
Me *ne* lyst not to doo hyt nowe,
Ne this nyl I graunte yowe.'
	Tho come ther lepynge in a route,
And gunne choppen al aboute
Every man upon the crowne,
That alle the halle gan to sowne,
And seyden, ' Lady, leefe and dere,
We ben suche folkes as ye mowe here.

To telle al tho talo aryght,
We ben shrewes every wyght,										740
And han delyte in wikkednes,
As goode folke han in godenes;
And joye to bo knowen shrewes,
And ful of vices and wikked thewes;
Wherefore wo prayen yow a rowe,
That oure fame suche be y-knowe,
In allo thing ryght as hit is.
Y graunte hyt yow,' quod sho, ' ywis.
But what art thow that seyst this tale,
That werest on thy hose a pale,										750
And on thy tipet suche a belle ?'
' Madame,' quod ho, ' sothe to telle,
I am that ylke shrewe, ywis,
That brende the templo of Ysidis
In Athenes, loo, that citee.'
' And wherfor didest thou so ?' quod she.
' By my thrift,' quod he, ' madame,
I wolde fayn han haddo a fame,
As other folke haddo in the toune,
Alle-though they were of grete renoune							760
For her vertue and her thewes,
Thought Y, as gret fame han shrewes,
(Though hit bo noght) for shrewedenesse
As goode folke han for godenesse;
And sith I may not have that oon,
That other nyl Y noght forgoon.
And for to gette of fames hire,
The templo set Y alle a-fire.
Now doon, our loos bo blowen swithe,
As wisly be thou ever blythe.'										770
' Gladly,' quod she.   ' Thow Eolus,

Herestow not what this folke prayen us ?'
' Madame, yis, ful wel,' quod he,
' And I wil trumpen *hit*, parde !'
And toke his blake trumpe faste,
And gan to puffen and to blaste,
Til hyt was at the wor*l*des ende.
　　With that Y gan aboute wende,
For oon that stoode ryght at my bake,
Me thought*e* goodely to me spake,
And seyde, ' Frende, what is thy name ?
Artow come hider to han fame ?'
' Nay, forsothe, frende !' quod I ;
' I cam noght hyder, graunt mercy
For no suche cause, by my hede !
Sufficeth me, as I were dede,
That no wight have my name in honde.
I wote my-self best how Y stonde,
For what I drye or what I thynke,
I wil my selfe alle hyt drynke,
Certeyn for the more parte,
As ferforthe as I kan my*n* arte.'
' But what doost thou here ?' quod he.
Quod Y, ' That wyl Y tellen the,
The cause why Y stonde here.
Somme newe tydyngis for to lere,
Somme newe thinge, Y not what,
Tydynges other this or that,
Of love, or suche thinges glade.
For, certeynly, he that me made
To come hyder seyde me
Y shulde bothe here and se,
In this place, wonder thynges ;
But these be no suche tydynges

As I mene of.—‘Noo?’ quod he.
And I answerede, ‘Noo pardé!
For wel Y wote ever yit,
Sith that first Y hadde wit,
That somme folke han desired fame
Diversly, and loos and name; 810
But certeynly I nyste howe,
Ne where that Fame duelled, er nowe;
And eke of her descripcioun,
Ne also her condicioun,
Ne the ordre of her dome,
Unto the tyme Y thidder come.’
‘ Why than, loo, be these tydynges,
That thou now hider brynges,
That thou hast herde?’ quod he to me;
‘ But now, no fors; for wel Y se 820
What thou desirest for to lere.
Come forth, and stonde no lenger here,
And Y wil the, withouten drede,
In suche another place lede,
Ther thou shalt here many oon.’
 Tho gan I forthe with hym goon,
Oute of the castel, sothe to seye.
Tho saugh Y stond in a valeye,
Under tho castel faste by,
An house, that domus Dedaly, 830
That Laboryntus ycleped ys,
Nas made so wonderlych ywis,
Ne half so queyntelych ywrought.
And evermo, so swyft as thought,
This queynte hous aboute wente,
That nevermo stille hyt stente.
And theroute come so grete a noyse,

That had hyt stonde upon Oyse,
Men myght hyt han herd esely
To Rome, Y trowe sikerly.
And the noyse which I have herde,
For alle the world right so hyt ferde,
As dooth the rowtynge of the stoon,
That from thengyne ys leten goon.
    And al thys hous of whiche Y rede,
Was made of twigges, salwe, rede,
And green eke, and somme weren white,
Swiche as men to these cages thwite,
Or maken of these panyers,
Or elles hattes or dossers ;
That for the swough and for the twygges,
This house was also ful of gygges,
And also ful eke of chirkynges,
And of many other werkynges;—
And eke this hous hath of entrees
As feele as of leves ben on trees,
In somer whan they grene ben,
And on the rove men may yet seen
A thousand holes, and wel moo,
To leten wel the soune oute goo.
And *eke* be day in every tyde
Been a*lle* the dores opened wide,
And *they* be nyght echoon unshet*te,*
No porter ther is noon to lett*e*
No manor tydynges in to pace ;
No never rest is in that place,
That hit nys filde ful of tydynges,
Other loude or of whisprynges ;
And over alle tho houses angles,
Ys ful of rounynges and of jangles,

Of werres, of pes, of mariages,
Of restes, of labour, and of viages,
Of abood, of deeth, of lyfe,
Of love, of hate, acorde, of stryfe,
Of loos, of lore, and of wynnynges,
Of hele, of sekenesse, of bildynges,
Of faire wyndes, of tempestes,
Of qwalme of folke, and eke of bestes ;
Of dyvers transmutacions,
Of estates and eke of regions ;   880
Of trust, of drede, of jelousye,
Of witte, of wynnynge, of folye ;
Of plenté, and of grete famyne,
Of ehepe, of derthe, and of ruyne ;
Of good or mysgovernement,
Of fire, and of dyvers accident.
    And loo, thys hous of which I write,
Syker be ye, hit nas not lyte ;
For hyt was sixty myle of lengthe,
Alle was the tymber of no strengthe ;   890
Yet hyt is founded to endure,
While that hit lyst to Aventure,
That is the moder of tydynges,
As the see of welles and of sprynges ;
And hyt was shapen lyke a cage.
    ' Certys,' quod Y, ' in al myn age,
Ne saugh Y suche a hous as this.'
And as Y wondrede me, ywys,
Upon this hous, tho war was Y,
How that myn egle, faste by,   900
Was perched hye upon a stoon ;
And I gan streghte to hym goon,
And seyde thus :—' Y preye the

That thou a while abide me
For goddis love, and lete me seen
What wondres in this place been;
For yit paraventure Y may lere
Somme good theron, or sumwhat here
That leef me were, or that Y wente.'
  'Petre! that is myn entente,'
Quod he to me; 'therfore Y duelle,
But certeyn oon thyng I the telle,
That, but I bringe the therinne,
Ne shalt thou never kunne gynne
To come into hyt, out of doute,
So faste hit whirleth, lo, aboute.
But sithe that Jovys, of his grace,
As I have seyde, wol the solace,
Fynally with these thinges,
Unkouthe syghtes and tydynges,
To passe with thyn hevynesse,
Soch routhe hath he of thy distresse,
(That thou suffrest debonairly,
And wost thy-selfen outtirly,
Disesperat of alle blys,
Syth that fortune hath made amys
Tho frot of al thyn hertes reste
Languish and eke in poynt to breste,)
That he thrugh hys myghty merite,
Wol do than ese, al be hyt lyte,
And yaf in expresse commaundement,
To whiche I am obedient,
To further the with al my myght,
And wisse and teche the aryght,
Where thou maist most tydynges here,
Shaltow here anoon many oon lere.'

With thi*lke* worde he ryght anoon,
Hente me up bytwexe his toon,
And at a wyndowe yn me broghte,
That in this hous was, as me thoghte;   940
And therwithalle me thought hit stente,
And nothinge hyt aboute wente;
And me set in the flore adoun.
But whiche a congregacioun
Of folke, as I saugh rome aboute,
Some within and some withoute,
Nas never seen, ne shal ben eft,
That, certys, in the worlde nys left,
So many formed be Nature,
Ne dede so many a creature,   . 950
That wel unnethe in that place
Hadde Y a fote brede of space,
And every wight that I saugh there,
Rouned in *eche* others ere,
A newe tydynge prevely,
Or elles tolde alle oppenly
Ryght thus, and seyde, ' Nost not thou
That ys betyd, *late or now.*'
  ' No,' quod he, ' Telle me what.'
And than he tolde hym this and that,   960
And swore therto that hit was sothe,
' Thus hath he sayde,' and ' Thus he dothe,'
And ' Thus shal hit be,' and ' Thus herde Y seye,'
' That shal be founde, that dare I leye.'
That alle the folke that ys a lyve,
Ne han the kunnynge to discryve,
Tho thinges that I herde there,
What aloude, and what in ere.
But al the wonder most was this :—

Whan oon had herde a thinge, ywis,
He come forthright to another wight,
And gan him tellen anon ryght,
The same *thynge* that him was tolde,
Or hyt a forlonge way was olde,
But gan sommewhat for to eche
To this tydynge in this speche
More than hit ever was.
And nat so sone departed nas
That he fro him thoo he ne mette
With the thridde; and, or he lette
Any stounde, he told hym als;
Were the tydynge sothe or fals,
Yit wolde he telle hyt natheles,
And evermo with more encres,
Than yt wase erst.   Thus north and southe,
Went every mothe fro mouthe to mouthe,
And that encresing evermoo,
As fire ys wont to quyk and goo
From a sparke sprongen amys,
Tille alle a citee brent up ys.

   And whan that *hit* was ful yspronge,
And woxen more on every tonge
Than ever hit was, and went anoon
Up to a wyndowe out to goon,
Or but hit myghte oute there pace,
Hyt gan oute crepe at somme crevace,
And flygh forthe faste for the nones.

   And somtyme saugh I thoo, at ones
A lesyng and a sad sothe-sawe,
That gonne of aventure thrawe,
Out to a wyndowe for to pace;
And, when they metten in that place,

They were acheked bothe two,
And neyther of hem most out goo;
For other so they gonne crowde,
Til eche of hem gan crien lowde,
' Lat me go first !'—' Nay, but let me !
And here I wol ensuren the
Wyth the *vowes* that thou wolt do so,
That I shal never fro the go,   1010
But be thyn oune sworen brother !
We wil us medle eche with other,
That no man, bo they never so wrothe,
Shal han *that* on *or* two, but bothe
At ones, al beside his leve,   .
Come we *a* morwe or on eve,
But we cried or stille yrouned.'
Thus saugh I fals and sothe, compouned,
Togeder flo for oo tydynge.

Thus oute at holes gunne wringe   1020
Every tydynge streght to Fame ;
And sho gan yeve eche hys name,
After hir disposicioun,
And yaf hem eke duracioun,
Some to wexe and *wane* sono,
As dothe the faire white mone,
And lete hem goon.   Ther myght Y seen
Wen*g*ed wondres faste fleen,
Twenty thousand in a route,
As Eolus hem blew aboute.   1030
And, lord ! this hous in al*le* tymes
Was ful of shipmen and pilgrimes,
With scrippes bret-ful of lese*yn*gs,
Entremedled with tydynges,
And eke allone bo hemselve.

O, many a thousand tymes twelve
Saugh I eke of these pardoners,
Currours, and eke messangers,
With boystes crammed ful of lyes,
 As ever vessel was with lyes.
And as I alther-fastest wente
About, and did al myn entente,
Me for to pleyen and for to lere,
And eke a tydynge for to here,
That I had herd of somme contré
That shal not now be tolde for me:
For hit no nede is, redely;
Folke kan hit synge bet than I.
For alle mote oute other late or rathe,
Alle the sheves in the lathe.

   I herde a grete noyse withalle
In a corner of the halle,
Ther men of love tydynges tolde,
And I gan thiderwarde beholde;
For I saugh rennynge every wight,
As fast as that they hadden myght;
And everyche criede, 'What thing is that
And somme sayde 'I not never what.'
And whan they were alle on an hepe,
Tho behynde begunne up lepe,
And clamben up on other faste,
And up the noyse an-highen kaste,
And troden faste on otheres heles,
And stampen, as men doon after eles.

   Atte laste I saugh a man,
Whiche that I nat, ne kan,
But he semede for to bo
A man of grete auctorité.

And therewithalle I abrayde
Out of my sleepe, halfe afraide; 1070
Remembring welle what I had*de* seene,
And how hye and ferre I hadde beene
In my goost; and had*de* gret wonder
Of that the god of thunder
Had*de* let me knowen; and began to write
Lyke as yee have herd me endite.
Wherefore to study and rede alway,
I purpose to do day by day.
 Thus in dreaming and in game,
End*eth* this lytel booke of Fame. 1080

HERE ENDETH THE BOOKE OF FAME.

THE PROLOGUE OF NINE GOODE WYMMEN.

A THOUSANDE tymes I have herd telle
There ys joy in hevene, and peyne in helle,
And I acorde wel that it ys so;
But, natheles, yet wot I wel also,
That ther is noon dwellyng in this countree,
That eythir hath in hevene or helle ybe,
Ne may of hit noon other weyes witen,
But as he hath herd seyde, or founde it writen;
For by assay ther may no man it preve.
But God forbede but men shulde leve   1
Wel more thing then men han seen with eye!
Men shal not wenen every thing a lye
But-yf hymselfe yt seeth, or elles dooth;
For, God wot, thing is never the lasse sooth,
Thogh every wight ne may it not ysee.
Bernarde, the monke, ne saugh nat alle pardé!
Than mote we to bokes that we fynde,
(Thurgh which that olde thinges ben in mynde)
And to the doctrine of these olde wyse,
Yeve credence, in every skylful wise,   2(
That tellen of these olde appreved stories,
Of holynesse, of regnes, of victories,
Of love, of hate, and other sondry thynges,

Of whiche I may not maken rehersynges:
And yf that olde bokes were awey,
Ylorne were of remembraunce the key.
Wel ought us, thanne, honouren and beleve
These bokes, there we han noon other preve.
And as for me, though than I konne but lyte,
On bokes for to rede I me delyte,   30
And to hem yive I feyth and ful credence,
And in myn herte have hem in reverence
So hertely, that ther is game noon,
That fro my bokes maketh me to goon,
But yt be seldom on the holy day,
Save, certeynly, whan that the monethe of May
Is comen, and that I here the foules synge,
And that the floures gynnen for to sprynge,
Fairewel my boke, and my devoeioun!
Now have I thanne suche a condicioun,   40
That of alle the floures in the mede,
Thanne love I most thise floures white and rede,
Suche as men callen daysyes in her toune.
To hem have I so grete affeccioun,
As I seyde erst, whanne comen is the May,
That, in my bed ther daweth me no day,
That I nam uppe and walkyng in the mede,
To seen this floure ayein the sonne sprede,
Whan it up rysith erly by the morwe ;
That blisful sight softneth al my sorwe,   50
So glad am I, whan that I have presence
Of it, to doon it alle reverence,
As she that is of alle floures flour,
Fulfilled of al vertue and honour,
And evere iliko faire, and fressh of hewe.
And I love it, and evere ylike newe,

And ever shal, til that myn herte dye;
Al swere I nat, of this I wol nat lye,
Ther lovede no wight hotter in his lyve.
And, whan that hit ys eve, I renne blyve,
As sone as evere the sonne gynneth weste,
To seen this flour, how it wol go to reste,
For fere of nyght, so hateth she derkenesse!
Hire chere is pleynly sprad in the brightnesse
Of the sonne, for ther yt wol unclose.
Allas, that I ne had Englyssh, ryme, or prose,
Suffisant this flour to preyse aryght!
But helpeth ye that han konnyng and myght,
Ye lovers, that kan make of sentement;
In this case oghte ye be diligent,
To forthren me somwhat in my labour,
Whethir ye ben with the leef or with the flour,
For wel I wot, that ye han herbiforne
Of makynge ropen, and lad awey the corne;
And I come after, glenyng here and there,
And am ful glad yf I may fynde an ere
Of any goodly word that ye han loft.
And thogh it happen me rehereen eft
That ye han in your fresshe songes sayede,
Forbereth me, and beth not evele apayede,
Syn that ye see I do yt in the honour
Of love, and eke in service of the flour,
Whom that I serve as I have witte or myght.
She is the clerenesse and the verray lyght,
That in this derke worlde me wynt and ledyth,
The hert in-with my sorwful brest yow dredith,
And loveth so sore, that ye ben verrayly,
The maistresse of my witte, and nothing I.
My worde, my werkes, ys knyt so in youre bond

That as an harpe obeieth to the hond,   90
That maketh it soune after his fyngerynge,
Ryght so mowe ye oute of myn herte bringe
Swich vois, ryght as yow lyst, to laughe or pleyne;
Be ye myn gide, and lady sovereyne.
As to my erthely God, to yowe I calle,
Bothe in this werke, and *in* my sorwes alle.
    But wherfore that I spake to yive credence
To olde stories, and doon hem reverence,
And that men mosten more thyng beleve
Then they may seen at eighe or elles preve;   100
That shal I seyn, whanne that I see my tyme;
I may nat all attones speke in ryme.
My besy gost, that trusteth alwey newe,
To seen this flour so yong, so fressh of hewe,
Constreynede me with so gredy desire,
That in myn herte I feele yet the fire,
That made me to ryse er yt wer day,
And this was now the firste morwe of May,
With dredful hert, and glad devocioun
For to ben at the resurreccioun   110
Of this flour, whan that yt shulde unclose
Agayne the sonne, that roos as rede as rose,
That in the brest was of the beste that day,
That Agenores doghtre ladde away.
And doune on knes anoon ryght I me sette,
And as I koude, this fresshe flour I grette,
Knelyng alwey, til it unclosed was,
Upon the smale, softe, swote gras,
That was with floures swote enbrouded al,
Of swich swetnesse, and swich odour over-al,   120
That for to speke of gomme, or herbe, or tree,
Comparisoun may noon ymaked be;

For yt surmounteth pleynly alle odoures,
And of riche beauté of floures.
Forgeten had*de* the erthe his pore estate
Of wyntir, that him naked made and mate,
And with his swerd of colde so sore greved ;
Now hath thatempre sonne alle that releved
That naked was, and clad yt new agayn.
The smale foules, of the seson fayn,   130
That of the panter and the nette ben scaped,
Upon the foweler, that made hem awhaped
In wynter, and distroyed hadde hire broode,
In his dispite hem thoghte yt did hem goode
To synge of hym, and in hir songe dispise
The foule cherle, that for his coveytise,
Had hem betrayed with his sophistrye.
This was hire songe, ' The foweler we deffye,
And al his crafte.'   And somme songen clere
Layes of love, that joye it was to here,   140
In worshippynge and in preysing of hir make ;
And, for the newe blisful somers sake,
Upon the braunches ful of blosmes softe,
In hire delyt, they turned hem ful ofte,
And songen, 'Blessed be seynt Valentyne !   .
For on his day I chees yow to be myne,
Withouten repentyng, myn herte sweto !'
And therewithalle hire bekes gonnen meete,
Yeldyng honour, and humble obeysaunces
To love, and diden hir othere observaunces   150
That longeth onto love, and to nature ;
Construeth that as yow lyst, I do no cure.
And thoo that hadde doon unkyndenesse,
As dooth the tydif, for nowfangelnesse,
Besoghte mercy of hire trespassynge,

And humblely songe hire repentynge,
And sworen on the blosmes to be trewe,
So that hire makes wolde upon hem rewe,
And at the laste maden hire acorde.
Al founde they Daunger for a tyme a lord,   160
Yet Pitee, thurgh his stronge gentil myght,
Forgaf, and made mercy passen ryght
Thurgh Innocence, and ruled Curtesye.
But I ne clepe yt nat innocence folye,
Ne fals pitee, for vertue is the mene,
As Et*h*ike seith, in swich maner I mene.
And thus thise fowcles, voide of al malice,
Acordeden to love, and laften vice
Of hate, and songe alle of oon acorde,
' Welcome Somer, oure governour and lorde.'   170
And Zepherus, and Flora gentilly
Yav to the floures, softe and tenderly,
Hire swoote breth, and made hem for to sprede,
As god and goddesse of the floury mede.
In whiche me thoght I myghte, day by day,
Dwellen alwey, the joly monyth of May,
Withouten slepe, withouten mete or drynke.
Adoune ful softely I gan to synke,
And lenynge on myn elbowe and my syde,
The longe day I shoope me for tabide   180
For nothing ellis, and I shal nat lye,
But for to loke upon the daysie;
That men by reson wel it calle may
The daisie, or elles the ye of day,
The emperice, and floure of floures alle.
I pray to God that faire mote she falle,
And alle that loven floures, for hire sake:
But, natheles, ne wene nat that I make

In preysing of the flour agayn the leef,
No more than of the corne agayn the sheef: 190
For as to me nys lever noon ne lother,
I nam withholden yit with never nother.
Ne I not who serveth leef, ne who the flour,
Wel browken they her service or labour,
For this thing is al of another tonne,
Of olde storye, er swiche thinge was begonne.

    Whan that the sonne out of the south gan weste,
And that this floure gan close, and goon to reste,
For derknesse of the nyght, the which she dredde,
Home to myn house full swiftly I me spedde   200
To goon to reste, and erly for to ryse,
To seen this flour sprede, as I devyse.
And in a litel herber that I have,
That benched was on turves fressh ygrave,
I bad men sholde me my couche make ;
For deyntee of the newe someres sake,
I bad hem strawen floures on my bed.
Whan I was leyde, and hadde myn eyen hed,
I fel on slepe, in-with an houre or twoo,
Me mette how I lay in tho medewe thoo,   210
To seen this flour. that I love so and drede ;
And from a fer come walkyng in the mede
The God of Love, and in his hande a quene,
And she was clad in real habite grene ;
A fret of gold she hadde next her heer,
And upon that a white corowne she beer,
With flourouns smale, and, I shal nat lye
For al the worlde ryght as a daysye
Ycorouned ys with white leves lyte,
So were the flowrouns of hire coroune white ;   220
For of oo perle, fyne, oriental,

Hire white coroune was imaked al,
For which the white coroune above the grene
Made hire lyke a daysie for to sene,
Considered eke hir fret of golde above.
Yelothed was this myghty God of Love
In silke enbrouded, ful of grene greves,
In-with a fret of rede rose leves,
The fresshest syn the worlde was first begonne.
His gilte here was corowned with a sonne   230
In stede of golde, for hevynesse and wyghte;
Therwith me thoght his face shoon so brighte
That wel unnethes myght I him beholde;
And in his hande me thoght I saugh him holde
Twoo firy dartes, as the gledes rede,
And aungelyke hys wynges saugh I sprede.
And, al be that men seyn that blynd ys he,
Algate me thoghte that he myghte se;
For sternely on me he gan byholde,
So that his loking dooth myn herte colde.   240
And by the hande he helde this noble quene,
Corowned with white, and clothed al in grene,
So womanly, so benigne, and so meke,
That in this world, thogh that men wolde seke,
Half of hire beuté shulde men nat fynde
In creature that formed ys by kynde.
And therfore may I seyn, as thynketh me,
This songe in preysyng of this lady fre.

Hyd, Absalon, thynne gilte tressis clere;
Ester, ley thou thy mekenesse al adown;   250
Hyde, Jonathas, al thy frendly manere;
Penelopee, and Marcia Catoun,
Make of youre wifhode no comparysoun;

Hyde ye youre beautes, Ysoude and Eleyne,
My lady comith, that al this may disteyne.

Thy faire body lat yt nat appere,
Lavyne; and thou Lucresse of Rome toune,
And Polixene, that boghten love so dere,
And Cleopatre, with al thy passyoun,
Hyde ye your trouthe of love, and your renoun, :
And thou, Tesbé, that hast of love suche peyne,
My lady comith, that al this may disteyne.

Hero, Dido, Laudomia, alle yfere,
And Phillis, hangyng for thy Demophoun,
And Canace, espied by thy chere,
Ysiphile betraysed with Jasoun,
Maketh of your trouthe neythir boost ne soun,
Nor Ypermystre, or Adriane, ye tweyne,
My lady cometh, that all this may dysteyne.

   This balade may ful wel ysongen be, :
As I have seyde erst, by my lady fre;
For certeynly al thise mowe nat suffise,
To apperen wyth my lady in no wyse.
For as the sonne wole the fire disteyne,
So passeth al my lady sovereyne,
That ys so good, so faire, so debonayre,
I prey to God that ever falle hire faire.
For nadde comfort ben of hire presence,
I hadde ben dede, withouten any defence,
For drede of Loves wordes, and his chere, :
As, when tyme ys, herafter ye shal here.
   Behynde this God of Love upon the grene
I saugh comyng of ladyes nientene
In real habite, a ful esy paas;

And after hem come of wymen swich a traas,
That syn that God Adam hadde made made of erthe,
The thridde part of mankynde, or the ferthe,
Ne wende I nat by possibilitee,
Had ever in this wide worlde ybee,
And trewe of love, thise women were echon.   290
Now wheither was that a wonder thing or non,
That ryght anoon, as that they gonne espye
This flour, which that I clepe the daysie,
Ful sodeynly they stynten al attones,
And knelede doune, as it were for the nones,
And songen with o vois, ' Heel and honour
To trouthe of womanhede, and to this flour
That bereth our alder pris in figurynge,
Hire white corowne beryth the witnessynge ?'
And with that word, a-compas enviroun,   300
They setten hem ful softely adoun.
First sat the God of Love, and syth his quene
With the white corowne, clad in grene ;
And sithen al the remenaunt by and by,
As they were of estaat, ful curteysly,
Ne nat a worde was spoken in the place,
The mountaunce of a furlong wey of space.
    I, knelyng by this floure, in good entente
Aboode, to knowen what this peple mente,
As stille as any ston ; til at the laste   310
This God of Love on me hyse eighen caste,
And seyde, ' Who kneleth there ?' and I answerde
Unto his askynge, whan that I it herde,
And seyde, ' It am I,' and come him nere,
And salwed him. Quod he, ' What dostow here,
So nygh myn oune floure, so boldely ?
Yt were better worthy trewely

A worme to neghen ner my flour than thow.'
' And why, sire,' quod I, ' and yt lyke yow?
' For thow,' quod he, ' art therto nothing able. 320
Yt is my relyke, digne and delytable,
And thow my foo, and al my folke werreyest,
And of myn olde servauntes thow mysseyest,
And hynderest hem, with thy translacioun,
And lettest folke from hire devocioun
To serve me, and holdest it folye
To serve Love.   Thou maist it nat denye,
For in pleyne text, withouten nede of glose,
Thou hast *translated* the Romaunce of the Rose,
That is an heresye ayeins my lawe, 330
And makest wise folke fro me withdrawe ;
And of Cresyde thou hast seyde as the lyste,
That maketh men to wommen lasse triste,
That ben as trewe as ever was any steel,
Of thyn answere avise the ryght weel,
For thogh thou reneyed hast my lay,
As other wrecches han doon many a day,
By seynte Venus, that my moder ys,
If that thou lyve, thou shalt repenten this
So cruelly, that it shal wele be sene.' 340
    Thoo spake this lady, clothed al in greene,
And seyde, ' God, ryght of youre curtesye,
Ye moten herken yf he can replye
Agayns al this that ye have to him meved ;
A God ne sholde nat be thus agreved,
But of hys deitee he shal be stable,
And therto gracious and merciable.
And yf ye nere a God that knowen alle,
Thanne myght yt be as I yow tellen shalle ;
This man to yow may falsly ben accused, 350

Ther as by right him oughte ben excused ;
For in youre courte ys many a losengeour,
And many a queinte totolere accusour,
That tabouren in youre eres many a sown,
Ryght aftir hire ymagynacioun,
To have youre daliance, and for envie.
Thise ben the causes, and I shal nat lye,
Envie ys lavendere of the court alway ;
For she ne parteth neither nyght ne day,
Out of the house of Cesar, thus seith Dante ;   360
Who so that gooth, algate she wol nat wante.
   ' And eke, parauntere, for this man ys nyce,
He myghte doon yt, gessyng no malice ;
For he useth thynges for to make,
Hym rekketh noght of what matere he take ;
Or him was boden maken thilke tweye
Of somme persone, and durste yt nat withseye ;
Or him repenteth outrely of this.
He ne hath nat doon so grevously amys,
To translaten that olde clerkes writen,   370
As thogh that he of malice wolde editen,
Despite of Love, and had himselfe yt wroght.
This shoolde a ryghtwis lord have in his thought,
And nat be lyke tirauntes of Lumbardye,
That han no reward but at tyrannye.
For he that kynge or lorde ys naturel,
Hym oghte nat be tiraunt ne crewel,
As is a fermour, to doon the harme he kan ;
He moste thinke yt is his leege man,
And is his tresour, and his gold in cofre.   380
This is the sentence of the philosophre :
A kyng to kepe hise leeges in justice,
Withouten doute that is his office.

Al wol he kepe hise lordes in hire degree,
As it ys ryght and skilful that they bee
Enhaunced and honoured, and most dere,
For they ben half goddys in this world here,
Yit mote he doon bothe ryght to poore and ry
Al be that hire estaate be nat yliche;
And han of poore folke compassyoun.
For loo, the gentil kynde of the lyoun!
For whan a flye offendith him or biteth,
He with his tayle awey the flye smyteth
Al esely; for of his gentrye
Hym deyneth nat to wreke hym on a flie,
As dooth a curre, or elles another best.
In noble corage oughte ben arest,
And weyen every thing by equytee,
And ever have rewarde unto his owen degree.
For, syr, yt is no maistrye for a lorde
To dampne a man, without answere of wor̈de,
And for a lorde, that is ful foule to use.
And it so be, he may hym nat excuse,
But asketh mercy with a dredeful herte,
And profereth him, ryght in his bare sherte,
To ben ryght at your owen jugement,
Than oght a God, by short avysement,
Consydre his owne honour, and hys trespas;
For syth no caus of dethe lyeth in this caas,
Yow oghte to ben the lyghter merciable;
Leteth youre ire, and beth sumwhat tretable!
The man hath served yow of his kunnyng,
And furthred wol youre lawe in his makyng.
Al be hit that he kan nat wel endite,
Yet hath he made lewde folke delyte
To serve you, in preysinge of your name.

He made the book that hight the Hous of Fame,
And eke the Deeth of Blaunche the Duchesse,
And the Parlement of Foules, as I gesse,
And al the Love of Palamon and Arcite   420
Of Thebes, thogh the storye ys knowen lyte;
And many an ympne for your haly dayes,
That highten Balades, Roundels, Virelayes.
And for to speke of other holynesse,
He hath in prose translated Boece,
And made the Lyfe also of Seynt Cecile.
He made also, goon ys a grete while,
Origenes upon the Maudeleyne.
Hym oughte now to have the lesse peyne,
He hath maade many a lay, and many a thynge. 430
    ' Now as ye be a God, and eke a kynge,
I your Alceste, whilom quene of Trace,
I aske yow this man, ryght of your grace,
That ye him never hurte in al his lyve,
And he shal sweren to yow, and that blyve,
He never more shal agilten in this wyse,
But shal maken, as ye wole devyse,
Of wommen trewe in lovyng al hire lyf,
Wher so ye wol, of mayden or of wyf,
And forthren yow as muche as he mysseyde,   440
Or in the Rose, or elles in Creseyde.'
    The God of Love answerede hire anoon,
' Madame,' quod he, ' it is so long agoon
That I yow knewe so charitable and trewe,
That never yit, syn that the worlde was newe,
To me ne founde Y better noon than yee;
If that ye wolde save my degree,
I may ne wol nat *werne* your requeste;
Al lyeth in yow, dooth wyth hym as yow liste.

I al foryeve withouten lenger space ;　　450
For who-so yeveth a yifte or dooth a grace,
Do it bytyme, his thank ys wel the more,
And demeth ye what he shal do therfore.
Goo thanke now my lady here,' quod he.
I roos, and doune I sette me on my knee,
And seyde thus :—' Madame, the God above
Foryelde yow that the God of Love
Han maked me his wrathe to foryive,
And grace so longe for to lyve,
That I may knowe soothly what ye bee,　　460
That han me holpe, and put me in this degree.
But trewely I wende, as in this cas
Naught have agilt, ne doon to love trespas ;
For-why a trewe man, withouten drede,
Hath nat to parten with a theves dede.
Ne a trewe lover oghte me not to blame,
Thogh that I spake a fals lovere som shame.
They oghte rather with me for to holde,
For that I of Creseyde wroot or tolde,
Or of the Rose, what-so myn auctour mente,　　470
Algate, God woot, yt was myn entente
To forthren trouthe in love, and yt cheryce,
And to ben war fro falsnesse and fro vice,
By swiche ensample ; this was my menynge.'
　　And she answerde, ' Lat be thyn arguynge,
For love ne wol nat countrepleted be
In ryght ne wrong, and lerne that of me ;
Thow hast thy grace, and holde the ryght therto.
Now wol I seyn what penance thou shalt do
For thy trespas, understonde yt here :—　　480
Thou shalt while that thou lyvest, yere by yere,
The moste partye of thy tyme spende

In makyng of a glorious legende,
Of goode wymmen, maydenes, and wyves,
That weren trew in lovyng al hire lyves ;
And telle of false men that hem bytraien,
That al here lyf ne don nat but asayen
How many women they may doon a shame,
For in your worlde that is now holde a game.
And thogh the lyke nat a lovere bee,   490
Speke wel of love; this penance yive I the.
And to the God of Love I shal so preye,
That he shal charge his servauntes, by any weye,
To forthren thee, and wel thy labour quyte :
Goo now thy weye, this penaunce ys but lyte.
And whan this book ys made, yive it the quene
On my byhalfe, at Eltham, or at Sheene.'
    The god of love gan smyle, and than he seyde :—
' Wostow,' quod he, ' wher this be wyf or mayde,
Or queene, or countesse, or of what degre,   500
That hath so lytel penanee yiven thee,
That hast deserved sore for to smerte ?
But pité renneth soone in gentil herte :
That maistow seen, she kytheth what she ys.'
And I answerde, ' Nay, sire, so have I blys,
No more, but that I see wel she is good.'
' That is a trewo tale, by myn hood !'
Quod Love, ' and thou knowest wel, pardee,
If yt be so that thou avise the.
Hastow nat in a book lyth in thy cheste,   510
The grete goodnesse of the quene Alceste,
That turned was into a dayesye ?
She that for hire housbonde chees to dye,
And eke to goon to helle, rather than he,
And Ercules rescowed hire, pardé,

And broght hir out of helle agayne to blys?'
And I answerde ageyn, and sayde, ' Yis,
Now knowe I hire.   And is this good Alceste,
The dayesie, and myn owene hertes reste?
Now fele I weel the goodnesse of this wyf,   520
That both after hir deth, and in hir lyf,
Hir grete bounté doubleth hir renoun.
Wel hath she quyt me myn affeccioun,
That I have to hire flour the dayesye.
No wonder ys thogh Jove hire stellyfye,
As telleth Agaton, for *hire* goodenesse,
Hire white corowne berith of hyt witnesse;
For also many vertues hadde shee,
As smale *florouns* in hire corowne bee.
In remembraunce of hire and in honoure   530
Cibella maade the dayesye and tho floure
Ycrowned al with white, as men may see,
And Mars yaf to hire *a* corowne reede, pardee,
In stede of rubyes sette among tho white.'
Therwith this queene wex reed for shame a lyte,
Whanne she was preysed so in hire presence.
Thanne seyde Love, ' A ful grete necligence
Was *yt* to the, that ilke tyme thou made,
' Hyd Absolon thy tresses' in balade,
That thou forgate hire in thy songe to sette,   540
Syn that thou art so gretly in hire dette,
And wost wel that kalender ys shee
To any woman that wol lover bee:
For she taught al the crafte of fyne lovyng,
And namely of wyfhode the lyvyng,
And *alle* tho boundes that she oghte kepe;
Thy litel witte was thilke tyme aslepe.
But now I charge the upon thy lyfe,

That in thy legende thou make of thys wyfe,
Whan thou hast other smale ymaade before; 550
And fare now wel, I charge thee na more.
But er I goo, thus muche I wole the telle,
Ne shal no trewe lover come in helle.
Thise other ladies sittynge here arowe,
Ben in thy balade, yf thou kanst hem knowe,
And in thy bookes alle thou shalt hem fynde;
Have hem in thy legende now alle in mynde,
I mene of hem that ben in thy knowyng.
For here ben twenty thousande moo sittyng
Thanne thou knowest, goode wommen alle, 560
And trewe of love for oght that may byfalle;
Make tho metres of hem as the lest;
I mot goon home, tho sonne draweth west,
To Paradys, with al thise companye;
And serve alwey the fresshe daysye.
At Cleopatre I wole that thou begynne,
And so forthe, and my love so shalthou wynne;
For lat see now what man that lover be,
Wol doon so stronge a peyne for love as she.
I wot wel that thou maist nat al yt ryme, 570
That swiche lovers dide in hire tyme;
It were to long to reden and to here;
Sufficeth me thou make in this manere,
That thou reherce of al hir lyfe the grete,
After thise olde auctours lysten for to trete.
For who-so shal so many a storye telle,
Sey shortly or he shal to longe dwelle.'
And with that worde my bokes gan I take,
And ryght thus on my legende gan I make.

INCIPIT LEGENDA CLEOPATRIE MAR-
TIRIS, EGIPTI REGINE.

FTER the deth of Tholomé the kyng,
That al Egipte hadde in his governyng,
Regned hys queene Cleopataras ;
Til on a tyme befel ther swich a cas,
That out of Rome was sent a senatour,
For to conqueren regnes and honour,
Unto the toune of Rome, as was usaunce,
To have the worlde at hir obeysaunce,
And sooth to seye, Antonius was his name.
So fil yt, as Fortune hym oght a shame,   10
Whanne he was fallen in prosperitee,
Rebel unto the toune of Rome ys hee.
And over al this, the suster of Cesar
He lafte hir falsly, er that she was war,
And wold algates han another wyf,
For which he took with Rome and Cesar strif.
    Natheles, forsooth this ilke senatour,
Was a full worthy gentil werreyour,
And of *his* deeth it was ful gret damage.
But Love had*de* brought this man in swich a rage, 20
And him so narwe bounden in his laas,
Allo for tho love of Cleopataras,
That al the worlde he sette at noo value ;
Hym thoghte ther was nothing to him so due
As Cleopataras for to love and serve ;
Hym roghte nat in armes for to sterve
In tho defence of hir and of hir ryght.

This noble queené ek lovede so this knyght,
Thurgh his desert and for his chivalrye;
As certeynly, but-yf that bookes lye,   30
He was of persone, and of gentilesse,
And of discrecion, and of hardynesse,
Worthy to any wight that liven may;
And she was faire, as is the rose in May.
And to maken shortely is the beste,
She wax his wif, and hadde him as hir leste.

The weddyng and the feste to devyse,
To me that have ytake swich emprise,
Of so many a storye for to make,
Yt were to longe, lest that I sholde slake   40
Of thing that beryth more effecte and charge;
For men may overlade a shippe or barge.
And forthy, to effect than wol I skyppe,
And al the remenaunt I wol let yt slyppe.

Octovyan, that woode was of this dede,
Shoop him an oost on Antony to lede,
Al outerly for his destructioun,
With stoute Romaynes, crewel as lyoun;
To shippe they wente, and thus I let hem sayle.

Antonius, that was war, and wol nat fayle   50
To meten with thise Romaynes, yf he may,
Took eke his rede, and booth upon a day
His wyf and he and al hys oost forthe wente
To shippe anoon, no lenger they ne stente,
And in tho see hit happed hem to mete.
Up gooth the trumpe, and for to shoute and shete,
And paynen hem to sette on with the sonne;
With grisly soune out gooth the grete gonne,
And hertely they hurtelen al attones,
And fro the toppe doune cometh the grete stones.

In gooth the grapenel so ful of crokes,   61
Amonge the ropes, and the sheryng hokes ;
In with the polax preseth he and he ;
Byhynde the maste begynneth he to fle,
And out agayn, and dryveth hym over borde ;
He styngeth hym upon hys speres orde ;
He rent the sayle with hokes lyke a sithe ;
He bryngeth the cuppe, and biddeth hem be blithe ;
He poureth pesen upon the hacches slidre,
With pottes ful of lyme, they goon togedre.   70
And thus the longe day in fight they spende
Til at the last, as every thing hath ende,
Antony is shent, and put hym to the flyght*e*,
And al hys folke to-goo, that best goo mygh*e*.
Fleeth ek the queene with al hir purpre sayle,
For strokes which that went as thik as hayle ;
No wonder was, she myght it nat endure.
And whan that Antony saugh that aventure,
‘ Allas,’ quod he, ‘ the day that I was borne !
My worshippe in this day thus have I lorne !’   80
And for dispeyre out of hys wytte he sterte,
And roof hymself anoon thurghout the herte,
Er that he ferther went out of the place.
Hys wyf, that koude of Cesar have no grace,
To Egipte is fled, for drede and for distresse.
But herkeneth ye that speken of kyndenesse.

    Ye men that falsly sweren many an oothe,
That ye wol dye yf that your love be wroothe,
Here may ye seen of women which a trouthe.
This woful Cleopatrie hath made swich routhe,   90
That ther nys tonge noon that may yt telle.
But on the morowe she wol no lenger dwelle,
But made hir subtil werkmen make a shryne
Of *ulle* the rubees and the stones fyne

In al Egipte that she koude espye;
And put ful the shryne of spicerye,
And let the corps enbawme; and forth she fette
This dede corps, and in the shryne yt shette.
And next the shryne a pitte than dooth she grave,
And alle the serpentes that she myght have,   100
She put hem in that grave, and thus she seyde:—
' Now, love, to whom my sorweful hert obeyde,
So ferforthely, that fro that blysful houre
That I yow swor to ben al frely youre;
(I mene yow, Antonius, my knyght,)
That never wakyng in the day or nyght,
Ye nere out of myn hertes remembraunce,
For wele or woo, for carole, or for daunce;
And in my self this covenaunt made I thoo,
That ryght swich as ye felten wele or woo,   110
As ferforth as yt in my powere lay,
Unreprovable unto my wifhood ay,
The same wolde I felen, life or dethe;
And thilke covenaunt while me lasteth breethe
I wol fulfille; and that shal wel be scene,
Was never unto hir love a trewer queene.'
And wyth that worde, naked, with ful good herte,
Amonge the serpents in the pit she sterte.
And ther she chees to han hir buryinge.
Anoon the neddres gonne hir for to stynge,   120
And she hir deeth receveth with good chere,
For love of Antony that was hir so dere.
And this is storial, sooth it ys no fable.
Now er I fynde a man thus trewe and stable,
And wolde for love his deeth so frely take,
  I prey God lat oure hedes nevere ake!

EXPLICIT LEGENDA CLEOPATRE MARTYRIS.

INCIPIT LEGENDA TESBE BABILON,
MARTIRIS.

T Babiloyne whylom fil it thus,
The whiche toune the queene Simyram
Leet dichen al about, and walles mak
Ful hye, of harde tiles wel ybake:
There were dwellynge in this noble toune,
Two lordes, which that were of grete renoune.
And woneden so neigh upon a grene,
That ther nas but a stoon wal hem betwene,
As ofte in grette tounes ys the wone.
And sooth to seyn, that o man had a sone,
Of al that londe oon the lusticste;
That other had a doghtre, the faireste
That esteward in the worlde was tho dwellynge.
The name of everyche gan to other sprynge,
By wommen that were neyghebores aboute;
For in that contre yit, wythouten doute,
Maydenes ben ykept for jelousye
Ful streyte, leste they diden somme folye.
    This yonge man was cleped Piramus,
Tesbé highte the maide (Naso scith thus).
And thus by reporte was hir name yshove,
That as they wex in age, wax hir love.
And certeyne, as by reson of hir age,
Ther myghte have ben betwex hem mariage,
But that hir fadres nold yt not assente,
And booth in love ylike soore they brente,

That noon of al hir frendes myghte yt lette.
But prevely sommtyme yit they mette
Be sleight, and spoken somme of hir*e* desire,
As wre the glede and hotter is the fire;   30
Forbeede a love, and it is ten times so woode.
    This wal, which that bitwixe hem bothe stoode,
Was cloven atwoo, right fro the toppe adoune,
Of olde tyme, of his foundacioun.
But yit this clyft was so narwe and lite
Yt was nat seene, deero ynogh a myte;
But what is that that love kannat espye?
Ye lovers twoo, yf that I shal nat lye,
Ye founden first this litel narwe elifte,
And with a soune as softe as any shryfte,   40
They leete hir wordes thurgh the clifte pace,
And tolden, while that they stoden in the place,
Al hir*e* compleynt of love, and al hire woo.
At every tyme whan they dorste soo,
Upon the o syde of the walle stood he,
And on that other syde stood Tesbé,
The swoote soune of other to receyve.
And thus *here* wardeyns wolde they disceyve,
And every day this walle they wolde threete,
And wisshe to God that it were doune ybete.   50
Thus wolde they seyn :—' Allas, thou wikked walle!
Thurgh thyn envye thow us lettest alle!
Why nyltow cleve, or fallen al atwo?
Or at the leest*e*, that thow wouldest so,
Yit woldestow but ones let us meete,
Or oones that we myght*e* kyssen sweete,
Than were we covered of oure cares colde.
But natheles, yit be we to the holde,
In as muche as thou suffrest for to goon

Our wordes thurgh thy lyme and eke thy stoon, 60
Yet oght*e* we with the ben wel apayede.'
    And whan these idel wordes weren sayde,
The colde walle they wolden kyssen of stoon,
And take hir leve, and foorth they wolden goon.
Alle this was gladly in the evetyde,
Or wonder erly, lest men it espyede.
And longe tyme they wroght in this manere,
Til on a day, whan Phebus gan to clere,
Aurora with the stremes of hire hete,
Had*de* dried uppe the dewe of herbes wete,   70
Unto this clyfte, as it was wont to bê,
Come Piramus, and after come Tesbé.
And plighten trouthe fully in here faye,
That ilke same nyght to steele awaye,
And to begile hire wardeyns everychone,
And forth out of the citee for to gone.
And, for the feeldes ben so broode and wide,
For to meete in o place at o tyde,
They sette markes; hire metyng sholde bee
Ther kyng Nynus was graven, under a tree;   80
(For olde payens, that ydoles heriede,
Useden thoo in feeldes to ben beriede)
And faste by *his* grave was a welle.
And shortly of this tale for to telle,
This covenaunt was affermed wonder faste,
And longe hem thoghte that the sonne laste,
That it nere *goon* under the see adoune.
    This Tesbé *hath* so greete affeccioun,
And so grete lykynge Piramus to see,
That whan she seigh hire tyme myghte bee,   90
At nyght she stale awey ful prevely,
With hire face ywympled subtilly.

For al hire frendes, for to save hire trouthe,
She hath forsake; allas, and that is routhe,
That ever woman wolde be so trewe,
To trusten man, but she the bet hym knewe!
And to the tree she gooth a ful goode paas,
For love made hir so hardy in this caas;
And by the welle adoune she gan hir dresse.
Allas! than comith a wilde leonesse   100
Out of the woode, withouten more arreste,
With blody moouth of strangelynge of a beste,
To drynken of tho welle ther as she sat.
And whan that Tesbé had espyed that,
She ryst hire up, with a ful drery herte,
And in a cave, with dredful foot she sterte,
For by the moone she saugh yt wel withalle.
And as she ranne, hir wympel leet she falle,
And tooke noon hede, so soore she was awhaped,
And eke so glad that she was escaped;   110
And ther she sytte, and darketh wonder stille.
Whan that this lyonesse hath dronke hire fille,
Aboute tho welle gan she for to wynde,
And ryght anoon the wympil gan she fynde,
And with hir blody mouth it al to-rente.
Whan this was don, no lenger she ne stent*e*,
But to the woode hir wey than hath she nome.
    And at the laste this Piramus ys come,
But al to longe, allas, at home was hee!
Tho moone shoone, men myghte wel ysee,   120
And in hys wey, as that he come ful faste,
Hise eighen to the grounde adoune he caste;
And in tho sonde as he behelde adoune,
Ho seigh the steppes broode of a lyoune;
And in his herte ho sodeynly agroos,

And pale he wex, therwith his heer aroos,
And nere he come, and founde the wimpel torne.
' Allas,' quod he, ' the day that I was borne !
This oo nyght wol us lovers boothe slee !
How shulde I axen mercy of Tesbee,   13
Whan I am he that have yow slayne, allas ?
My byddyng hath *i*-slayn yow in this caas !
Allas, to bidde a woman goon by nyghte
In place thereas a peril fallen myghte !
And I so slowe ! allas, I ne hadde bee ··
Here in this place, a furlong wey or yee !
Now what lyon that be in this foreste,
My body mote rente, or what beste
That wilde is, gnawen mote he now my herte !'
And with that worde he to the wympel sterte, 14
And kiste it ofte, and wepte on it ful sore ;
And seyde, ' Wympel, allas ! ther nys no more,
But thou shalt feele as wel the blode of me,
As thou hast felt the bledynge of Tesbé.'
And with that worde he smot hym to the herte ;
The blood out of the wounde as brode sterte
As water, whan the conduyte broken ys.
    Now Tesbé, which that wyste nat this,
But syttyng in hire drede, she thoghte thus :—
' Yf *it* so falle that my Piramus   15
Be comen hider, and may me nat fynde,
He may me holden fals, and ek unkynde.'
And oute she comith, and after hym gan espien,
Booth with hire hert, and with hire eighen ;
And thoghte, ' I wol him tellen of my drede,
Booth of the lyonesse and al my dede.'
And at the laste hire love than hath she founde,
Betynge with his helis on the grounde,

Al blody; and therwithal abak she sterte,
And lyke the wawes quappe gan hir herte,   160
And pale as boxe she wax, *and* in a throwe
Avised hir, and gan him wel to knowe,
That it was Piramus, hire herte dere.
    Who koude write which a dedely chere
Hath Tesbé now? and how hire heere she rente?
And how she gan hir selve to turmente?
And how she lyth and swowneth on the grounde?
And how she wepe of teres ful his wounde?
How medeleth she his blood with hir compleynte?
How with his blood hir selven gan she peynte?
How clippeth she the dede corps? allas!   171
How dooth this woful Tesbé in this cas?
How kysseth she his frosty mouthe so colde?   .
· Who hath doon this? and who hath ben so bolde
To sleen my leefe? O speke Piramus!
I am thy Tesbé, that thee calleth thus!'
And therwithal she lyfteth up his heed.
    This woful man that was nat fully deed,
Whan that he herde the name of Tesbé crien,
On hire he caste his hevy dedely eyen,   180
And doune agayn, and yeldeth up the gooste.
    Tesbo rist uppe, withouten noyse or booste,
And saugh hir wympel and his empty shethe,
And eke his swerde, that him hath doon to dethe.
Than spake she thus:—'Thys woful hande,' quod
        she,
'Ys strong ynogh in swiche a werke to me;
For love shal me yive strengthe and hardynesse,
To make my wounde large ynogh, I gesse.
I wole the folowen deede, and I wol be
Felawe, and cause eke of thy deeth,' quod she. 190

' And thogh that nothing save the deth oonly,
Myghte the fro me departe trewely,
Thou shal noo more now departe fro me
Than fro the deth, for I wol goo with the.
    ' And now ye wrecched jelouse fadres oure,
We that weren whilome children youre,
We prayen yow, withouten more envye
That in oo grave we moten lye,
Syn love hath us broght this pitouse ende.
And ryghtwis God to every lover sende,
That loveth trewely, moore prosperité
Than ever hadde Piramus and Tesbé.
And let noo gentile woman hire assure,
To putten hire in swiche an aventure.
But God forbede but a woman kan
Ben as trewe and lovynge as a man,
And for my parte I shal anoon it kythe.'
And with that worde his swerde she took as-swith
That warme was of hire loves blood, and hoote,
And to the herte she hire selven smoote.
    And thus are Tesbé and Piramus agoo.
Of trewe men I fynde but fewe moo
In al my bookes, save this Piramus,
And therfore have I spoken of hym thus.
For yt is deyntee to us men to fynde
A man that kan in love be trewe and kynde.
    Here may ye seen, what lover so he be,
A woman dar and kan as wel as he.

EXPLICIT LEGENDA TESBE.

INCIPIT LEGENDA DIDONIS, MARTIRIS

CARTHAGINIS REGINE.

GLORIE and honour, Virgile Mantuan,
Be to thy name! and I shal as I kan
Folowe thy lanterne as thou goste byforn,
How Eneas to Dido was forsworne,
In thyne Eneyde. And of Naso wol I take
The tenour and the grete effectes make.
    Whan Troy i-broght was to destruccion
By Grekes sleight, and namely by Synon,
Feynyng the hors offred unto Minerve,
Thurgh which that many a Trojan moste sterve,   10
And Ector had after his deeth appered;
And fire so woode, it myghte nat ben stered,
In al the noble tour of Ylion,
That of the citee was the cheef dungeon;
And al the contree was so lowe ybroght,
And Priamus the kyng fordoon and noght;
And Eneas was charged by Venus
To fleen away; he tooke Ascanius
That was his sone in his ryght hande and fledde,
And on his bakke he baar, and with him ledde   20
His olde fader, cleped Anchises;
And by the wey his wyf Creusa he lees,
And mochel sorowe hadde he in his mynde,
Er that he koude his felawshippe fynde.
But at the laste, whan he hadde hem founde,
He made him redy in a certeyn stounde,
And to the see ful faste he gan him hye,

And sayleth forth with al his companye
Towarde Ytayle, as wolde destanee.
But of his aventures in the see,　　　　　　　　　30
Nys nat to purpos for to speke of here,
For it acordeth nat to my matere.
But as I seyde, of hym and of Dydo
Shal be my tale, til that I have do.
　So longe he saylled in the salte see,
Til in Lybye unneth arryved he,
So was he with the tempest al to-shake.
And whan that he the havene had ytake,
He had a knyghte was called Achates,
And him of al his felawshippe he ches　　　40
To goon with him, the contree for tespye.
He toke witn him na more companye,
But forth they goon, and lafte hise shippes ride,
His fere and he, withouten any guyde.
　So longe he walketh in this wildernesse,
Til at the last he mette an hunteresse,
A bowe in hande, and arwes hadde shee;
Hire clothes were knytte unto the knee.
But she was yit the fairest creature
That ever was yformed by nature;　　　　　50
And Eneas and Achates she grette,
And thus she to hem spak whan she hem mette.
　'Sawe ye,' quod she, 'as ye han walked wide,
Any of my sustren walke yow besyde,
With any wilde boor or other beste,
That they han hunted to in this foreste,
Ytukked up, with arwes in hire cas?'
　'Nay soothly, lady!' quod this Eneas;
'But by thy beauté, as yt thynketh me,
Thou myghtest never erthely woman be,　　60

But Phebus suster artow, as I gesse.
And yf so be that thou be a goddesse,
Have mercy on oure labour and oure woo.'
  'I nam no goddesse soothely,' quod she thoo;
'For maydens walken in this contree here,
With arwes and with bowe, in this manere.
This is the regne of Libie ther ye been,
Of which that Dido lady is and queene.'
And shortly tolde al the occasioun
Why Dido come into that regioun,   70
Of which as now me lusteth nat to ryme;
It nedeth nat, it nere but los of tyme.
For this is al and somme; it was Venus
His owene moder, that spake with him thus;
And to Cartage she bad he sholde him dighte,
And vanysshed anoon out of his sighte.
I koude folwe worde for worde Virgile,
But it wolde lasten al to longe while.
  This noble queene, that cleped was Dido,
That whilom was the wife of Sicheo,   80
That fairer was than the bryghte sonne,
This noble toune of Cartage hath begonne;
In which she regneth with so grete honoure,
That she was holde of al*le* quenes floure,
Of gentilesse, of fredome, of beautee,
That wel was him that myght hir oones see.
Of kynges and of lordes so desired,
That al the worlde hire beauté hadde yfired,
She stoode so wel in every wyghtes grace.
  Whan Eneas was come unto that place,   90
Unto the maistre temple of al the toune,
Ther Dido was in hir devocioun,
Ful prively his wey than hath he nome.

Whan he was in the *large* temple come,
I kannat seye yf that hit be possible,
But Venus hadde him maked invisible;
Thus seith the booke, withouten any les.
　And whan this Eneas and Achates
Hadden in the temple ben over-alle,
Than founde they depeynted on a walle,　　　100
How Troy and al the londe destrued was.
' Allas, that I was born !' quod Eneas.
'Thurghout the worlde oure shame is kid *so* wide
Now it is peynted upon every side.
Wo that weren in prosperitee,
Be new disclaundred, and in swiche degre,
No lenger for to lyven I ne kepe.'
And with that worde he braste out for to wepe
So tendirly that routhe it was to scene.
　This fressho lady, of the citee queene,　　　110
Stoode in the temple, in hire estat royalle,
So richely, and eke so faire withalle,
So yonge, so lusty, with hire eighen glade,
That yf that God that hevene and erthe made,
Wolde han a love, for beauté and goodenesse,
And womanhode, and trouthe, and semlynesse,
.Whom sholde he loven but this lady swote?
Ther nys no woman to him halfe so mete.
Fortune, that hath the worlde in governaunce,
Hath sodeynly broght in so newe a chaunce,　　　120
That never yit was in so fremde *a* cas.
For al the companye of Eneas,
Which that he wende han loren in the see,
Aryved ys noght fer fro the citee.
For which the grettest of his lordes, some
By aventure ben to the citee come

Unto that same temple for to seke
The queene, and of hire socour hir beseke;
Swich renowne was ther spronge of hir goodnesse.
  And whan they had*de* tolde al hire distresse,
And al hir tempeste and hire harde cas,   131
Unto tho queene appered Eneas,
And openly beknew that it was he.
Who had*de* joy thanne, but his me*y*nee,
That hadden founde hire lord, hire governour?
  The queene sawgh they dide him swich honour,
And had herde ofte of Eneas er thoo,
And in hir herte *had*le* routhe and woo,
That ever swiche a noble man as hee
Shal ben dishereted in swiche degree.   140
And sawgh the man, *that he* was lyke a knyghte,
And suffisaunt of persone and of myghte,
And lyke to ben a verray gentilman.
And wel hys wordes he besette kan,
And hadde a noble visage for the noones,
And formed wel of brawnes and of boones;
And after Venus hadde swich fairenesse,
That no man myght*e* be half so faire I gesse,
And wel a lorde him semede for to bee.
And for he was a straunger, somwhat shee   150
Lyked him the bette, as God do boote,
To somme folke often newe thinge is swoote.
Anoon hire herte hath pitee of his woo,
And with pitee, love come alsoo;
And thus for pitee and for gentillesse,
Refresshed mote he ben of his distresse.
  She seyde, certes, that she sory was,
That he hath had swich peril and swiche cas;
And in hire frendely speche, in this manere

She to him spake, *and* seyde as *ye may here.*   160
  ' Be ye nat Venus sone and Anchises ?
In good faythe, al the worshippe and encres
That I may goodly doon yow, ye shal have ;
Youre shippes and your meynee shal I save.'
And many a gentil worde she spake him too,
And comaunded hire messageres goo
The same day, withouten any faylle,
Hys shippes for to seke and hem vitaylle.
Ful many a beeste she to the shippes sente,
And with the wyne she gan hem to presente, 170
And to hire royalle paleys she hire spedde,
And Eneas alwey with hire she ledde.
What nedeth yow the feste to discryve ?
He never better at ese was his lyve.
Ful was the feste of deyntees and richesse,
Of instruments, of songe, and of gladnesse,
And many an amorouse lokyng and devys.
   This Eneas is comen to Paradys
Out of the swolowe of helle ; and thus in joye
Remembreth him of his estaat in Troye. 180
To daunsyng chambres ful of parements,
Of riche beddes, and of pavements,
This Eneas is ladde after the meete.
And with the queene whan that she hadde seete,
And spices parted, and the wyne agoon,
Unto hyse chambres was he lad anoon
To take his ease, and for to have his reste
With al his folke, to doon what so hem leste.
   Ther nas coursere wel ybridled noon,
No stede for the justyng wel to goon, 190
No large palfrey, esy for the noones,
No juwel frette ful of riche stoones,

Ne sakkes ful of gold, of large wyghte,
Ne rubee noon that shyneth by nyghte,
Ne gentil hawteyn faukone heroneer,
No hound for hert, or wilde boor or deer,
Ne coupe of golde, with floryns newe ybette,
That in the londe of Lybye may ben gette,
That Dido ne hath hit Eneas isente;
And al is payed, what that he hath spente.   200
Thus kan this honourable queene hir gestes calle,
As she that kan in fredome passen alle.
  Eneas soothly eke, withouten les,
Hath sent to his shippe by Achates
After his sone, and after ryche thynges,
Booth eeptre, clothes, broches, and eke rynges;
Somme for to were, and somme for to presente
To hire, that alle thise noble thinges him sente;
And bad hys sone how that he sholde make
The presentynge, and to the queene it take.   210
  Repeyred is this Achates agayne,
And Eneas ful blysful is and fayne,
To seen his yonge sone Ascanius.
For *unto* him yt was reported thus,
That Cupido, that is the god of love,
At prayere of his moder hye above,
Hadde the liknesse of the childe ytake,
This noble queene enamoured to make
On Eneas.   But of that scripture
Be as be may, I make of yt no cure.   220
But sooth is this, the queene hath made swich chere
Unto this childe that wonder is to here;
And of the present that his fader sente,
She thanked him *ful* ofte in goode intente.
  Thus is this queene in pleasaunce and in joye,

With al this newe lusty folke of Troye.
And of the dedes hath she moore enquered
Of Eneas, and all the storie lered
Of Troye; and al the longe day they tweye
Entendeden for to speke and for to pleye.   230
Of which ther gan to breden swich a fire,
That sely Dido hath now swich desire
With Eneas hir newe geste to deele,
That she loste hire hewe and eke hire heele.

Now to theffecte, now to the fruyt of al,
Why I have tolde this storye, and tellen shal.

Thus I bygynne :—It fil upon a nyght,
Whan that the moone upreysed hadde hire lyght,
This noble queene unto hire reste wente.
She siketh soore, and gan hire selfe turmente ; 240
She waketh, walwithe, maketh many a brayde,
As doone thise lovers, as I have herde sayde ;
And at the laste, unto hire suster Anne
She made hir mone, and ryght thus spake she thanne.

‘ Now dere suster myn, what may it be
That me agasteth in my dreme ?’ quod she.
‘ This ilke Trojane is so in my thoghte,
For that me thinketh he is so wel ywroghte,
And eke so likely to ben a man,
And *ther*withal soo mykel good he kan,   250
That al my love and lyf lyth in his cure.
Have ye nat herde hym telle his aventure ?
Now certes, Anne, yif that ye rede me,
I wil fayne to him ywedded be ;’
(This is theffect ; what sholde I more seyn ?)
‘ In him lith alle, to doo me lyve or deyn.’

Hir suster Anne, as she that kouth hire goode,
Seyde as hire thoght, and somedel yt withstoode.

But herof was so longe a sermonynge,
Yt were to longe to make rehersynge.   260
But, finally, yt may nat be withstonde ;
Love woll love, for no wyght wol yt wonde.
    The dawenyng upryst oute of the see,
This amorouse queene chargeth hire meynee
The nettes dresse, and speres brood and kene ;
An huntynge wol this lusty fresshe queene,
So priketh hire this newe joly woo.
To hors is al hire lusty folke ygoo ;
Unto the courte the houndes ben ybroughte,
And up on coursere, swyfte as any thoughte,   270
Hir yonge knyghtes heven al aboute,
And of hir women eke an houge route.
Upon a thikke palfrey, paper white,
With sadel rede, enbroudet with delyte,
Of golde the barres, up enbosed heighe,
Sitte Dido, al in golde and perrey wreighe.
And she is faire as is the bryghte morwe,
That heeleth seke folkes of nyghtes sorwe.
Upon a coursere, startlyng as the fire,
Men myghte turne him with a lytel wire,   280
Sitte Eneas, lyke Phebus to devyse,
So was he fressh arrayed in hys wyse.
The fomy bridel, with the bitte of golde,
Governeth he ryght as himselfe hathe wolde.
And foorth this *noble* queene, this lady ride
On huntyng, with this Trojan by hire syde.
The heerde of hertes founden ys anoon,
With 'Hay ! goo bet ! prike thou ! lat goon, lat goon !
Why nyl the lyoun comen, or the bere,
That Y myght hym ones meten with this spere ?'   290
Thus seyn thise yonge folke, and up they kylle

The wilde hertes, and han hem at here wille.
    Amonges al this, to romblen gan the hevene;
The thonder rorede with a grisly stevene;
Doune come the rayne, with haile and sleet so faste,
With hevenes fire, that ys so sore agaste
This noble quene, and also hire meynee,
That yche of hem was glad awey to flee;
And shortly, fro the tempest hire to save,
She fled hire selfe into a lytel cave,   30(
And with hire wente this Eneas alsoo.
I not with hem yf ther went any moo;
The auctour maketh of hit no mencioun.
And here beganne the depe affeccioun
Betwix hem two; this was the firste morwe
Of hire gladnesse, and gynnynge of hir sorwe.
For there hath Eneas yknyled soo,
And tolde hir al his herte and al his woo;
And sworne so depe to hire to be trewe
For wele or woo, and chaunge for noo newe,   310
And as a fals lover so wel kan pleyne,
That sely Dido rewed on his peyne,
And toke hym for housbonde, and became his wife
For evermor, while that hem laste lyfe.
And after this, whan that the tempest stente,
With myrth, out as they come, home they wente.
    The wikked fame up roos, and that anoon,
How Eneas hadde with the queene ygoon
Into the cave, and demed as hem liste.
And whan the kynge that Yarbas hight, hit wiste,   32(
As he that had hire loved ever his lyfe,
And wowed hire to have to hys wife,
Swiche sorowe as he hath maked, and suche chere,
Yt is a rewthe and pitee for to here.

But as in love alday it happeth soo,
That oon shal lawghen at anotheres woo;
Now lawghed Eneas, and is in joye,
And more riches than ever was in Troye.
    O sely woman, ful of innocence,
Ful of pitee, of trouthe, and conscience,   330
What maked yow to men to trusten soo?
Have ye suche rewthe upon hir feyned woo,
And han suche ensaumples olde yow beforne?
So ye nat alle how they ben forsworne?
Where so ye oon that he ne hath lafte his leefe?
Or ben unkynde, or don hir some myscheefe?
Or pilled hir, or bosted of hys dede?
Ye may as wel hit seen as ye may rede.
Take hede now of this grete gentilman,
This Trojan, that so wel hire plese kan,   340
That feyneth him so trewe and obeysinge,
So gentil, and so privy of his doynge;
And kan so wel doon al his obeysaunce
To hir, at festes and at daunce,
And whan she gooth to temple, and home agayne,
And fasten til he hath his lady sayne;
And beren in his devyses for hire sake
Wot I not what; and songes wolde he make,
Justen, and doon of armes many thynges,
Send hire letres, tokens, broches, and rynges.   350
Now herkneth how he shal his lady serve.
    Ther as he was in peril for to sterve
For hunger and for myscheef in the see,
And desolate, and fledde fro his contree,
And al his folke with tempeste al to-driven,
She hath hir body and eke hir reame yiven
Into his hande, theras she myghte have beene

Of other lande than of Cartage a queene,
And lyved in joy ynogh; what wolde ye more?
   This Eneas, that hath thus depe yswore,   360
Ys wery of his crafte within a throwe;
The hoote erneste is al overblowe.
And prively he dooth his shippes dyghte,
And shapeth him to steele awey by nyghte.
   This Dido hath suspecion of this,
And thoughte wel that hit was al amys;
For in his bedde he lythe a nyght and siketh,
She asketh him anoon what him mysliketh;
' My dere herte which that I love mooste?'
   'Certes,' quod he, 'thys nyght my fadres gooste
Hath in my slepe me so sore turmentede,   371
And eke Mercure his message hath presentede,
That nedes to the conqueste of Ytayle
My destany is soone for to saylo,
For whiche me thynketh, brosten ys myn herte.'
Therwith his false teeres oute they sterte
And taketh hir within his armes twoo.
   'Ys that in ernest?' quod sho; 'wol ye soo?
Have ye nat sworne to wife me to take?
Allas, what woman wol ye of me make?   380
I am a gentil woman, and a queene;
Ye wol nat fro your wyfe thus foule fleene!
That I was borne, allas! what shal Y doo?'
   To telle in short, this noble queene Dido
She seketh halwes, and doothe sacrifise;
She kneleth, crieth, that routhe is to devyse;
Conjureth him, and profereth him to bee
Hys thral, hys servant, in the lest degre.
Sho falleth him to foote, and swowneth there,
Disshevely with hire bryghte gelte here,   390

And seith, 'Have mercy! let me with yow ryde;
These lordes, which that wonnen me besyde,
Wol me destroien oonly for youre sake.
And ye wole now me to wife take,
As ye han sworn, than wol I yive yow leve
To sleen me with your swerd now soone at eve,
For than shal I yet dien as youre wife.
I am with childe, *and* yive my childe his lyfe!
Mercy lorde, have pitee in youre thought!'
But al this thing avayleth hire ryght nought,   400
For on a nyght sleping he let hir lye,
And staal awey upon his companye,
And as a traytour forthe he gan to sayle
Towarde the large countree of Ytayle.
And thus hath he lefte Dido in woo and pyne,
And weddid there a lady highte Lavyne.
A clooth he lefte, and eke his swerde stondynge
(Whan he fro Dido staale in *hire* slepynge,)
Righte at hir beddes hed: so gan he hye,
Whanne that he staale awey to his navye.   410
    Which clooth, whan sely Dido gan awake,
She hath *i*-kyste ful ofte for hys sake;
And seyde, 'O swete clooth, while Jupiter hit leste,
Take my soule, unbynde me of this *un*reste,
I have fulfilled of fortune al the course.'
And thus, allas, withouten hys socourse,
Twenty tyme yswowned hath she thanne.
And whan that she unto hir suster Anne
Compleyned had, of which I may not write,
So grete routhe I have hit for to endite,   420
And bad hir noryce and hir sustren goon
To fecche fire, and other thinges anoon,
And seyde that she wolde sacrifie;

And whan she myght hir tyme wel espye,
Upon the fire of sacrifice she sterte,
And with his swerde she roof hire to the herte.
But, as myn auctour seythe, yit thus she seyde,
Or she was hurte, beforne or she deide,
She wroot a letter anoon, that thus biganne.
   ' Ryght so,' quod she, ' as the white swanne 430
Ayenst his deeth begynneth for to synge ;
Ryght so to yow I make my compleynynge,
Nat that I trowe to geten yow agayne,
For wel I woot *that* hit is al in vayne,
Syn that the goddys ben contrariouse to me.
But syn my name ys loste thurgh yow,' quod she,
' I may wel leese a worde on yow, or letter,
Albeit I shal be never the better.
For thilke wynde that blew your shippe away,
The same wynde hath blowe awey your fay.'   440
But who-so wool al this letter have in mynde,
Rede Ovyde, and in him he shal hit fynde.

EXPLICIT LEGENDA DIDONIS, MARTIRIS,
CARTAGENIS REGINE.

INCIPIT LEGENDA YPSIPHILE ET MEDEE,
MARTIRIS.

THOU roote of false lovers, duke Jason !
Thou slye devourer, and confusyon
Of gentil women, gentil creatures !
Thou madest thy reclaymynge and thy
    lures

To ladies of thy staately aparaunce,
And of thy wordes farsed with plesaunce,
And of thy feyned trouthe, and thy manere,
With thyne obeysaunce and humble chere,
And with thy countrefeted poyn and woo!
Ther other falsen oon, thou falseste twoo!   10
O, ofte swore thou that thou woldest deye
For love, whan thou ne felteste maladeye,
Save foule delyte, which that thou callest love!
If that I lyve, thy name shal be shove
In Englyssh, that thy sleighte shal be knowe;
Have at the, Jason! now thyn horn is blowe!
But certes, it is bothe rowth and woo,
That love with false lovers werketh soo;
For they shalle have wel better and gretter chere
Than he that hath *i*-bought love ful dere,   20
Or had in armes many a blody box.
For ever as tender a capon eteth the fox,
Though he be fals, and hath the foule betrayed,
As shal the goode man that therfor payed;
Alle thof he have to the capon skille and ryghte,
The false fox wil have his part at nyghte.
On Jason this ensample is wel yseene,
By Isiphile and Medea the queene.
   In Tessalye, *as* Ovyde telleth us,
Ther was a knyght that highte Pelleus,   30
That had a brother whiche that hight Eson.
And whan for age he myghte unnethes gon,
He yaf to Pelleus the governynge
Of al his regne, and made him lorde and kynge.
Of whiche Eson this Jason geten was;
That in his tyme in al that lande ther nas
Nat suche a famouse knyghte of gentilesse,

Of fredome, of strengthe, and of lustynesse.
After his fader deeth he bar him soo,
That there nas noon that lyste ben his foo,
But dide him al honour and companye.
Of which this Pelleus hath grete envye,
Imagynynge that Jason myghte bee
Enhaunced so, and put in suche degree,
With love of lordes of his regioun,
That from hys regne he may be put adoun.
And in his witte a nyghte compassed he
How Jason myghte beste destroyed be,
Withoute sclaunder of his compassemente.
And at the laste he tooke avysemente,
To senden him into some fer contre,
There as this Jason may distroyed be.
This was his witte, al made he to Jasoun
Grete chere of love and of affeecioun,
For drede leste his lordes hyt espyede.
So felle hyt so as fame renneth wide,
Ther was suche tidynge overalle, and suche los,
That in an ile that called was Coleos,
Beyonde Troye estewarde in the see,
That ther was a ram that men myghte see,
That had a flees of golde, that shoon so bryghte,
That no wher was ther suche another syghte,
But hit was kept alway with a dragoun,
And many other mervels up and doun ;
And with twoo booles maked al of bras,
That spitten fire ; and muche thinge ther was.
But this was eke the tale nathelees,
That who-so wolde wynne thilke flees,
He moste booth, or he hit wynne myghte,
With the booles and the dragoun fyghte ;

And kyng Otes lorde was of that ile.
This Pelleus bethoughte upon this wile,
That he his nevywe Jason wolde enhorte
To saylen to that londe, him to disporte.
And seyde, ' Neviwe, yf hyt myghte be,
That suche worshippe myghte falle the,
That thou this famouse tresor myghte wynne,
And brynge hit my regyoun wythinne,
It were to me grette plesaunce and honoure ;
Thanne were I holde to quyte thy laboure, - 80
And al the costes I wole my-selfe make ;
And chese what folke thou wilte wyth the take.
Let see nowe, darstow taken this viage ?'
    Jason was yonge, and lustie of corage.
And undertooke to doon this ilke emprise.
Anoon Argus his shippes gan devyse.
    With Jason wente the stronge Hercules,
And many another that he with him ches.
But who-so axeth who is with him goon,
Let him rede Argonauticon, 90
For he wol telle a tale longe ynoughe.
Philoctetes anoon the sayle up droughe,
Whan the wynde was good, and gan him hye
Out of his contree called Tessalye.
So longe he sayled in the salte see,
Til in the ile of *Lemnos* arryved he.
Al be this not rehersed of Guydo,
Yet seyth Ovyde in hys Epistoles so ;
And of this ile lady was and queene,
The faire yonge Ypsiphile the shene, 100
That whilom Thoas doughter was, the kynge.
    Ypsiphyle was goon in hire pleynge,
And romynge on the clyves by the see.

Under a brake anoon espiede shee
Where lay the shippe that Jason gan arryve.
Of hire goodnesse adoun she sendeth blyve,
To weten, yf that any straunge wyghte
With tempest thider were yblow anyghte,
To doon hem socour, as was hir usaunce,
To forthren every wyghte, and don plesaunce   110
Of very bountee, and of curteysie.
    This messagere adoun him gan to hye,
And founde Jason and Ercules also,
That in a cogge to londe were ygo,
Hem to refresshen, and to take the eyre.
The morwenyng atempree was and faire,
And in hys wey this messager hem mette;
Ful kunnyngely these lordes twoo he grette,
And did his message, askynge hem anoon
If they were broken, or woo begoon,   120
Or hadde nede of lodesmen or vitayle;
For socoure they shulde nothinge fayle,
For it was outerly the quenes wille.
    Jason ansuerde mekely and stille;
' My lady,' quod he, ' thanke I hertely
Of hire goodnesse; us nedeth trewely
Nothing as now, but that we wery bee,
And come for to pley out of tho see,
Til that the wynde be better in oure weye.'
    This lady rometh by the clyffe to pleye   130
With hire meynee, endelonge the stronde,
And fyndeth this Jason and thyse other stonde
In spekynge of this thinge, as I yow tolde.
    This Ercules and Jason gan beholde
How that the queene it was, and faire hir grette,
Anoon ryght as they with this lady mette.

And she tooke hede, and knywe by hir*e* manere,
By hire array, by wordes, and by chere,
That hit were gentil men of grete degree.
And to the castel with hir ledeth shee   140
These straunge folke, and dooth hem grete honour;
And axeth hem of travaylle and labour
That they han suffred in the salte see;
So that withynne a day two or three
She knywe by the folke that in his shippes bee,
That hyt was Jason, full of renomee,
And Ercules, that hadde the grete los,
That soughten the aventures of Colcos.
And did hem honour more than before,
And with hem deled ever the lenger the more;   150
For they ben worthy folke withouten les.
And, namely, she spake most with Ercules,
To him hir herte bare, he shulde bee
Sad, wise, and trewe, of wordes avysee,
Withouten any other affeccioun
Of love, or any other ymaginacioun.
    This Ercules hathe this Jason preysed,
That to the sonne he hath hyt up reysed,
That halfe so trewe a man ther nas of love
Under the cope of hevene, that is above;   160
And he was wyse, hardy, secre, and ryche;
Of these thre poyntes ther nas noon hym liche.
Of fredome passed he, and lusti*h*ede
Alle thoo that lyven, or ben dede.
Therto so grete a gentil man was he,
And of Tessalye likly kynge to be.
Ther nas no lakke, but that he was agaste
To love, and for to speke shamefaste;
Him lever had himselfe to mordre and dye,

Than that men shulde a lover him espye.　17
As wolde God that I hadde iyive
My bloode and flessh, so that I myght*e* lyve
With the *bones*, that he hadde oughe-where a wif
For his estaat! for suche a lusty lyfe
She sholde lede with this lusty knyghte!
And al this was compassed on the nyghte
Betwix him Jason, and this Ercules.
Of these twoo here was a shrewede les,
To come to house upon an innocent,
For to bedote this queene was her entent.　18
Thise Jason is as coy as ys a mayde;
He loketh pitousely, but noght he sayde
But freely yafe he to hir counselleres
Yiftes grete, and to hire officeres,
As God wolde that I leyser had and tyme,
By processe al his wowyng for to ryme!
But in this house yf any fals lover be,
Ryght as himselfe now dothe, ryght so did he,
With feynynge, and with every sotil dede.
Ye gete no more of me, but ye wol rede　19
The original that telleth al tho cas.
　　The sothe is this, that Jason weddid was
Unto this queene, and toke of hire substaunce
What-so him lyste unto hys purveyaunce;
And upon hir begate he children twoo,
And drough his sayle, and saugh hir never moo.
A letter sente she to hym certeyn,
Which were to longe to written and to seyn;
And him repreveth of his grete untrouthe,
And prayeth him on hir to have some routhe.　20
And of his children two, she sayede him this;
That they be lyke of alle thinge, ywis,

To Jason, save they couthe nat begile.
And prayed*e* God, or hit were longe while,
That she that had his herte yrefte hir fro,
Most him fynden to hir untrewe alsoo;
And that she moste booth hir children spille,
And al*le* thoo that suffreth hym his wille;
And trew*e* to Jason was she al hir lyve,
And ever kept hir chaste, as for his wyve;   210
And had*de* never she joye at hir herte,
But dyed*e* for his love of sorwes smerte.

 To Colcos comen is this duke Jasoun,
That is of love devourer and dragoun,
As nature appeteth forme alwey,
And from a forme to forme it passen may;
Or as a welle that were botomeles,
Ryght so kan Jason *ne* have no pes,
For to desiren, thurgh his appetite,
To doon with gentil wymmen hys delyte;   220
This is his luste, and his felicité.
Jason is romed forthe to the cité,
That whylom cleped was Jasonicos,
That was the maister toune of al Colcos,
And hath ytolde the cause of his comynge
Unto Æetes, of that contree kynge;
Praynge him that he moste doon his assay
To gete the flese of golde, yf that he may.
Of which the kynge assentith to hys bone,
And dothe him honour as hyt is *to* done,   230
So ferforthe, that his doghtre and his eyre,
Medea, which that was so wise and feyre,
That feyrer saugh ther never man with ye,
He made hire doone to Jason companye
Atte mete, and sitte by him in the halle.

Now was Jason a semely man withalle,
And like a lorde, and had a grete renoun,
And of his loke as rial as lyoun,
And goodly of his speche, and famulere,
And koude of love al crafte and arte plenere
Withoute boke, and everyche observaunce.
And as fortune hir oughte a foule meschaunce,
She wex enamoured upon this man.
'Jason,' quod she, 'for oght Y se or kan,
As of this thinge the whiche ye ben aboute,
Ye, and your-selfe ye put in moche doute ;
For who-so wol this aventure acheve,
He may nat wele asterten, as Y leve,
Withouten dethe, but I his helpe bo.
But nathelesse, hit ys my wille,' quod she,
'To furtheren yow, so that ye shal nat dye,
But turne sounde home to youre Tessalye.'
'My ryghte lady,' quod thys Jason, ' thoo,
That ye han of my dethe or of my woo
Any rewarde, and doon me this honour,
I wote wel, that my myght, no my labour,
May not deserve hit in my lyves day ;
God thanke yow, ther Y ne kan nor may.
Youre man am I, and louly yow besecho
To ben my helpe, withoute more speche ;
But certes for my dethe shal I not spare.'
Thoo gan this Medea to him declare
Tho peril of this case, fro poynt to poynte
Of hys batayle, and in what disjoynte
Ho moto stonde ; of whiche no creature
Save oonly she no myght hys lyfe assure.
And shortely, ryght to the poynt to goo,
They been accorded ful betwex hem two,

That Jason shal hir wedde, as trewe knyght,
And terme ysette to come soone at nyght   270
Unto hir chambre, and make there hys oothe
Upon the goddys, that he for leve ne loothe
Ne shulde hire never falsen, nyght ne day,
To ben hir husbonde while he lyve may,
As she that from hys dethe hym saved there.
And here upon at nyght they mete yfere,
And doth his oothe, and goothe with hir to bed*de*,
And on the morwe upwarde he him sped*de*,
For she hath taught him how he shal not faile
The flese to wynne, and stynten hys batayle;   280
And saved him his lyfe and his honour,
And gete a name as a conquerour,
Ryght thurgh the sleyghte of hir enchauntement.
     Now hath Jason the fleese, and home ys went
With Medea, and tresoures ful grete woone;
But unwiste of hir fader she is goone
To Tessalye, with duke Jason hir leefe,
That afterwarde hath broght hir to myschefe.
For as a traytour he ys from hire goo,
And with hir lefte yonge children twoo,   290
And falsly hath betrayed hir, allas!
And ever in love a cheve traytour he was;
And wedded yet the thridde wife anon,
That was the doghtre of kynge Creon.
     This ys the mede of lovynge and guerdoun,
That Medea receyved of Jasoun
Ryght for hir trouthe, and for hir kyndenesse,
That loved hym beter thane hir-selfe, Y gesse;
And lefte hir fadir and hire heritage.
And of Jason this is *the* vassalage,   300
That in hys dayes nas never noon yfounde

So fals a lover goynge on the grounde.
And therfore in her letter thus she sayde,
First whan she of hys falsnesse hym umbrayae.—
' Why lykede me thy yelow heere to see,
More than the boundes of myn honesté ?
Why lykede me thy youthe and thy fairenesse,
And of thy tonge the infynyte graciousnesse?
O, haddest thou in thy conquest ded ybe,
Ful mykel untrouthe hadde ther dyed with the !'
  Wel kan Ovyde hir letter in verse endyte. 311
Which were as now to longe for me to write.

EXPLICIT LEGENDA YSIPHILE ET MEDEE

MARTIRUM.

INCIPIT LEGENDA LUCRECIE ROME,

MARTIRIS.

OW mote I sayne thexilynge of kynges
Of Rome, for *the* horrible *doynges*
Of the laste kynge Tarquynyus,
As saythe Ovyde, and Titus Lyvyus.
But for that cause telle I nat thys story,
But for to preysen, *and* drawen to memory
The verray wife, the verray Lucresse,
That for hir wifehode, and hir stedfastnesse,
Nat oonly that these payens hir comende,
But that *i*-cleped ys in oure legende 10
The grete Austyne, hath grete compassyoun
Of this Lucresse that starfe in Rome toun.

And in what wise I wol but shortly trete,
And of this thynge I touche wil but the grete.
   Whan Ardea beseged was aboute
With Romaynes, that ful sterne were and stoute,
Ful longe lay the sege, and lytel wroghten,
So that they were halfe ydel, as hem thoghten.
And in his pley Tarquynyus the yonge
Gan for to jape, for he was lyghte of tonge ;   20
And sayde, that hyt was an ydel lyfe ;
No man dide ther more than hys wife.
' And lat us speke of wives that is best ;
Preise every man hys owne as him lest,
And with oure speche let us ease oure herte.'
   A knyght, that highte Colatyne, up sterte,
And sayde thus :—' Nay, for hit ys no nede
To trowen on the worde, but on the dede.
I have a wife,' quod he, ' that as I trowe
Ys holden good of alle that ever hir knowe.   30
Go we to Rome, to nyght, and we shul se.'
Tarquynyus answerde, ' That lyketh me.'
To Rome they be come, and faste hem dighte
To Colatynes house, and doun they lyghte,
Tarquynyus, and eke this Colatyne.
The housbonde knywe the estres wel and fyne,
And ful prevely into the house they goon,
For at the gate porter was there noon :
And at the chambre dore they abyde.
This noble wyfe sate by hir beddys syde   40
Disshevely, for no malice she ne thoghte,
And softe wolle, sayeth our boke, that she wroghte,
To kepen hir fro slouthe and ydilnesse ;
And bad hir servauntes doon hir besynesse ;
And axeth hem, ' What tydynges heren ye ?

How sayne men of the sege ? how shal yt be ?
God wolde the walles werne falle adoune !
Myn housbonde ys to longe out of this toune,
For which the drede doth me so to smerte ;
Ryght as a swerde hyt styngeth to myn herte,
Whan I thenke on these or of that place.
God save my lorde, I pray him for *his* grace !'
And therwithalle ful tendirly she wepe,
And of hir werke she toke no more kepe,
But mekely she let hire eyen falle,
And thilke semblant sat hir wel withalle.
And eke the teeres ful of hevytee,
Embelysshed hire wifely chastitee.
Hire countenance ys to her herte digne,
For they acordeden in dede and in signe.
And with that worde hir husbonde Colatyne,
Or she of him was ware, come stertyng ynne,
And sayede, ' Drede the noght, for I am here !'
And she anoon up roos, with blysful chere,
And kyssed hym, as of wives ys the wone.

  Tarquynyus, this prowde kynges sone,
Conceyved hath hir beauté and hir chere,
Hire yelow heer, hir bounté, and hire manere,
Hir hywe, hir wordes that she hath compleyned,
And by no craft hire beauté was not feyned ;
And kaughte to this lady suche desire,
That in his herte brent as any fire
So wodely that hys witte was foryeten,
For wel he thoghte she shulde nat be geten.
And ay the more he was in dispaire,
The more he covetyth, and thoght hir faire ;
Hys blynde lust was al hys covetynge.
On morwe, whan the brid began to synge,

Unto the sege ho cometh ful pryvely,
And by himsolfo ho walketh sobrely,   80
The ymage of hir recordyng alwey newe;
Thus lay hir heer, and thus fressh was hir hewe,
Thus sate, thus spake, thus spanne, this was hir
        chere,
Thus fairo sho was, and thys was hir manere.
Al this conceyte hys herte hath new ytake,
And as tho see, with tempesto al to-shake,
That after whan tho stormo ys al agoo,
Yet wol tho watir quappe a day or twoo;
Ryght so, thogh that hir forme were absent,
The plesaunce of hir forme was present.   90
But natheles, nat plesaunce, but delyte,
Or an unryghtful talent with dispite,
' For mawgree hir, sho shal my lemman be:
Happo helpeth hardy man alway,' quod ho,
' What endo that I make, hit shal be soo!'
And gyrt hym with his swerde, and gan to goo,
And ho forthe-ryght til ho to Rome ys come,
And al allon hys way than hath ho nomo,
Unto the house of Colatyne ful ryght;
Doune was tho sonne, and day hath lost hys lyght.
And inne ho come unto a prevy halke,   101
And in tho nyght ful thefely gan he stalke,
Whan every wyght was to hys reste broght,
No no wyghte had of tresoun sucho a thoght,
Whether by wyndow, or by other gynne.
With swerde ydrawe, shortly ho cometh ynne
There as sho lay, thys noble wyfe Lueresse,
And as she woko, hir bed sho felte presso:
' What best ys that,' quod sho, ' that weyeth thus?'
' I am the kynges sono Tarquynyus,'   110

Quod he; ' but and thow crye, or noyse make,
Or yf thou any creature awake,
Be thilke God that formede man on lyve,
This swerde thurgh thyn herte shal Y ryve.'
And therwithal unto hir throte he sterte,
And sette the swerde al sharpe unto hir herte.
No worde she spake, she hath no myght therto,
What shal she sayne? hir wytte ys al agoo !
Ryght as a wolfe that *fint* a *lomb allone*,
To whom shal she compleyne or make mone ?   120
What? shal she fyghte with an hardy knyghte?
Wel wote men a woman hath no myghte.
What! shal she crye, or how shal she asterte,
That hath hir by the throte, with swerde at herte ?
She axeth grace, and seyde al that she kan.
      ' Ne wolt thou nat?' quod this cruelle man ;
' As wisly Jupiter my soule save,
I shal in the stable slee thy knave,
And lay him in thy bed, and lowde crye,
That I the fynde in suche avowtrye ;   130
And thus thou shalt be ded, and also lese
Thy name, for thou shalt not chese.'
Thise Romaynes wyfes loveden so hir name
At thilke tyme, and dredden so the shame
That what for fere of sklaundre, and drede of dethe,
She loste both attones wytte and brethe ;
And in a swowgh she lay, and woxe so ded,
Men myghten smyten of hir arme or hed,
She feleth nothinge, neither foule ne feyre.
      Tarquynyus, thou art a kynges eyre,   140
And sholdest as by lynage and by ryght
Doon as a lorde and *as* a verray knyght,
Why hastow doon dispite to chevalrye ?

Why hastow doon thys lady vylanye?
Allas, of the thys was a vilenouse dede!
But now to the purpose; in the story I rede,
Whan he was goon al this myschaunce ys falle.
Thys lady sent aftir hir frendes alle,
Fader, moder, housbonde, alle yfere,
And dysshevelee with hir heere clere,   150
In habyte suche as wymmen usede thoo
Unto the buryinge of hir frendes goo,
She sytte in halle with a sorowful syghte.
Hir frendes axen what hir aylen myghte,
And who was dede, and she sytte aye wepynge.
A worde for shame ne may she forthe out-brynge,
Ne upon hem she durste nat beholde,
But atte laste of Tarquyny she hem tolde
This rewful case, and al thys thing horryble.
Tho woo to telle hyt were impossible   160
That she and al hir frendes made attones.
Al hadde folkes hertys ben of stones,
Hyt myght have maked hem upon hir rewe,
Hire herte was so wyfely and so trewe.
She sayde that for hir gylt ne for hir blame
Hir housbonde shulde nat have the foule name;
That nolde she nat suffre by no wey.
And they answerde alle unto hir fey,
That they forgaf hyt hyr, for hyt was ryght.
Hyt was no gilt; hit lay not in hir myght.   170
And seyden hire ensamples many oon.
But al for noght, for thus she seyde anoon:
' Be as be may,' quod she, ' of forgyfynge;
Y wol not have noo forgyft for nothinge.'
But pryvely she kaughte forth a knyfe,
And therwithalle she rafte hir-selfe hir lyfe;

And as she felle adoun she kaste hire loke,
And of hir clothes yet hede she toke;
For in hir fallynge yet she had*de* care,
Lest that hir fete or suche thynge lay bare,   18(
So wel she loved*e* clennesse, and eke trouthe !
Of hir had al the toune of Rome routhe,
And Brutus hath by hir chaste bloode swore,
That Tarquyny shulde ybanysshed be therfore,
And al hys kynne; and let the peple calle,
And openly the tale he tolde hem alle;
And openly let cary her on a bere
Thurgh al the toune, that men may see and here
The horryble dede of hir oppressyoun.
Ne never was ther kynge in Rome toun   19
Syn thilke day; and she was holden there
A seynt, and ever hir day yhalwed dere,
As in hire lawe.   And thus endeth Lucresse
The noble wyfe, Titus beryth wittnesse.
I telle hyt, for she was of love so trewe,
Ne in hir wille she chaunged*e* for no newe,
And in hir stable herte, sadde and kynde,
That in these wymmen men may al day fynde,
Ther as they kaste hire herte, there it dwelleth.
For wel I wot, that Criste himself telleth,   2(
That in Israel, as wyde as is the londe,
That so grete feythe in al the londe he ne fonde,
As in a woman; *and* this is no lye.
And as *for men*, loketh which tirannye
They doon al day, assay hem who-so lyste,
The trewest ys ful brotil for to triste.

INCIPIT LEGENDA ADRIANE DE
ATHENES.

JUGE infernal Mynos, of *Crete* king,
Now cometh thy lotte; now com
    mestow on the rynge.
Nat oonly for thy sake writen ys this
    story,
But for to clepe ageyn unto memory
Of Theseus the grete untrewe of love,
For which the goddis of heven above
Ben wrothe, and wreche han take for thy synne.
Be rede for shame ! now I thy lyfe begynne.
Mynos, that was the myghty kynge of Crete,
That wan an hundred citees stronge and grete, 10
To scole hath sent hys sone Androgeus
To Athenes, of the which hyt happeth thus,
That he was slayne, lernynge philosophie,
Ryght in that citee, nat but for envye.
The grete Mynos of the whiche I speke,
His sones dethe ys come for to wreke,
And the citee besegeth harde and longe ;
But natheles, the walles be so stronge,
And Nysus, that was kynge of that citee,
So chevalrouse, that lytel dredeth he ; 20
Of Mynos or hys oste toke he no cure.
Til, on a day, befel an aventure,
That Nisus doghtre stode upon the walle,
And of the sege sawe the maner alle.
So hyt happede, that at a skarmysshynge,
She caste hir hert upon Mynos the kynge,

For hys beauté, and hys chevalrye,
So sore, that she wende for to dye.
And, shortly of this processe for to pace,
She made Mynos wynnen thilke place,
So that the citee was al at his wille,
To saven whom hym lyst, or elles spille.
But wikkidly he quytte her kyndenesse,
And let hir drenche in sorowe and distresse,
Ner that the goddys had of hir pité;
But that tale were to longe as now for me.
Athenes wanne this kynge Mynos also,
As *Alcathoe* and other tounes mo;
And this theffect, that Mynos hath so dryven
Hem of Athenes, that they mote hym yiven
Fro yere to yere hir owne children dere
For to be slayne, as ye shal after here.
    Thys Mynos hath a monstre, a wikked beste,
That was so cruelle that withouten areste,
Whan that a man was broght into hys presence
He wolde hym ete; ther helpeth no defence.
And every thridde yere, withouten doute,
They casten lotte, as hyt came aboute,
On ryche, on pore, he most hys sone take,
And of hys childe he moste present make
To Mynos, to save him or to spille,
Or lat his best devoure him at his wille.
And this hath Mynos doon *right* in dyspite,
To wreke hys sone was sette all his delyte;
And make hem of Athenes hys thralle
Fro yere to yere, while he lyven shalle;
And home he saileth whan this toune ys wonne
This wikked custome is so longe yronne,
Til of Athenes kynge Egeus,

Moste senden his oune sone Theseus,   60
Sith that the lotte is fallen hym upon,
To bo devoured, for grace is ther non.
And forth is lad thys woful yonge knyght
Unto the countree of kynge Mynos ful of myght,
And in a prison fetred faste ys he,
Til the tyme he shulde yfreten be.
    Wel maystow wepe, O woful Theseus,
That art a kynges sone, and dampned thus!
Me thynketh this, that thow depe were yholde
To whom that savede the fro cares colde.   70
And now yf any woman helpe the,
Wel oughtestow hir servant for to be,
And ben hir trewe lover yere by yere!
But now to come agayn to my matere.
    The tour, ther this Theseus ys ythrowe,
Doure in the bothome derke, and wonder lowe,
Was joynynge to the walle of a foreyne,
And hyt was longynge to the doghtren tweyne
Of Mynos, that in hire chambres grete
Dweltene above the maystre strete   80
Of Athenes in joy and in solace.
Wot I not how hyt happede parcase,
As Theseus compleyned hym by nyghte,
The kynges doghtre that Adriane hyghte,
And eke hir suster Phedra, herden alle
Hys compleynt, as they stode on the walle,
And loked upon the bryghte mone;
Hem liste nat goo to bedde so sone.
And of hys woo they hadde compassyoun;
A kynges sone to be in swiche prisoun,   90
And be devoured, thoughte hem grete pitee.
Than Adriane spake to hir suster free,

And seyde, ‘ Phedra, leve suster dere,
This woful lordes sone may ye not here,
How pitousely compleyneth he hys kynne,
And eke his pore estate that he ys ynne ?
And gilteles ; certes now hit ys routhe !
And yf ye wol assente, by my trouthe,
He shal be holpen, how soo that we doo.’
    Phedra answerde, ‘ Ywys, me ys as woo   100
For him, as ever I was for any man ;
And to his helpe the beste rede that I kan,
Ys, that we doon the gayler prively
To come and speke with us hastely,
And doon this woful man with him to come ;
For yf he may the monstre overcome,
Than were he quyte ; ther ys noon other bote !
Lat us wel taste him at hys herte rote,
That yf so be that he a wepne have,
Wher that hys lyfe he dar kepe or save,   110
Fighten with this fende and him defende.
For in the prison, ther as he shal descende,
Ye wote wel that the best is in a place
That nys not derke, and hath roume and eke space
To welde an axe, or swerde, or staffe, or knyffe.
So that me thenketh he shulde save hys lyffe ;
Yf that he be a man, he shal do so.
And we shal make *him* balles eke alsoo
Of wexe and towe, that whan he gapeth faste,
Into the bestes throte he shal hem caste,   120
To sleke hys hunger, and encombre hys tothe.
And ryght anoon whan that Theseus sethe
The beste asleked, he shal on hym lepe
To sleen hym or they comen more to *kepe*.
This wepen shal the gayler, or that tyde,

Ful prively within tho prisoun hyde :
And for tho houso is crynkled to and fro,
And hath so queynte weyes for to go,
For yt is shapen as the mase is wroght ;
Thcrto have I a remedy in my thoght,   130
That by a clywe of twyne, as ho hath goon,
The same way ho may rcturne anoon,
Folwynge alway tho thredc, as ho hath come.
And whan this bcste ys overcome,
Thanne may ho fleen away out of this stede,
And cke tho gayler may he wyth him ledo,
And him avaunce at home in his contree,
Syn that soo grcte a lordes sone ys he.'
Thys ys my redo yf that ye dar hyt take ;
What shulde I lenger *sermoun* of hyt make ?'   140
Tho gayler cometh, and with hym Thescus,
Whan these thynges ben acorded thus.
Doune sytte Theseus upon hys knee,
' The ryghte lady of my lyfe,' quod he,
' Y sorwful man, ydampned to the deth,
Fro yow, whiles that me lasteth breth,
I wol not twynne aftir this aventure,
But in youre serviso thus I wol endurè ;
That as a wrechche unknowe I wol yow serve
For evermore, til that myn herte sterve.   150
Forsake I wol at home myn herytage,
And, as I sayde, ben of your courte a page,
Yf that ye vouchesafe that in this place,
Yo graunte mo to have suche a grace,
That I may have not but my mete and drinke ;
And for my sustenaunco yet wol I swynke,
Ryght as yow lysto ; that Mynos ne no wyght,
Syn that ho sawe me never with eighen syght,

Ne no man elles shal me konne espye, ·
So slyly and so wele I shal me gye, 160
And me so wel disfigure, and so lowe,
That in this worlde ther shal no man me knowe,
To han my lyfe, and to have presence
Of yow, that doon to me this excellence.
And to my fader shal I sende here
This worthy man that is your gaylere,
And him so guerdone that he shal wel bee
Oon of the gretest men of my contree.
And yif I durste sayne, my lady bryght,
I am a kynges sone and eke a knyght, 170
As wolde God, yif that hyt myghte bee,
Ye weren in my contree *alle* three,
And I with yow, to bere yow companye.
Than shulde ye seen yf that I therof lye.
And yf that I profre yow in lowe manere,
To ben youre page and serven yow ryght here,
But I yow serve as lowly in that place,
I prey to Marce to yove me suche grace,
That shames dede on me ther mote falle,
And dethe and poverte to my frendes alle, 180
And that my spirite be nyghte mote goe
After my dethe, and walke to and froo,
That I mote of traytoure have a name,
For which my spirite mot goo to do me shame!
And yif ever Y clayme other degre,
But ye vouchesafe to yove hyt me,
As I have seyde, of shames doth Y deye!
And mercy, lady! I kan no more seye.'
 A semely knyght was this Theseus to see,
And yonge, but of twenty yere and three. 190
But whoso hadde yseen hys contenaunce,

He wolde have wepte for routhe of his penaunce :
For which this Adriane in this manere,
Answerde to hys profre and to hys chere.
    ' A kynges sone, and eke a knyght,' quod she.
' To ben my·servant in so lowe degre,
God shelde hit, for the shame of wymmen alle,
And lene me never suche a case befalle !
And sende yow grace and sleyght of hert also
Yow to defende, and knyghtly sleen your fo !   200
And lene hereaftir I may yow fynde
To me and to my suster here so kynde,
That I ne repente not to yeve yow lyfe !
Yet wer hyt better I were your wife,
Syn ye ben as gentil borne as Y,
And have a realme nat but faste by,
Then that I suffrede your gentillesse to sterve,
Or that I lete yow as a page serve ;
Hyt is not profet, as unto your kynrede.
But what is that, that man wol not do for drede ?
And to my suster syn that hyt is so,   211
That she mote goon with me yf that I goo.
Or elles suffre deth as wel as I,
That ye unto your sone as trewely,
Doon hir be wedded at your home comynge.
This ys the fynal ende of al this thynge ;
Ye, swere hit here, upon al that may be sworne !'
    ' Yee, lady myn,' quod he, ' or elles torne
Mote I be with the Minotawre to morowe !
And have here of myn herte bloode to borowe,   220
Yif that ye wol ! Yf I hadde knyfe or spere,
I wolde hit laten out, and theron swere,
For then at erst, I wote ye wol me leve.
By Mars, that ys chefe of my beleve,

So that I myghte lyven, and nat faylo
To morowe for to taken *my* batayle,
Y nolde never fro this place flee,
Til that ye shulde the verray prefe see.
For now, yf that the sothe I shal yow saye,
I have loved yow ful many a day*e*,   230
Thogh ye ne wiste nat, in my contree,
And aldermoste desirede yow to see,
Of any erthely lyvynge creature.
Upon my trouthe I swere and yow assure,
These seven yere I have your servant bee.
Now have I yow, and also have ye mee,
My dere hert, of Athenes duchesse !'
     This lady smyleth at his stedfastnesse,
And at hys hertely wordys, and at his chere,
And to hir suster sayde in this manere :—   240
     ' And softely now, suster myn,' quod she,
' Now be we duchesses both I and ye,
And sykered to the regals of Athenes,
And both heraftir lykly to be queenes,
And saved fro hys deth a kynges sone
As ever of gentil wymen ys the wone,
To save a gentilman, enforthe hir myght,
In honest cause, and namely in his ryght.
Me thinketh no wyght ought us heroof blame,
No beren us therfore an evel name.'   250
     And shortely of this matere for to make,
This Theseus of hir hath love ytake,
And every poynt was performed in dede,
As ye have in the covenant herde mo rede ;
Hys wepne, his clyw, hys thing that I have sayde
Was by the gayler in the house ylayde,
Ther as this Mynatowre hath hys dwellyng,

Ryght faste by tho dorre at hys entrynge,
And Theseus ys ladde unto hys dethe;
And forthe unto this Mynatauro he gcthe,   260
And by the techynge of thys Adriane,
Ho overcome thys beste and was hys bane,
And oute ho cometh by the clywe agayne
Ful prively.   When he thys beste hath slayne,
And by the gayler gotten hath a barge,
And of his wives tresure gan it charge,
And tok hys wif, and eke hir suster free,
And by the gayler, and wyth hem alle three
Ys stole away out of the londe by nighte,
And to tho contree of Ennopye hym dyghte,   270
There as ho had a frende of his knowynge.
There festen they, there dauncen they and synge,
And in hys armes hath thys Adriane,
That of the beste hath kepte him from hys bane.
And gate him there a noble barge anoon,
And of his countre folke a grete woon,
And taketh hys leve, and homewarde sayleth hee;
And in an yle, amydde tho wilde see,
There as ther dwelleth creature noon
Save wilde bestes, and that ful many oon,   280
He made his shippe a-londe for to sette,
And in that ile halfe a day he lette,
And sayde on tho londe he moste him reste.
Hys maryners han don ryght as hym leste;
And, for to telle schortly in thys case,
Whanne Adriane hys wyfe aslepe was,
For that hir suster fairer was than she,
Ho taketh hir in hys honde, and forth gooth he
To shyppe, and as a traytour stale hys way,
While that thys Adriane aslepe lay,   290

And to hys contree-warde he sayleth blyve,
(A twenty devel way the wynde him dryve!)
And fonde hys fader drenched in the see.
Me lyste no more to speke of hym, pardee!
These false lovers, poyson be her bane!
    But I wol turne ageyne to Adryane,
That ys with slepe for werynesse ytake;
Ful sorwfully hir herte may awake.
Allas, for the myn herte hath pitee!
Ryght in the dawenynge awaketh shee,   300
And gropeth in the bed, and fonde ryght noght.
    'Allas,' quod she, 'that ever I was wroght!
I am betrayed,' and hir heer to-rente,
And to the stronde barefote faste she wente,
And cryede, 'Theseus, myn herte swete!
Where be ye, that I may not wyth yow mete?
And myghte thus with bestes ben yslayne.'
The holowe roches answerde hir agayne.
No man she sawe, and yet shone the mone,
And hye upon a rokke she wente sone,   310
And saw hys barge saylynge in the see.
Colde waxe hir hert, and ryght thus sayde she :—
    'Meker than ye fynde I the bestes wilde!'
(Hath he not synne, that he hir thus begylde?)
She cried, 'O turne agayne for routhe and synne,
Thy barge hath not al thy meyny ynne.'
Hir kerchefe on a pole stykede shee,
Ascaunce that he shulde hyt wel ysee,
And hym remembre that she was behynde,
And turne agayne, and on the stronde hir fynde.
But al for noght; hys wey he ys i-goon,   321
And doune she felle a-swowne on a stoon;
And up she ryste, and kyssed in al hir care

The steppes of hys fete, there he hath fare,
And to hir bedde ryght thus she speketh thoo :—
  'Thow bedd,' quoth she, 'that haste receyved
        twoo,
Thow shalt answere of twoo and not of oon,
Where ys the gretter parte away *i*-goon ?
Allas, where shal I wreched wyght become ?
For though so be that bote noon here come,   330
Home to my contree dar I not for drede ;
I kan my selfe in this case not rede.'
    What shulde I telle more hir compleynynge ?
Hyt ys so longe hyt were an hevy thynge.
In hyr epistil Naso telleth alle,
But shortly to the ende tel I shalle.
The goddys have hir holpen for pitee,
And in the sygne of Taurus men may see
The stones of hir corowne shyne clere ;   ·
I wol no more speke of thys matere.   340
But thus these false loveres kan begyle
Hire trewe love ; the devel quyte hym hys while !

EXPLICIT LEGENDA ADRIANE DE ATHENES.

INCIPIT LEGENDA PHILOMENE.

THOW yiver of the formes, that hast
        wroght
      The faire worlde, and bare hit in thy
        thoght
Eternally or thow thy werke began*ne*,

Why madest thow unto the sklaunder of man*ne*,—
Or al be that hyt was not thy doyinge,
As for that *fine* to make suche a thynge,—
Why suffrest thow that Tereus was bore,
That ys in love so fals and so forswore,
That fro thys worlde up to the firste hevene
Corrumpeth, whan that folke hys name nevene? 1
And as to me, so grisly was hys dede,
That whan that I this foule story rede,
Myn eyen wexen foule and sore also;
Yet laste the venym of so longe ago,
That infecteth hym that wolde beholde
The story of Tereus, of which I tolde.
Of Trase was he lorde, and kynne to Marte,
The cruelle god that stante with blody darte,
And wedded had*de* he, with blisful chere,
King Pandyones faire doghter dere,   2
That hyghte Proygne, floure of hir contree;
Thogh Juno *luste* nat at the feste bee,
No Ymeneus, that god of weddyng is.
But at the feste redy ben, ywys,
The furies thre, with al hire mortel bronde.
The owle al nyght about the balkes wonde,
That prophete ys of woo and of myschaunce.
This revel, ful of songe, and ful of daunce,
Laste a fourtenyght or lytel lasse.
But shortly of this story for to passe,   3
(For I am wery of hym for to telle)
Fyve yere hys wyfe and he togedir dwelle;
Til on a day she gan so sore longe
To seen hir suster, that she sawgh not longe,
That for desire she nyste what to soye,
But to hir husbonde gan she for to preye

For Goddys love, that she moste ones goon
Hir suster for to seen, and come anoon.
Or elles but she moste to hyr wende,
She preyde hym that he wolde aftir hir sende.　40
And thys was day be day al hir prayere,
With al humblesse of wyfehode, worde and chere.
　This Tereus let make hys shippes yare,
And into Grece hymselfe ys forthe yfare,
Unto hys fader in lawe, and gan hym preye,
To vouche-safe that for a moneth or tweye,
That Philomene, his wyfes suster, myghte
On Proigne hys wyfe but ones have a syghte;
'And she shal come to yow agayne anoon,
My selfe with hyr, I wil bothe come and goon,　50
And as myn hertes lyfe I wol hir kepe.'
　Thys olde Pandeon, thys kynge, gan wepe
For tendernesse of herte for to leve
Hys doghtre goon, and for to yive hir leve;
Of al thys worlde he lovede nothinge soo;
But at the laste leve hath she to go.
For Philomene with salte teres eke
Gan *of* hir fader grace to beseke,
To seen hir sustre that hir longeth soo,
And hym enbraceth with hir armes twoo.　60
And ther-with-alle so yonge and faire was she,
That whan that Tereus sawgh hir beauté, ·
And of array that ther nas noon hir lyche,
And yet of bounté was she too so ryche,
He caste hys firy hert upon hir soo,
That he wol have hir how-soo that hyt goo,
And with hys wiles kneled and so preyde,
Til at the laste Pandeon thus seyde:—
　'Now sone,' quod he, 'that arte to me so dere,

I the betake my yonge doghtre dere,   70
That bereth the key of al myn hertes lyfe.
And grete wel my doghter and thy wyfe,
And yeve hir leve sommetyme for to pley*e*,
That she may seen me oones or I dey*e*.'
And sothely he hath made him ryche feste,
And to hys folke, the moste and eke the leste,
That with him come : and yaf him yeftes grete,
And him conveyeth thurgh the maistir strete
Of Athenes, and to the see him broght*e*,
And turneth home ; no malyce he ne thoght*e*. 80
The ores pulleth forthe the vessel faste,
And into Trace arryveth at the laste ;
And up into a forest he hir ledde,
And into a cave pryvely hym spedde,
And in this derke cave, yif hir leste,
Or leste noght, he bad hir for to reste ;
Of which hir hert agrosse, and seyde thus :—
  ' Where ys my suster, brother Tereus ?'
And therewithal she wepte tendirly,
And quok for fere, pale and pitously,   90
Ryghte as the lambe that of the wolfe ys byten,
Or *as* the colver that of theglo ys smyten,
And ys out of *his* clawes forthe escaped,
Yet hyt ys aferde and awhaped
Lest hit be hent eftesones : so sate she.
But utterly hyt may none other be,
By force hath this traytour done a dede,
That he hathe refte hir *hir* maydenhede
Maugree hir hede, be strengthe and by his myght.
Loo, heere a dede of men, and that aryght !   100
She crieth ' Suster !' with ful longe stevene,
And ' Fader dere ! helpe me God in hevene !

Al helpeth nat.   And yet this false thefe,
Hath doon thys lady yet a more myschefe,
For ferde lest she sholde hys shame crye,
And done hym openly a vilanye,
And with his swerde hire tonge of kerf he,
And in a castel made hir for to be,
Ful prively in prison evermore,
And kept hir to his usage and to hys store,   110
So that she ne mighte never more asterte.
O sely Philomene, woo ys in thyn herte!
Huge ben thy sorwes, and wonder smerte!
God wreke the, and sende the thy bone!
Now ys hyt tyme I make an ende sone.
This Tereus ys to hys wyfe ycome,
And in hyse armes hath hys wyfe ynome,
And pitously he wepe, and shoke hys hede,
And swore hire that he fonde hir suster dede;
For which the sely Proigne hath suche woo,   120
That nyghe hire sorwful herte brake atwoo.
And thus in teres lat I Proigne dwelle,
And of hir suster forthe I wol yow telle.
This woful lady ylerned had in yowthe,
So that she werken and enbrowden kowthe,
And weven in stole the radevore,
As hyt of wymmen hath be woved yore.
And, shortly for to seyn, she hath hir fille
Of mete and drynke, of clothyng at hire wille,
And kouthe eke rede wel ynogh and endyte,   130
But with a penne she kouthe nat write;
But letteres kan she weve to and froo,
So that by the yere was agoo,
She hadde woven in a stames large,
How she was broght from Athenes in a barge,

And in a cave how that she was broght,
And al the thinge that Tereus hath wroght,
She wave hyt wel, and wrote the story above,
How she was served for hir' suster love.
And to a knave a rynge she yaf anoon,   14
And prayed hym by signes for to goon
Unto the quene, and beren hir that clothe;
And by sygne sworne many an othe,
She shulde hym yeve what she geten myght*e*.

 Thys knave anoon unto the queene hym dyght*e*
And toke hit hir, and al the maner tolde.
And whanne that Proigne hath this thing beholde,
No worde she spake for sorwe and eke for rage,
But feyned hyr to goon on pilgrymage
To Bachus temple.   And ih a lytel stounde   15
Hire dombe suster syttyng hath she founde
Wepynge in the castel hir-self allone.
Allas, the woo, constreynt, and *eke* the mone
That Proigne upon hir dombe suster maketh!
In armes everych of hem other taketh;
And thus I lat hem in her sorwe dwelle.

 The remnant ys no charge for to telle,
For this is al and somme, thus was she served,
That never harme agylt*e* no deservede
Unto thys cruelle man, that she of wyste.   18
Ye may be war of men yif that yow lyste.
For al be that he wol not for *the* shame
Doon as Tereus, to lese hys name,
No serve yow as a mordcrere or a knave,
Ful lytel while shul ye trowe hym have.
That wol I seyne, al were he nowe my brother,
But hit so be that he may have another.

EXPLICIT LEGENDA PHILOMENE.

INCIPIT LEGENDA PHILLIS.

BY preve, at wel as by auctorité,
That wikked frute cometh of wikked tree,
That may ye fynde yf that hyt liketh yow.
But for thys ende I speke thys as now,
To telle yow of fals Demophone.
In love a falser herde I never none,
But hit were hys fader Theseus;
God for hys grace fro suche oon kepe us!
Thus these wymen prayen that hit here;
Now to theffect turne I of my matere.   10
    Distroyed ys of Troye the citee;
This Demophon come saylyng in the see
Towarde Athenes to hys paleys large.
With hym come many a shippe, and mony a barge
Ful of folke, of whiche ful many oon
Ys wounded sore, and seke, and woo begoon,
And they han at a sege longe ylayne.
Byhynde him come a wynde and eke a rayne,
That shofe so sore, hys saylle myghte not stonde.
Hym were lever than al the worlde a-londe,   20
So hunteth hym the tempest to and fro!
So derke hyt was, he kouthe no-wher go,
And with a wawe brosten was hys stere.
Hys shippe was rent so lowe, in suche manere,
That carpenter koude hit nat amende.
The see by nyght as any torche brende
For wode, and posseth hym up and doune;
Til Neptunus hath of hym compassyoun,
And *Thetis*, Chorus, *Triton*, and they alle,

And maden him upon a londe to falle,
Wherof that Phillis lady was and quene,
Lycurgus doghtre, fayrer on to sene,
Than is the floure ageyn the bryghte sonne.
Unneth ys Demophoon to londe ywonne,
Wayke and eke wery, and his folke forpyned
Of werynesse, and also enfamyned,
And to the dethe he was almoste ydreven,
Hys wise folke counseyle han hym yeven,
To seken helpe and socour of the quene,
And loken what hys grace myghte bene,
And make in that londe somme chevissaunce,
To kepen hym fro woo and fro myschaunce.
For seke he was, and almoste at the dethe;
Unnethe myght he speke, or drawe brethe;
And lyeth in Rhodopeya hym for to reste.
Whan he may walke, hym thoght hit was the be
Unto the contree to seken for socoure.
Men knewe hym welle and dide hym honoure;
For at Athenes duke and lorde was hee,
As Theseus hys fader hath ybe,
That in hys tyme was grete of renoun,
No man so grete in al hys regioun;
And lyke hys fader of face and of stature,
And fals of love; hyt came hym of nature,
As doothe the fox Renarde, the foxes sone;
Of kynde he koude hys olde fadres wone
Withoute lore, as kan a drake swymme
Whan hit ys kaught and caried to the brymme.
    Thys honourable quene doth him chere,
And lyketh wel hys porte and hys manere.
But I am agroteyd here beforne,
To write of hem that in love ben forsworne

And eke to haste me in my legende,
Which to performe, God me grace sende
Therfore I passe shortly in thys wyse.
Ye have wel herde of Theseus the gyse,
In the betraysyng of faire Adriane,
That of hir pitee kepte hym fro hys bane;
At shorte wordes, ryght so Demophone,
The same way, the same path hath gone,   70
That did his false fader Theseus.
For unto Phillis hath he sworne thus,
To wedden hir, and hir his trouthe plyghte,
And piked of hyr al the good he myghte,
Whan he was hole and sounde, and had hys reste,
And doth with Phillis what-so that him liste,
As wel kouthe I, yif that me leste soo,
Tellen al hys doynges, to and fro.
    He sayede to hys contree moste him sayle,
For ther he wolde hire weddyng apparaylle   80
As fille to hir honour and hys also,
And openly he tok his leve tho,
And to hir swore he wolde not sojourne,
But in a moneth ageyn he wolde retourne.
And in that londe let make hys ordynaunce,
As verray lorde, and toke the obeisaunce,
Wel and hombely, and his shippis dyghte,
And home he gooth the nexte wey he myghte.
For unto Phillis yet come he noght,
And that hath she so harde and sore yboght,   90
Allas, that the story *doth* us recorde,
She was hir oune dethe with a corde,
Whanne that she segh that Demophon her trayede.
But firste wrote she to hym, and faste hym prayede
He wolde come and delyver hir of peyne,

As I reherse shal oo worde or tweyne.
Me lyste nat vouche-safe on hym to swynke,
Dispenden on hym a penne ful of ynke,
For fals in love was he ryght as hys syre;
The Devel set hire soules both on a fire!
But of the letter of Phillis wol I wryte,
A worde or tweyne althogh hit he but lyte.

  'Thyn hostesse,' quod she, 'O Demophone,
Thy Phillis, which that is so woo begone,
Of Rhodopey, upon yow *mot* compleyne,
Over the terme sette betwix us tweyne,
That ye ne holden forwarde, as ye seyde.
Your anker, which ye in oure haven leyde,
Hyght us that ye wolde comen out of doute,
Or that the mone ones went aboute;
But tymes foure, the mone hath *hid* hir face
Syn that thylke day ye wente fro this place;
And foure tymes lyghte the worlde ageyn.
But for al that, yet I shal soothly'seyn,
Yet hath the streme of Sit*hon* nat *i*-broght
From Athenes the shippe; yet come hit noght.
And yf that ye the terme rekne wolde,
As I or other trowe lovers sholde,
I pleyne nat, God wot! beforne my day.'
But al hir letter writen I ne may
By ordre, for hit were to me a charge;
Hir letter was ryght longe, and therto large.
But here and there, in ryme I have hyt layde
There as me thoghte that she hath wel sayde.

   She seyde, 'The sayllos cometh nat ageyn,
Ne to the worde there nys no fey certeyn,
But I wote why ye come nat,' quod she;
' For I was of my love to yow so fre.

And of the goddys that ye han forswore,
That hir*e* vengeaunce fal on yow therfore,   130
Ye be nat suffisaunt to bere the peyne.
To moche trusted I, wel may I seyne,
Upon youre lynage and youre faire tonge,
And on youre ter*e*s fals*e*ly out-wronge.
How kouthe ye wepe soo be crafte?' quod she;
' May there suche ter*e*s *i*-feynede be?
Now certes yif ye wolde have in memorye,
Hyt oughte be to yow but lytel glorie,
To have a sely mayde thus betrayed!   139
To God,' quod she, ' prey I, and ofte have prayed,
That hyt be nowe the gretest prise of alle,
And moste honour that ever yow shal befalle.
And when thyn olde auncetres peynted be,
In which men may her worthynesse se,
Then pray I God, thow peynted be also,
That folke may reden, forth by as they go :—
    ' Lo this is he, that with his flaterye
Betrayed hath, and doon hir vilanye,
That was his trewe love in thoghte and dede.'
    ' But sothely of oo poynt 'yet may they rede, 150
That ye ben lyke youre fader, as in this;
For he begiled Adriane, ywis,
With suche an arte, and suche soteltee,
As thou thy selven haste begiled me.
As in that poynt, althogh hit be nat feire,
Thou folwest *hym* certeyn, and art his eyre.
But syn thus synfully ye me begile,
My body mote ye seen, within a while
Ryght in the havene of Athenes fletynge,
Withouten sepulture and buryinge,   160
Though ye ben harder then is any stone.'

And whan this letter was forthe sent anon*e*,
And knyw how brotel and how fals he was,
She for dispeyre fordidde hir-self, allas!
Suche sorowe hath she for *he* beset hire so!
Be war ye wymmen of youre sotile fo!
Syns yet this day men may ensample se,
And as in love trust*eth* no man but me.

EXPLICIT LEGENDA PHILLIS.

INCIPIT LEGENDA YPERMYSTRE.

N Grece whilom weren brethren twoo
Of which that oon was called Danoo,
That many a sone hath of hys body
wonne,
As suche false lovers ofte konne.
Amonge hys sones alle there was oon,
That aldermoste he loved of everychone.
And whan this childe was borne, this Danoo
Shope hym a name, and called hym Lyno.
That other brother called was Egisto,
That was in love as fals as ever hym lysto.
And many a doghtre gate he in hys lyfe;
Of which he gate upon his ryght*e* wife
A doughter dere, and did hyt for to calle,
Ypermystra, yongest of hem alle.
The whiche childe, of hir natyvité,
To alle goode thewes borne was sho,
As lykede to the goddes or she was borne,

That of the shefe she shulde be the corne.
The wirdes that we clepen destanye,
Hath shapen hir, that she moste nedes be   20
Pitouse, sad, wise, trewe as stele.
And to this woman hyt acordeth wele;
For though that Venus yaf hir grete beauté,
With Jubiter compouned so was she,
That conscience, trouthe, and drede of shame,
And of hir wyfehode for to kepe hir name,
This thoghte hire was felicité as here.
And rede Mars, was that tyme of the yere
So feble, that his malice ys him rafte;
Repressed hath Venus hys cruelle crafte.   30
And *what* with Venus, and other oppressyoun
Of houses, Mars hys venym ys adoun,
That Ypermystra dar not handel a knyfe
In malyce, thogh she shulde lese hir lyfe.
But natheles, as heven gan thoo turne,
To badde aspectes hath she of Saturne,
That made hir to dye in prisoun.
And I shal after make mensioun,
Of Danoo and Egistis also.
And thogh so be that they were brethren twoo,   40
For thilke tyme nas spared no lynage,
Hyt lyketh hem to maken mariage
Betwix Ypermestra and hym Lyno,
And casten suche a day hyt shal be so,
And ful acorded was hit wittirly.
The array ys wroght, the tyme ys faste by
And thus Lyno hath of his fadres brother
Tho doghter wedded, and eche of hem hath other.
The torches brennen, and the lampes bryght*e*,
The sacrifices ben ful redy dyght,   50

Thencence out of the fire reketh sote,
The floure, the lefe, ys rent up by the rote,
To maken garlandes and corounes hye ;
Ful ys the place of sounde of mynstraleye,
Of songes amorouse of mariage,
As thilke tyme was the pleyne usage.
And this was in the paleys of Egiste,
That in his house was lorde, as hym lyste.
And thus that day they driven to an ende ;
The frendes taken leve, and home they wende ;   60
The nyght ys comen, the bride shal go to bed*de*.
Egiste to hys chambre fast hym sped*de*,
And prively he let his doghter calle,
Whanne that the house voyded was of alle.
He loked on hys doghter with glad chere,
And to hir spak as ye shal after here.

  ' My ryght*e* doghter, tresoure of myn hert*e*,
Syn firste day that shapen was my shert*e*,
Or by the fatale sustren hadde my dome,
So ny myn hert*e* never thinge me come   70
As thou, Ypermystra, doughter dere !
Take hede what thy fader seythe the here,
And wirke after thy wiser ever moo.
For alderfirste, doghter, I love the soo
That al the worlde to me nys halfe so lefe,
Ne nolde rede the to thy myschefe,
For al the good under the colde moone,
And what I meene, hyt shal be seyde ryght soone,
With protestacioun, as seyn these wyse,
That but thou do as I shal the devyse,   80
Thou shalt be ded, by hym that al hath wrought !
At shorte wordes thou ne schapest nought
Out of my paleyse or that thou be dede,

But thou conscente and werke aftir my rede ;
Take this to the for ful conclusioun.'
This Ypermystra caste hir eyen doun,
And quoke as dooth the lefe of aspe grene ;
Ded wex hir hewe, and lyke as ashe to scne ;
And seyde, ' Lorde and fader, al youre wille,
After my myght, God wote I shal fulfille,   90
So hit be to me no confusioun.'
     ' I nyl,' quod he, ' have noon excepcioun.'
And out he kaughte a knyfe as rasour kene.
' Hyde this,' quod he, ' that hyt be not i-sene ;
And whan thyn housbonde ys to bedde goo,
While that he slepeth kut hys throte atwoo ;
For in my dremes hyt is warned me,
How that my nevywe shal my bane be,
But which I not ; wherfore I wol be siker.
Yif thou say nay, we two shal make a byker,   100
As I have seyde, by him that I have sworne !'
     This Ypermystra hath nygh hire wytte forlorne,
And, for to passen harmlesse of that place,
Sho graunted hym ; ther was noon other grace.
And therwithal a costrel taketh he tho
And seyde, ' Hereof a draught, or two,
Yife hym to drynke whan he gooth to reste,
And he shal slepe as longe as ever the leste,
The narcotikes and opies ben so stronge.   109
And goo thy way, lest that hym thynke to longe.'
     Oute cometh the bride, and with ful sobre chere,
As ys of maidenes ofte the manere,
To chambre broght with revel and with songe.
And shortly, leste this tale be to longe,
This Lyno and she beth i-broght to bedde,
And every wight out at the dore hym spedde.

The nyght ys wasted and he felle aslepe;
Ful tenderly begynneth she to wepe;
She riste hir up, and dredefully she quaketh,
As dothe the braunche that Zepherus shaketh, 1:
And hussht were alle in Argone that citee.
As colde as eny froste now wexeth shee,
For pite by the herte streyneth hir soo,
And drede of dethe doth hir so moche woo,
That thries doun she fil in swich a were,
She ryst hir up and stakereth her and there,
And on hir handes faste loketh she.
‘Allas, shal myn handes blody be?
I am a mayde, and as by my nature,
And be my semblant, and by my vesture,   1:
Myn handes ben nat shapen for a knyfe,
As for to reve no man fro hys lyfe!
What devel have I with the knyfe to doo?
And shal I have my throte korve a twoo?
Than shal I blede, allas, and be i-shende!
And nedes coste thys thing mot have an ende:
Or he or I mot nedes lese oure lyfe.
Now certes,’ quod she, ‘syn I am hys wyfe,
And hathe my feythe, yet is hyt bet for me
For to be ded in wyfely honesté,   14
Than be a traytour lyvyng in my shame.
Be as be may, for erneste or for game,
He shal awake and ryse and go hys way
Out at this goter, or that hyt be day.’
And wepte ful tendirly upon his face,
And in hir armes gan hym to embrace,
And hym she roggeth and awaketh softe,
And at the wyndow lepe he fro the lofte,
Whan she hath warned hym and doon hym bote.

This Lyno swyft was and lyght of fote,   150
And from hir ranne a ful goode pace.
This sely womman ys so wayke, allace,
Helpeles, so that er she fer*r*e wente,
Her crewel fader did hir for to hente.
  Allas, Lyno, why art thou so unkynde?
Why ne hast thou remembred in thy mynde,
And taken hir, and ledde hir forthe with the ?
For when she saw that goon away was he,
And that she myght*e* not so faste go,
Ne folowen hym, she sate *hir* doun ryght thoo, 160
Til she was kaught and fetred in prisoun.
This tale ys sayde for this conclusioun.

HERE ENDETH THE LEGENDE OF GOODE WOMEN.

END OF VOL. V.

CHISWICK PRESS:—PRINTED BY WHITTINGHAM AND WILKINS,
TOOKS COURT, CHANCERY LANE.